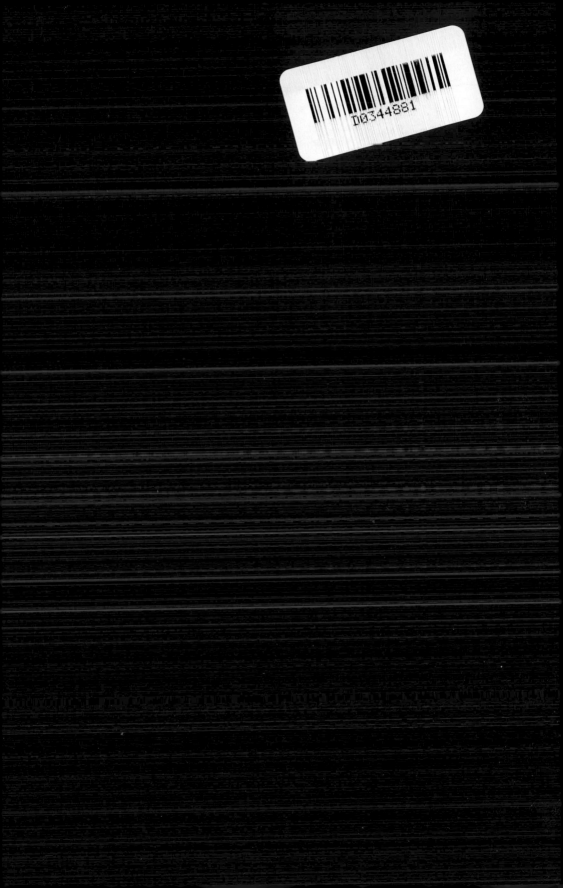

D0344881

THE
KEEPER
OF
NIGHT

**Books by Kylie Lee Baker
available from Inkyard Press**

The Keeper of Night

THE KEEPER OF NIGHT

KYLIE LEE BAKER

ISBN-13: 978-1-335-40566-1

The Keeper of Night

This edition published by arrangement with Harlequin Books S.A.

Inkyard Press
22 Adelaide St. West, 40th Floor
Toronto, Ontario M5H 4E3, Canada

Printed in the United States of America

To my wonderful mom and dad,
who (thankfully) are nothing like Ren's parents.

CHAPTER 01

LATE 1800s
LONDON, ENGLAND

The legend they tell about me goes something like this:

First, you'll see a streak of silver across the sky, like a comet burning through the fog.

Then, the clock hands will still halfway between this second and the next.

The world will fall silent, and the Reaper will knock three times on your bedroom door.

Whether you answer or not, Death will enter through the light in the keyhole.

She will reach down your throat and pull your soul out from deep, deep inside you, like an endless length of rope, and you will die in a world entirely your own. There will be no one but you, and the Reaper, and her unblinking green eyes.

But, of course, urban legends are rarely ever true.

On one particular collection night, the man was already awake when I opened his bedroom window and came in to take his soul. Humans, especially the very sick ones, always sensed when one of us was coming for them.

I stepped in through the window, pulling my long skirts after me, and found the man staring at me from his bed. He lay so still that I might have thought him dead already, but his eyes tracked me as I turned to slam the window shut. I pulled my clock from my pocket and closed my fingers around the silver-and-gold casing, locking the world into a time freeze.

The sounds outside of our little room silenced. No wind beat against the glass panes, no footsteps crunched through snow on the sidewalk outside, no floorboards creaked from the tenants below. The human lay frozen in his blankets, as if already dead. I crossed the room and pressed a finger to the hollow of his cheek.

With the touch of my cold skin, the time freeze unlatched its teeth from his throat and he jolted awake, joining me in our frozen infinity between moments. Our tiny world filled with his ragged exhales and scraping inhales, his wet blinks of fever-bright eyes, his twitching limbs shifting against the stiff sheets.

"Are you going to kill me?" he said.

Technically, I wasn't. His time of death had been written in the high ledgers since the day he was born, and I had done nothing to interfere with that destiny. I was not his executioner but his deliverer, and I couldn't extract a soul that wasn't ready to abandon its body.

"Yes," I said. I stepped closer and my shadow loomed over his bed, a wraith casting darkness over his pale face.

He closed his eyes and took several croaking breaths. When he opened his eyes again, tears pooled in the corners.

"Will it hurt?" he whispered.

I let him wait in suspense for my answer. I did not blink, did not breathe, only looked down at him with an unchanging expression.

"I wouldn't know," I said. "I've never died."

It wasn't what he wanted to hear, but that wasn't my problem. He'd asked a question and I'd answered. His pupils grew wide, like two yawning chasms of black, his bones quivering against the thin tarp of his skin. He reached out a shaking hand as if to touch me. I watched him struggle but made no move to help him, taking a small glass vial from my pocket.

"Is there a Heaven?" the man said, his frail hand somehow latching on to the sleeve of my robe. I looked down at the grayed skin stretched taut over bones, wrapped in the shimmering silver fabric and trembling hard. "Please, Reaper, tell me. Will I go to Heaven?"

I smirked. His trembling stilled, maybe in breathless anticipation of my answer, or maybe in horror that I'd smiled so cruelly over his deathbed. That look in his eyes—like I was horrible and magnificent and could tear the whole universe to ribbons if I wanted to—was the only part of the process that I truly liked. No one but humans looked at me with that kind of reverence.

In truth, I didn't know where souls went after we released them. The High Reapers spoke of Heaven and Hell, but I had never seen such places and suspected they were fantasies conjured to absolve us of responsibility. Those places were no more real to me than Santa Claus, or unicorns, or God.

But the humans believed in them so fervently, just like they believed that I came from a comet and slid through keyholes. The man wasn't the first to ask me for answers, thinking I was Death and not one of his children playing messenger. When they asked me, I always answered.

"There is no Heaven," I said. The man's twisted expression went gray, his grip on my sleeve suddenly weak. "There is no Hell, either," I said. "There is nothing but Death."

The tears that bled from his eyes told me that if there was a Heaven, I would never see it. But my teachers always said that tainted souls like mine would burn for eternity anyway, so what difference did this brief unkindness make?

He started calling out names, probably those of the humans in the rooms next door who would never hear him as long as I kept the clocks frozen. But I didn't like the sound of begging. I could tolerate threats and bribes and rage, but something about begging made my body wither into itself like a dried flower, as if every desperate word was being scratched into my skin in scars that only I could see. Long after the begging stopped, my skin always itched for hours and the words always rang in my head, shaking me from shallow dreams.

I looped the chain of my clock around my neck like a pendant, making sure the metal still touched my bare skin, and got to work.

I pressed one hand to his forehead and held it still while I forced his jaw open with my thumb. He choked and cried as I crammed my hand down his throat. When my fingertips finally brushed the milky edges of his soul, I grabbed hold and yanked it out.

From between his lips, a cloud of gold mist rose into the

air, speckled with bright lights that moved in tandem like a chain of constellations. I'd seen souls made of black tar and bile, others of pale pink candy floss, and even ones that sizzled and burst like fireworks. Just like every human life, souls were unique and beautiful for a single moment, and then they were nothing but dust.

His soul spun aimlessly in the air until I uncorked my glass vial with my thumb. The soul rushed inside, magnetized by the bone glass. As soon as I sealed it shut, the soul turned murky gray and settled as ashes at the bottom. I carved a 7 onto the lid with my pocketknife, for it was my seventh collection of the night, then dropped it into the drawstring bag in my pocket, where it clinked against the other six vials.

The man lay dead in his sheets, jaw hanging open and eyes still wet with tears that dripped down to his pillow. I closed his mouth and eyes, then whispered a compulsory prayer to Ankou, the Father of Death and King of the Reapers.

Though I had never met him, I felt his presence everywhere the same way that humans felt love or hate or other intangible things. All Reapers were his servants, born halfway between the realm of humans and gods, bound to serve him and keep the human world in balance. Though the humans spoke of us as villains or nightmares, they needed us more than they would ever understand. Death brought humans fear, and fear made humans interesting. Without Death, humans would grow complacent and stale. Even we Reapers would one day surrender to Death's scythe.

In Britain, we served Ankou, but the Reapers beyond our borders answered to a different Death. In China, they served Yanluo, ruler of the Fifth Hell of Wailing, Gouging, and Boiling. In Mexico, they served Santa Muerte, a skeletal saint in brightly colored robes who granted protection to society's forgotten children. And in Norway, there was Pesta the plague hag who dealt out death with a dusty broom. At least, that was what the legends said.

But I knew better than anyone that legends were nothing but overgrown trees sprouted from tiny seeds of truth.

As I whispered my prayer to Ankou, the language of Death numbed my lips, the sacred words reaching out for his blessing for both my own damned soul and the human's. The language of the dead always hung suspended in the air for longer than any mortal language, like its words had been carved into the universe. It was a crooked and cursed language that all could understand but only creatures of Death could speak. Once the frozen night inhaled my prayer, I threw open the window and climbed out into the petrified darkness.

Snowflakes hovered in midair like stars in a soundless galaxy, ravens suspended in their flight overhead with black wings spread wide. Snow fell beyond the barrier just a block away, for I was still a young Reaper, and I couldn't yet control time in too large a space.

I would have liked to stay in the freeze forever, where the world was silent and peaceful, but of course I never could.

Time is not created, but stolen, the Timekeepers had always said when reprimanding me for taking too long on collections. *You must pay for every second you steal.* Of course, to keep the universe in balance, the extra time we stole through collections was shaved off our own lifespans by Ankou himself. We were meant to spend our stolen minutes collecting souls in stopped time, for it was the only way to guarantee that humans never saw us until their Death Day, that we remained nothing but urban legends and superstitions. We sacrificed those moments of our lives so that humans would never know the dangerous truth. Humans instinctively fought Death at all costs, but they could never fight us if they didn't know we existed until the very end.

In a lifetime of thousands of years, a loss of minutes mattered little to us. But hours, days, even months were stolen only by reckless fools. For every time we stopped the clock, we could hear a distant ticking that grew louder as the stolen moments passed, reminding us that one day, no matter how much time we tried to steal back, Death would come for us.

I pressed a hand to the clock still hanging around my neck, cold inside my blouse. My clock, made of pure silver and gold, was the key that unlocked my control over time. Every Reaper received one on their hundredth birthday. They allowed the Timekeepers to see the fingerprints I left on the timeline, every single second I stole that would be added to my debt. Time pulsed from the silver and gold into my bloodstream, then spread from my fingertips to wherever, or whoever, I chose. Each clock was unique, nontransferable, and took months to make. We were meant to protect them more fiercely than our own children. After all, Reapers without children were still Reapers, but Reapers without clocks were just very slow-aging humans.

I unwound the chain from my neck, pulled up my hood, and dropped the clock into my pocket.

Time came unstuck the moment my fingers left the metal, the howling snowstorm yanking my hood back in an icy blast. I pulled it back down, not caring how quickly the hail burned my hand, because I couldn't let anyone see the color of my hair. If anyone noticed me, trouble would follow.

I needed to get back home before Last Toll, or I'd be trapped outside until tomorrow's dusk. Then my brother would break curfew to come looking for me, and we'd both be outside when the church grims began their hunt. I could handle them, but Neven would surely get hurt. Church grims looked like dogs, and Neven would sooner eat his own clock than kill a dog.

Besides, walking around with a pocket full of unprocessed souls always left me uneasy—the glass was sturdy but not indestructible. If, for instance, I fell from a clock tower or was impaled on a wrought-iron fence or thrown under a carriage again, the vials would shatter and the souls would be trapped in the mortal plane.

I ran through Belgrave Square, which the deep night had left near-deserted. Prodigious white estates surrounded the block, their fourth-story windows like prison watchtowers leering down on the streets. I kept running past the curved redbrick buildings of Wilton Crescent, then veered away from such exposed areas and slipped into the darker side streets, hoping the shadows would conceal me.

I'd just turned the corner to Cadogan Place when time changed again.

I felt the ghost of a hand on my throat and spun around, but I stood alone on a frozen street. There was no distant clanking of pipes or faraway echo of hoofs on cobblestone or blurred conversations a block away, just a barren expanse of silence, my every breath louder than a scream.

I lifted my hood and peered up at a million snowflakes frozen in midair, not by my own doing.

It didn't matter then if I walked or ran or crawled—their cold hands had dragged me into their frozen world. They were watching me, waiting for my next move while they hid in the shadows.

They knew the longer they waited in the silence, the more my mind would spiral and fragment and imagine all the ways they'd pull me apart, bone by bone. Unlike humans who had the privilege of seeing them once and only once before their souls went into the void, I'd spent nearly two centuries with them.

The urban legends should have told of Reapers like them, not ones like me. Because even though I was a terrible person, I was not the kind of Reaper one should have feared.

Here is the tale that humans should have told:

First, you feel their hands on your face, their skin cold with Death's chill as they wake you from sleep.

Second, the clocks stop ticking and you're alone in the silence, where all you can hear are your breaths getting faster and faster.

When you're somewhere between consciousness and death, vision hazy from lack of oxygen, a figure in a silver cloak will come to ruin you.

Time is ribbons in their hands, to cut or twist or tie around your throat.

They can freeze time so solidly that you're no longer a part of the world, caught inside a painting.

They can grind time forward so slowly that you're trapped

in a viscous amber, spending centuries taking a single breath but agonizingly conscious.

They can dig their white nails into your heart and pull out your worst moments, then play them on an eternal loop.

They cull the weak from their own families and snap the spines of their lovers, and as long as they want you, you are never, ever safe.

"Hello, Wren."

The words came from behind me, a woman's voice in my left ear that hummed through my whole body like a death knell. The name sounded wrong in my head. *Wren Wren Wren*, like the little brown birds that eat spiders and die in the winter, and it wasn't even my real name.

My mother, whom I couldn't remember, had named me Ren, the word for *lotus* in Japanese. I knew, because just like all Shinigami, the kanji was burned into my spine in strokes of black ink that wouldn't wash away. But my father had put my name down as *Wren* in the ledgers because that was an acceptable, albeit meek, name for a British Reaper. And while the pronunciation was similar, I always knew who was calling my real name and who was calling me a little bird.

"What's wrong, Wren?" someone said, in my right ear this time, a different voice.

They loved to say the name that wasn't even mine, stretching out the vowel like thick taffy because they loved to disrespect me. We were meant to address each other as *Reaper* outside of our families, but of course I didn't warrant that kind of decency.

"You're awfully quiet tonight," said another voice, and this one I knew. But before I could answer, a pair of hands grabbed each of my arms and wrenched me onto my back in the snow. The time-frozen snowflakes spanned upward as far as I could see until they dissolved into the frozen infinity of gray-black sky.

A boot collided with my jaw and crushed my face into the street. My vision flashed white while my brain crashed against the walls of my skull. The heel dug harder into my temple, and I could only lie there like a dead thing until she was done with me, no better than the souls in my pocket.

Hellfire simmered in my fingertips, the gas streetlights burning dangerously bright. But before my flames could shatter the glass, I choked down a breath of cold air and squeezed my eyes shut, forcing the searing light down.

With my one eye that wasn't scraping against snow crystals, I looked up at my assailants.

There was Ivy's boot on my cheek, of course, because Ivy always appeared where I didn't want her. Her silver cloak rippled like a clear river behind her, the fabric made of silk and moonlight. Ash blond hair, the color of bones, hung in soft curls around her face. She was beautiful in exactly the way Reapers were supposed to be—so fair that the snowflakes seemed to pass through her, like she had faded halfway into another world, features sharpened by the edges of her bones, eyes every color of the northern lights, shifting between jewel tones and faraway starlight.

I didn't look like her, or any of the other Reapers.

My eyes and hair were the color of Yomi, the Japanese underworld and Realm of Perpetual Night, the place that light didn't dare touch. To call it a color was too generous—it was the absence of everything. For that reason, I always braided my hair back and hung my hood low over my eyes—to be seen was to be targeted.

The hands on my left arm ground my bones harder into the street, and I guessed it was Sybil because of the strength. Where Sybil went, Mavis usually followed, though it didn't much matter who held me down. All of the High Reapers had their fun with me at some point, but Ivy always loomed somewhere close.

The boot lifted and the tremendous pressure on my skull subsided, leaving me light-headed. The bruises would melt away in a few minutes, but Ivy would certainly make more before they could heal. I tensed up when she moved again, but this time she only kicked my hood back.

My black hair poured out like an oil spill onto the snow, half of it fallen loose from my braid after Ivy's violent kick.

"As if anything could hide what you are," she said.

"Half-breed," Mavis said under her breath, crushing my arm another degree into the pavement.

"Won't you look at a High Reaper when they're addressing you?" said Ivy.

I dragged my gaze skyward and locked eyes with Ivy, her irises a nauseating swirl of purple and green.

She reached down for me and I couldn't help closing my eyes again, imagining the thousand different kinds of pain she could inflict. Every muscle in my body pulled taut, flinching away from expected agony. My legs kicked out half-heartedly, but I was no stronger than a pinned butterfly. I clenched my jaw so hard that my teeth scraped together, and I imagined a world where I could fight back without consequences from the High Council, where there was anyone in power who cared what happened to me.

The pain didn't come for an agonizing stretch of time. My muscles wound tighter and tighter, shaking from the force.

Then, with uncharacteristic gentleness, Ivy gathered my hair and lifted it from the snow. I opened my eyes just as a pair of scissors crossed my line of vision, gleaming in the weak streetlight.

"No!" I said, surging against the arms that slammed me back into the street. I lunged up again, but the hands ground deeper into my bones. I couldn't get up without hurting them, and if I hurt them, the High Council would hear about it. So instead I thrashed like a speared fish and glared up at the unmoving snow above me and tried to make the process as difficult as possible for them.

I knew my hair was the wrong color and that nothing I did with it would ever make me beautiful, but it was *mine*, not Ivy's to take.

She grabbed my jaw with one hand and held it still, the scissors suspended a breath away from my eye.

"Stop moving, or I'll take your eye instead," she said. Her words sent a numbing chill through my bones. It must have been the voice she used on humans before she took their souls, because her words made my whole body want to wither like a dying plant. Though cuts on my skin zipped themselves up and shattered bones always snapped back into place within minutes, I'd never had the displeasure of regrowing eye jelly and didn't particularly want to find out how it felt.

I went still, afraid to move in case the silver blades dropped down even a millimeter. It wasn't the threat of pain that stilled me, but the anticipation of the squishing sensation, how it would feel to have scissors plunged through my eye, the way my vision would fracture and kaleidoscope. I grew nauseous at the thought, unable to do anything but stare at the sharpness of the blades, the polished twinkle of silver in the streetlight.

The background softened into a dreamy haze and I realized too late that Ivy was turning time on me, stretching the moment longer and longer. I lay trapped in a world of only me and the scissors and the breathless promise of the blades plunging into my eye. She could keep me here for centuries if she wanted to. I started to panic even though I couldn't breathe or move, my slow-beating heart racing and my lungs screaming for oxygen they didn't need. I stared and stared and couldn't look away and the blades only seemed to grow sharper and more sinister, moving closer and closer to my open eye, and suddenly I wanted Ivy to gouge my eye out just to *end it end it end it*—

The scissors disappeared from my line of vision and I gasped, falling limp against the snow while Sybil and Mavis laughed on either side of me. Cold sweat caked my skin and my eyes burned with dryness, even though only a second had passed.

"Look how scared she is," Sybil said, jamming her finger into my cheek. "This is supposed to be the heir of a High Reaper?"

"She'll never ascend," Mavis said, grabbing a fistful of dirty snow and shoving it in my face.

Surely nothing would anger them more, and part of me wanted to ascend as a High Reaper just to spite them. But it would never happen. My father would never train me for ascension, even though I was his firstborn.

Ivy yanked my half-undone braid and I remembered why she'd had the scissors in the first place. I clenched my jaw at the sharp snip of scissors and my own hair falling into the snow, dropping my gaze to the gas streetlight caught in our time freeze, the light still casting a weak circle onto the snow around us.

It doesn't matter, I told myself. *It's fine, you're fine, and it doesn't matter at all.*

But the words whispered under my breath didn't reach my brain. The flame of the streetlight contorted angrily against its glass cage, echoing my despair. A severed piece of hair blew over my shoulder and I clawed my fingertips into the snow, forcing my eyes shut and praying that the dark sanctuary would calm me. But even with my eyes pressed closed, I could see the light burning brighter than before.

I needed to calm down before the light got any brighter. I remembered being half a century old and my father grabbing me by the shoulders and shaking me so hard that I couldn't see, shards of exploded light bulb all around us. *Reapers don't control light*, he'd said. *Don't let anyone see.* Keep it a secret. Be a good little bird and don't ever do that again.

And he was right, because British Reapers didn't control light. But Japanese Reapers—Shinigami—did.

My heritage was hardly a secret, but we both knew nothing good could come from High Reapers feeling threatened. They could turn time with more finesse than I ever would, but how effective would that be if they couldn't see me? Who knew what lengths they'd go to just to keep me restrained, to keep themselves in power?

I might have hated my father, but he was right—I couldn't show them my Shinigami powers.

"Aww, I think you made her cry," Mavis said.

The sound of scissors stopped. Ivy grabbed my chin.

Was I really crying? I couldn't feel my face anymore, could only feel the tremors through my entire body as I tried not to shower us all in fire and glass shards. The line between control and chaos was so very thin, and it took every part of my concentration to hold myself back. I needed Ivy to finish quickly before I got too angry and ruined everything.

"Poor thing," Ivy said, cuffing a tear from my burning cheek. Her nails cut into my face, sharp like a snake bite. "And what did I tell you about looking at a High Reaper when they're addressing you?"

I wrenched my eyes open and the words spilled out before I could stop them.

"Just finish, already."

Ivy's smile dropped. She grabbed my jaw and pulled it closer until it made a cracking sound and pain knifed through my face.

"Is that what you want, half-breed?" she whispered. "For me to end you?" Her words slithered across my skin, curling around my throat and wrists. Her eyes churned indigo, a dark undertow pulling me deeper.

Yes, a secret part of me whispered.

I knew it was an idle threat, but sometimes I wished it were possible.

Reapers lived for nearly two millennia unless a more powerful being cut them off early. Humans were weak creatures who could flay me and sever my limbs and carve my heart out of my chest, but they would never succeed in killing me. The church grims and demons were slightly stronger beings that could eat my flesh down to the bone, but still they couldn't end me. But Ivy was a High Reaper, and if she wanted to crush every one of my bones into the pavement until I was nothing but powder and then collect my soul, she could.

But she never would, because Ankou extracted the memories of all his Reapers when they died, so my murder could never remain her little secret. Even Ivy wasn't above Ankou's punishing scythe.

Yet, sometimes, when my heart felt dark as the night that I carried in my eyes, I wished she would do it anyway.

Ivy leaned closer and her hair fell in a curtain in front of me, sealing us away from the rest of the world.

"What would happen if we tied you to this streetlamp until daybreak?" she whispered. "Would your little brother come to pluck the church grims off your bones?"

"Don't," I said, the word a shuddered exhale. My fingers twitched, already unnaturally warm. I hated when Ivy talked about Neven, and she knew it. My poor little half brother, lucky enough to be full Reaper but unlucky enough to be chained to me.

When Neven took the souls of children, he held their hands and sang them lullabies. He let the older ones pray and told them stories about what awaited them in Heaven, how everything there was beautiful and nothing would ever hurt them again. But because of me he would never have friends, never join the High Council, never be anyone but the Shinigami's brother. He could have forsaken me like our father, but instead he brought me stray cats and built book towers over me while I slept and cast shadow puppets on the walls while I tried to read.

His name didn't belong on Ivy's lips.

"Would he cry when he saw they'd nibbled off your fingers and drunk your eyes from their sockets?"

"Don't," I said again, but the word was dead and heavy in my mouth.

"Or would he be happy that he was finally free?"

I bit hard into my lip and prayed that the pain would help me center, draw my focus away from the light of the streetlamp that was getting brighter with the promise of broken glass and fire, because words could only hurt you if you knew they were true.

"How long would it take him to forget about you?" Ivy whispered. "Half a century, maybe?"

My teeth gnawed deeper into my lip. Ivy was right. The lives of Reapers spanned millennia, and Neven had barely spent a century with me. Time would scrub my face from his memories whether he liked it or not.

The streetlight burned bright against the glass casing, orange and blue and sun-hot white. I closed my eyes, but all I could see was my hair on the snow and scissors and moonlight and my soul cast into an empty eternity and Neven's face and *it's fine it's fine it doesn't matter at all*, but the snow began to reflect the increasing light from the streetlamp and our little circle of refuge from the winter darkness was now a boiling spotlight in the middle of London and *I couldn't stop it*.

Ivy leaned in closer, her cold lips brushing my ear.

"Then no one would remember you," she said, "like you'd never existed at all."

My control flew away from me all at once, a tether yanked out of my hands, spiraling fast and far away.

The streetlamp's weak light swelled to fill its glass cage, no longer a dying flame but a searing starlight that bleached away the night sky and ripped the colors from the street. The High Reapers began to turn around.

"Don't look!" I said, but they ignored me as always, and the light scorched through the soft flesh of their eyes.

They screamed and released me, clapping their hands over their eyes and crumpling to the ground. I held my sleeve over my face as the glass panes of the lantern burst outward and thousands of sharp crystals rained down like hellfire, singeing holes in my cloak with white-hot sparks. The time freeze collapsed, snow pelting my face and turning the lingering flames to swirling steam. I slapped the embers off my skirt, then turned to the three blind and sobbing High Reapers, collapsed in melted snow puddles, their cloaks steaming quietly, surrounded by pieces of my hair.

The image forced a sneer to my lips before I could stop myself. *This is what they deserve, to be on their knees in front of me.* But the feeling drained away as fast as it had come, like a sudden eclipse of darkness. I looked down at my trembling hands, scored with glass shards, my sheared hair blowing across my face, the sobbing Reapers at my feet trying to rub the blood from their eyes.

I had ruined everything.

I dashed into the snow, slipping on a patch of ice and clawing my way back to my feet. I prayed that the light would keep them incapacitated. As long as they couldn't see, they couldn't trap me again or make their way back home. No matter what, I had to stay ahead of Ivy. As soon as the High Council got word that I'd assaulted three High Reapers, one of them the great granddaughter of Ankou himself, I could safely say I'd be chained up in a mausoleum for the next millennium. I had to turn in my soul vials to Collections, then get home to tell Neven what happened.

I looked over my shoulder as I ran, taking in the ice-polished cobblestones and evergreen garlands and redbrick chimneys scratching the stars through the eyes of someone seeing them for the last time. Every step was a goodbye to a place I'd never really loved but that had made up my entire world.

I turned and looked ahead again, because in the end it wasn't even a choice. I wouldn't wait around for them to put me in chains. I would leave London, and I would never come back.

CHAPTER 02

At the far edge of London, somewhere between nightmares and formless dreams, the Reapers slept by daylight.

The only way to enter our home was through the catacombs of the Highgate Cemetery, through a door that no longer existed. It had been built there long ago, when the Britons first came to our land and Ankou carved a hole in their world so that Death could enter. But humans had sealed it shut with layers of wood, then stone, then brick and mortar, all in the hopes of keeping Death out.

By the nineteenth century, humans had mostly forgotten about the Door and what it meant. Then, when the London churchyards began to overflow with bones, the humans had searched for a place just outside of London to bury their dead. By chance or fate, they'd built their new cemetery right on top of the Door. It turned out that Death drew all of us close, even if we weren't aware of it.

No streetlights lit the path through Highgate at night, but I didn't need them to find my way home. Before I'd even passed through the main gate, Death pulled me closer. All Reapers were drawn to him, our bones magnetized to the place of our forefather. As soon as I entered the cemetery, a humming began just under my skin, like a train's engine beginning to whir. My blood flushed faster through my veins as I brushed aside the branches of winter-barren lime trees and low-hanging elms. My boots crunched shattering steps into the frosted pathways as I ran.

I stumbled through jagged rows of ice-cracked tombstones on uneven ground and through a village of mausoleums, finally reaching the gothic arched doorway of the catacomb entrance. The pull had grown unbearable, dragging me along in a dizzy trance as I descended the stairs into the cool quietness of damp bricks and darkness. The labyrinth would have been unnavigable if not for the fervent pull.

At last, my hands came out to touch the wall where the Door used to be, but now there were only damp bricks and an inscription on the arch overhead that read *When Ankou comes, he will not go away empty* in rigid script. I dug one hand into my pocket and clutched my clock, pressed my other hand to the bricks, then closed my eyes and turned time all the way back to the beginning.

Time flowed through the silver-and-gold gears, up into my bloodstream and through my fingertips, dispersing into the brick wall. Centuries crumbled away, the mortar growing wet and bricks falling loose. One by one, they leaped out of their positions in the wall and aligned themselves in dry stacks on the ground, waiting once again for construction. Objects were easy to manipulate with time, for I could draw from their own intrinsic energy rather than siphoning off my own. Bricks could last for centuries before they crumbled to dust, so it was easy enough to borrow years from them rather than paying in years of my own life, quickly repaying the time debt when I put them back in place.

I stepped through the doorway and the pull released me all at once. I breathed in a deep gasp of the wet night air, then turned around and sealed the door behind me. The bricks jumped back to their positions in the wall, caked together by layers of mortar that dried instantly, the time debt repaid.

The catacombs beyond the threshold spanned infinitely forward, appropriated as resting places for Reapers rather than corpses. Mounted lanterns cast a faint light onto the dirt floors and gray bricks. It was almost Last Toll, so only the last of the Reapers returning from the night shift still milled around, their silver capes catching the dim light of the tunnels, but most had retreated to their private quarters for the morning.

I turned right and hurried down the block. The low ceilings gave way to high-arched doorways and finally opened up to a hall of echoing marble floors and rows of dark wood desks. Luckily, there was no line for Collections this close to Last Toll.

I hurried to the first Collector and all but slammed my vials into the tray, jolting him awake in his seat. He was a younger Reaper and seemed perplexed at having been awoken so unceremoniously. When his gaze landed on me, he frowned and sat up straight.

"Ren Scarborough," I said, pushing the tray closer to him.

"I know who you are," he said, picking up my first vial and uncapping it with deliberate slowness. Of course, everyone knew who I was.

He took a wholly unnecessary sniff of the vial before holding it up to the light to examine the color, checking its authenticity. The Collectors recorded every night's soul intake before sending the vials off to Processing, where they finally released the souls into Beyond. He picked up a pen from his glass jar of roughly thirty identical pens, tapped it against the desk a few times, then withdrew a leather-bound ledger from a drawer. He dropped it in front of him, opened the creaky cover, and began flipping through the pages, one by one, until he reached a fresh one.

I resisted the urge to slam my face against the desk in impatience.

I really didn't have time to waste, but Collections was a necessary step. I didn't consider myself benevolent in times of crisis, but even I was above leaving souls to expire in glass tubes instead of releasing them to their final resting place, wherever that was. And besides, a blank space next to my name in the Collections ledger meant a Collector would pay a visit to my private quarters to reprimand me. The last thing I needed was someone realizing that I'd left before Ivy could even report me.

But when the Collector uncorked my fourth vial and held it up to the lamp, swirling it in the light for ten excruciating seconds, I began to wonder if I'd made the right decision.

The bells of Last Toll reverberated through the bricks all around us, humming through the marble floors. In this hazy hour between night and day, the church grims came out in search of Reaper bones to gnaw on. Night collections had to be turned in by then, while day collections had to be processed by the First Toll at dusk.

The Collector sighed as he picked up my fifth vial. "I'm afraid I'll have to mark your collections as late."

My jaw clenched. "Why?"

"It's past Last Toll, of course," he said.

My fingers twitched. The lamp on the Collector's desk flickered with my impatience, but I took a steadying breath.

"I was here before Last Toll," I said, trying to keep my voice even.

"According to my ledger, your collections still have not been processed," he said, spinning my fifth vial in his left hand.

I sighed and closed my eyes. Of course, I knew what he was doing. Chastising a "latecomer" would earn praise from higher management. It was the easiest way for him to climb the ranks—to exert his power over the half-breed. He would be praised for his steadfastness and gain a reputation as a strict and immovable Collector, while I could do nothing to complain. I could explode his lamp and send glass shards into his eyes, but that wouldn't make him process my vials any faster. The fastest way to get out of there was subservience.

"Forgive me, Reaper," I said, bowing my head and dropping my shoulders. I let my voice sound timid and afraid. "I apologize for being late."

The Collector blinked at me for a moment, as if surprised that I'd given in so quickly. But he looked young and power-hungry and not particularly perceptive, so I wasn't too afraid that he'd see through my tactic. As expected, he sneered as if I truly had offended him, finally beginning to process the fifth vial.

"It's a great inconvenience to both Collections and Processing," he said, "though I wouldn't expect a half-breed to understand the workings of the educated Reapers."

The only believable response to his goading was humiliated silence, so I hung my head even further and tried to make myself as small and pathetic as possible. It wasn't hard, because the memory of the night's events was still wringing my heart out like a wet rag and my skin prickled with nerves so fiercely that I wanted to claw it all off and escape before Ivy could find me, yet here I was, brought to my knees before a glorified teller. I imagined being a High Reaper, being able to reach over and smash his face into his blotter and shatter his owlish glasses into his eyes for delaying and insulting me.

His lamp flickered more violently and he paused to smack it before finally finishing with my last vial. He placed all seven in a tray and pressed a button that started the conveyor belt, sending the souls down to Processing. The moment he put a black check next to my name in the ledger, I stood up straight and turned to leave.

His hand twisted into my sleeve, yanking me back.

I shot him a look that could have melted glass, but he only pulled me closer.

"There's the matter of your sanction," he said.

"My sanction," I said, glancing around the office to see how many people would notice if I simply twisted the Collector's neck. Too many.

"For your tardiness, of course," he said, smirking sourly.

From his position stretched across the desk, the lamplight caught in his glasses and turned them into two beaming white moons.

The standard punishment for failing to make curfew was a night on the pillory, hands and feet nailed to the wood and head locked in a hole that was just slightly too tight, letting you breathe but not speak. The other Reapers could pull your hair or pour mead over your head or call you a thousand names when you couldn't talk back. But the worst part wasn't the nails or the insults. It was the Reapers who did nothing but look at you and sneer like you were nothing but an ugly piece of wall art, like they were so perfect that they couldn't fathom being in your place. And far worse than that was my own father and stepmother walking past me and pretending not to see.

"Come back at First Toll," the Collector said. "We'll find a nice place to hang you up by the Door."

It took every ounce of restraint I had left to keep my expression calm. This was the part where I was supposed to say, *Yes, Reaper*, and bow, but he was lucky that I hadn't smashed his glasses into his face with my fist.

As if he could smell my defiance, he pulled me closer. His glasses fell out of the lamplight, revealing a deep frown.

"Scrub that look from your face," he said. "Remember that I'll handle your collections in the future."

The future, I thought.

Luckily, I didn't have a future.

The light bulb flashed with a sudden surge of power, then burst. Glass shards rained down over the desk, forcing the man to release me as hot glass scored his hands. Some of his pa-

perwork caught fire, and he frantically patted out the flames
with hands full of shards.

"Yes, Reaper," I said, bowing deeply so he wouldn't see
my smirk as he sputtered about "bloody light bulbs, I knew
we should have kept the gas lamps."

Then I turned and rushed off to the West Catacombs.

I threw open the door to 857 West, locked it, and stopped
time for the world outside of my room in the widest radius
I could manage. That would envelop the West Catacombs,
at least, stopping any Reapers from breaking down our door
before I could slip out again. That is, unless a High Reaper
came looking for us and sensed the time turn, but it would
at least buy me a few minutes to prepare.

Up in the loft, Neven's hand hung between the banister
bars. I smacked it, jolting him both out of the time freeze
and out of sleep.

"Why'd you do that?" his sleep-crackled voice said from
above.

One greenish-purple eye glowed from between the slats,
the other hidden behind white blond hair and pillows. Neven
couldn't sleep in the dark, so he'd left all the candles burning
in the corners of our studio and from the precariously suspended candelabra overhead.

I waved my hand and every candle in the room doubled in
brightness, switching from a romantic orange glow to sterile white. Neven made a strangled noise, but I was already
tearing through the trunk at the foot of my bed, digging for
some sort of bag to take with me. When I found nothing
of use, I pulled out the drawers of my wardrobe and turned

them over, sending broken quills and origami stars spilling across the floorboards.

Our room was a stark cage of bricks, chilled from both the clay and the deep earth around it. Neven slept in the loft surrounded by sparkling cogs and gears and bits of glass from little machines that he'd disassembled. I occupied the lower half of the room, my mattress surrounded by a small fortress of stolen books in eleven languages. I'd taken an interest in botany lately and had gathered some of the most beautiful and poisonous flowers I could find in London: hemlock, foxglove, and wolfsbane. I'd dried them and strung them up on the wooden slats of Neven's loft, because Reapers were drawn to Death, and my plants were both very deadly and very dead.

I brushed aside the withered petals and ducked into my alcove, then dumped out the plants that I'd stuffed into a brown leather bag.

Neven hung his head over the edge of the loft, squinting down at me.

"Why are you redecorating at five in the morning?" he said. "And the time lock? Ren—"

"I have to leave," I said, tearing through my wardrobe for something besides a glittering silver cloak that might keep me warm. I could steal a disguise off some unfortunate Londoner, but I'd need to go out in public first and sparkling silver cloaks weren't exactly in fashion. I tried to focus on packing rather than answer Neven's question, because all the words I wanted to say felt rotten in my mouth and, maybe, if I didn't speak, none of it would be true.

"I heard Last Toll," Neven said, rubbing his eye with the

back of his hand and sliding his legs through the slats. "It's too late to go out."

"I made a mistake," I said.

Something in my tone must have alerted Neven to the gravity of the situation, because he straightened and fumbled for his glasses, knocking down gears from the loft. He blinked down at me, his eyes magnified behind his glasses making him look a bit like a dragonfly, then rushed down the ladder.

"Your hair," he said, frowning.

My hand shot up to grab what was left of my braid. I'd almost forgotten about it in my panic, since my hood had concealed it, but the reminder made my eyes burn with something close to tears. Part of my braid still barely hung on, while the rest had been cut to my collarbone. I stormed past Neven and yanked open a desk drawer, then another, then another, sending cogs and buttons flying. I grabbed a pair of scissors and tried to contort myself to finish the job.

"Ren, stop," he said, taking my wrist and sliding the scissors from my fingers before I could jab them into my shoulder blades.

"I want it off," I said, holding my hand out for the scissors.

A million questions spun behind his violet eyes, but he didn't voice any of them. "Turn around," he said. "I'll do it."

"You've never cut hair," I said.

"And you can't see the back of your head."

I sighed and closed my eyes, turning around.

I hated the sound of scissors slicing through my hair again and tried not to picture myself held down in the snow, but luckily Neven finished quickly.

"Ivy again?"

I said nothing, turning to the mirror on the inside door of my dresser and trying to tie my hair back so I wouldn't have to see it.

"Ren, what did you do?" Neven said from behind me.

I glanced at his reflection in my mirror, his eyes spinning cool purple and infinite patience. I shut the door.

"I have to leave," I said again, shedding my silver cloak and replacing it with a long black coat that had a hood to hide my hair. "Ivy knows what I can do, and they're going to come for me. I can't stay in England anymore, Neven, I'm sorry." The words came out stilted and mean, like I was arguing. But my eyes watered and I couldn't explain more, or I'd never finish packing. It was so much easier to be angry than to be cracked open.

For the last century, I'd dreamed of leaving England, but never like this. It was supposed to happen in broad daylight, when Ivy was asleep. I was supposed to have my bags packed and my forged papers ready. I was supposed to be so prepared that there was almost no chance of failure. But the chance for that perfect escape had come and gone. I could leave now or not at all.

At least I'd already mapped out the first steps. The hardest part was escaping England, where Reapers had eyes everywhere and all of them knew my face. The fastest way out was the ferry to France that ran three times a day. The French Reapers, still bitter about Napoleon's wars at the turn of the century, wouldn't take kindly to large numbers of British Reapers tearing France apart to find me. I would have time to regroup and the Reapers would lose my trail. From there, I could safely make my way to Japan.

I'd seen every photograph and painting of Japan the library had to offer—sepia snapshots of palaces with sloped roofs, kimonos of a thousand patterns, painted parasols and paper fans. Having never known anywhere but London, Japan seemed more like a vivid dream than a place I'd come from.

And it was the only place in the world where there was someone who might help me. Maybe my mother had given me to my father, Ambrose, because she hadn't wanted me. Maybe he'd stolen me. Maybe she was dead. But if she was still alive, she owed me answers, if not help. Even coldhearted Ambrose had given me food and a place to stay. Surely my mother, who had given me nothing but my name, could offer me that much.

I'd never tried to escape, because whenever I sat down to write out my plans, Neven would appear, smiling and pulling me up to his loft to show me a telephone that he'd deconstructed, or a new pair of glasses he'd made himself, or a baby squirrel he'd rescued. And for those small moments, I would forget about Ivy and her friends, about Ambrose and my stepmother, Corliss, and everyone else but Neven. He'd talk to me about his latest gadget or rescued pet and I'd think about how Reapers weren't supposed to feel love, but whatever this feeling was, it made it so hard to leave Neven.

Now I had no choice.

"I'm sorry," I said again, because the silence had stretched on for too long and I couldn't look at Neven, couldn't bear to see his face.

"Okay," Neven said quietly. "Okay, I just need to pack a few things."

My hands froze over the gray dress I was folding. "Neven,"

I said, "you don't have to come with me. I came to say good-bye."

But Neven was already climbing back up to the loft. He looked over his shoulder and frowned like I'd gravely insulted him, then grabbed a bag and started jamming socks into it.

"Don't be ridiculous," he said. He hurried back down the ladder and inspected the gears on the table, then swept everything into his bag.

"Neven," I said, pulling his bag away as he tried to stuff another handful of cogs into a pocket.

"Hey! Let me—"

"Neven," I said, setting my hands on his shoulders, "if you leave with me, you can never come back."

The determination behind his eyes dimmed. Unlike me, Neven had parents to think about. He lived in a world where he could be something, especially if I left.

"I know," he said.

"You can't say goodbye to Father or Corliss."

"I *know*," he said again, closing his eyes. He took a ragged breath, then opened his eyes and laid his hand on top of mine with a small smile. "I won't let you go alone, Ren."

He gently moved my hands off his shoulders and went back to packing while I stood there, speechless and unworthy of everything he was giving up for me. I should have tried harder to make him stay in London, where he was safe. But I desperately didn't want to go alone, and even the sight of him packing made the burning in my eyes recede. *Selfish,* my brain said.

I hoped that this would be at least a little good for Neven, too. Neven was never meant to be a Reaper. He still spent nights crying after taking souls, showing guilt that Reapers weren't supposed to feel.

"He doesn't have enough Death in him," our father always said. He'd tried to make Neven practice extracting the souls of squirrels and rabbits as a child, but Neven had always cried and screamed until Ambrose relented. Corliss had tried reading him ghastly bedtime stories about royal beheadings and medieval torture—tales that most Reaper children found exciting—but he would just sob and hide under his blankets.

"This is why Ankou warns us that High Reapers are meant to have only one child," Corliss had whispered to Ambrose. "One of them comes out weak."

Neven and I, huddled in my bed with our ears pressed to the wall, heard everything.

But now Neven was busy packing his jeweler's tools and deciding which socks to take with him when he left his entire world behind for me, so perhaps Corliss had been wrong.

We finished packing in a matter of minutes. I'd taken only some clothes, an extra knife, and a book of Tennyson's poems. I wished there was a way to carry all my books with me, but in the end I'd randomly chosen one from the precarious piles around my desk, and hadn't been overly disappointed to see Tennyson's name printed on the cover. He'd written a poem called "All Things Must Die," so it was little surprise that his work appealed to a Reaper. But he'd also written of Ulysses, who had left home in search of a better place, not unlike what I was trying to do. *'Tis not too late to seek a newer world*, he'd said. But "late" was relative when you could turn time, and the cold metal of the clock still clutched in my sweaty palm told me that I was already far too late.

Into the inner pocket of my bag, only big enough to fit a few sheets of paper, I crammed the pictures of Japan that I'd ripped from library books. I hadn't told Neven that this was my final destination, too afraid that he'd say no to something so far away and foreign. After all, there was a big difference between traveling across the Channel and traveling across the world. Maybe I could show him the pictures once we were safe in France, and maybe he'd be just as enchanted as I was.

"Okay," Neven said, wrapping a scarf around his extra pair of glasses and placing it in his suitcase. "Okay, okay, I think that's everything." He latched his suitcase and turned toward the door, then froze and dropped the luggage, eyes going wide. "Oliver!" he said, rushing up to the loft.

"Oliver?"

Neven shoved aside his sheets and hefted an enormous gray cat into his arms.

"Another stray?" I said, pressing my eyes closed. "Neven, I've been storing poisonous plants in here."

"Oliver just sleeps," Neven said, waving his hand dismissively and tucking the cat under one arm, grabbing for his suitcase with the other. "He's lazy."

"And morbidly overfed," I said. "We're sneaking him out, too, I suppose."

"I can't leave him here!" Neven said. "We're never coming back!"

I sighed. "Fine. But if he makes too much noise, you better leave him. I'm not dying over a stray cat."

"He's fine," Neven said, squishing the limp cat tighter against his side.

I rolled my eyes and tightened my grip on my bag. "Are you ready?"

Neven nodded. Oliver blinked.

I opened the door and stepped out into the catacombs.

We hurried through the tunnels, not even daring to breathe. In this hushed hour between darkness and daybreak, the spectral planes parted and the monsters came out in the world above. For this reason, most Reapers were already asleep in their quarters or waiting for the day shift to begin. Only a handful of High Reapers were allowed out during the twilight hour.

Our footsteps slapped wetly against the stones as we moved through the tunnels that glowed at only half light, some of the lanterns left extinguished until the guards came to relight them when the hour had passed. Our shadows rolled across the walls as we walked, dark and contorted in the weakly changing light.

I was just about to turn a corner when the sharp shadow of another Reaper announced their presence from the adjoining hallway. Stronger Reapers must have overridden my time lock, as they could if they drew close enough.

I swept Neven into an alcove and extinguished the nearby lanterns with a wave of my hand, pulling darkness over us like a thick blanket. I hugged my bag against my chest with one arm and nudged Neven's suitcase back with my knee until he got the hint and tucked it flat against the wall. Despite all the stereotypes that female Reapers were more frivolous, I had packed only clothes and a book while Neven had tried to cram half his room into a suitcase, leaving us with a dense and somewhat lumpy shadow. I wished he had packed lighter, but when my brother was giving up his home for me, I could hardly begrudge him a few extra pairs of socks.

With Neven pressed against me, the panicked pounding of his heart echoed through my bones. I couldn't verbally re-assure him without risking other Reapers overhearing, so I squeezed his arm in a way that hopefully told him *it's all right, they won't find us.* He swallowed and held his breath.

Two Reapers rushed around the corner a moment later and flew past us. They hadn't seen us through my wall of darkness. Neven let out a quivering breath and huddled closer to me.

The Reapers stopped at the far end of the hallway, just out-side our room. They tried the handle and found it locked, then one of them stepped back while the other pressed his hand to the door.

The black paint on the door flaked and shuddered to the ground, like a serpent shedding it skin. Then the wood it-self began to rot, fading into sickly shades of gray-green and cleaving into chunks that crumbled to the floor. Without a word, they stormed into the apartment.

I dreaded to think what that Reaper's hands could do if they ever touched my skin. Just like with objects, High Reap-ers could steal from my own lifespan if they turned time on me and only me.

This was the great danger of upsetting High Reapers. With time as powerful and volatile as it was, only Ankou's chosen few and their descendants were allowed to ascend as High Reapers and learn how to wield time not as a tool but as a weapon. The Low Reapers collected souls, and the High Reapers maintained order among the soul collectors.

"They know," Neven said, as if I needed any confirmation that Ivy had returned. His eyes glowed a nauseous green, and I suspected that the reality of running away with me had finally set in. But it was too late for either of us to turn back.

I tried to think of something comforting to say, but I couldn't think of anything that wasn't a lie, and I didn't like lying to Neven. I wished I could promise him that I had a perfect plan, that I could defeat any Reaper that got in our way, that I could keep him safe.

But nothing that day had gone according to plan. All I could do, all I had ever done, was find a way to survive.

"We have to go now," I said, releasing the cloak of darkness and grabbing Neven's hand. Neither of us dared to mention that there was only one door out of the catacombs.

CHAPTER 03

The Door, of course, was guarded.

Neven and I had run through the shadows all the way to the main tunnel, where we crushed ourselves into an alcove and I pulled a sheet of darkness over us. Two High Reapers were standing in front of the Door, questioning the Collector I'd seen earlier that evening.

"She broke my glasses!" he said, holding his shattered lenses in one hand as pieces of them sparkled to the cobbled ground. I didn't recall breaking his glasses, but it wasn't the first time someone had tried to frame me. "She seemed suspicious, so I tried to detain her, but she just smashed my glasses into the desk and ran off! I wanted to stop her, but my astigmatism—"

"All right, Lester," said the High Reaper, holding up a

hand. The Collector jolted like he expected to be struck across the face. "Go back to your quarters, you're finished for today."

Lester's spine snapped into a ninety-degree bow. "Yes, Reaper," he said. Then he turned and hurried out of the main hall.

I hoped the High Reapers would leave as well, but they simply turned and stood in front of the door with their arms crossed. Ivy had definitely escaped the time freeze and reported me, and Lester had confirmed that I'd returned to the catacombs. The lower division of the High Council was probably running around the tunnels searching for me, hoping to secure their eternal positions as High Reapers by being the first to drag me to the courtroom. They would have had better luck working together to freeze all the catacombs at once, but Reapers were selfish creatures who didn't like to share glory. As it was, all the different time turns had started to not only cancel each other out but to make me feel a bit timesick, yanked back and forth off the natural timeline.

There was still the matter of escaping. I glanced at the swinging chandeliers and wall-mounted candles and wondered if a sudden flash of bright light could incapacitate the other Reapers long enough for us to escape, like what had happened with Ivy.

But that had been a massive accident. I'd never felt rage quite like that before, never felt the light build up within me and surge out in every direction like I was an ancient star exploding to its death. I wouldn't tell Neven just yet, but I was worried. I'd spent my entire life learning to keep candles from turning into sun-white hellfire when I lay at another Reaper's feet swallowing my own blood, but suddenly

I couldn't hold it back. They said that a Reaper's powers got stronger with age, but did a Shinigami's? I didn't know, and there was no one who could tell me, no book I could steal from the library that would enlighten me.

Regardless, I couldn't do it again, not intentionally. It had taken several minutes for the light to build up to that degree, and the High Reapers had surely been warned of what had occurred. They would be prepared, because Reapers never failed the same way twice.

Wielding time against a High Reaper wasn't an option that I particularly liked, either. Ivy had been incapacitated, but in their normal form, High Reapers were practically invincible. While Low Reapers like me and Neven finished our studies once we could freeze time and manipulate objects, High Reapers were trained to inflict time torture on other Reapers, ensuring that no one used time as their toy and irrevocably broke the timeline. Ivy and her High Reaper friends had always edged the line between bullying and time torture, and I didn't want to see what happened when she had permission from the High Council to cross it.

The other option was waiting in the darkness until the guards left, but I doubted that they would give up until they'd searched behind every single brick.

Neven tapped my shoulder, then pointed to the hallway. I looked over and saw nothing, then turned back at him and raised an eyebrow. He pointed to the High Reapers, then his ears, then made an X motion with his fingers. I nodded in understanding and picked up my suitcase. He wanted to speak somewhere the High Reapers wouldn't hear us.

We crept through the shadows and back out to the hall

where we hid in another alcove. Luckily, the Reapers seemed too busy checking rooms to pay attention to a connecting hallway with no doors.

"I think we can get out through the vents," Neven said.

"Vents?"

I looked up, scanning the walls for some kind of grate. Neven nodded toward the far end of the hallway, where a lattice-patterned iron grate about the size of my Tennyson book was fixed to the ceiling.

"You are vastly underestimating the circumference of my hips," I said.

Neven shook his head. "If you move the bricks to get in, it's big enough to crawl through."

"And how would you know that?"

He lifted the cat, who blinked sleepily at me.

"It's where I found Oliver," he said. "I heard him crying in the walls, so I climbed inside to try and get him. He was scared and ran away, but I bribed him with some rats."

"You had a collection of dead rats at your disposal?"

"They weren't dead."

I groaned and clapped a hand over my eyes.

"I didn't pack them!" Neven said.

"Small mercies," I said, dropping my hand from my face. "All right, let's try it."

I froze the entire hallway and prayed that it held while Neven got to work opening the grate. Doing so required standing on his suitcase and time-turning the bricks away like we did at the Door until the opening was large enough to climb through. It was difficult to perform two different time turns at once, so I was once again infinitely glad Neven was with me. Hopefully a stronger Reaper wouldn't come by and sense the change.

I moved a safe distance from the bricks raining down from the ceiling until Neven finished. He climbed into the vent, then reached down for me to hand him the cat, then the bags, and finally my own hands so he could pull me up.

I climbed up into a round tunnel carved into the stone prison of the catacombs, about the width of my shoulders. The vent left me enough space to hunch over and crawl with my bag in one hand, but not much else. It smelled of dampness and mold, the stone slick beneath my fingers.

Neven repaired the bricks and I waved away the time freeze in the hallway below.

"I don't suppose you know which way is out?" I said.

"Well..."

Oliver squeezed under Neven's arm, crawling through my legs and strutting through the vent.

"Let's follow him," Neven said. "He must have come here from the outside, so maybe he'll go there again."

I sighed but nodded, thrilled by the fact that Reapers— some of the strongest creatures in the land—were on their knees crawling after a stray cat.

We shuffled through the dim passageway, my knees growing soaked from the suspicious-smelling wetness, the jagged edges of the stones scraping my elbows raw. Whenever we passed over a grate, Neven or I would freeze the room below us so no one would notice the sounds of shuffling clothes and dragging luggage. All the Reapers frantically searching wouldn't notice one extra time turn among all the others they were casting, and none of them thought to try to freeze a place they couldn't see.

Suddenly, the voice of a High Reaper thundered through the vents, echoing with the language of Death. The words blasted the warmth from my bones and raked coldness across my skin, as if my whole body had been flayed.

"Where is the Shinigami?"

Both Neven and I froze. I imagined Ankou's skeletal hands coming through the grate and dragging me to the darkest and coldest depths of the catacombs.

Oblivious to our terror, the conversation continued in the room directly below us.

"She couldn't have gotten far," said a man's voice, muted through the vents but still tight with anger.

"She's a monster," Ivy's voice said, sore and strained. "She can probably bleed through walls or turn into a roach and crawl away."

I held my breath and crawled closer to the grate, peering down.

It was the High Council chamber, that much I could tell from the arrangement of thirty throne-like chairs around the perimeter, each one with a tall back that loomed like a shadow, different beasts carved into each of the arms—lions, bears, spiders, dragons.

Ivy occupied the twenty-fifth seat, white bandages wrapped around her face, concealing her eyes. I found that odd, considering I was an inferior Reaper and shouldn't have been able to cause much lasting harm to her. Either she was weaker than she pretended to be, or I was much stronger than I thought.

"We'll find her," said the first man, the one who spoke in

Death and occupied the first chair. High Councilor Cromwell, the primogenital grandson of Ankou himself, and Ivy's
father. His face looked as if time had grabbed it and stretched
it downward like white clay, fingernails scoring lines of age
into his forehead and the skin around his thin lips. Even
the flesh under his eyes drooped, a sweeping penumbra of
shadow in contrast to the startling brightness of his ice-blue
eyes. Signs of age didn't show on Reapers until they neared
two millennia. My nearly two centuries of collecting had
rendered me the appearance of a young adult by human stan-
dards, while Neven's one century of life made him more of
a scrawny and graceless teenager. But eventually, the Death
that we delivered to humans would come for us, too, a slow
repayment for our sins.

"She is too dangerous to let live any longer," Cromwell said.

The words, because he spoke them in our language, were
not an opinion, but a promise.

My fingers trembled against the damp stone. I'd assumed
that my punishment would be a few centuries in one of Highgate's mausoleums with only corpses for company, as was the
case for most transgressors. But death was a far more terrify-
ing prospect. I thought of all the souls I'd collected and tossed
into a void without thinking about what became of them.
What would become of someone like me? If there was such
a thing as Hell, I would burn there. But I didn't believe in
silly Christian tales. In the way that some people believed in
God, I believed that nothing awaited us after death. And the
idea of closing my eyes and being nothing at all was far worse
than an eternity on fire.

I couldn't let them catch me.

Cromwell turned, his bones creaking like weary furniture, and looked directly at the thirtieth chair of the Council. *"Ambrose,"* he said. *"She's your charge, is she not?"*

The man flinched at the sound of his name in our language, hands curling into fists in his lap as all eyes in the room settled on him.

He was the father that Neven and I shared. The illustrious Ambrose Scarborough, Thirtieth High Reaper on the Council.

Having a bastard daughter with a Shinigami had demoted him from Fourth to Thirtieth chair, the very lowest of the High, but his reputation as an otherwise upstanding High Reaper had been enough to save him from being ejected entirely from the Council. When word of my birth got out, he'd quickly married a respectable Reaper—Corliss—and had Neven to show the Council he wasn't loyal to a Shinigami.

Neither he nor Corliss had ever been cruel to me. They'd fed me, bought me new shoes and cloaks as I grew taller, brushed and braided my black hair to hide it beneath my hood.

But when I was young and woke up crying from nightmares of church grims eating my bones and pounded on their bedroom door, it was always locked, no matter how loudly I screamed. When I told them the other Reapers tormented me in our training groups, they wiped the tears from my face with a rag and told me to go to bed. Once, I'd run away for three nights, sleeping in the rafters over Big Ben while the church grims barked below, and no one had searched for me.

From that perch I'd watched the humans, how they carried their children on their shoulders and kissed their cheeks and held their hands and said they loved each other. Even when they had five or six children trailing after them, one was never left behind or ignored. Something sour had settled in my stomach, as if everything inside me had started to rot. The children all looked so sickeningly happy. Was this the reason that humans found so much joy in their pitifully short lives, while I, who had already outlived most of them, found nothing about life to be all that pleasant?

Reaper families were not meant to love like humans. Reapers married for alliances and had children to continue their lineage, and good Reapers had no practical need for love in order to be successful. In fact, those who cast too many fond glances at their wives or spoiled their children too readily were the first to see their families culled, the objects of their weakness eliminated. I knew this, and yet, as I'd watched families rushing through the market and couples stopping to kiss in shadowed alleys, I couldn't help but wonder how it would feel to be human.

I'd returned home only because I'd gotten too scared of the rats, but my father and Corliss hadn't even asked where I'd gone. When I'd come back to our quarters, dirty and trembling, my father's eyes had dimmed with disappointment.

They'd tried to keep me away from Neven at first, but Neven had no reason to hate me the way they did. At night, I'd teach him new words from the language books I studied— French and Greek and Russian and (secretly) Japanese. He'd show me the mechanical toys that he'd pried open with jeweler's tools, laying their sparkling carnage across my desk, where Corliss wouldn't comment on it. And when the other Reapers smashed my clock, he'd gather the pieces and put them back together for me with skilled precision. When he realized that his parents acknowledged his high marks with stoic praise while any news of my success at school went ignored, he'd bring me dead flowers and shiny rocks and tell me I'd done well today, like Ambrose sometimes deigned to say to him. And when he'd turned one hundred and had the choice of living with his parents or living with me, he hadn't hesitated.

"I've relinquished her," my father said in the High Council chamber below, his words impassive, the same gentle coldness that I'd always known. "You know this."

The words stung but didn't surprise me. Though he'd never told me, I'd learned quite young that the population of High Reapers was never meant to increase beyond Ankou's chosen few, to ensure that the High Reapers could never overpower Ankou himself. Couples with only one High Reaper, like Ambrose, could have only one child unless the child died or was formally renounced. I was very much not dead, and yet I had a younger brother. It wasn't difficult to see what had happened. Before I'd even graduated, Ambrose must have signed away my rights to inheritance, both of his estate and his spot on the Council. On paper, I was an orphan, graciously allowed to live in his home because having the death of a child on his soul was apparently too great a weight to bear. For a while, I hadn't even known whether I would be allowed to collect souls, but with the population of London increasing so rapidly in the last century and the death rate multiplying in turn, it seemed even High Reapers knew that turning me away would have been a waste.

Neven had gone very still beside me. He looked at me searchingly, but I shook my head. I couldn't think about Ambrose right now, couldn't risk losing control just a few meters above Cromwell.

"She's taken your son, as well," said another Councilor. "What do you propose we do about this, Ambrose?"

The question was meant as a taunt, a shift of blame, because of course none of them could do anything but wait.

"Neven will return," Ambrose said with complete certainty. "He's a coward who runs from shadows. He doesn't know what it's like beyond."

Neven's fingers curled tighter around his suitcase, his lips pressed together.

Despite all the ways his parents had tried to twist him into something colder, he still looked at them as if they'd breathed the universe into existence and hand-placed every star in the sky. He clung to their small compliments and cried at their admonishment, then cried more when they told him Reapers weren't supposed to cry. Neven's heart was soft like a sponge, and Ambrose insulting him so casually made me want to wring his neck.

Before Cromwell could respond, the doors to the council room burst open, two High Reapers dragging in a Low Reaper whose arms and legs had been bound with thick rope.

Neven tensed, shooting me a panicked look as his eyes flashed between purple and green. I squinted at the captured Reaper's face, but I didn't recognize him. He couldn't have been more than a century old.

The High Reapers dragged him toward Cromwell and forced him into a chair, chaining his ankles down. He kicked and tried to throw his weight off the chair, but the High Reaper struck him across the face and he fell still.

"High Councilor," the Reaper said, "we've found Gray Westbrook, a friend of the Shinigami's brother."

As soon as the High Reaper said his name, I realized why Neven had looked so alarmed. He had mentioned Gray's name before, but *friend* was a bit of an overstatement. Because of me, neither of us had friends—at least, not in public. No one wanted to be associated with a Shinigami, but some Reapers, like Gray, felt bad enough for Neven to help him on occasion.

Neven was too squeamish to extract souls with any kind of efficiency, so he was perpetually falling behind on his collections. Gray had reaped some of the souls on Neven's list for him, and in return, Neven had lent him one of my books on the Salem Witch Trials. I'd told him it was a bad idea, but he'd been so determined thank Gray somehow, even though he knew that Reapers had eyes everywhere.

Sure enough, the High Reaper threw my book at Gray's feet, the pages spilling open to the bookplate I'd pasted in the front, my name in curled script inside a wreath of ivy. Usually the bookplates kept other Reapers from stealing my books, since anyone with Shinigami property would be taunted by High Reapers. But Gray was facing something much worse than schoolyard taunts.

"He's the Scarborough boy's friend," the High Reaper said. "He says the book is from him and not the Shinigami."

Cromwell leaned forward in his chair, eyes seething. *"Tell us where the Shinigami has gone,"* he said.

Gray tried to bow, but his hands tied behind the chair stopped him from going very far. Instead, he just hung his head, sweat dripping from his forehead to the marbled floor.

"High Councilor," Gray said, his voice trembling, "I never met the Shinigami. I don't know where she's gone."

"But you're friends with her brother!" said the High Reaper who had dragged him in. "You must know where he is!"

"No!" Gray shook his head. "No, we weren't friends, I just felt sorry for him."

Neven didn't say a word, but his unnatural stillness told me enough. Like always, no one cared about him when the High Reapers were watching.

Cromwell didn't move. His pale blue eyes shifted toward the second seat of the High Council, and that was all the instruction needed before the second chair Reaper rose to his feet.

Gray shook his head and surged back, nearly toppling his chair as the High Reaper drew closer.

"No, no, I swear, I have no idea!" Gray said, thrashing against the ropes.

But the High Reaper didn't so much as hesitate, stepping forward and placing his hand on Gray's head.

All at once, Gray's skin grew loose and sallow, wrinkles appearing around his eyes and veins bulging from his hands where he gripped the chair. The sound of his scream withered from a young man's voice to an old man's grating wails, his spine contracting as he shrank down and hunched over in his seat, the pain of a lifetime tearing through his bones.

Neven closed his eyes and pressed his forehead to the cool stone tunnel, trying to breathe quietly. I set a hand on his spine and rubbed gently up and down. Sometimes Neven knew what I was thinking without me saying it, and I hoped that this was one of those times. I hoped he understood that this was all because of me and my mistakes and everything I wasn't, that none of it could ever be his fault. Neven could look away, but I forced myself to watch, not to stop time and run away like a coward.

Three Low Reapers—one in chains—stood no chance at all against the entire High Council. Helping Gray would mean almost certain death for both me and Neven, and I didn't know Gray well enough to make that kind of sacrifice. Neven was too scared and too loyal to me to take any action, and I was too selfish to risk my life for someone I didn't know. But I would not look away from Gray Westbrook and pretend that he wasn't suffering because of me.

At last, the High Reaper withdrew his hand.

"I will ask you again," Cromwell said as Gray sat panting in his chair, now as old as Cromwell. *"Where has the Shinigami gone?"*

Gray closed his eyes, whispering prayers in the language of Death as tears followed the jagged path of his wrinkled skin down to his chin.

"I don't know," he said at last. "Please, I don't know."

The High Reaper turned to Cromwell, his hands twitching and eyes begging for permission to continue, but Cromwell only sighed.

"He knows nothing," Cromwell said. *"We are wasting time here while the Shinigami gets away. Send him back."*

The High Reaper guarding Gray scowled but bent down and unlocked the shackles from around his ankles and then his wrists. Gray fell forward, groaning as his bones collided with the marble floors. Before Cromwell could issue another order, he lurched to his feet and limped from the room, shoving past the High Reapers, who watched him with mild pity as he burst through the door and disappeared into the dark hallways.

"It's time to take more drastic measures," Cromwell said, turning to the court aid, who brought forward a massive leather-bound book embossed with gold. He dropped it heavily on Cromwell's desk, then bowed deeply and backed away.

I had seen this book only once before, on my hundredth birthday, when I'd signed my name on its infinite pages and received my clock. This was Ankou's register, the book that all new Reapers had to sign to enter into a contract with him.

Death, which made us and guided us, was volatile and ever-hungry. Creatures born of Death could either serve it or be devoured by it. By signing our names in Ankou's book and beginning our Reaper duties, we agreed to do the work Death asked of us in exchange for its guidance, a long life, and more strength than humans could ever dream of. It was like when humans fed fires in their hearths, keeping them burning for the warmth and light they provided. But fire stayed trapped in a hearth only if it wanted to, if there was nothing else nearby to devour. Fire had no shape or limit, could swallow cities whole if no one stopped it. Death was as endless as fire, and we carried it inside of us. The contract was our agreement with Ankou that kept it contained.

As Cromwell turned the pages, I peered around the bars of the grate and read the names scratched into the ancient surface with deep indigo ink.

Beowulf Hale
Everleigh Lancaster

Synne Churchill
Wren Scarborough

The High Councilor dipped his quill into a well of viscous black ink, then slashed a clean line through my name. I held my breath as the letters began to fade from dark blue to a pale gray, then disappeared into the paper. What would happen now that I was untethered? Would the spirit of Ankou descend and point the Council to my hiding place? Or would great invisible hands drag me to Ankou himself to be torn apart with his scythe?

"*There,*" Cromwell said. "*She has no contract with us now. Death will find her.*"

I frowned and looked at Neven, but he still hadn't opened his eyes. What could Cromwell possibly mean? Death didn't need to find me because it was always there, in my blood and bones. I was made of Death.

"And the boy?" said another councilor.

"He'll return," Ambrose said.

"*And when we find the girl,*" the High Councilor said, turning sharply to Ambrose, "*you will take her to Ankou yourself.*"

Ambrose placed his hand over his heart, bowed in Cromwell's direction, and then promised in the language of Death:

"*Yes, Reaper.*"

CHAPTER 04

We made it to the surface just before daylight broke over the cemetery. The rabbits and birds had gone into hiding and the snowstorm held its breath, as if even the snowflakes were too scared to fall down to earth in this dark hour.

I replaced the grate and bricks from the mouth of the tunnel, sealing away the yawning chasm that led back to Death's home. We were far enough from the Door that Reapers probably wouldn't be lurking around here, but I didn't want to stay long enough to find out. Neven scooped up Oliver and tucked him into his coat, then stared out at the blaze of new sunlight filtering through the fingerlike branches of the trees, his expression pale.

"Don't think about him," I said, because it was too easy to read Neven's face.

"But Gray—"

"There was nothing you could have done," I said. "If you'd tried to stop them, we all would have died."

Neven's eyes looked wet, but he nodded and turned away. I wished I could take all of his guilt for myself. Unlike Neven, I was good at tucking it away somewhere deep inside myself and pretending it wasn't there, at least until I fell asleep and my dreams reminded me of the long list of things I would one day have to atone for.

As I set the last brick in place and picked up my suitcase, something black flashed along the tree line.

A church grim was watching us.

From a distance, it could be mistaken for a black dog, but the closer you looked, the more contorted it became—the black fur that seemed soft from a distance grew needle-sharp, the golden eyes turned sickly yellow, and the hunched legs resembled the muscled calves of a human.

A warning growl hummed through the grim's body, cracking the thin sheet of ice below us and rippling the dead winter grass.

Church grims were meant to protect the parishioners of London, which was all well and fine, except they saw Reapers as the greatest threat of all. Never mind that death was necessary and technically not our doing; they tried to destroy us all the same.

The grim turned and vanished into the twilight.

"Have your clock ready," I said. "He'll be back."

Neven fished his clock out of his pocket, the jostling causing Oliver to squirm with disapproval. He clenched his clock in a tight fist, ready to stop time if the grim jumped out of the shadows.

We followed the footpath to the main gates, past head-stones shaped like Celtic crosses and concrete angels gazing forlornly at the earth. I had never walked through the cemetery in the soft light of daybreak before, when I could clearly see the stony eyes of the frozen angels and the names of the souls I'd taken carved forever into marble—a glaring accusation that night had always blurred away.

But even more unsettling than the starkness of morning was the feeling of being hunted. I couldn't see the grim anymore, but I could sense it in the nervous shifting of the trees and the way the shadows wavered, as if someone had disturbed them.

As we crested a small hill, the main gates of the cemetery came into view. Neven's stride mimicked the confident gait of High Reapers, but his eyes spun colors like carnival lights and gave away his fear.

The cat made a rumbling sound of displeasure and bared his fangs.

"Oliver?" Neven said, hitching the cat higher against his chest.

Oliver hissed and tried to climb Neven's torso like a tree, his front claws hooking into Neven's lips.

"Ow! Oliver, stop—"

The cat launched away from Neven in a desperate bid to escape and landed on my shoulder, claws caught in my cloak and scratching at my neck with its hind paws.

"Neven, get your damned cat off of me!" I said, dropping my suitcase and yanking the cat away with both hands, then casting it to the ground.

The air to my right whistled as if something had slashed it in half, then a grim sank its teeth into the cat's spine and crunched hard. Grims might have been dumb dogs, but they were the fastest creatures I'd ever seen.

"Oliver!" Neven said, rushing forward as the grim shook the cat before tossing it to the side, still crunching on its bones, jowls dripping with blood.

The grim would do the same to Neven, and though it wouldn't kill him, it would hurt.

I'd dropped my clock somewhere in the dirt to peel the cat away, and though it was still chained to my clothing, I didn't have time to search for it in the dim light. Instead, I threw myself in front of Neven as the grim spun and launched toward us, its hairy human legs kicking off the ground.

Its teeth sank into my right forearm and sent me crashing back onto Neven, his head smashing into the dirt and my spine crushing into his neck. The pain set in belatedly, dulled by the adrenaline but still sharp and white-hot. The teeth tore through the tendons in my wrist and sank into the bone, leaving my fingers limp and unresponsive.

I felt around for my clock's silver chain, the fingers on my left hand alarmingly cold and numb as they closed around the thick metal links and pulled hard, tossing my clock into the air above me.

The grim's eyes caught the sudden blaze of silver and gold in the moonlight, its jaw unhinging with long strands of yellow drool, finally releasing me. That was when my arm started to hurt, blood boiling hot against my chilled skin and tendons screaming as they tried to twist themselves back into place, wriggling like worms deep in my flesh.

The grim opened its mouth to catch my clock, but before it could clamp it between its teeth, I reached out with my left hand and snatched the clock from the air.

The sounds of the cemetery went silent and the grim froze, jaws wide and unbreathing just inches from my face, three rows of jagged teeth and a forked tongue on display.

I felt behind me for Neven, just in case he hadn't been touching my skin during the time freeze, but he was already rolling out from under me, breathing hard and scrambling for his clock. My right arm was throbbing deadweight pulling at my shoulder socket as I rose to my feet. I kicked the grim's flank and he tipped over, legs sticking out rigidly.

"Oliver!" Neven said, his voice cracking as he knelt by the cat's remains. He reached out as if to pet him, but his hand shook and his eyes watered at all the blood spilling in the soil.

"Neven, don't look," I said, still trying to catch my breath.

He turned to me, his eyes a stormy blue, then his gaze fell to the blood slowly dripping down my arm.

"Ren!" he said, crawling the few feet between us and rolling up my sleeve.

"It's fine," I said before I'd even looked at it. I could tell, because the pain was ebbing away. Blood had soaked the white sleeve of my inner shirt, but the tooth marks were already shrinking, sealing themselves up. Grims, no matter their speed, were still inferior creatures, after all. They couldn't do much lasting damage. Luckily, my dark coat could hide the blood stains.

"I'm sorry, Ren," Neven said, clutching my sleeve. "I didn't help you."

"You are helping me," I said, cutting off some of the soaked fabric with my pocketknife. He had no idea just how much he was helping me. "Besides, it's done. We're fine."

Neven bit his lip and turned to the chewed-up remains of the cat a few feet away from us. He took a shuddering breath, then turned away and picked up his suitcase.

"I'm sorry," he said again, this time staring at his shoes, speckled dark with my blood. "Ren, I'm really sorry."

"Neven, stop."

"Father said—"

"*Stop,*" I said, taking Neven's scared face in my hands, even though I was smearing blood into his cheek. In that moment I hated Ambrose even more for reducing Neven to this. *He's a coward who runs from shadows*, Ambrose had said, as if Neven needed a reminder of how little Ambrose thought of him. Ambrose's opinion no longer mattered to me, but to Neven it surely did.

"You're helping me," I said again, staring hard into Neven's mournful blue eyes so he would know it was true. He swallowed and nodded, even as my hands fell away. I used my clean sleeve to scrub away the blood on his cheek.

"We have to get to the docks," I said.

Neven nodded, brushing the dirt from his knees. When we closed the cemetery gates and headed into town, Neven did not once look back.

We stopped time just long enough to steal the clothes off a young couple. I took a hand-sewn shawl, along with a dirty white bonnet that helped to hide my shorn hair. We weren't in rags—after all, impoverished humans could never afford a ticket—but we needed to seem poor enough to blend in with the steerage passengers, where the mass of people would hide

Neven's color-shifting eyes and my Asian features. Neven
liberated a heavy brown overcoat and gray cap from the man
before we hurried back to the dock.

Evading the fare was a simple matter of stopping time just
long enough to slip past the ticket collectors, and without
much delay, we had boarded a ship rapidly moving toward
France, away from everything we'd ever known.

Neven stared at the retreating shoreline with wonder, even
as the packed crowd shuffled us back and forth on the deck.
The sea air felt new and clean. My chest filled with lightness
at the idea that Ivy, Ambrose, and all of London would from
now on be only a memory.

But yet, every time I blinked, I could see my name in
Ankou's book, slashed through with a single thin line.

And I could hear Cromwell's age-crackled voice as clearly
as if he were standing beside me, fingers cupped and whispering into my ear:

"Death will find you."

We descended into steerage, the dim and crowded under-
belly of the ship where we would pretend to be humans for
the next few hours. Despite the chill of early January over the
water, the air on the lower deck simmered from the warmth
of so many compacted humans. Not a single window let in
light or even a breath of ocean air into the smothering wood-
paneled cage. The waves rocked the floor, sending us col-
liding into other passengers, elbows jabbed in stomachs and
feet stomping on feet.

Maybe it was a result of being free from a contract, but the
edges of the human world looked soft and unreal in the day-

light, like beautiful illusions that would disappear and leave me back in my stone-cold loft. I felt untethered, the weight of my clothes and the suitcase in my right hand the only things keeping my feet on the ground.

I kept glancing over my shoulder, the same restless way I turned over in bed on long mornings that melted into evenings when sleep wouldn't come. A ship at sea was a cage, and if the High Reapers caught up to me, there was no place I could run.

If they knew you were here, you wouldn't be standing here thinking about them, I told myself. But that wasn't entirely true. While High Reapers didn't need to delay, they could if they wanted to watch me squirm. I thought of Ivy's scissors and rubbed my eye at the ghost sensation, then pushed the stray pieces of my hair back under my bonnet and tried to make myself seem small and insignificant.

I'd rarely paid attention to the mannerisms of humans, and now I wasn't quite sure how to mimic them. I'd hardly even touched humans, apart from wrenching their jaws open during collections. Suddenly crushed together with so many of them, their arms and chests pressed against me, I found their skin oddly warm. The heat of their blood burned even through their clothes. Reapers' bodies, though we still had blood and hearts, always ran gravely cold. I tried to press closer to Neven, concerned that my icy touch might startle one of the humans and cause a disturbance.

"Are you all right?" Neven said.

"Fine." I tensed as a man bumped into me, pushing me into Neven. Luckily, Neven was taller than me and quite difficult to knock over, but that also made him more visible.

Especially when he was surveying the room like a slowly ro-tating lighthouse beacon.

"Stop looking around," I said, grabbing the brim of his hat and yanking it over his eyes. "You're too tall to be subtle."

"I'm keeping watch!" Neven said, straightening his hat. "What if we've been followed?"

"Yes, exactly," I said, yanking his hat down again so it cov-ered more of his startlingly white blond hair. "If we have, they're going to see a boy with color-changing eyes gaping like a fish at everyone else. Keep your head down."

"My eyes are still blue," Neven said under his breath, look-ing down at the floor anyway. "That's a standard human eye color."

"They're navy," I said. "Try a few shades lighter."

Neven squinted for a moment, and when he blinked again his eyes were closer to sapphire, shockingly bright but passable so long as he didn't get distracted and lose control.

I scanned the room and spotted a darkened corner near a door marked NO PASSENGERS just beneath a large over-hanging vent on the opposite wall. It would be a perfect shadow to sink into, if we could somehow squeeze through all the other passengers and make it there.

I grabbed Neven's arm and started to pull him toward the corner.

"Ren—"

"Shh!" I stopped and elbowed him in the chest, forcing a winded cough out of him. "Don't say my name."

Reapers had impeccable hearing—we knew the sounds of snowflakes landing on windowpanes, of blades of grass break-ing through soil, of eyes closing and hearts stopping. A word whispered across a room might as well have been screamed in our ears. A High Reaper would have no problem hearing my name, even among all the human voices.

We shoved through the torrent of humans, heads down and trying to be as unobtrusive as one could possibly be while pushing people aside. I wished Neven had walked in front of me to carve the path, but there was no room to switch places. While humans were weak and I could have parted this human sea with one hand, sending full-grown men flying across the room wasn't the best way to go unnoticed.

I bumped into the broad chest of a middle-aged man, the bronze buttons of his coat stamping into my face. I couldn't easily push past him, blocked by children on one side and an elderly woman on the other.

"Pardon me," I said.

But he didn't move. Instead, he glared down at me, his long nose casting shadows like a sundial under the singular overhead light. He stood close to a woman with a similarly sour countenance, brightened up marginally by a thin coating of white powder. His eyes were pearly blue and the woman's were a misty green, both on the Reaper spectrum of colors.

They've found us, I thought, my knees starting to shake. *They're going to drag us back to England in chains along the ocean floor.*

Then the crowd behind me pushed us closer, pressing me against the man's warm chest. I exhaled. Even High Reapers couldn't change the temperature of their blood. These people had static eyes and no chains for clocks in their pockets. They had to be human. I leaned back against Neven, every muscle relaxing. I wasn't dead just yet.

I glanced at the children on their left and the old woman on their right and decided to split the difference, sliding between the couple while Neven sputtered apologies in English and French.

"Whore," the man mumbled as I shouldered past him. Another human might not have heard it in the chaos of steerage, but my sensitive ears picked it up easily. "Just what we need, more Chinese selling themselves in Poplar."

I nearly whirled around and shattered his nose, but Neven nudged me forward, the crowd drawing us in deeper.

I clenched my jaw and shoved across the room with more force than necessary until we reached the corner. I shuffled into the shadow, dismayed that it wasn't as dark as I'd originally thought. Neven finally caught up and stood beside me, letting me tuck him into the darkened space as I dimmed it even more. I couldn't hide us entirely—it wasn't dark enough for that without someone noticing us vanishing—but I could at least make us harder to see.

In the reduced light, the tightness of my shoulders began to ease. Darkness meant safety. I so rarely experienced the privilege of being unnoticeable.

Only an elderly man reading a French book and a younger man holding a bouquet of roses stood near us. I leaned against the wall and closed my eyes.

"Nothing will be different in France," I said, so quietly that only Neven would hear. The ferry no longer felt like a passage to freedom but merely a longer chain. "Anywhere I go, it will be like this."

Neven shook his head, shuffling closer to me in the shadows. The cold from his bones bled into mine, soothing in the chaotic heat around us.

"We'll make it different," he said.

"How?" I said, crossing my arms.

"I think there are good people everywhere," Neven said. "I've met a lot of them while collect—"

I elbowed him in the ribs.

"—while working," he continued, rubbing his side. "I think people who aren't...like us...they're less set in tradition."

"Why would they be?"

"They don't live more than half a century," Neven said. "Old ideas die with them. With us, it takes a lot longer for the new to replace the old."

"You better hope nobody overheard that," I said, turning my head away so I wouldn't have to actually respond to his theory. It was dangerous to hope for things. My lament had merely been a statement of fact, not a call for his optimism.

"No one knows us outside of England," Neven said. "We can be anyone. We can be students—"

"*Men* can be students."

"Oh." Neven paused. "Well, we could work. What if we were librarians?"

I scoffed. "Who would hire a woman, much less a Japanese one?"

Neven sighed. "Well, what was your amazing plan, then?"

I glared at him. "Not dying. This isn't a holiday for me, Neven."

He wilted against the wall. "You're being belligerent," he said.

"I'm contending with my reality."

"Ren, I was only trying to..." He shook his head and looked down. "Never mind."

I tipped my head back against the wood paneling, staring at the cracked white ceiling. Neven meant to help, but he didn't understand and probably never could. I sagged against the wall and curled into the shadows, wishing that I hadn't taken out my frustration on Neven. It was so easy to be brave and calm for him when all he feared was darkness and church grims and ghost stories. It was much harder to do when my own death chased after me. After all, Neven wasn't the one who would be executed if we were caught. I had no doubt that Ambrose would deliver me to the High Council in chains and beg on his knees for Neven's life. Then Ankou would crack open my rib cage like a treasure chest and rip out my soul, tossing it into the void. Every time I imagined it, I thought I might shatter into white light and glass like the streetlamp that had started the whole mess.

"A flower, madam?"

I turned to the man on my left, who had plucked a pale rose from his bouquet and extended it to me. I wanted to yank the shadows over me like a human child hiding under her covers from monsters. Humans never looked at me without fear, never smiled at me or offered me flowers.

"I don't mean to suggest anything," he said, misreading my hesitation, "but you looked like you could use one.

I looked between the slightly damaged flower and the man's earnest brown eyes. I didn't particularly want a human present, but I got the impression that declining would read as a rather un-human behavior, so I accepted the flower with stiff fingers.

"Thank you," I said, trying to sound human and sincere, but the words sounded more like they'd been forcibly squeezed from my throat. I turned away so the man couldn't continue the interaction.

"See?" Neven whispered. "Not all humans are the same."

"Perhaps," I said, lifting the flower to my face. The scent triggered a vivid recollection of the cemetery in spring. Would London truly follow me everywhere for the rest of my life, hiding out in scents and colors just to remind me that my freedom could end at any moment?

When I pulled the flower back from my face, it was dead.

The petals had stiffened and turned a wicked brown, the leaves dried and curled in on themselves. The whole bulb tipped back with a dry cracking sound and fell to the floor, where someone's leather shoe crushed it.

I frowned, examining the brittle stem. It hadn't been so withered a moment ago, had it? What sort of bizarre flower had the human given me?

Before I could consider it any further, a man with white blond hair shoved his way into the steerage compartment at the other end of the room.

He wore a tailcoat two sizes too big and an undone cravat—clothes that were not only too expensive for a steerage passenger but clearly didn't belong to him. His face was the sickly pale color of nightshift workers and was twisted into the most thoroughly displeased expression I'd ever seen, like he'd been tasked with cleaning public toilets. He scanned the room, his irises darkening from light blue to stony indigo.

I dropped to the floor, dragging Neven down with me and slapping a hand over his mouth so he couldn't ask questions.

He squawked out a sound of surprise against my palm, but went still when he saw my face.

I'd expected any Reapers pursuing us to use the full extent of their powers and rip me from frozen time, but perhaps I hadn't considered what a full search of London would entail. Even if they forced every off-duty Reaper to spend all day combing through London to find me, how many days or weeks would it take to thoroughly search every nook and cranny, every basement and attic, every civilian home and shop and church? Of course most Reapers wouldn't want to shorten their own lifespans by freezing time to search for me. Maybe someone like Ivy would do it, but this was clearly a young Reaper woken up on his off-shift who seemed more inconvenienced than vengeful. As long as he didn't see us, we would be fine. Regardless, steerage was no longer safe for us.

I abandoned my suitcase and pulled a denser shadow over the emergency exit, keeping my back to the Reaper as I shouldered it open and slid through the opening. Neven followed close behind me, quietly closing the door.

We emerged in a dim hallway of pipes and portholes and dozens of signs that said NO PASSENGERS, which I ignored. I closed the emergency door and snapped the handle off, tossing it to the ground.

"Hey!" a crew member called out, appearing around the corner. "You can't be down here!"

I grabbed Neven's suitcase and swung it into the human's face, knocking him back against the wall where he slumped down, unmoving.

"Ren!" Neven said, grabbing his suitcase back. "Don't use my luggage to hurt people!"

"He's fine! I aimed away from his nose and teeth."

"You hit his *head*!"

"Bone heals faster than cartilage!"

Neven let out a shaky sound of frustration but dropped the argument once satisfied that the human was breathing.

"Now what?" he said, clutching his suitcase to his chest like some sort of hard rectangular pillow. Of course he expected me to have a plan, as if I'd spent my life drawing up escape strategies instead of learning languages and reading poetry.

We couldn't stay on the ferry, that was certain. Even if the Reaper on board was exhausted and disgruntled, he didn't need to catch us to win, he only needed to see us. The moment he did, it would all be over. I wouldn't stake my life on another Reaper's potential fatigue. Fighting him wasn't ideal, either, as a fight among so many humans would quickly get messy.

I looked out the porthole at the endless stretch of gray sea sloshing against the boat.

"Out there," I said, pointing.

Neven's eyes went wide. "You want to swim to France?"

"Well, I don't want to be dissected by High Reapers."

The swirl of colors in Neven's eyes told me how little he liked my plan, but what choice did we have?

"Come on," I said, setting a hand on his arm that I hoped conveyed some sort of warmth instead of the panicked urgency I felt hammering through my whole body. "Most of the sharks in the channel are harmless."

"Is that your idea of reassurance?" Neven said, shuddering but allowing me to drag him down the hall.

We hurried up a wet staircase to the next level, sunlight

spilling out from the doorway. I froze a small part of the upper deck just before we emerged into the light, to keep any humans from seeing us go overboard, then grabbed Neven and clambered up onto the lip of the boat before I could change my mind. I'd already stepped off and started falling when I realized Neven was frozen with fear, peering down at the steep drop into black waters. It was too late to try to convince him to jump, and once I hit the water I wouldn't be able to climb back up to help him.

Sorry, Neven, I thought, letting go of my clock and grabbing the hem of his coat, pulling him down after me.

When we crashed into the water, it felt like I'd been buried alive—the bone-coldness of frozen dirt packed six feet underground, no air or light, only the damp chill of forever curling cold around my skin. Neither the water nor the cold could kill me, but it could still freeze my bones to brittle ice and fill my lungs with salt water.

I swam deeper and deeper underwater to stay out of sight from the surface, Neven following close behind me. Above us, pale sun cast ribbons of light through the black waters, and before us the side of the ferry spanned forever forward like some great white sea beast. The muffled sounds of the deep ocean all around us rivaled the pure silence of stopped time. Maybe this was how it felt to float in the ether once your soul was extracted but before you went Beyond—floating in a hazy world that unfolded before you in slow motion, your limbs so cold that they hardly felt like part of you anymore, a distant light overhead just beyond your grasp.

The salt stung my eyes and blurred my vision, but I kept them open anyway, looking up for any signs that we'd been followed. The humans had probably seen Neven go over or at least heard the splash, which might draw attention to us.

As the sunlight fractured in the waves overhead, a glint of silver caught my eye.

That was the only warning I had before all the world's weight crushed my throat and something dragged me toward the surface. Neven floated unmoving in the water below me, the fish around us suspended like a galaxy of strange stars. The Reaper must have frozen time and awakened me with the touch of their arm around my neck.

As we broke the surface, the only sound in the frozen sea was my frantic kicking and splashing as the Reaper wrenched me farther away from Neven, his silver cloak billowing in the water around us. He held his clock in his left hand while his right arm snaked around my throat, crushing me against him.

I grabbed my knife from my sleeve and stabbed at the Reaper's arm, but he had the strength of iron chains and kept crushing my throat and twisting me around in the water. I kicked and scratched his face and elbowed his ribs, but none of it helped—he only pressed harder into my throat, my vision blurring and fingers going numb.

I bit down on my tongue until I tasted blood, desperate to stay awake. Every part of me screamed at the Reaper's touch, as if he'd set my blood on fire. He was going to drop me at Ankou's feet and laugh as he opened me up rib by rib, unraveling my soul before the other High Reapers. I clenched my teeth and fought back as dying humans did, with no plan or skill, just a mindless desperation to outrun death at any cost.

But, like always, it didn't make any difference. Was this really how I would end? My whole life over after only two centuries, sad and short and meaningless? Just when I'd been on the cusp of something better, they dragged me away.

I looked at the horizon, where France was supposed to be. Even as the Reaper choked me and pulled me away and shook me so hard that salt water filled my mouth and stung my eyes, I couldn't look away. I reached out toward that faraway place at the end of the horizon, clawing through the water as if I could grab handfuls of the ocean to drag myself there.

Don't bring me back, my mind screamed, for my lungs couldn't draw in the air to speak. Just the thought of London made my blood run cold, like I was already dead. I had lived there all my life, but it had never been my home.

I thought of the pictures of Japan in my suitcase, now abandoned in the ferry charging farther and farther away from us. The lush mountains with cherry blossoms, palaces like tiered cakes, bamboo forests, and embroidered kimonos. My home was somewhere in those photographs, with people who looked like me and would call me their own.

What right did Reapers have to take that away, to punish me by their laws, when they wouldn't even call me a Reaper? I would not die at the hands of a Reaper, not before I'd set foot in Japan.

The Reaper kept choking me and my gaze fell to the black waters, silver glinting just below the surface.

Instead of trying to rip his face off or stab my knife into his eye, I plunged my hands into the water and grabbed his clothes, cutting long slashes through his robes.

"Your aim is terrible," he said. "I can't believe someone as pathetic as you managed to take down Ivy. You can't even give me a paper cut."

I don't need to, I thought, clenching my teeth as my fingers felt around the water. *I can win without even touching you.*

My hand closed around the chain of his clock and pulled.

The metal, wet with salt water, slipped from his left hand and sank into the water. It should have caught on the clip attached to his pocket and stayed tethered to him. It would have, if I hadn't cut a hole in his robe.

The clock plummeted with the heavy weight of gold and glass, straight for the ocean floor.

The High Reaper released me instantly, diving after his clock with a startled gasp. I coughed and grabbed my throat as the ocean came back to life, the waves slapping me across my face. I could barely stay afloat, but I reached down and cast clouds of darkness through the sea around the Reaper, so thick that even the clear water near the surface looked like the depths of night. That would keep him occupied long enough for us to escape.

Neven must have noticed my sudden disappearance, for he was swimming toward me, glasses in one hand.

"What happened?" he said. "Are they here?"

"There's a Reaper down below chasing after his clock," I said, my voice raw and every word painful. "Let's go before he comes back."

Neven turned and looked at the ferry heading toward the horizon. It hadn't seemed to move very fast when we were on it, but in the short moments that time had turned since we'd jumped off, it had grown much smaller in the widening distance. Even with inhuman strength, we could never catch up to it.

I'm sorry, I thought as Neven shivered and began swimming

in the direction of the ship. I could never say it out loud, because there were too many things to apologize for. For throwing him into freezing waters. For bringing him with me. For being his sister and ruining his life.

For a small infinity, we swam to shore, shrouded in a blanket of shadows. We couldn't grow tired in such a mundane way as swimming, so the passing hours mattered little. For a while, I appreciated the isolation, with nothing but gray sky and dark ocean in every direction. We didn't speak for the rest of the journey as the cold numbed our lips.

By the time we reached France, night had grown heavy enough to conceal our arrival on the rocky shore. I turned time just long enough to pickpocket some francs from humans passing by, then led us through the doors of the closest hotel, sopping wet. I slapped the francs on the desk and argued with the concierge, who steadfastly pretended not to understand my French but somehow understood Neven perfectly, even though his accent was worse. By the time we reached the room, it felt like years had passed.

As I shut the door behind us, Neven sat on the floor by the window in a wet heap and gestured toward the bathroom.

"Go ahead," he said, his voice sore from swallowing salt water.

"Neven?"

He looked up, his eyes dull. Exhaustion had drawn his features down, his glasses blurred from salt water.

"I didn't…" I pressed my lips together, numbed from hours in the frigid sea. Our journey had only just started and already I'd nearly been killed and forced Neven to swim until his lips turned blue. Neven was going to realize how much of an ordeal this was and regret coming with me, even though he would never say it out loud. He deserved so much better than me. "I didn't think that…"

But Neven shook his head before I could finish the sentence, waving a hand as if to wipe the words from the air. He always knew what I was trying to say.

"The worst is over," he said, offering a soft, fake smile. "But I'm soaked, so could you please…" He gestured to the bathroom again.

Without another word, I entered the bathroom, closing the door behind me. I turned on the water in the bathtub and the gas furnace on the side, then peeled off my wet clothes and wrung them out over the sink.

I climbed into the lukewarm water, rubbing the soap first through my hair and then over every inch of my body. I thought of the Reaper with his arm around my throat and scrubbed harder, the soap slipping from my fingers and sliding across the floor. When I no longer smelled of salt, I had the sudden urge to get as far away from water as possible.

I nearly slipped out of the tub but caught myself on the rim and dried myself with shaking hands. Thanks to my newly cut hair, the mirror reflected the kanji inked into my spine between my shoulder blades: 蓮.

My name was the only thing my mother had ever given me. According to Ambrose, all Shinigami were born with their names painted on their spines in black ink that would never wash away. I wondered who I would have been if I'd grown up in Japan as Ren and not Wren, if someone would have loved me there, if I still would have had to flee and drag my poor brother along with me.

I twisted my arm back to touch the tattoo, but couldn't quite reach it. Like everything else about Japan, it was just barely out of reach.

I thought once more of the High Reaper dragging me through the water, my hands reaching for the horizon. For a brief moment, I had thought I was going to die. I'd seen that moment in the eyes of so many humans whose souls I'd collected. Confronting your final end made you realize what was important, because death stripped away all the comfortable and convenient lies you told yourself. And in that moment, all I had wanted was to reach a place that could be my home.

"Neven," I whispered, knowing he would hear me even through the closed bathroom door.

"Are you all right?" he said, his voice cracked and weary.

I grabbed a towel off the shelf and wrapped it around myself, then threw open the door.

Neven was sitting on the floor in a puddle, still in his wet clothes, glasses in one hand. I knelt down in front of him.

"I need to go to Japan," I said. It was the first time I'd spoken the thought aloud, to him or to anyone. "The Shinigami there won't be afraid of my light powers like the Reapers. I can find my mother and live there with her and the other Shinigami."

Neven rubbed his right eye and said nothing, letting his hand drop to the floor where it splashed in a shallow puddle.

"How will you find her?" he said at last, his words so heavy and waterlogged that I wanted to cry for him. But at least his first response hadn't been a resounding *no*.

"I don't know," I said, "but I have to try. I know it's easier to stay in Europe, but anywhere I go here, they'll look at me the same way the Reapers do, and I can't live like that anymore."

Neven was still staring at me, his expression too tired to read.

"You don't have to come," I said, dropping my gaze to the wet floorboards. "You can stay in France and be a student, like you wanted. I'll come back and visit in a few years—"

"Stop saying that."

I looked up. Neven was frowning, slipping his dirty glasses back on.

"Stop saying what?"

He glared at me through fogged lenses. "Stop acting as if I'd want to be anywhere without you."

Once again I thought of a thousand ways I should have talked him out of it. I should have told him that living among the humans in France would be far different from living among the Shinigami in Japan, where everyone would know at first glance that he didn't belong. I should have told him that all the books I'd read about Japan were old and likely inaccurate, that I truly had no idea what monsters waited in the Japanese underworld.

But then I thought about swimming through the loneliness of the dark ocean all alone, and how, without Neven, I would be Wren and not Ren. In the end, I didn't try to stop him.

He tipped his head back against the wall, dampening the curled lilies of the wallpaper.

"Well," he said, a faint smile curling the corner of his mouth, "I guess you'll have to start teaching me Japanese again."

CHAPTER 05

I stepped onto the shores of Yokohama and took a deep breath of the October air. It had been nearly nine months between the different legs of the journey—around Spain and Portugal, through the Strait of Gibraltar and then Indonesia, boarding a different ship on the coast of China, and finally arriving at the port of Yokohama, Japan.

Throughout the journey I'd stayed mostly hidden in our cabin, wary of any Reapers that might be searching for me, but Neven had ventured outside. He'd talked to the humans, coming back every few hours to bring me stolen trinkets or books in different languages, some I'd never seen before. He told me stories like he had when we were kids, this time claiming he'd met a female pirate with one eye, and the founder of a ginger candy company who gave him samples that tasted like spices and dust.

It wasn't until six months had passed without event that I'd felt certain the Reapers had given up hope of finding me, perhaps deciding I wasn't worth the effort and resources. I started venturing out to the upper docks with Neven, and though I had little interest in making human friends, as Neven seemed inclined to do, I heard languages that I'd only ever seen on paper, saw people who didn't wear corsets or elaborate hats, and smelled spices that I hadn't known existed. Of course I had always known that the world was vast, but until then, everything but London had seemed like a fairy tale. Every time I went to sleep, I was sure I would wake up again in the catacombs, ripped away from this new dream.

The months spun by in a blur of sunrises and sunsets and endless ocean from behind the fingerprinted glass of my cabin window. While it was one of the duller periods of my existence, in a lifetime of two millennia, a year lasted no more than a breath, and this time was inconsequential. For a while, as I floated farther and farther away from Ivy and Ambrose and the dark winter of London, the quiet hours spent alone had felt meditative and necessary. But the closer we came to Japan, the more I lay awake at night, my stomach twisting. Neven blamed it on seasickness, but I knew he was wrong because I felt the sensation down in my bones. For over a century I'd dreamed of reaching Japan, and in a few short weeks, I would see it not through the lens of a camera or a painter's reproduction but with my own eyes.

When the final ship in our journey docked in Yokohama and we emerged from the cramped cabin onto the shores of

Japan, I clung to Neven's sleeve, afraid that I would wake up if I didn't keep myself tethered.

We'd arrived in the early stages of autumn, when leaves had started to crisp at the tips and the whole world looked like it was dying. While London was made of stone and brick, Japan was made of wood—every house wore panels of unpainted cypress and pine as armor, the bare wooden buildings like skeletons of houses long forgotten. Closer to the port, spidery wooden legs elevated the coastal homes above the shore. I imagined the houses crawling away into the sea and drowning all the humans inside.

In another world, this could have been my home. I might have grown up running barefoot on the shore instead of on rain-slick cobblestones. Maybe *home* would have meant the smell of brine and sight of merchant ships on the horizon, rather than the taste of burnt coal dust in the air and rain-clouds over stone steeples.

Everything I saw was a story that had been stolen from me. The ships that shifted sleepily in the glassy port waters, the footprints in the fine dirt roads, the perfect pale white shade of the sky—all of it should have been mine. I shouldn't have returned to Japan with the eyes of a tourist but of a native. I would never truly be native to anywhere in the world, because my father had stolen this world from me and shoved me into another one.

I understood so little about my origins, but I was reasonably certain that I'd been born in Japan and not England. Whenever I'd asked Ambrose about it, he'd always murmured something vague before suddenly needing to leave on Coun-

cil business. The only thing he'd ever truly confirmed was
that my mother was Japanese, and she was not in England.

In response to his silence, I'd liberated some library books
and read that around the time I was born, the shogun had
closed off Japan from the rest of the world. The Japanese
couldn't leave, so neither could the Shinigami. But the Japanese had still traded with the Dutch, and it would have been
feasible for Ambrose to sail to the Netherlands and then Japan.
It was far less likely that my mother had fled Japan and then
returned for punishment.

I would never understand why my father had been the one
to take me, when I'd so clearly been unwanted. Nor did I
understand how Ambrose, who was about as romantic as a
slab of moldy bread, could be seduced by a Shinigami when
he knew very well what the consequences would be. But he
was far away and would never tell me the answer.

Maybe my mother would, once I found her.

There was always the chance that I wouldn't find her, but
somehow that didn't feel like my destiny. I'd read so many of
the humans' novels about children with dead parents, loving
mothers lost to childbirth or plagues. But I was not a hero
with a tragic backstory, I was just a girl nobody wanted. Creatures of Death did not die as easily as humans, so it was far
more likely that my mother had simply handed me to Ambrose and sent him away. That had been nearly two hundred
years ago—long enough for her to change her mind, or regret, or wonder what might have been.

The first step to finding her was to locate Yomi, the Realm
of Perpetual Night.

No Reaper had ever documented a journey to Japan's un-

derworld, so I'd turned instead to the human books about
Japanese legends of Death. After all, the English mythology
that the humans believed was at least partially correct—they'd
had legends of the Grim Reaper since plague days, and correctly associated him with Chronos, the ancient god of time.
It was likely that Japanese mythology would be at least partially based in reality.

The legend that seemed most reasonable to me was that of
Yomi, the underworld bathed in darkness. I already knew that
Shinigami could control light, so it made sense that they'd
been granted that power to adapt to a world of darkness. But
even the Shinto myths were strangely cryptic—the only de-
tails of the dark underworld I could find were: it was where
humans went when their lives ended, and once you ate the
food of Yomi, you could never leave. Surely the reality would
be more complex than that. Once we made it to Yomi, we
could look for other Shinigami to help us.

I wasn't certain that we could find Yomi from Yokohama,
but most of the merchant ships from China had been headed
there. If we couldn't find it on our own, I hoped that we'd at
least be able to find some Shinigami after nightfall.

"Where should we go?" Neven said, his gaze tracing the
path of a brown pheasant with its wings stretched across the
white sky.

"Let's find a graveyard and start from there." After all, we
were looking for the land of the dead. It made sense to follow Death's pull to its most concentrated place.

We stepped onto more level ground, past the wet slope of
the shore and beyond a row of burnt red maple trees guarding
the town. As I passed the barrier of the tree line and brushed

a stray branch from my face, all the crimson leaves withered to crisp black and a sudden wind ripped them all from the branches, showering us in dead leaves.

Neven sputtered at the leaves in his eyes and hair, but didn't seem to notice how suddenly they'd died. I thought back to the rose I'd killed on the ferry to France. Once was strange, twice was a pattern. Cromwell had promised that Death would find me, and now it was spreading from my fingertips. But if the only consequence was a few dead plants, I wasn't going to agonize over it. Perhaps whatever curse he'd cast had been unable to follow me to the other side of the world and would grow weaker over time.

"Ren?" Neven said, pausing when he realized I'd stopped walking. "Are you all right?"

I brushed the leaves from my coat. "Yes," I said, looking away. I wouldn't worry Neven over something I didn't fully understand. He had enough to worry about as it was. "Let's go."

A few fishermen carrying their boat to the sand stopped and stared as we walked past them. I'd expected as much, considering that we were wearing British clothes and not kimonos, like everyone else.

A group of women walked by, holding up umbrellas even though it wasn't raining. They wore kimonos patterned with pinstripes and cotton flowers, their hair pinned back in the same loose but elegant bun that I had no idea how to imitate. They said something in Japanese that I didn't quite understand, and I suddenly wished that I'd studied more.

As we drew closer to the town, the crowd began to thicken.

I pressed closer to Neven, jumping when a woman brushed the fabric of my skirts.

Men pulling people on two-wheeled carts cut through the crowd, one nearly crushing my toes. To stay out of the way, we moved to the edge of the path, elevated from the shallow water a few feet below. All around us, fishermen hauled their massive nets through the crowd, women knelt before their looms and wove red fabric, and children ran through the streets with their wooden sandals thwacking against the dirt.

I stopped at the intersection of what seemed to be the main road, store wares spilling onto the street. Old women advertised their silk hanging from clotheslines and waving in the breeze, scarlet red with gold flowers, pale peach with embroidered emerald cranes. Others held ceramic plates painted with the purple silhouette of the distant mountains. More of the two-wheeled carts rolled down the street carrying crates, and children ran around with damp and sand-caked feet. The air smelled of ocean and smoked fish.

It felt like a home. Not my home, but a place that could be home to someone. London had felt like a place to live, but not a place that could ever be home.

A child barreled toward us, screaming and laughing. Neven took a step back to get out of his way and nearly slipped off the path and into the water. I grabbed his shirt to keep him from falling, and we teetered on the edge for a moment before we both tipped the other way and fell into the dirt road. The people shuffling past us stared and whispered in Japanese, giving us a wide berth.

"I don't think we're blending in very well, Ren."

I sighed and stood up, wiping my hands on my skirt. "As if we ever stood a chance in these clothes."

I looked longingly at the kimonos that all the women wore. I wanted their floral fabrics and wooden sandals and paper parasols instead of the barely tied corset and heavy skirts I was wearing. Just like in England, I was a spectacle.

"We should find a cemetery quickly," Neven said, standing protectively over me, nearly backing me into the water again. He was right. If there was anywhere to find Death—and hopefully, Yomi—in Japan, it would be where the dead rested.

I pounded a fist into his shoulder blade until he took a step forward and let me step away from the ledge.

"I don't feel Death pulling anywhere, do you?" I said.

Neven shook his head. "You could ask someone?"

I looked around at the crowd flowing down the street, picking up pieces of conversations in accents I'd never heard, words I'd never studied. My tongue suddenly felt like lead in my mouth.

"Let's head farther inland," I said, turning away. "Humans don't tend to bury their dead on beaches. The bodies resurface too quickly."

"All right," Neven said, his gaze tracing a great horned ox hauling a carriage of carved stones down the street.

A gong rang somewhere far away, the vibrations humming under our feet.

I had no idea what such a sound meant in Japan, but everyone else seemed to know with certainty.

All at once, people began to walk faster. The street became a current dragging us forward. I grabbed a fistful of Neven's coat so we wouldn't be separated as people pushed to get past us. Someone stepped on my skirt, the fabric ripping behind me. I gathered up my skirts in one hand and reached for my clock with the other, but then someone crashed into Neven's back and sent us both spilling forward.

My right foot slipped off the ledge, the world slid upside down, and I hit the water below. Neven tumbled down with me because I hadn't let go of his coat, his weight compacting me into the sand.

I slid out from under Neven and got to my feet in the shallow water, then grabbed up my skirts and wrung them out. Ever since the ship incident, I hated being submerged. I kicked off my shoes and emptied them of water while Neven groaned and got to his knees.

"My glasses," he said, feeling around underwater.

Above us, the people continued to rush down the street. The gong rang again, the sound pealing across the shore.

"Ren, my glasses!"

I looked down and spotted Neven's glasses in the sand beneath the rippling water just in front of my toes.

"Stand up," I said, picking up his glasses and shaking off some of the salt water before waving them in front of his face. He grabbed them and scrubbed the brine from his eyes.

"Where are they going?" I said to myself.

Neven shook the water off his glasses a bit more, then put them on and squinted through the dirty lenses. "I think they're going…inside?"

He seemed to be right. The crowd had thinned out from the panicked mob that drove us into the water. The sound of doors sliding shut repeated endlessly down the streets. Only shopkeepers remained outside, packing up their wares.

I sank my hands into the dirt road and climbed back up onto the path, clothes heavy with water. Neven hopped up behind me as I turned to follow the main road, now easily able to dodge the few lingering humans.

The town suddenly seemed so much larger, the streets vast when empty. White lanterns with painted red dots hung in a garland running all the way down the street, eerily resembling a thousand bloodshot eyes. The sky beyond had begun to dim, pure white to gray ashes, the blood orange sun sinking toward the mountains beyond the curtain of clouds.

I walked toward a group of women hurriedly folding the silk scarves that they'd been selling, packing them into boxes and rushing the boxes indoors. The third toll of the gong made them all jump like a pack of startled pigeons, and they gave up on folding and simply crumpled their silk into balls and crammed them into their boxes.

We needed to know what was going on, and sooner or later I would need to speak to someone in Japanese. I took a deep breath and stepped closer.

"Excuse me?" I said.

But none of the women looked at me, too busy trying to pack up their silk, even when the slippery surface eluded their fingers. Others were collapsing the tented arches and locking their shop doors.

"Go inside, dear," one of the women said, kneeling on the ground and hurrying to pack up the last of her fabrics. It took me a moment to understand, for no one had ever spoken Japanese to me before. I'd studied the phonetic alphabet and memorized the sounds as best as I could from my books, but papers couldn't mimic the intonation, the song of all the sounds melted together.

"Why?" I asked, kneeling beside her. "Why is everyone leaving?"

The woman paused, fingers hovering over green silk. She looked behind her at the other women carrying their wares away.

"Omagatoki," she whispered. She spoke the word like a curse, as if the syllables cut her tongue. Her fingers trembled as she folded her fabric. I didn't know what the word meant but felt too embarrassed to ask. "It wasn't always this way," the woman said, "but every year since the new Emperor ascended, it's gotten worse."

"What's gotten worse?"

"Shh!" the woman hissed, looking behind her again. "We're not like Tokyo," she said. "We're still a fishing village. Things are starting to change, more foreign ships are coming into port. But we're still traditional people. We still believe. We still know what there is to be afraid of."

"What should you be afraid of?"

One of the doors opened and a younger woman yelled something that I guessed was the older woman's name, because she gathered her boxes and stood up.

"Go inside and don't come out," she said. Then she turned and hurried into her house. The door slammed behind her.

I stood up and turned to Neven. "They're hiding from something, but I don't know what."

Neven's eyes simmered dark blue. "Should we hide, too?"

I looked around at the street of locked doors and abandoned tents. "Maybe," I said, "but where?"

Neven didn't answer, shifting closer to me.

"It's too soon to worry," I said. "Humans are skittish because they die easily. They don't fear the same things we do."

"Right," Neven said, sounding far from convinced.

"Come on, let's find that graveyard now." I tugged his arm.

It wasn't yet dark, but the dimming sky and swelling shadows cast a gray tinge over the empty street. A fragile breeze stirred the shop banners around us, and they bowed deeply as we passed, brushing us with their silk. Something about their touch felt too deliberate, too gentle.

I raised a hand in the air and ignited the red-and-white lanterns around us with a weak glow. I thought it would disperse some of the darkness and put Neven at ease, but it had the opposite effect. The painted red circles in the vast whiteness of the paper lanterns became demon-red pupils, and with the backdrop of light behind them, it seemed as if the whole street had suddenly opened its eyes and looked directly at us.

From the end of the street came the sound of wooden sandals on the dirt road.

CHAPTER 06

The breeze faded away, and the only sound in the world was the *thwack* of wooden sandals. Beyond the paper doors, the murmurs of the humans in hiding fell silent, as if they'd gone to another world we could no longer touch. The sun descended into the jagged line of mountains before us, the orange glare of dusk deepening into crimson that bled unstopped across the entire skyline.

And still, behind us came the unhurried footsteps in a town that was supposed to be hidden away. Whatever walked down this road was not afraid like all the humans. Was this omagatoki?

Neven started to look over his shoulder, but I grabbed his sleeve and pulled him hard around a corner.

"Don't," I whispered. "We're going to avoid confrontation with things that we don't understand."

"Okay," Neven said, sticking close to my side even when I released his arm.

The crisp sound of sandals rounded the corner behind us, louder than before. Each grain of sand crunched and burst under its weight.

I took Neven's sleeve and pulled him faster, glancing around for any door left partially open, any sort of hotel or church or unlocked place that we could hide in. But the houses and stores on either side of us looked less and less like dwellings and more like paintings of scenery, too far away and unreal to touch.

The footsteps came faster behind us.

"Ren?" Neven said, his eyes a queasy clash of colors. But I didn't have the answers he wanted, and he must have seen the helplessness in my eyes.

He started to run.

"Neven!" I said, lifting my damp skirts off the ground and sprinting after him.

The footsteps behind us began to run as well, drawing closer.

I reached into my pocket and pulled out my clock, yanking time to a stop as I grabbed Neven's hand.

He jolted backward from the force of my pull, falling to the dirt and breathing heavily. He must have noticed me pulling him from the time freeze, or I was sure he would have kept running until he reached the mountains. He turned around, lips parted like he was about to speak, but then his gaze settled on the road behind me and his face went gray.

"Ren," he whispered. "What's going on?"

I turned around slowly, imagining a time-frozen beast inches from my ankles, jaw unhinged and claws striking out in the still air.

But the street was empty.

Carriage wheels had carved scars into the dirt road, filled with shallow rainwater. There was nothing but the utility poles standing as thin sentinels and the faraway hills blurred with mist.

An invisible creature? I thought. I hadn't read about anything like that in Japan, except...

My throat went dry. I thought of all the Japanese ghost stories I'd read as a child, tales of evil spirits that cut your face open with scissors and drowned you with their hair. Japan had thousands of different spirits that wreaked havoc on humans, but they were supposed to be urban legends and children's tales, not part of the mythology that built the universe.

Apparently, I was standing in the middle of one of my childhood stories.

"I think I know what this is," I said.

"What?" Neven said, still transfixed by the empty road.

"Stand up," I said, pulling his sleeve. He rose, holding my arm for balance when his knees shook.

I put my clock back in my pocket, and time released its breath. Weak wind flowed down the street again, stirring the dirt around our ankles. The footsteps had stopped.

I took a slow step sideways, off the path, pulling Neven along with me.

"After you," I said in Japanese to the empty air.

For a moment the street was silent. Even the weak breeze

seemed to still, the street static as a photograph. Then the sound of footsteps picked up again from right in front of us and continued down the path, the sound slowly fading as it headed toward the mountains.

"What was that?" Neven said, his voice tightly wound, as if a single wrong word could send him sprinting off again.

"That was Betobeto-san," I said, pulling Neven back into the street. We had to find the cemetery, especially now that I knew what was after us.

"And what, exactly, is Betobeto-san?"

"He's a Yokai," I said, trying my best to sound calm for Neven's sake while focusing more energy on feeling out the pull of Death. "I thought he was a ghost story, but I guess he's more like a spirit. He tries to scare travelers until they let him pass."

"And there are other Yokai?"

I looked down a passing street, delaying my answer. I'd read about many benign Yokai like Betobeto-san, ones that manifested as flat white walls to block your path, or sentient brooms that swept away autumn leaves. But I'd also read about Yokai with hungry jaws on the back of their heads, severed torsos that ran after you on their hands, demon children born from dead leaves and rainwater. If Betobeto-san was real... were all of them real?

"Ren?" Neven said, panic rising in his voice. I didn't need to answer his question anymore, because my silence had given it away. "Are they dangerous?"

I wanted to reassure him, but I couldn't lie to Neven.

"Some are, some aren't," I said, trying my best to sound flippant. The more important question was, could they kill us? I didn't know how the power structure worked in Japan among creatures of Death. I doubted that someone as benign as Betobeto-san could kill a Reaper, but was that true of all Yokai?

"All the humans wouldn't go into hiding just because of Betobeto-san," Neven said, his voice wavering. "There must be Yokai worse than him out here, right?"

I pulled Neven to a stop.

"We're Reapers, Neven," I said, because sometimes Neven needed reminding that he was made not out of flesh and blood but Death and Time. "We don't need to fear children's tales. They should fear us."

"But they're trying to scare us off, Ren," Neven said

A rush of autumn air blew through the street. The complicated plaits of my hair had started to come undone, so I began to tug them out and let my hair down, reveling in how long it had grown since Ivy cut it.

"Let them try," I said.

I yanked my fingers through the final knot and let my hair blow back in the wind.

We walked in silence until the pull of Death intensified, the distant gravity of a faraway star reaching out to pull us closer.

"It's this way," I said, pointing down a street where merchants' banners hung limp in the streets, sunless flowers of blue and violet inked with brush strokes of kanji.

Neven nodded. "I can feel it, too."

The sky darkened as we drew closer to the graveyard. Though the horizon still burned red, night had begun to deepen the shadows of the buildings. The distance became blurred with darkness, as if the shore and all its ships were a hazy memory.

Soon, I could see the cemetery's stone gates at the end of the road, the headstones jutting out of the earth like crooked teeth, the pull magnetizing.

Then a light appeared at the gate.

A young woman stood vigil, a red peony lantern in one hand. Her kimono hung off her thin frame, the fabric the color of storm clouds, embroidered with summer flowers. It was hard to see her face from far away, aside from the glow of the lantern in her eyes.

Neven didn't slow down, but he took my hand and pressed it to the inside of his elbow, silently asking me not to let go of his arm as we moved forward. The closer we came to the cemetery gates, the more the air around us reeked of Death.

The woman's gaze tracked us as we came to a stop in front of her, the lantern illuminating her soft, young face. Though she didn't block the entrance, something about her presence still compelled me not to enter before confronting her. I could safely assume that no one we met at this hour was human, but as long as she kept up a human appearance, I couldn't gauge how dangerous she was to us.

Rather than speaking, she stared at Neven. It wasn't the morbid fascination of humans who happened to see the northern lights shifting in his eyes. It wasn't lust or even curiosity. Instead, her dark eyes read him with a fevered intensity, as if cracking open his skull in her mind and examining the contents. Neven held her gaze, the lights in his eyes spinning faster, flashing blue and violet and emerald and blue again in panic that only I could read.

"Not many are brave enough to come here during omaga-toki," she said.

Neven blinked back at her, uncomprehending.

"So we've heard," I said in Japanese, crossing my arms. "What, exactly, is omagatoki?"

She tore her gaze from Neven, looking at me like she wanted to peel away my skin and count my bones.

"The hour between day and night when the borders between the realms are thinned," she said. "When the sky is red, the spirits can come out."

That explains things, I thought. "Anyway," I said, "we're just passing through."

"One cannot 'pass through' this place," she said.

A spider dropped down from her ear, dangling by its silvery web like an earring. Neven's lip curled, his arm tense against mine.

"Will you try to stop us?" I said, not bothering to hide the impatience in my voice.

She tilted her head, eyes flickering down to my toes and back up to my face.

"You may enter, if you wish," she said, "but you will not pass through."

Another spider crawled across her cheek and crept down the arch of her neck until it came to rest on her collarbone.

Neven stood transfixed, his gaze following the spider with thinly veiled horror.

"What is she?" he said, more to himself than to me.

"An obstacle," I said.

She turned back to Neven and smiled, her lips cracked with thin black lines.

"I've been waiting for you," she said. But Neven didn't understand much Japanese, so he said nothing. Another spider crawled out of the girl's mouth and past her red lips, leaving tiny speckles of red in its path down her chin. Her fingers twitched as she reached out and touched Neven's face. I would have snapped her wrist off had the motion not been so unnervingly gentle.

"You won't leave like all the others, will you?" she said. She turned her hand over, caressing his cheek with black nails. Her fingers brushed over his eyelashes and down to his lips.

"Neven?" I said. She hadn't hypnotized him into stillness, had she?

My voice seemed to snap him out of his trance. His gaze darted to me, then down to the pale hand and black nails on his lips.

"I suggest you remove your hand," he said, this time using his Reaper voice—polite, because he was Neven, but with an undeniable authority. She wouldn't notice how he kept his shaking hands in his pockets, close to his clock, just in case.

I didn't know if she understood, but her hand floated away from his face, leaving clear strings attached to his lips, tethering him to her fingertips. A single spider crawled across the tightrope, inching slowly toward his face. Neven froze, his gaze tracing the strings leading to the girl's palm, then floating back to the spider's eight red eyes suspended in front of him.

It took one step closer and all of Neven's resolve shattered.

He choked out a panicked noise and ripped the strings from his face. They cut like fine glass and lashed blood onto his palm when he cast them to the ground.

The girl frowned and made an odd clicking sound in the back of her throat. I had officially run out of patience.

"Just who do you think we are?" I said, taking a step forward. My words in the language of Death shattered the sacred quiet of the graveyard, the black cherry trees quivering. I hadn't traveled a year among humans to be toyed with and delayed by an insect.

A burst of spiders scurried down from the girl's hair at the sound of my voice. She took a step back, her spine stretching taller, her fingers curling into a clawlike shape.

"You dare to raise your voice at me?" she said. "I don't an swer to foreigners."

"You answer to Death," I said, my words ripping the dying leaves from their branches.

The woman's arms stretched past the sleeves of her kimono, her nails sharp as talons.

"Your foreign gods have no place here," she said, and this time when she spoke, fangs hung over her bottom lip.

Your foreign gods. Even now, she had no idea what I was. The Reapers had looked at me and seen nothing but a Shinigami, but this creature saw only a foreigner. I'd traveled across the world to be respected as a Shinigami, so how dare she tell me that I still didn't belong?

I would pluck off her limbs like children did with helpless insects, squash her under my heel and scrape her into the dirt. I would destroy her, because we weren't in England anymore and there was no one to stop me from punishing those who deserved it.

I grabbed her wrist, which grew thinner and oddly hairy in my hand, yanking her lantern to my face. It burned searingly bright, casting the whole cemetery in daylight. The whites of my eyes burned black, light glowing just beneath my skin.

"I'm no foreigner," I said. I leaned in, my face close to her jeweled eyes, which multiplied until eight yellow orbs blinked at me. *"The graves that you're standing on belong to me."*

She frowned, her gaze shifting between my face and the graves around us. As the black eclipsed the whites of my eyes, her twitching limbs froze like an insect that knew it was cornered, her eyes wide and yellow as she stared into mine.

"Shinigami?" she said.

The lantern light seared through the graveyard like a star explosion, leaving nothing but blackness in its wake. She reared back against my grip, her arm pulling upward as she doubled in height.

The chain of Neven's clock jingled, his hand touched mine, and everything froze.

I waved my hand toward the crushed lantern and it sparked back to life, casting a flickering yellow haze over the graves. The girl was reared back, her kimono torn open where an extra set of black arms had burst from her middle. Her legs spread wide and black and hairy, fingers merged into claws. Eight eyes decorated her face like tiny yellow pearls.

"Jorogumo," I whispered, circling around her and running my fingers across her new limbs. "Spider woman." Another Yokai, more troublesome than the previous one, since this one had an appetite for young men. In the book of Yokai that I'd read as a child, she'd been taller than a building. But I supposed that the book had valued entertainment more than accuracy.

"She's horrifying," Neven said, stepping slightly behind me.

He shook the webs from his fingers, the clock in his other hand glinting in the dim light.

"She didn't hurt you, did she?" I said, grabbing Neven's jaw and turning his head to the side where she'd touched him. "Was she venomous?"

"I'm fine," he said, setting a gentle hand on my wrist.

That matter settled, I turned back to the Jorogumo, grabbing her by her long black hair and yanking hard. The time freeze had stiffened her body, but eventually I cranked her head down to my level. I pulled the switchblade from the band at my skirt, but just as I moved toward her throat, Neven caught my wrist.

"Ren," he said quietly, his eyes a weak blue.

"She attacked us," I said, even though we both knew that wasn't the reason.

"Ren."

I looked down at my hand, tangled in her hair, her glassy black eyes still staring straight ahead.

Your foreign gods have no place here.

Her words spun endlessly in my head. How dare she look at me and call me a foreigner. I looked like a Shinigami—that was what I'd been told since I was old enough to retain memories. *Go back to Japan and play with your Shinigami friends, Ren. Feed yourself to the faerie dogs, Ren, because dying would be the only thing you're good for. Just let your brother reap your soul so he can live without shame.*

I yanked my wrist from Neven's grip and slit her throat.

For one single moment as I released her, I saw a flash of white inside my hand, as if my skin had turned translucent and revealed my bare bones wrapped in ribbons of red veins.

But when I blinked, the hand was the same as it had always been, and still clean, because the blood wouldn't fall until time restarted.

I kept staring at my left hand as Neven let go of me. Reapers did not have impeccable vision, so perhaps it had been a trick of light.

I didn't look at my brother as I put my knife away, then picked up the Jorogumo's lantern and followed the pull across the graveyard, Neven a few paces behind me.

We followed a dirt path to a torii gate made of weathered stone. As we passed through, the night fell silent. Beyond the gate, an open-air structure with a sloped roof awaited us at the end of the path. White flags with emerald circles hung around the half walls, unmoving in the quiet night.

The strength of Death's pull had my feet moving faster and faster until it dropped me at the stairs of the building.

"Is it a grave?" Neven said from behind me.

I shook my head. "It's a shrine."

My hands brushed dirt from the stone platform, revealing the kanji carved into it.

"Izanami," I whispered, my fingers dusting over her name.

"Izanami?"

I nodded, rising slowly to my feet. "The Goddess of Death," I said. "She created all the islands of Japan."

"She sounds more like a goddess of creation," Neven said.

I shook my head, toeing my shoes off and abandoning them on the stairs. "She died giving birth to the god of fire and fell into the underworld."

I could feel her presence around the shrine, the same way that I could feel Ankou back in England—a sense that someone was there, watching you in the trees and grass and stars. But unlike Ankou, this felt less like I was being hunted and more like I was coming home, no longer alone in a new country. Perhaps I could ask Izanami where my mother was, rather than searching through all of Yomi for a face I'd never seen.

Neven took his shoes off and followed me onto the stone platform. The shrine was empty inside, letting the night pass through it. The coldness of the stone floor numbed my bare feet and sent pinpricks up my legs.

"Her husband, Izanagi, went down to bring her back to Earth," I said, circling the perimeter and running my hands across the smooth wood banister, "but when he held a torch to her face, he saw that her flesh had been eaten by maggots, and she was no longer beautiful, so he ran away from her."

I finished my circuit of the room and knelt down, feeling along the stone tiles. "She chased him and said that if he didn't come back, she would take one thousand of the living to join her in the darkness every day. And guess what he did?"

Neven watched me, still standing in his socks near the entrance. "He left her," he said quietly.

I nodded. "She must be in charge of the Shinigami, like Ankou is in charge of us. She must know where my mother is."

My hands stilled. I'd felt all the stone tiles but found no give, nothing that might be a passage to another world. Death had pulled us to her door, but wouldn't open it for us.

"Can I help?" Neven said.

I shook my head. "I just need to think."

He nodded and leaned back against the doorway. When

he turned, the moonlight fell across half his face, casting it in cadaverous gray.

I stood up and moved to the half wall, sticking my head outside. Dying leaves shrouded the graveyard from the rest of the town, so the only light that reached the shrine came from the thin slice of moon and faraway stars. But that was probably too much light, since we were looking for the Land of Eternal Darkness.

"Take my hand," I said.

Neven crossed the space between us, and his hand fell into mine. I raised my other hand to the sky, and with one swift arc of my arm, extinguished the moon and stars.

Darkness crashed over us. The same color as my hair and eyes, the blackness from before time began, when there was nothing in all directions. I held Neven's hand tighter when the chill of the stone floor crept up my legs and prickled up my rib cage, a million tiny pinpricks cutting me open.

"Ren," Neven said, his palm sweaty in mine, his grip growing looser. I had no reassurance except to crush his hand tighter.

Then the stones dissolved and our feet sank into wet sand. I heard the whisper of waves crawling onto shore, the sound of leaves shivering against each other, the wind that hummed from far away.

We saw nothing at all in the endless night, and that could mean only one thing. I gripped Neven's hand harder.

"We're here."

CHAPTER 07

Every part of the underworld was speaking.

The hush of leaves in the wind was a thousand formless whispers, both in my ear and a hundred miles away. Ocean waves sighed over our feet and shattered like glass. Even the air resonated with the heavy and faraway hum of a bell toll. The underworld felt alive in a way that the living world never did.

I took a step forward, pressing my foot deep into the sand. Like the water, it had no temperature, just a distant pain, like my foot was falling asleep. Neven must have heard the crunch of sand and thought I was walking away, because his hand snatched my wrist.

"Don't..." He trailed off, his grip loosening slightly as if he were embarrassed, but not enough to let go of me entirely.

"Some light would be nice," he said, clearly trying hard to sound impatient, even though his voice wavered.

"There's no source of light that I can manipulate," I said. "Let's go find one."

I took another step and Neven's hand went tight on my wrist again as he hurried to keep pace with me.

We followed the edge of the water to make sure we didn't walk in circles, careful never to wade too deep. After a few minutes, the darkness became less oppressive and more familiar, as if I'd always lived in total blackness. Though I could see nothing, I could feel the whole landscape—the plum blossoms and magnolias draped in a canopy over the river, the golden flash of koi fish beneath the water, the distant slope of mountains. Had my senses heightened as a Shinigami, or was the darkness making me hallucinate and paint pictures in my mind? I was trapped in a dreamscape, where everything felt tangible, but if you reached out to touch something or focused too closely on any one detail, the whole picture dissolved. It was more of a feeling than any kind of vision.

With this odd half sight, I led us to a stone lantern by the water's edge. I laid my hand on it, just to be sure that it really existed, then ignited the flame.

The light formed a pale circle around us, a small shelter from the blackness on all sides. The trees that I'd imagined in the darkness appeared overhead, sickly pale in the dim light. Neven let go of my sleeve and reached out to touch the leaves.

"I forgot what it was like to see for a moment," he said, running his thumb across the branch. "That's strange, isn't it? We were only walking for a few minutes, but I forgot what the world looked like. What I looked like."

"Strange," I said, burning the light a little brighter and extending our circle of visibility. Apparently the underworld affected us both in ways I didn't understand. I knelt down beside the stone lantern and peered through the openings to where a small candle burned, then carefully slid my hand inside and separated the wax from the stone, removing the candle from the lantern and rising to my feet.

"Let's go," I said, forcing Neven to follow as I walked away with his only source of light.

The shallow bank of the river expanded, the numbing water rising to our ankles no matter which way we turned. With the light in front of me, I could no longer make out shapes in the darkness the way I'd been able to without light. Were we doomed to wander like this forever? It felt like years had already passed.

Something thin and silky brushed my toes. I looked down, expecting seagrass, but instead saw endless strands of silver swaying back and forth under the clear water. Neven had already stopped and was bending down to run his fingers through the silver thread. It swirled around us, caressing our ankles, as if it knew we were there. Neven pulled some of it above the water, then instantly dropped it and shot to his feet.

"It's hair," he said.

I lifted my foot out of the water, pulling up gray strands that turned to a clinging web. What kind of creature had so much hair?

"So it is," I said, managing to disguise the horror in my voice but unable to keep the disgust off my face.

"This is worse than that spider touching me," Neven said, grimacing.

We walked for a few more minutes until the hair began to lift out of the river as if someone had pulled it, hanging in dripping knots that gradually rose higher and higher.

Our circle of candlelight inhaled an old woman sitting cross-legged on a small boulder in the river. Her skin was the color of dust, pruned and folded and speckled with age. Her eyes burned a searing gold, her lips pulled back in a smile showing oddly immaculate teeth. Kimonos of a thousand different colors hung from the tree branches behind her, forming an impenetrable wall of fabric.

"Hello, travelers," the old woman said, her voice cracked like autumn leaves. "Do you seek to cross the river?"

I looked out across the waters to our left, seeing no determinable end to them.

"Is that possible?" I said.

The woman's smile grew wider, almost so wide that it no longer fit on her face. My whole body wanted to shudder at the sight, but I kept my feet planted firmly in the sand.

"It is possible," she said, "but only if you shed the outside world."

"Our clothes?" I said, looking up at the kimonos. "And what happens if we do?"

The old woman gestured to the water. "A bridge will appear over the river, and you may enter into the town of Yomi."

I turned to Neven. "She wants our clothes in exchange for a bridge across the river," I said in English.

He looked up at the hanging kimonos with unease. "You're not considering it, are you?"

I bit my lip and watched the different colors of fabric stir in a silent breeze. Shinto texts hadn't spoken of an elderly gatekeeper to Yomi, so I had no idea if she meant us any harm. I turned and looked across the black waters leading forever into the distance.

"Well, the alternative is that we can swim across, and there's no way I can hold a candle while doing it."

Neven shook his head quickly. "I don't know what's in that water."

I imagined us swimming through the water in total darkness, no idea of what was above or below us. If we became disoriented, we'd never find our way back to shore. No, I wouldn't do that to Neven.

I turned back to the old woman.

"I will go, but my brother will stay here," I said.

The woman nodded, eyes crawling over my clothing.

"What did you tell her? Ren?"

I handed him the candle. "Just keep your eyes on her," I said, shedding the first layer of my skirt. I handed it to the old woman, who snatched it from me, her long fingernails scraping the back of my hand. She examined my skirt and pressed it to her face. As she did so, I slid my clock from my pocket into Neven's.

"When the bridge appears," I said, "use your clock."

He held my gaze for a long moment, then nodded and turned back to the old woman, one hand in his pocket.

I'd expected to feel cold as I stepped out of my clothes, but the underworld apparently had no temperature. I finally handed the old woman my slip, detesting that my brother was standing so close to me at that moment, but at least he was determined to look absolutely anywhere but at me.

"There," I said.

The old woman shook her head. "Continue, dear."

I frowned. "I've given you everything."

"Continue," she said again. "You must shed the outside world."

"There's nothing more to shed," I said.

"Continue."

"Ren," Neven said.

"We had a deal."

"Continue," the woman said. Something stringy tickled the back of my ankles.

"Ren!"

The light from the candle shifted sharply, illuminating another withered tree to Neven's right. Strips of flesh draped over the branches, great blankets of skin hanging dead and torn around the edges. I could make out flattened faces and stretched scalps with black hair that shuddered in the breeze.

The gray hairs in the water locked around my ankles and pulled.

"Neven!" I said as the ground fell out from under me and I splashed backward onto my elbows. The hair climbed up to my waist in long stringy tendrils, razor sharp on my bare skin.

Then all at once, the river roared up and devoured the woman.

Waves rocked the water, submerging me and dragging Neven down, too. The grip of a thousand needlelike hairs fell away, their sting soothed by the tepid water. The river had swallowed the candle, plunging us into darkness and so much water that I couldn't tell whether I was swimming to the surface or deeper into the darkness. I thought of the freezing waters of the channel, of the monster with the silver hair that could seize me by the toes and drag me down, of Neven tossed and spun around in the darkness that he feared so much.

Then the water rolled over the shore and laid me down on the sand like a child tucked into bed, the current still lapping at my feet.

"Neven?" I said, sinking my hands into the sand and pushing myself up. "Neven, where are you?"

The only answer was the ripple of settling waters and the crunch of sand beneath my hands as I clawed across the shore, feeling around for Neven. A light in the distance arced closer, like a distant star shooting across the night sky, but I couldn't worry about that until I found Neven. If he wasn't here, I would have to go under the water again. I would sooner drain the whole river and dig through its hollow trench in total darkness than leave him out here alone.

Then the water surged with a sudden wave that splashed against my side, and a heavy weight crunched into the sand near me.

"Neven?"

I crawled toward the sound, my fingers slapping against metal buttons, then someone's face and eyeglasses.

"Ow, Ren!" Cold hands slapped mine away. "Do you know how hard it was to hold on to my glasses underwater? Don't break them!"

I sank back on my knees. In the privacy of the darkness, I took a moment to fold into myself, biting the side of a hand to hold back the urge to scream from relief. I hadn't lost everything, not yet.

"Ren?" Neven said, all annoyance gone from his voice. I heard him shuffle backward in the water. "Ren, is that you?"

"Of course it's me," I said, my voice sounding strange even to my own ears, rigid with false anger. I uncurled myself and remembered the approaching light, getting to my feet.

I hit my head against a low-hanging tree branch as I stood up, knocking some kimonos down from the monster's tree.

"Ren?"

I heard Neven moving closer.

"Stay back for a moment," I said, swiping my hand through the air to ward off Neven, just in case he was feeling for me in the darkness. I grabbed a wet kimono from the branches and wrapped it around myself. Our next attacker was coming, and I wasn't about to confront him while naked.

This one, at least, was kind enough to carry his own lantern.

The approaching light revealed a young man running toward us with an uneven gait, the long sleeves of his kimono flapping behind him in shifting shades of blue. The lantern in his left hand illuminated his silver-white skin and dark eyes. Neven squared his stance and tossed me my clock, which I caught with the hand that wasn't holding my kimono closed.

"Are you all right?" the man said, limping the last few steps toward us. He stopped a careful distance away, seeming to notice our defensive stances, the light from his lantern enclosing the three of us in a dim circle. Beneath the shallow water, his right foot curved inward, his weight resting on the side of his foot rather than the sole.

Perhaps I should just knock him out and steal his lantern to save us all some time, I thought. I'd run out of patience for entertaining Japan's tricksters.

But then he shifted to his left foot and the lantern light fell over his face.

For the first time in my life, I stared back at another pair of black eyes, filled with all the endless darkness of the underworld.

The notes about Shinigami in the Reaper records had contained absolutely no useful information, other than few soppy notes about how they were "hauntingly beautiful, eyes and hair of endless black, skin that glows like moonbeams." I hadn't given the description much weight, because I wasn't beautiful and my skin certainly didn't glow. But the man before me looked like the protagonist of an exquisite nightmare, his face as haunting and magnificent as the dead of night.

He loomed over us with his lantern held high, his frame stretched tall and narrow, wrapped in layers of shimmering fabric. His deep blue kimono was embroidered with ocean waves and koi fish in silver thread that glimmered in the lantern light, creating the illusion that the waves churned and the fish leaped across his clothes.

The curse of Death's presence loomed all around him, in the harsh lines of his jaw and cheeks, the skeletal joints of the hand that held the lantern aloft, the syrupy thickness of his shadow behind him. But something about him transcended the weight of Death in a way I'd never learned how to do myself. His eyes, though dark as all of Yomi, somehow looked more like a night full of stars than a vacuum of nothingness.

"You're a Shinigami," I said.

He dropped his gaze to the sand, a faraway sadness softening his features. "By birth, yes," he said, "but I'm not serving at the moment."

"Then what is he?" Neven asked me, clearly getting the gist of the conversation with his limited Japanese.

"Right now, just Hiro, a fishing spirit," the man replied in English. He smiled and turned around, pointing to a basket of fish on his back. "You can have one if you want, but if you eat the food of the underworld, you can never leave."

I took a few steps closer through the shallow water, unable to look away from him. More than anything, I wanted Hiro to keep talking. His words had a distant ring to them, like the ghost of a note played on the piano when it's almost faded away.

"A fishing spirit?" I said. "So you controlled the river just then?"

Hiro nodded and turned back around to face me. "Datsueba has a habit of trying to skin people before they can cross over. A wonderful way to greet the newly dead, isn't it? It's not an issue for everyone, but some people lose their Shinigami guides on the journey down. Don't worry, she knows I'll wash away all her kimonos if she tries anything again."

"So what are you doing here?" Neven said. "Shouldn't a fishing spirit be up with the living?"

I sighed at Neven's politely toned bluntness. Neven didn't seem quite as enamored with Hiro as I was. I didn't blame him for his suspicion, after everything that had happened to us since setting foot in Japan.

If the question offended Hiro, he didn't show it. "I have friends here," he said, shrugging. "And it's hard to stay away, if this is where you're from." Then he turned to me. "You must feel it, too, right? You're a Shinigami, aren't you?"

Finally, someone had recognized me without prompting.

I held back a smug smile. "Yes," I said, "but it's my first time here."

Hiro hummed. "Well, that's unusual, but all right. What's your name?"

"Ren," I said. "This is my brother, Neven. We've come from London."

Hiro's eyes widened. "Reapers?"

"You know about Reapers?" Neven said.

Hiro laughed, rippling the still water. "Japan isn't as closed off as one might think." Then he turned to me again, his deep eyes drinking me in, his attention unravelling me so quickly that I wanted to melt into the black waters. "So that would make you half Reaper and half Shinigami, I suppose?"

I nodded slowly. "Is that a problem for you?" I said, my words lacking their usual bite as his eyes explored my face.

He smiled and shook his head. "What an interesting day I'm having," he said. "Well, Ren of London, your kimono is on backward."

I looked down at my sopping wet clothes and wished I could disappear. The worst part was that I had no idea how to fix my clothing.

"I got dressed in the dark," I said, glaring down at my feet in the clear water.

"Most of us do, down here," Hiro said. He walked to Datsue-ba's tree and pulled off what looked like a thin white dress. "Even if you're from London, we expect you to wear underwear here," he said, smirking and handing me the slip.

I am standing in a single layer of soaking wet silk in front of my brother and a handsome stranger, my brain helpfully reminded me, now that I was no longer worried about the dangerous hairy woman or drowning in the darkness. I snatched the slip from Hiro's hand, my face burning.

"Turn around," I said. "Both of you."

Neven turned around wordlessly, but kept himself angled so that Hiro remained in his line of sight. Hiro, meanwhile, turned away from both of us, seemingly unconcerned that we might attack him from behind. I slung my wet kimono over a branch and hurried to put on the undershirt.

"So what brings you two here?" Hiro said, talking loudly up at the endless black sky. "We don't get very many tourists."

I hesitated, my hand hovering over the kimono. *It might be dangerous to tell a stranger our purpose, even if he's a Shinigami,* I thought. Hiro swung his arms back and forth like a child who couldn't stand still, totally defenseless against any attack. I wished I could meet Neven's eyes to know what he was thinking. It was more likely that Hiro would help us than hurt us, given that he'd already saved us once when he could have left us for dead.

"Hello?" Hiro said. "Have you run away in the darkness and left me standing here like a fool?"

"We're here to see Izanami," I said.

Hiro froze. Silence stretched across the darkness, the distant murmur of trees falling silent, the ripples around Hiro's feet stilling until the water was once again solid black glass.

"Why?" he said, the word more of a threat than a question.

"That's not your concern," Neven answered before I could respond. Neven had hardly ever snapped at anyone so quickly, aside from the Reapers who'd bullied me. Clearly, Hiro didn't impress him.

"Everything about the Goddess is my concern," Hiro said,

standing up straighter. His shadow grew taller in the dim light of his lantern, and an image of the towering Jorogumo flashed in my eyes. Then he shook his head and the hard line of his shoulders slumped. "I'm sorry, it's just...she and I have a complicated history. Me being a demoted Shinigami and whatnot."

"And why did that happen?" I said, slipping on the kimono the opposite way that I'd done it before. If Hiro planned to turn on us, I at least wanted to be fully dressed for it.

"Nothing like what you're imagining," he said, not offering any further explanation. He must have known it was an unsatisfying answer, but for the moment it wasn't worth potentially upsetting him to pry.

"I'm done," I said. "Neven, help me tie this."

"Can I turn around, too?" Hiro said.

"If I weren't decent, why would I let my brother see me?"

Hiro turned around, smiling as if the whole world hadn't darkened around our conversation. "I didn't want to tread on your decency, Ren of London."

"Just 'Ren' is fine," I said as Neven took the cord around my waist and tightened it so much it nearly sliced my torso in half.

"Careful!" I said, coughing. "It's not a corset, Neven! Just tie it so it won't fall open."

"That part ties in the front, actually," Hiro said. He hung his lantern from a branch, then stepped forward and extended a hand. "May I?"

Neven withered when Hiro came closer, all of his previous bravado gone. Without waiting for permission, Hiro gently slid the cord from Neven's hands and stepped in front of me.

"Hold this," he said, taking my hand and pressing it just above my hip to hold the fabric in place. His fingers seared my corpse-cold skin, the ghost of his touch sparkling with warmth on my hand even when he moved away.

His arms came around my waist to cross the cord over itself in the back, and for a moment I couldn't breathe with his sudden closeness. The skin around his neck glowed with a ghostly haze and smelled of brine and sand. Like the landscape in the darkness, he seemed barely a part of reality.

The closeness only lasted a moment before he knelt in front of me and tied the cord, then tucked it under the fabric. The moment I could breathe again, my stomach ached with a gnawing humiliation. I was so incompetent in my own culture that he'd had to dress me like a child.

Hiro's eyes searched the trees above us, then he pulled a purple sash from the branches and wound it around my waist before moving behind me.

"This is the part that ties in the back," he said, pulling at the fabric. It tightened for a moment before he released it and stepped back in front of me, surveying me from head to toe. "Lovely," he said.

The word warmed every inch of my skin. I looked away, raking my damp and tangled hair out of my face and focusing on finding a place for my clock. Unlike a Reaper's cloak, the kimono had no pockets, so I clipped it to the purple sash around my waist and tucked the clock inside the fabric.

"I've done my best, but I'm glad you can't see the bow I did in the back," Hiro said, scratching the back of his neck. "Sorry, but I haven't put a kimono on my sisters since they were about three feet tall."

"Shinigami can have more than one child?" Neven said.

"Well, no," Hiro said simply, turning and gesturing across the water with his lantern. "I take it you wanted to cross the river?"

I glanced at Neven, who looked mildly confused at the blunt response, then nodded at Hiro. "If that's where Izanami is," I said.

Hiro turned and pointed over the water, though we couldn't see beyond the scope of the light. "The mainland is across the river. There's a boat downstream that will take you there."

He took off walking past us, waving for us to follow. Apparently he planned to escort us there. Neven and I had to hurry after him, since he'd taken the only light source with him.

"Are you injured?" I said, looking down at Hiro's foot.

He let out a sharp laugh. "Not recently, no. I sustained a severe paper cut on Tuesday, though, and I'll have you know that I didn't even cry."

"I mean…" My gaze drifted to his foot again.

"Oh, that? Well, my mother always insisted that I eat my peppers as a child, but I never listened. Of course, she was right, because one day I woke up and my foot had changed. I swallowed crates and crates full of peppers after that. But tragically, it was too late for me."

"Oh." I frowned. What a mundane reason. "Is that problem common for Shinigami?"

Hiro sighed. "Have you heard of 'jokes' in England? My humor is wasted on you."

I said nothing, deciding not to press any further. It was only fair that Hiro was entitled to secrets, too.

He stopped so suddenly that I bumped into him. Neven stumbled into both of us, pushing me into Hiro's back.

"Why did you—"

"Shh!" Hiro said, waving a hand and extinguishing his lantern.

In the sudden darkness, Neven grabbed my kimono and pressed himself closer.

"Look over there," Hiro whispered.

I couldn't see where he was pointing, but my eyes focused on a circle of pale light about a hundred meters to our right. I felt Neven move around me to get a better look.

Two figures stood before the river, one in a bloodred kimono, holding a lantern like Hiro, the other in a white burial gown.

"Who are they?" I said.

"How should I know?" Hiro said. "I just love a good soul extraction."

Soul extraction? But that would mean…

I squinted, my eyes adjusting to the light. The figure in red had the same ghostly glow as Hiro, the same hazy aura of Death steeping in the darkness around him. This was another Shinigami.

The few texts I'd read in England had no information on soul collecting outside of England. It made sense, for collections were a sacred act that Reapers preferred to do in private, so people of other cultures were probably just as secretive. But surely the process couldn't be that different?

Before I could ask any other questions, the Shinigami's fingernails sharpened like talons, and he plunged his hand straight through the human's chest.

I gasped, slapping a hand over my mouth to silence the sound. Behind me, Neven's fingers twisted in my clothes. But I shouldn't have worried, because the human and Shinigami were too engrossed in the extraction to notice us.

The human's lips parted, tinged with blood, hands clinging to the Shinigami's arm as red painted the pure white kimono. Then the Shinigami withdrew his hand, pulling out a pulsing heart and a cloud of silver dust that twinkled like distant stars. *His soul*, I thought. I'd seen enough souls to recognize one on sight, even when they were unique to every person.

The human fell to his knees, a hand clapped over the bleeding wound, while the Shinigami stood over him, blood dripping down his robes as he raised the heart to his lips and took a wet bite.

"He's *eating* it?" I whispered.

"Isn't it enthralling?" Hiro said. I could hear his grin, even if I couldn't see it.

"But why?" I said, wincing as the Shinigami took another bite and devoured the rest of the heart, then wiped his lips on his red robes. Perhaps this was why his robes were the exact shade of blood.

"As Shinigami, we are part of Izanami," Hiro said. "We're her eyes and ears on earth, and in Yomi, her mouth. This is how she receives the souls. Humans must forfeit them before they cross the river."

"Then what's left of them to cross the river?" Neven said.

"A shell," Hiro said. "When they reach the city, they will be whole again, but their soul will forever belong to Izanami. They can never leave Yomi with their soul intact."

I felt a bit nauseous at the thought of eating pulsing flesh, but there was something enthralling about it, as Hiro had said. It should have been a repulsive act, but was it really any worse than jamming my arm elbow-deep down a human's throat to rip out their soul through the mouth? It was alarming how captivating the act appeared to me, like an instinctive part of me had always wanted to collect in this way but hadn't realized it until I'd seen the bright gleam of fresh blood in near-total darkness, the ethereal contrast of stark white and violent red. I couldn't help picturing myself in bright red robes, my lips painted with blood, standing on the shores of Yomi with my lantern like a beacon of light in the endless darkness. Was eating hearts all it took to be called a Shinigami, not as an insult but as a respected title?

The Shinigami lifted the human to his feet as easily as if he was made of paper. Something about the human's presence seemed lighter, the shadows of darkness now a thick blanket over him, as if he'd become more translucent. The Shinigami turned and pointed in our direction, and together they began to walk toward us.

"And that's our cue to leave," Hiro said, hurrying down the shore. "They're headed for the boats, too, and I don't want to run into them." He didn't bother relighting his lantern, so I followed his footsteps and Neven grabbed onto my sleeve.

"Why not?" I said. But Hiro only took off walking faster, leaving me and Neven trailing behind.

"Are you sure about this?" Neven whispered, hand still twisted tight in my wet kimono. Hiro could probably hear us from only a few feet away, but graciously pretended not to. "Should we really be following him?"

Of course I wasn't sure. But I hadn't expected to find a

paved golden road leading to Izanami. Of all the creatures that we'd met in Japan so far, Hiro appeared the most innocuous. After all, we'd been standing in his waters, which could have drowned us at any moment, but hadn't. He'd taken the time to help me dress properly and turned his back to us as if he trusted us. There was a chance that he wanted to drag us deeper and sacrifice us to some river monster, but there was also a chance that he was just a Shinigami helping another Shinigami. Besides, I had no idea how to reach Yomi without him.

"Yes," I said.

We dragged our feet through the shallow waters for a few silent minutes before Hiro finally lit his lantern and a wet dock came into view. Ten fishing boats sat perfectly still in the water, unbothered by any current.

"Here we are," Hiro said, picking up a paddle from a small pile on the dock, then gesturing to the boats. "Pick any one you like!"

I knelt down by the first boat, looking inside for any obvious holes or traps. Before I could get inside, Neven blocked my path.

"After you," he said to Hiro.

I wanted to smack Neven for his impertinence, but Hiro merely smiled and said, "Sure!" before stepping into the boat. Neven untied the rope and held it in one hand, gesturing for me to get in.

I gripped his wrist. "Don't anger him," I whispered, squeezing until the rope went slack in his hand.

Neven frowned but didn't argue back. I stepped carefully

into the boat and sat in the middle beside Hiro's lantern as Neven followed behind, pushing us off.

Hiro started to paddle, and we set off from shore. Soon, the boat gained momentum, cutting through the water as if the universe had tied a string to the bow and was pulling us along. Hiro seemed to know where we were going, even with the lantern only illuminating a small circle around us. He started to hum, the sound echoing as if the waters had turned to a great expanse of marble.

The song carried across the darkness, distant and sad, like an old lullaby. The moment it reached my ears, a tingling settled in my bones. I'd heard that song before. I was positive. But how was that possible?

His song filled up the endless dark with sadness, and I wondered if the melody and not the direction of the boat had carried us across the river.

As he hummed the final notes, the boat began to slow. Shallow water gave way to soft sand, and we slid silently onto the shore. Hiro set his paddle down but did not turn around.

"Welcome to Yomi."

CHAPTER 08

As the boat slid into the sand, Hiro got up and moved as if to help me out, but Neven somehow materialized in front of him and offered me a hand. I ignored both of them and hopped out on my own, the sand damp under my bare feet.

In the distance, hazy lantern light glowed beyond a grove of trees, warm amber and red. The gleam of lights in the stark darkness blurred the edges of the buildings, as if the whole landscape was a fever dream.

"I thought there was no light in Yomi," I said.

"There's not much of it," Hiro said, setting his lantern in the sand and tugging the boat farther up onto the shore. "There's total darkness near the shrines and most people's homes, but this is where a lot of new arrivals come, so we try not to scare them too much."

"You don't?" Neven said. "Isn't this Hell?"

Hiro laughed, brushing the sand off his hands and picking up his lantern.

"Ah, that's right. You're from London. You might have Heaven and Hell, but in Japan, there is only Yomi."

"You mean that creature who tried to skin me wasn't hellish to you?" I said.

Hiro smiled, gesturing for us to follow him down a trodden path in the sand where the beach grass hadn't grown.

"Even the land of the living has hellish creatures, but that doesn't make it Hell," he said. "There are some malicious spirits down here, sure. After all, this world was created with pain. But it's not meant to be a place of suffering any more than the world above. It's just that, when you have enough souls in one place, suffering is inevitable."

The beach grass and sand gave way to soil that softened to the shape of my feet. We approached the grove of trees, their branches blocking the city lights under a canopy of white blossoms. Even without the light of Hiro's lantern, the sky of flowers had an eerie glow of their own.

"How do they survive with no light?" I said.

Hiro smiled. "What makes you think they're alive?"

We followed him through the grove. The ground sloped gently upward, leading us away from sea level and closer to the blurred voices of the city. Light burned through the spaces between the blossoms, the petals star-bright in the darkness.

Hiro reached forward and parted the branches, and suddenly we stood at the gates of the city.

Yomi was an oasis of light in the infinite darkness, garlands of red lanterns strung between the awnings of every building.

The houses wore their roofs like extravagant hats, massive slopes of black clay tiles with gently curved brims. Just like in Yokohama, the city was stark unpainted wood and paper doors and shadows. But unlike Yokohama's spacious roads, the houses in Yomi crowded together too tightly to breathe. People moved in a rushing torrent in both directions, filtering into the fish shops and bookstores and tea stands that lined the road.

All the dead wore white kimonos, silky and pale as the moon. The fabric was translucent at the sleeves and hem, as if the dead were slowly dissolving into Yomi's darkness. I looked down at my pink kimono with trepidation, but Hiro—dressed unashamedly in ocean blue—didn't seem concerned.

He led us from the soft soil of the grove to the paved ground of the city, under the painted vermillion archway that marked the entrance to Yomi. The throng of dead souls pulled us in, sweeping us through the barrage of sounds and colors. Everything in the streets tried futilely to combat the crushing darkness—the red lanterns strung in zigzags back and forth overhead like a sky of ruby stars, the open-air restaurants with archways revealing the elaborate chandeliers inside, the pastry cases backlit with white and green lights. But darkness fell like heavy rain, and all the lights cast only small and ghostly circles of brightness around themselves—their light could not combine to cast an artificial daytime across the street. They could barely break through the darkness at all.

The sum effect was a kaleidoscopic assault on the eyes. It hurt to stare in any one spot for too long, so my eyes jumped from image to image without truly processing any of them.

Hiro pressed through the crowd, Neven and I stumbling

along behind him. I'd never truly seen the dead before, as the souls in England all went Beyond, where Reapers couldn't trespass. The dead in Yomi looked much like the humans I'd seen in Yokohama, but with an eerily dim presence. Rather than actual humans, they looked like memories of humans pieced together from a thousand hazy images. Their eyes and noses and smiles seemed real enough in passing, but the longer you looked, the stranger their features became, as if their faces weren't real but painted onto their blank skin. Many of them turned to stare at us in our colored clothes, their gazes lingering long after we'd passed them.

"Hey, fish boy!" a woman's voice called in Japanese.

Hiro stopped in front of a mask maker's store, where a woman in a red-and-white cat mask leaned against a banister. Her masks decorated the outside walls and the pillars holding up the awning, the open door revealing a thousand more faces wallpapering the store inside.

Neven and I stopped close behind Hiro, the crowd parting seamlessly around us. The masks covering the windows leered down at us, white-faced geishas and blue devils, old men with stringy beards and horned dragons.

"Hayashi!" Hiro said, reaching into his basket and tossing the woman a fish.

She caught it with one hand, then removed her mask and took a vicious, juicy bite. She turned to look at me as she chewed, juices running down the long line of her neck. She looked young, her eyes a bit hollow with Death, but exquisite in the way that ageless things always were, like insects cased in amber.

"Interesting souvenirs you've brought back," she said, speaking to Hiro, but staring at me and Neven.

Hiro laughed, though I didn't find it funny. "I made some friends over by Datsue-ba's tree."

"Friends," she said, eyes scanning up and down Neven's frame. "This one's in a costume."

"It's not a costume," I said in Japanese. "It's what humans wear in England."

The woman stared at me for a long moment, so long in fact that I started to wonder if I'd accidentally stopped time. My eyes flickered to Hiro, who watched Hayashi like one might watch a tiger outside of its cage.

"You're a long way from England," she said, "and you speak Japanese like your mouth is full of sand. Who taught you?"

Hiro let out a sound like a strangled bird, though I thought it might have been an attempt at a laugh. "Hayashi, they don't know your sense of humor yet," he said. "She's joking," he said, turning to me.

I glared at the woman but said nothing, because saying anything else in Japanese would only prove her point. She had no idea how many decades I'd spent studying Japanese just to reach the fluency of a child. My studies had been my dark and precious secret, my Japanese books hidden in the floorboards so Corliss wouldn't burn them again. I'd practiced kanji by painting the letters onto my skin and washing away the evidence by nightfall. But none of that mattered because Hayashi wasn't wrong—I knew she wasn't, and perhaps that was why her words cut so deeply. My fingertips burned white-hot from my anger, but I hid them in my pocket, even as it felt like I'd dipped my hands in lava.

"Ah, yes," the woman said. "I tend to joke a lot."

She ripped off another bite of fish with her teeth, then slapped the remains on her worktable.

Something about her indifference cut through me, like an iron poker jammed straight through my stomach. I clenched my burning hands into fists to try to stop it, but it was no use. The light surged from my hands, and all three of the red lanterns above her shop burst into flames.

Hayashi jumped back and Neven threw himself to the ground, shielding his face from flying sparks. All around us, the dead hesitated in their paths and turned toward us, drawn like moths to the sudden brightness. Hiro waved his hand and instantly extinguished the flames, leaving behind only scorched black strips of paper and a cloud of smoke, the mask shop now dimmer than the rest of the street.

Hayashi turned to Hiro, her face twisted into a scowl.

"Is she trying to ruin my business, or is she just incompetent?" she said, extinguishing some errant sparks by pounding her fist onto a display table.

"I'm sure it was an accident," Hiro said, looking between us like he couldn't decide who was more dangerous. "Ren, your powers are still developing, aren't they?"

"Excuse me?" I said, crossing my arms.

"I mean, how old are you? Two centuries? Three?"

"Nearly two," I said. "How did you know that?"

"See? Her powers haven't settled yet," Hiro said, turning back to Hayashi.

"She needs to be house-trained," Hayashi said, her tone still bitter, but her eyes no longer murderous.

But this time her insult didn't register, for I was too dis-

tracted by what Hiro had said. Because of the delicate nature
of time, a Reaper's powers didn't really develop unless they
received advanced training. But apparently, a Shinigami's
powers grew with age, and outbursts of light like this seemed
to be excusable in that stage.

I thought back to the exploded streetlight in London that
had ruined everything, how I'd suddenly been unable to control the light that I'd always wielded so easily. Could I have
prevented it if I'd known? If anyone had been there to help
me, would I even be in Japan right now?

"And why, exactly, haven't you taken them to an Overseer
yet?" Hayashi said.

I tensed up. Hiro was meant to take us somewhere? I looked
to Neven, but he was busy examining all the different masks
on the walls. I'd forgotten that he didn't understand much
Japanese.

"They're not human or dead," Hiro said.

"Obviously, but they'll deal with them all the same,"
Hayashi said. Then she pulled a mask down over her face.

She was no longer a beautiful woman, but a red-faced beast
with sloped black eyebrows, golden pupils, and a long beaked
nose. When she spoke, her lips moved with the mask, as if it
had become part of her face.

"You don't need to play guardian angel," she said. The mask
had altered her voice as well—still her own, but deeper and
raspier. "You should take them to a Shinigami who's actually
practicing. It's their responsibility, not yours."

Hiro turned away from Hayashi, but I suspected it had less
to do with the mask than her abrasive words.

"She *is* a Shinigami," Hiro said, gesturing to me. "She doesn't need to be watched by one."

"Except for you?"

Hiro sighed, then reached back into his basket and tossed another fish to Hayashi, who snatched it from the air with one hand, lifting her mask and taking another wet bite.

"Don't worry about Shinigami business," Hiro said. "We'll be going now."

"Neven," I said, the sternness of my voice making him jump and hurry away from the mask he was about to touch.

Hayashi laughed and pulled a fox mask from the wall, then slipped it over her face.

"Come back soon, travelers!" she said, this time in English, as we walked away. Her voice had become high-pitched, the sound of a mosquito buzzing in my ear. "I have all the masks in the world. You can be anything you want!"

Almost anything, I thought.

"Lovely friend," I said, as soon as the woman was out of earshot.

Hiro sighed. "Hayashi is rather...traditional. She's from my hometown. She died a few centuries—"

"What do you want?" I said, grinding to a stop in the middle of the road. I didn't care about the tragic backstory of the woman who had just insulted me to my face. I didn't care to know what redeeming qualities she had when she'd made me feel smaller than a speck of dust, and yet Hiro was defending her. "Why are you helping us?"

"I... I don't want anything," Hiro said, eyes wide. "I just wanted to help—"

"Do you think we're fools?" I said. "Do you think we came here all the way from England through sheer idiocy?"

"Of course not," Hiro said. "Ren—"

"You're breaking the rules by escorting us," I said. Neven tensed behind me at this new information. "Why would you do that?"

"I…" Hiro grappled for words, looking desperately between me and Neven as if one of us would save him. Whatever deception he'd been weaving was rapidly unravelling. I should have felt relieved that my intuition had been right, and that we hadn't followed him any farther than here. But instead, a hollow darkness opened in my stomach as he floundered for words. I'd wanted him to conjure up magic lies that explained his behavior. Something about him made me want to trust him, but I wouldn't follow him against all logic.

"It's really not a problem for me to help you," Hiro said at last, shoulders slumping because even he knew that was too little too late.

"It's a problem for us," Neven said. He set his hand on my shoulder, as if showing Hiro that we were a team. Neven had probably been waiting patiently for this moment, relieved that whatever girlish enchantment I'd been under had dissolved. But I didn't want to be on Neven's team at that moment. I didn't want to be with anyone at all.

"Goodbye, Hiro," I said, sliding out of Neven's grip, away from Hiro, away from everyone. I'd come too far to lose everything to an enchanting river spirit.

A hand gripped my sleeve.

"Wait," Hiro said.

I turned around, but Hiro was staring at the ground and not me, fingers closed around my sleeve.

"Please," he said quietly, "let me explain."

I looked to Neven, who had his clock in one hand and his arms crossed. I stood beside him. "All right."

Hiro dropped my sleeve. "I wanted to deliver you to Izanami," he said to the dirt road.

I frowned. "Why?"

"I thought she might reward me for bringing one of her children home," he said, his words growing quieter with shame.

"Izanami is not my mother."

"Yes, yes," Hiro said, waving his hand dismissively. "Biologically you're not, but all Shinigami are like her children. We exist because of her."

"I thought you didn't like her," Neven said, "so why are you so eager to deliver us to her?"

"It's not quite so simple as liking or disliking her," Hiro said. "She denies me the title of 'Shinigami' and the only way to restore it is by earning her favor. She's the only one who can give me what I want."

"And why, exactly, aren't you a Shinigami anymore?" I said.

Hiro closed his eyes, hands falling to his sides. The ghostly glow around his skin dimmed until he no longer looked like a prince of nightmares but a tormented human, the same as corpses after I'd torn out their souls and left them still and hollow in their beds.

"You asked me why my foot looks this way," he said at last. "Izanami asked the same thing when I was a child. 'How could a Shinigami, a creature made of moonlight and star-dust, look so broken?' That's what she said to me."

He hung his head lower, eyes open but unseeing. "My condition was worse back then," he said. "She sent me away to be raised by humans. They took care of me and treated me like their own children. I know that I can work like all her other Shinigami, but she won't even let me in her palace, much less speak to me."

He looked up, staring at me with startling intensity. "I'm no fool," he said. "It will take more than escorting you there for her to restore my title. But maybe it would be a start. I have to try, Ren. So please, let me do this."

Hiro no longer resembled the carefree river spirit we'd met in the shallow waters. I thought of the mournful song he'd sung as he'd rowed us across the waters, how it had chilled my blood with the rawness of its beautiful anguish. I no longer had to wonder where that sadness had come from. I could hardly blame Hiro for not telling us the whole truth all at once, when it was something so personal. I too knew how it felt to want something more than anything else in the world.

"Okay," I whispered.

Neven went rigid behind me. *"Okay?"* he said.

"You want to take us to Izanami, and we want to go there," I said to Hiro. "I don't see why we can't both get what we want."

For a moment, Hiro didn't move. Then his eyes closed and his lips curled in a gentle smile. The weight of his worry lifted off him, his skin glowing brighter than before. He bowed deeply and took my hand, surprising me again with his warmth.

"You don't have to worry," Hiro said, this time in Japanese. "I will look after you, Ren of London. I promise."

"And my brother," I said.

Hiro nodded. "As you wish, though I think he would prefer it if I didn't." He straightened his stance. "The palace is this way," he said in English.

We rejoined the crowd, tight in a single-file line. Neven refused to look at me, no matter how I tried to catch his gaze. I knew he wasn't pleased with my decision, but I didn't expect him to understand. Hiro's motivations would never make sense to someone like Neven, but that didn't mean they were lies. Neven understood so little of the nuances of being unwanted.

Hiro led us to the outskirts of the market, where the lights grew dimmer. Beyond their glow, the world turned inky black, heavy and viscous. There was no slow transition into the darkness, just a steep drop into the void.

Hiro hung his lantern on a hook at the border of the darkness.

"There is no light allowed at Izanami's court," he said.

I remembered the story of her origin, when Izanami's husband had shone a light on her and seen her rotting corpse, setting off the chain of events that led to the creation of Death for humankind. The rule made sense, all things considered.

Neven finally turned to me, eyes sickly green with alarm before he remembered to be mad at me and turned away. I took his arm, and he pretended the touch was unwanted for a few seconds before his muscles relaxed.

Hiro looked back at us, then stepped out into the darkness and disappeared.

I followed him, sensing Neven's resistance in the heaviness of his steps. A thick blanket of night dropped over us. The city lights over my shoulder grew small and distant as we followed the sound of Hiro's footsteps.

"Don't wander far from me," Hiro said. "You might find yourself sucked into a swamp in the deep darkness, where you can never climb back out." His tone implied that he might be joking, but Neven's grip around my arm tightened enough to bruise bone.

"The deep darkness?" Neven said.

"Yes," Hiro said. "There are monsters out there that no one has ever seen. It is said that they enjoy disassembling humans into all their constituent parts, then hoarding the bones to build their nests. They can smell fear and love the sound of screams."

"But we're not going anywhere near them," I said, squeezing Neven's wrist until he unlatched from my forearm, letting blood start to circulate again. "Isn't that right, Hiro?"

Hiro laughed. "Don't worry," he said. "I have no desire to walk close enough to the deep darkness to deliver you there. You both will live to see another day."

If this reassured Neven, he gave no sign of it, plastering himself to my side as we followed Hiro deeper into the night.

As we moved through the dark and the city behind us shrank into a distant star, once again my other senses opened their eyes and I could picture the world in vivid detail without actually seeing it.

The dirt road beneath my feet turned into a stone walkway and a great carved staircase that led up into the dark sky.

I raised my foot for the first step, but Neven tripped into it, nearly pulling me down.

"Ah, sorry, mind the stairs," Hiro said from somewhere in front of us. "You can hear my footsteps, yes?"

"It's fine," I said. Neven crushed my hand tighter against his arm and stumbled up the first step.

"I forget that not everyone can navigate the darkness when they first arrive," Hiro said. "You'll get used to it, I promise."

As we climbed upward, the endless staircase opened up to a stone courtyard with a massive archway, three layers of sloped roofs rising like a tremendous crown above it. As we passed under it, our footsteps rang as hollow echoes against the stone walls. Other footsteps joined Hiro's, and soon a crowd of worshippers swallowed the sound of his steps and breathing.

"What's happening?" Neven said, pressing closer to me.

"Other people came to pray," Hiro said. "Let's not disturb them."

I sensed him moving through the crowd, but I struggled to follow his path as the murmurs of the worshippers covered the sound of his footsteps. I couldn't merely scan the crowd and locate him, because everyone had melded into a homogenous People, my senses duller than if I could actually see. I sensed them bowing and taking off their shoes, but I couldn't comb Hiro from the mass.

I felt a magnetic pull to my left, not unlike the pull of Death, and turned around in instinctive obedience.

Hiro stood by the wooden archway of a nearby garden, watching me. His face was the sharpest image I'd sensed in the dreamy hellscape of the darkness. His eyes were the smooth black of stones washed up on the shore, patient and impartial.

His skin glowed brighter than I'd ever seen, like the shimmer of moonlight on the changing waves. Even though the world felt hazy, he was perfectly clear.

But something about his expression was strange. Perhaps my weak night vision couldn't parse the nuances of his face, but his eyes seemed to watch me too deeply, like they were unwrapping the layers of skin and flesh and trying to determine the color of my soul.

I pulled Neven toward Hiro, and as we drew closer, the strange hollowness in his eyes disappeared. A gentle breeze sighed through the garden behind us and blew the scent of lake and lotus to us as he uncrossed his arms.

"You can see in the dark," Hiro said.

Neven flinched, clearly not expecting his voice so close.

"Yes," I said.

"You can?" Neven said, with the clear implication of *why didn't you tell me?*

"Shinigami can," Hiro said, smiling. "How interesting."

"Were you testing me?" I said, frowning.

Hiro laughed, somehow melting away my anger. "I was only curious what a half Shinigami can do," he said. Then he turned and walked off through the garden, his footsteps loud on the jagged stone path.

I led Neven through the garden to a large open-air shrine crowded with worshippers. The fevered whispers of their prayers echoed in my ears as I stepped around their bodies. I tugged Neven closer to me so that he wouldn't step on any of the dead and followed Hiro through the masses. We slid through the crowd and arrived at the biggest building yet—a castle mounted on a gray stone foundation high above the ground.

Like an ink painting, the edges of the monochrome castle bled into the wet darkness. The lines between reality and illusion blurred, not like the dreamy haze of Yomi's town center but as a nightmarish smear of blackness raked across the sky. The castle towered ten stories high, each story marked with a sloped rooftop that flared up and out, the corners sharp as claws. What an extravagant castle that most people would never see.

"This is her palace," Hiro said. "I can't promise that she'll see you, but you can ask for an audience."

Before I could thank him, the shadows of the dream haze wrapped around him like a crashing wave, sucking him into the blackness with a startled breath. Where he'd once stood, only darkness remained.

"Hiro?" I said. I held Neven tighter, lest he disappear next.

"What happened?" Neven said.

"He's gone."

Then, with a sound like parchment ripping in half, the darkness parted and Hiro tumbled out, falling to his hands and knees.

"Dammit," he said, panting into the ground. He got to his feet and glared at the darkness "I'm not on palace grounds yet, damn you!"

"Hiro, what—"

The words caught in my throat when the darkness thickened, swirling into itself and forming the silhouette of a man.

"You're not supposed to be here."

CHAPTER 09

The guard had no face or shape, only a blurred silhouette painted with deep darkness, shifting and endless like a portal to outer space.

"I can come this far," Hiro said, brushing the dirt from his coat. "I'm not trespassing."

"You shouldn't be here at all, leech," the guard said, his voice vibrating in my bones like the language of Death, but a deeper frequency, a warm hum that ran down to my toes.

Hiro gripped the straps of his fish basket and glared at the ground. "I've brought the Goddess one of her children," he said.

The guard turned to me. Though he had no eyes to see me, the air shifted in my direction from the force of his gaze. Neven shuddered next to me.

"And what are you?" the guard said.

I forced my spine to remain straight, rather than wither under the force of his energy.

"I am Ren, of London," I said. "My mother is a Shinigami. I am here to speak to Izanami."

"The Goddess," the guard corrected, the air stirring with the weight of an impending storm. His silhouette dissolved and spun toward me, whispering over my face and neck like silk scarves, then quickly reforming into a human shape.

"You are not a Shinigami," he said.

My jaw locked, my blood beginning to simmer. "That's not for you to decide," I said, regretting the words as soon as they were out in the darkness. Who was I to question this specter when I had no idea what he was capable of? I should have been groveling on my knees for permission to see Izanami, but something in my blood had churned viscerally at his accusation. Why was it so hard for everyone in Japan to see that I was a Shinigami when it was the only thing the Reapers had seen?

If my outburst had ruined my chances of meeting Izanami, the guard gave no indication of it. He remained still except for the galaxies churning inside the blackness of his silhouette.

"She can see in the darkness," Hiro said.

The guard's silhouette stretched into thin ribbons that knotted around Hiro's neck and threw him to the ground. "Silence, leech!" he said, yanking the cords tighter as Hiro clawed at his throat, unable to make a sound.

"Stop!" I said, rushing forward and raking my hands through the ribbons, which slid through my fingers like particles of dust.

As I lunged forward, Neven grabbed on to my skirt and crashed to the ground with me. "Ren, what's happening? Ren?"

But I couldn't answer, too busy trying to seize something that didn't exist. I turned to Hiro's neck and tried to tear away the ribbons but did little more than scratch at the white skin of his throat as his legs kicked out and eyes rolled back.

Then the ribbons dissolved into black dust, and Hiro gasped and rolled onto his side, coughing.

"You can see," the guard said, voice rumbling behind me.

"You couldn't have just taken my word for it?" Hiro said, sitting up and rubbing his throat. He set a hand on my knee as if to thank me for my attempt.

"And who are you, boy?" the guard said to Neven, ignoring Hiro's complaint.

I elbowed Neven, who stood up straight, staring somewhere in the approximate direction of the guard. "Introduce yourself," I whispered.

He swallowed and nodded. "My name is Neven Scarborough," he said in faltering, clunky Japanese. "I am a London Reaper. I'm here to...to—"

"He's my brother, here to accompany me," I said.

The guard hummed in thought, the sound droning deep in the dirt. "I will take you to the Goddess and ask if she wishes to speak with you," he said to me. "But only Shinigami can enter her palace."

Hiro scrambled to his knees. "Could I—"

"You are not a Shinigami," the guard said, the venom in his words harsh enough to melt flesh from bone.

Hiro withered, sinking back down to the ground.

"Come now," the guard said.

I nodded and let go of Neven's hand.

"Ren?" he said, reaching out.

"Stay with Hiro until I return," I said, setting a hand on his shoulder. I looked at Hiro. "You will take care of my brother," I said in Japanese.

He bowed, one hand on his heart. As I stepped away, his white skin blurred into watercolors in the dream fog.

Then the guard turned and raked his fingers through the air, tearing a hole in the darkness that yawned open like a gaping wound. He pulled back one of the edges and the void stretched wider, a shade just as dark as the rest of Yomi but with a twisting undertow, the night spinning in tight circles. I forced myself not to look back at Neven and Hiro, not to show the guard my hesitation. I took one step into the void, and the darkness breathed me in.

It felt like I'd jumped into a warm and lightless sea, my body weightless in the never-ending night. An invisible current pulled me through until I broke the surface and the void spat me out on wooden floors.

The darkness in the palace dulled my Shinigami senses. I could barely make out the shape of paper doors in front of me, painted with golden mountain ranges and red waterfalls. I pressed a hand to the doors, where voices murmured behind the screen. The painted scenery revealed itself to my mind under the touch of my fingers—images of Izanami looking off a heavenly floating bridge into the unborn world, Izanagi by her side among the clouds, the beginning of their ancient story before everything would one day be ruined.

The door slid open on its wooden track and I yanked my fingers away.

"The Goddess wishes to see you," the guard's voice said from somewhere above me.

I rose to my feet and tripped over a lip in the wooden floor. I felt my way through the doorway, barely one step inside when the doors slammed shut, leaving me in complete darkness.

Here, my Shinigami senses found only solid darkness in all directions. It bruised my bones with its immense weight, pulsing behind my eyes with the crushing pressure of the ocean's depths. As I took another step away from the door, the darkness forced me to my knees. I tried to get to my feet but could only crawl forward with trembling limbs, as if fighting gravity itself just to exist.

"*Speak,*" a voice said, nearly pinning me to the floorboards with its force. This was not only the language of Death, but the voice of Death herself.

I had never met a Death God before. Even in London, I'd never met our forefather, Ankou, for I'd never had a reason to. And yet, here I was, in a foreign land, kneeling before the woman who had built Japan herself, who had created Death for these people and kept the souls of all the dead in her belly. I folded forward until my hands and forehead pressed to the ground in a crushing bow.

"My name is Ren," I said in Japanese. "My father is a Reaper and my mother is a Shinigami. I've come here to find her and live in the land where I was born."

Izanami did not reply. The seconds stretched out, my breath loud against the floor, my forehead damp with sweat.

"Show me your face," came the reply. The words scraped through my ear canals, the sound of torn and rotten vocal cords a thousand years dead.

I peeled my forehead from the floor and lifted my face, staring into the blackness.

"You are no Shinigami," the voice said. "You have the face of a Reaper."

Then the hands of darkness shoved me back to the ground, my face pressed once more against the mat.

"I am a Shinigami," I said, even though the words trembled. If there was any one truth in my life, it was this. It was what I'd been told my whole life. It was the reason I'd had to flee my home. I had to be a Shinigami because if I wasn't, then I was nothing at all.

"My Shinigami live and die in Yomi," the voice said, "but you've come from afar. Why do you return to me now, expecting hospitality?"

I swallowed and wished Neven were here. Not only for comfort, but to force me to pretend I was brave.

"I can no longer live in England," I said.

"Speak louder, girl."

"They wanted to kill me!" I said, my hands curling into fists against the mat. "I was hated there for what I am. They learned of my light powers and would have killed me if I'd stayed. My own father didn't even stop them. I've come to you now because I have nowhere else to go."

The air in the room had grown warmer, the scent of rot stronger against my tongue.

"I know who you are, Ren of Yakushima," the voice said at last.

I froze. "Yakushima?" I whispered.

"I know where you are from, and I know your mother. But that does not make you a Shinigami."

"You know my mother?" I asked, all the air leaving my body.

"She lost her title for her transgressions," Izanami said. "She is no longer a servant of mine."

"Do you know where she is now?" I said, unable to stop the words from rushing out, even though I wasn't sure I wanted to know.

"Yes."

I held my breath, starting to worry that I might faint from the heat and pressure of the room. If Izanami knew where my mother was, that meant she was still under Izanami's domain, somewhere in Japan.

"Could you tell me where—"

"Foreigners do not come into my palace and ask favors of me," Izanami said. "I owe you nothing, do you understand? You aren't supposed to be in Yomi."

I wanted to crumble under the harshness of her rebuke, but I forced myself to stay unmoving, my arms trembling on the mat. I'd come this far, and now Izanami planned to banish me from Yomi because she didn't like my face? I fought against the crushing pull of Death and rose to my forearms, raising my face to Izanami even though it felt like the weight of one thousand universes wanted to crush me back down.

"I am a Shinigami," I said in Death, so that Izanami would know my words were true. "Yomi is my birthright. I will find my mother on my own if you refuse to help me, but I will not be turned away from my own country."

In the silence that stretched out after my words, I realized my mistake.

How could I have talked so brashly to Death herself? She could snap my ribs off one by one and grate my skin into ribbons. She could kill me and keep my soul suspended in the ether, then go after my brother.

I was about to throw myself to the ground and beg for her forgiveness when she started to laugh.

At least, that was how I interpreted the dry, grating sound that came from the darkness.

"You may not have the face of a Shinigami," she said, "but perhaps you have the soul of one."

I let out a breath of relief, my whole body suddenly warm. No one had ever paid me a higher compliment than that.

"We do not entertain tourists in Yomi," Izanami said. "You can pledge yourself to me, body and soul, as my eternal servant, or you can leave and never return."

"Yes," I whispered, rising up as much as the crushing power of Death allowed, "yes, I will serve you." I thought of the Shinigami on the shore, his crimson robes, his perfect, elegant power.

"Serving me is a privilege," Izanami said. "You served Reapers for one hundred years instead of me. Now you must prove your worthiness."

"I'll do anything," I said.

Izanami said nothing for a moment, as if contemplating something of great importance.

"Come closer," she said.

Before I could even try to move, the force that had crushed me into a bow dragged me forward. I crawled through the thick mud of darkness, my knees and palms so sweaty that they stuck to the bamboo mats. The closer I came, the stronger the pull of Death and the stench of rot grew. A deep hum vibrated in my ears, like the lowest pedal tone of a church organ. At any moment, my bones would shatter under the immense weight of Izanami's power. I remembered the story of Izanami's origin, how her husband had cast his light on her and seen her rotten body eaten by maggots. What must she look like now, so many centuries later?

The pull finally stopped, holding me at some indeterminable place in the darkness. I tensed at the sound of scratching. Somewhere in the dark void, something sharp raked against wood in quick movements.

"There is something you must understand about Japan," Izanami said above the scratching. "We value harmony, even in death. There must be cooperation between wraiths both above and belowground. That is, the Shinigami and the Yokai. You know about the Yokai, don't you?"

"Yes," I said, the word barely audible.

"When the Yokai devour a soul, it no longer belongs to me," Izanami continued, the scratching growing louder. "They are allowed one thousand souls between them every day, and the rest are mine. Any more, and the population of Japan begins to decrease rapidly. Do you understand?"

"Yes," I said again.

The scratching stopped, leaving only the low hum of Izanami's power ringing deep in my ears.

"Hold out your hands," she said.

I extended my hands, palm side up, and waited, trying

not to tremble as I imagined a thousand terrible things that Izanami might lay on my palms.

Then something flat and wooden pressed into my hands. A tablet of some sort. As Izanami withdrew her hand, her fingers brushed over mine, bare bones scratching against my flesh.

"This is a list of Yokai who have taken more than their fair share," she said. "I want you to destroy them. When you do, return to me, and you may serve as one of my Shinigami."

"And my brother?" I said. I could hardly form the words, my teeth chattering even though I wasn't cold. "H-he came to Japan with me. He's a Reaper, he can serve you, too."

The air went still, the humming in my skull suddenly silent. I'd made a terrible mistake, and Izanami was going to withdraw her offer.

"Japan has opened up its doors," Izanami said after a moment. "I suppose Yomi can as well, if they are deserving. He cannot be a Shinigami, but perhaps he can serve Yomi in some way."

I pressed myself to the floor in a boneless and relieved bow. Finally, I had a chance at building a life that I actually wanted. First, I would secure my place in Yomi as a Shinigami, then I would find my mother.

"Thank you," I whispered into the mat. Then I remembered Hiro and tried to sit up, my arms too weak against Izanami's force to support me. "I was helped here by one of your Shinigami," I said. "His name is Hiro."

Izanami said nothing, the weight of Death suspended in the air as the moment stretched out longer and longer.

"I have no such Shinigami," she said at last. "Now go. Do not make me wait for long."

Then the crushing weight dragged me back toward the door. I scrambled to keep up with the pull, crawling with one damp hand while the other curled around the wooden tablet. My shaking fingers felt the screen door and pulled it open, the weight all but shoving me out the door, where I tumbled into the warm darkness of limbo again. I couldn't breathe or move, could only clutch desperately to the tablet as the current pulled me through.

The world ripped open and I fell onto cold dirt, the tablet still clutched in my right hand. Without the weight of Izanami's presence, my bones suddenly felt too light, like I might float off into the dark sky.

"Neven?" I called into the darkness. "Hiro?"

"Ren!"

Neven's voice broke through the darkness, followed by two sets of footsteps and fingers clumsily patting down my hair and shoulders.

"Are you all right?"

"I'm fine," I said, clearing my throat and sitting up. My eyes took a moment to readjust to the darkness and the strange half sight, my vision oddly skewed and dizzy. Hiro stood behind Neven, his eyes unreadable. I remembered how Izanami had denied him and decided not to repeat her words to Hiro, for it would accomplish nothing other than hurting him.

"What did she say?" Hiro said.

I looked down at the tablet in my hands and ran my fingers over the deep scratches, trying to decipher them. But it was hard enough to read Japanese even in good lighting, and I didn't recognize some of the characters that Izanami had written.

"She gave me an assignment," I said. "If I complete it, she'll accept me as a Shinigami and let me and Neven live in Yomi."

Hiro's hands reached out, becoming clearer as he drew closer, as if he'd reached from underwater and broken the surface.

"May I?"

I slid the tablet into his hands, explaining to Neven what had happened as Hiro examined it. When my explanation was finished and Hiro still stared at the tablet, I grew unsettled.

"Hiro, do you know these Yokai?" I said.

"I know of them, but I don't know them," he said, lowering the tablet. "I have met many Yokai, but never these three."

"And is there a reason for that?" Neven said.

Hiro handed the tablet back to me, his expression blurred by the darkness. "They have killed Shinigami."

I swallowed, thinking of all the horrific Yokai I'd read about as a child and which ones I'd soon have the privilege of meeting. If they were capable of killing Shinigami, they had to be much scarier than the ones we'd seen in Yokohama.

"And Izanami expects Ren to kill them," Neven said, crossing his arms. "Ren, don't you think this is strange? Reapers aren't meant to kill."

"Izanami isn't asking me to be a Reaper," I said, my nails biting into the wood tablet. "Wouldn't you do whatever Ankou asked of you?"

Neven said nothing.

"Is this even possible?" I said, turning to Hiro. "Has Izanami given me an impossible mission just to get rid of me?"

For a moment, Hiro didn't answer. The dark fog had cleared slightly, and once again he was the only thing I could see with clarity. The icy sternness of his expression was so different from his usual brightness.

"I don't know," he said at last, "but does it really matter?"

I frowned. "How can it not matter?"

"I don't know your story, Ren," Hiro said, "but I can assume that someone like you doesn't end up in Yomi unless she has no other choice."

Of course, Hiro was right. I might die trying to become a Shinigami, but what was the alternative? To live among humans who treated me just as badly as the Reapers? To hide away and live in isolation?

"Tell me who they are," I said, holding the tablet out to Hiro again.

He moved next to me, fingers tracing the scratches. No matter how hard I looked, I couldn't see words but only the claw marks of a rabid animal.

"Yuki Onna," Hiro said, pointing to the top line, "the Snow Woman."

His finger moved down another line. "Iso Onna, the Sea Vampire."

Finally, the last line: "Tamamo No Mae."

When Hiro didn't offer an explanation, I turned to him. "Who is she?"

He shook his head, finger drifting away from the tablet. "I don't want to lie to you."

"So don't."

"I don't think I should tell you."

I wanted to yell at him, but something in the graveness of his expression sobered me.

"You will tell me eventually," I said.

He nodded. "When it becomes necessary."

I gripped the tablet in both hands and stared hard through the murky darkness at the names of the souls I would soon destroy. I would secure my place as a Shinigami and build a home for myself and my brother in Yomi, where we were both safe. And then I would find my mother, even if Death herself wanted to keep her from me.

CHAPTER 10

Hiro led us away from the court and back into the sea of darkness, promising to find us an inn for the night. Neven clung to my right arm while I clutched the tablet in my left and followed close behind Hiro, weaving deeper and deeper into the endless black.

As the extravagance of the palace and throngs of worshippers faded away behind us, the world dissolved into nothing but dirt roads and night sky. For a while, we walked down the endless path to nowhere under a sky of infinite nothing.

Gradually the road narrowed and I sensed buildings on either side of us—walls of paneled wood and heavy thatched roofs. The wood dampened the noises of people inside, filling the darkness with formless murmurs in all directions. The houses, already hazy to my new senses, swirled together in their infinite sameness. Were we actually moving forward, or just walking forever in place?

Hiro whistled the same song that he'd hummed as he rowed our boat to Yomi, lonely and gentle. The notes echoed up into the great cathedral of darkness overhead.

"What is that song?" I said.

Hiro stopped whistling, looking over his shoulder.

"It's a siren song, actually," he said. "I'm luring you to your death."

"Funny."

Neven found it less amusing and took out his clock preemptively, forgetting that Hiro could see him in the dark.

"It's what you're both thinking," Hiro said. "No offense taken, truly. But I promise there's no need to clobber me to death with your pocket watch."

Neven dropped the clock in surprise, barely catching it by the chain before stuffing it in his pocket.

"You've threatened me with that watch quite a few times, Neven," Hiro said, smiling over his shoulder. "Is that the Reaper weapon of choice? You'll use it to bash my teeth in?"

"I…it wasn't a threat," Neven said, fingers tense around my arm. "Just a precaution. They're time turners, not weapons."

"Could I see?"

Neven said nothing, lips pressed tightly together.

"I've overstepped. My apologies." Hiro bowed dramatically even though Neven couldn't see it. "Are they made from the bones of Englishmen? What makes them so special?"

"Just silver and gold," I said when Neven made no attempt to answer.

Hiro hummed in acknowledgment. "Could I have a dem-onstration of this fantastical time-turning?"

"That's not possible," Neven said.

"Please?" Hiro said, clasping his hands together in front of his chest as if praying. "I can offer you something in return." He turned around and pulled one of his fish from his basket, waving it in front of Neven, who couldn't see it. "Have you ever seen fish dance?"

"As tempting as a dead fish circus is, we don't play with time," I said.

Hiro nodded, tossing the fish back in his basket. "All right. Very professional. Maybe I'll get a demonstration while you're killing those Yokai."

"You mean you plan to accompany us?" I said, my pace slowing.

Hiro laughed. "You want so desperately to get rid of me?"

"This is not a small favor that you do for strangers out of kindness," I said, coming to a stop in the road. "This is dan-gerous. You said so yourself."

Hiro sighed and nodded as if he'd been expecting this.

"I know you two are brave, or you wouldn't have come this far," he said, "but you don't know Japan, and you don't know the Yokai. I worry that if I let you go off on your own, you'll never come back."

I thought back to Datsue-ba and wondered if my skin would have been hanging off her tree had Hiro not come. When I'd imagined traveling through Japan, the image in my head had always been me and Neven and only the two of us forever. But now I could see Hiro walking beside us, whistling his siren song and telling jokes and passing out fish, as if he'd been there all along.

The image made my skin prickle the way it did when Ivy was tracking me, as if at any moment the sky was going to collapse and crush me to dust. Not because I found Hiro suspicious, but because I *didn't*, and that alone was cause for alarm. Neven was the only person I could trust. I'd learned that lesson a thousand times over, but some stupid, weak part of me wanted to trust Hiro anyway.

"Do you really intend to take us all over Japan?" Neven said. "Don't you have other duties?"

"You mean as a fishing spirit?" Hiro said, tilting his head. "It's nearly winter. The lakes will freeze over soon."

"How does a Shinigami even become a fishing spirit?" I said, pressing a hand to my temple and rubbing hard, as if I could erase every worry in my mind through sheer force.

"By growing up in a fishing village," Hiro said, shying away from our interrogation. "As I said, I was raised among humans. I'm not trying to deceive you."

"Why would you go so far to help us?" Neven said. "We're strangers."

"It's not for *you*," Hiro said, frustration finally cracking through his patient expression. His whole body tensed, the darkness simmering like hot oil around him. Then his shoulders drooped and his skin went dim, his face growing hazy in the darkness, as if he was drifting farther away.

"If it's what the Goddess wants, then I have to be a part of it," he whispered. He looked up, not at me or Neven but at a fixed point in the hollow darkness. "I have a chance to help her with something of importance. Maybe it will start to change her mind about me. Maybe she'll keep me out in the darkness forever. I don't know, but I have to try. I've spent so long locked outside in the dark."

For a moment, the three of us stood in the empty darkness with only the sounds of our breaths and a distant wind. Hiro's form had grown dim and blurry, as if he was wrapping himself in a blanket of darkness. The night had become physically heavy on my shoulders with the weight of Hiro's anguish. It tasted of soot on my tongue, crawling down my throat and filling up my lungs. I too knew how it felt to be crushed under the weight of the entire night sky.

I didn't know if Neven could feel any of those things. I was sure he already resented me for letting Hiro take us so far without properly asking him about it, and I wouldn't compromise our entire journey unless he agreed.

I was about to tell Hiro that we'd discuss it in the morning, but Neven spoke first.

"I think," Neven began, his voice small in the darkness, "it would be helpful if you came with us."

Both Hiro and I turned to Neven in surprise.

"I mean, if Ren thinks it's all right," he added, kicking at the dirt road. He must have felt us staring at him, but he refused to look at either of us. Hiro's eyes had gone so wide that one would have thought Neven had offered his hand in marriage. What had changed his mind so suddenly? I nearly dragged Neven aside to make sure he hadn't sustained a head injury in my absence, but it took all of three seconds for me to understand.

Sweet Neven, who stood up for me against the other Reapers, even when it meant that I would be his only friend until the day he died. Neven, who'd come with me across the world because he would never let me go alone. Neven, who always did what he knew was right. I could tell from his clenched jaw and hands stuffed stiffly in his pockets that he was wary of Hiro, but he couldn't bear to turn him away.

I linked my arm with Neven's, and he relaxed at the grounding touch in the endless night.

"I think so, too," I said.

The shock melted off Hiro's face and he bowed deeply.

"I won't lead you astray," he said. "I swear to you." Then he turned and gestured for us to follow him deeper into the darkness.

Soon, our feet no longer crunched on dirt but over the wooden panels of a bridge that dipped under our weight. I sensed a glassy surface of still water and lily pads below us and a monstrous building before us that grew taller as we approached.

Only two lanterns hung on either side of the massive doorway, illuminating the white paper doors and protective row of potted bonsai trees around the first story. The building spanned forever upward, with layers and layers of extravagant awnings over glass balconies that disappeared up in the dreamy darkness.

Hiro slid open the front door and the sudden influx of light scorched my eyes. I dropped both Neven's hand and my tablet to cover them, Neven mumbling a complaint behind me.

"Come on, don't let the light out," Hiro said, waving us inside.

I blinked the stars out of my eyes and picked up the tablet, stepping over the threshold where a thousand mazelike hall-ways of sliding doors lined the main lobby. The soft sound of doors sliding open and shut played a soothing rhythm in the distance. The dead in their white kimonos shifted back and forth across the hallways, sliding like specters into their rooms.

Hiro walked up to an ornate desk at the far wall, where an elderly woman with a tight gray bun and eyes sunk deep into her sockets didn't look up to acknowledge him.

"Two rooms, please," Hiro said, reaching into his pocket and putting some sort of gold coin on the desk.

The woman reached out with shocking speed and snatched the coin off the desk, like a feral animal whose food had been threatened, yet her expression remained stony. She reached into a drawer and pulled out two keys tied to thin pieces of wood with room numbers scratched into them. She set them on the desk, then her other arm shot out in the opposite di-rection, pointing a skeletal finger down a hallway to her left.

Hiro bowed and thanked her, taking the keys and waving for us to follow.

"I assumed you wanted to share a room with each other," Hiro said, tossing me one of the keys as he walked backward down the hall. "That way I can sneak in and murder you both at once instead of walking to two separate rooms."

"Exactly how many jokes about murdering us do you think it will take before we start to find them funny?" I said, glanc-ing at Neven with sympathy.

"Clearly more than I've attempted thus far," Hiro said, grinning.

"I sleep with knives under my pillow," I said, reaching for my sleeve out of habit before I remembered that both of my knives had been washed away with my clothes. "At least, I did before we met Datsue-ba. Do you know where I can get new knives in Yomi?"

"You can control time and light, but you prefer human weapons?" Hiro said, raising an eyebrow.

"How else will I actually kill the Yokai? Do you expect me to clobber them with my clock? Sparkle them to death with candlelight?"

Hiro shook his head. "That's not how Yokai—"

"I need knives."

Hiro sighed. "I'll see what I can find for you," he said. "And I didn't ask, but I assume Reapers don't need to eat?"

I shook my head.

"Good," Hiro said, "because that might have been a problem. Don't eat or drink anything you see here, or you—"

Hiro collided with a man coming out of his room, sending them both to the floor. As Hiro tumbled forward on top of the man, fish spilled out of his basket and onto the man's startled face.

The man sputtered and hurled a fish at the wall, sitting up on his elbows. Unlike all the dead clad in white, he wore a bright red kimono embroidered with gold dragons. His skin burned bright like an overheated light bulb moments from shattering, his eyes a furious black. I took a step forward, drawn to him the same way I was to Hiro.

Death drenched his skin. His face looked like the last one you would ever see, iron-cold in its sternness. The weight of his anger curled the wallpaper and warped the floorboards.

Shinigami, I thought. And this time, up close.

I'd been enchanted by the Shinigami on the shore, but

this time I could see the embroidery of the crimson robe, the blood under his fingernails, the dignified way that he carried himself. It was surreal to now have seen so many Shinigami in the flesh after only imagining them for so long. Was red the only uniform of working Shinigami? Could all of them control the brightness of their skin? A thousand unspoken questions went through my mind as the Shinigami set his eyes on Hiro.

"*You*," he said, eyes narrowing.

Hiro, who had been scrambling to stuff his fish back in his basket, froze.

"Forgive me," he said, throwing himself into a deep bow against the floorboards.

But the Shinigami was apparently not in a forgiving mood, for he reeled back and kicked Hiro in the face.

Hiro crashed into a door and lay still as the dead. I sucked in a sharp breath and stood frozen as the Shinigami spat on the ground, barely missing Hiro's face. I thought of Ivy, and all I could see was myself lying in the street under the flickering streetlight, a moment that felt like a thousand years ago but was only last year. Weren't the Japanese supposed to value politeness and harmony? Reapers were cruel and deceitful, but Shinigami were supposed to be different.

"Stay out of my way, leech," the man said, turning and storming past me down the hallway.

Hiro had already pushed himself up on his knees and was gathering what was left of his fish. I was too busy thinking about the darkness in the Shinigami's face to bother helping him. Hiro stood up and instantly crumpled back down with a wince, but Neven caught his arm and pulled him back to his feet. He was favoring his left foot and wouldn't meet my eyes.

"Do all Shinigami treat you like this?" I said, because it was all I could manage to say. "Are they all so…"

"Cruel?" Hiro said, gently pulling away from Neven. "Yes."

"Why?" I hadn't thought anyone could be as heartless as Reapers, but the look in the Shinigami's eyes—a rage that could shatter the whole universe—told me that maybe that wasn't true.

"Because Izanami tells them to," Hiro said, turning away. "She can't stop a Shinigami from coming to Yomi, but that doesn't mean she wants me in her city."

He started walking away, not bothering to check if Neven and I followed him.

"And why do they call you that?" I said. Both the guard and the Shinigami had called Hiro *leech*, a strangely specific insult. I'd never heard anyone called a leech in England, but perhaps it made more sense in Japanese.

"Call me what?" Hiro said, but his shoulders had formed a rigid line, so I knew he understood.

"Leech," I said. "Where did that name come from?"

"You'd have to ask them," he said without turning around. "I'm not the one who came up with it."

He stopped in front of a door and jammed his key into the lock.

"Good night, Ren, Neven."

Then he slid inside and shut the door.

I looked at Neven, who shrugged, then unlocked the room next door.

A hotel in Yomi apparently meant nothing more than a

small space with reed mats, a lantern, and supplies to set up a futon on the floor. I waved a hand over the lantern to ignite it, then Neven and I got to work rolling out the bedding. He took off his shoes and glasses while I shed the wrinkled outer layer of my kimono, then dimmed the lantern to a warm glow and slid under the sheets.

Neven slid in beside me and turned toward the lantern, facing me.

"Ren," he whispered. "Do you really trust him?"

I stared up at the thatched ceiling, then rolled onto my side to face Neven, his face lit only by the weak lantern light behind me. Did Shinigami have good hearing like Reapers? Was Hiro listening to us?

"I think so," I said. "But clearly, you don't."

"We should help him," Neven said without conviction.

"I won't let him hurt us, Neven."

Neven sighed, pulling the sheet tighter around himself and rolling onto his back. "Okay."

"I can tell just how much you believe me by that melo-dramatic sigh."

His lips crinkled in what might have been a half-hearted attempt at a smile.

"Hey." I waved my hand in front of his face and smiled in the way I only could when it was just me and Neven. "Four-eyes, I'm over here."

Neven swiped at my hand, missing horribly and jamming his middle finger into my eye. Without his glasses, his hand-eye coordination was lacking at best.

"Watch it!" I said, shoving a retaliatory finger in his ear. He laughed and flinched away, but I grabbed both his wrists before he could accidentally scrape my brain out through my nose.

"I win," I said, smirking over Neven even though he probably couldn't see it without his glasses.

He gave a token struggle before falling limp against the futon. "I surrender, but only because I know what you're capable of."

"And that's exactly why you should trust me," I said, releasing his wrists and settling back.

Neven glowered. "I trust *you*, Ren, it's just that...he's unsettling."

I agreed, but likely for a different reason. Unless Neven was about to tell me he also found Hiro disarmingly attractive.

"Have you noticed," Neven whispered, "that when he laughs, he doesn't really sound happy?"

"You just saw a Shinigami spit on his face. Would you be happy about that?"

He shook his head. "No, that's not what I mean. When I see him, I feel like I'm watching a shadow puppet. There's something important happening on the other side of the screen, but I can't see it."

I said nothing, too stunned at the depth of Neven's distrust. It was reasonable to question Hiro's motives, but what Neven was describing alarmed me.

"It's his eyes, I think," Neven went on. "They're too dark."

"They're just like mine, Neven."

"*No,*" he said. "Even in the dark, I can still see his eyes, Ren. There's not just darkness in them, there's nothingness. The total absence of color. I feel like that's how the world looks when you die."

"He's just a Shinigami," I said. "Maybe he's a little different from me because he's full Shinigami."

"The other ones weren't like him!"

"Shh!"

I looked around, as if Hiro would burst through the paper doors at any moment, but the night remained still and silent.

"I wouldn't turn him away for his eye color alone," Neven said, quieter this time, "but I'm not sure about him, Ren."

"I'm not sure of anything we've seen here," I said, "but I think he's the least of our worries."

Neven looked at me for a long moment, his eyes hazy blue. Without his glasses, I could see the purple darkness under his eyes.

He turned away from me and curled into the sheet. "Good night, Ren."

I rolled onto my back and stared up at the ceiling again, then waved my hand toward the lantern and extinguished the flame.

What felt like a few hours later, Hiro knocked on our door. He smiled as if he'd never been struck by another Shinigami in all his life, making me question whether anything I remembered was real. All of Yomi seemed like a distorted dream, since half of it existed only in my mind and not my visual memory. At least Neven was with me to tether me to reality.

Somehow, while we slept, Hiro had managed to procure kimonos for me and Neven—both ghostly white, as that was the only color non-Shinigami could get in Yomi, and technically he wasn't a Shinigami. While Neven still had his weathered boots from England, my shoes had been lost to the river, so Hiro gave me wooden sandals that just barely fit and socks that split between the toes.

My knives had been lost in my clothes given to Datsue-ba, so Hiro had found me a couple throwing knives too dull to slice butter and cheekily handed me a river rock with which to sharpen them. Mercifully, he had elected to leave his basket of raw fish behind.

Clothed and armed, we needed a plan to destroy the Yokai. As much as I hoped it would be a matter of simply finding them and slitting their throats like the Jorogumo, something told me that Izanami would not have given me such a simple task.

"Where can I research the Yokai?" I said as Hiro started tying Neven's kimono.

In London's library there had been books to teach me almost anything in the world—how to read Japanese poetry, how to draw paralytic poison out of flowers, how to understand why humans acted so brashly despite their short life spans. With no friends to speak of, I had always spent my time outside of collecting with Neven and books and nothing else, just the two of us and all the words in the universe at our disposal, and that was the way I preferred it.

I needed books to understand the Yokai beyond the watercolor portrayals of my children's anthology. I needed their backstories and urban legends and written records of their sightings, anything to help me understand why they were so special, why Izanami had sent me to destroy them.

"You can't," Hiro said. "At least, not easily."

I caught Neven's startled gaze in the mirror of our hotel room as Hiro finished tying his belt.

"Why not?" I said.

"There were many books written about the Yokai," Hiro said, "but almost all of them have been lost or destroyed."

"I had a book of Yokai in England," I said, frowning.

"Yes, I've heard of other countries writing about Yokai," Hiro said, grimacing. "Those stories are for entertainment, not research. I don't suppose your book told you how to defeat any Yokai?"

"No." I thought back to the illustration of the Jorogumo, portraying her as taller than a ten-story building. Perhaps my children's-book knowledge of Yokai wouldn't be enough any longer.

Hiro sat cross-legged on the floor. "There is only one remaining text about the Yokai that I would trust, and few people even know where to find it anymore," he said. "Its location is one of Yomi's many dark secrets, the knowledge lost to all but a few souls."

Though his words were morose, Hiro's eyes glowed and his lips twitched like he was trying desperately not to smile. Was I missing some sort of joke?

"How can we find it?" I said.

"Well," Hiro said, crossing his arms and leaning back against the wall, "you would have to find someone who knows where it is. Someone with connections all across both Yomi and Earth, someone incredibly trustworthy and knowledgeable."

Hiro still looked far too delighted to be delivering news of an impossible quest. I looked at Neven in case he understood, but he only shrugged. Hiro looked at me expectantly, then gave his own reflection a pointed glance in the mirror.

I sighed. "Hiro," I said, "do *you* know where it is?"

A smile broke across Hiro's face. He reached under one layer of his kimono and pulled out a long scroll from under his belt, then tossed it to me.

"You *have* it?" I said, snatching the scroll from the air. I nearly fell over from its unexpected heaviness. The knobs at each end were made of gold, the white washi paper held together with a braided red bow.

"Well, technically it's a copy," he said. "An unsanctioned one, so take care not to wave it around in front of any Shinigami, but yes. If you feed people enough high-quality tuna over the years, they don't mind doing you favors now and then."

"Are all your friends made by peddling fish?" I said.

"I do not 'peddle' fish," Hiro said, scowling, "I award them to others in exchange for their friendship and undying gratitude."

"Maybe that's why your charm is falling flat on me and my brother," I said. "We haven't had this magnificent tuna."

"I offered!" Hiro said, eyes wide as if he'd been seriously affronted.

I rolled my eyes and turned to the scroll, consciously forcing a smile off my lips. Hiro's theatrics probably should have annoyed me for the time they wasted, but somehow I couldn't despise the way he made me forget about the magnitude of my task for a few moments. Neven came up beside me, sliding his glasses down his nose to squint at the title painted down the side.

"What does it say, Ren?"

"The Book of…Hakutaku?" I read, looking to Hiro for confirmation.

Hiro nodded, patting the floor before him. I set the scroll down and began to unroll it.

"Hakutaku was one of the first Yokai," Hiro said. "He was a white ox with nine eyes who could speak all human languages. He told a Chinese emperor about all 11,520 Yokai. His words were recorded in this book. Hopefully, this will tell us more about the Yokai that Izanami wants you to kill."

"You don't already know everything about them?" I said, unwinding more and more of the paper. "Didn't you just tell us you were infinitely knowledgeable?"

"I just said that there are over eleven thousand distinct Yokai in Japan," Hiro said, pouting. "I have only met about five thousand of them. I hope you can forgive my severe shortcomings."

I ignored Hiro as I kept unrolling the paper in search of Yuki Onna's name. The writing on the scroll seemed to have no end. No matter how many meters of washi paper I unrolled, the scroll never changed in size, never looked like it was nearing its endpoint.

"Wait, it's here." Hiro leaned over and rested his warm hand on mine to stop me from rolling up any more paper. I looked up and met his eyes, far too close to mine. I caught myself cataloging the different shades of black in them, forgetting for a moment that time was not, in fact, frozen, and I did not have all the time in the world to observe him.

Hiro pulled his hand away and I dropped my gaze to the paper, my cold skin feeling too warm.

"Here," Hiro said, pointing to the center of the paper. I

frowned at the thin brush strokes, as if glaring at the page might make the words clearer. I'd never read so much hand-written Japanese before. The characters were so different from the clean printed ones in my textbooks.

"What does it say?" Neven said, looking at me.

I remained perfectly still, too ashamed to tell Neven that I couldn't read it, but not able to pretend in front of Hiro, who would know if I lied. Neven looked to me for guidance in a country and language he didn't understand. How could I tell him that a simple change in handwriting had rendered me mostly illiterate?

"May I?" Hiro said.

I looked up. Hiro wasn't asking Neven, but me. Were my thoughts really so transparent? Was he trying to rescue me, or did he just enjoy playing storyteller?

"Go ahead," I said.

Hiro cleared his throat, sat up straight, and told us the legend of Yuki Onna.

In the cold, lonely mountains of Niigata, at the top of a tall, tall hill, an old man and his wife opened their inn to travelers.

On the darkest night of winter, when snow fell thick and blazing white, a young woman knocked seven times on the door. She had long, black hair and eyes like jagged ice, her skin the same crystal-white shade of new snow.

The innkeeper and his wife gave her food, but she would not eat. They offered her a bed, but she would not sleep. She merely sat by the irori, warming herself as the darkness grew deeper, the storm louder.

When the storm began to beat its fists against the windowpanes, the lights in the inn went out, as did all the stars in the sky.

Only then did the young woman stand up and walk toward the door.

"Please don't leave," the old man said. "You will die in the storm."

But the young woman didn't listen, and walked out into the night.

"I have to find her," the old man said at last. He put on his coat and ventured into the freezing darkness.

The long night never seemed to end as the old woman waited for her husband to return. The sunrise never came, the mountains only growing colder and darker. Eventually, the old woman put on her coat and went out to find her husband.

She found him only three paces from the front door.

His skin was blue and his whole body had turned to ice, like he was trapped in a glass chrysalis. When the old woman bent down to touch him, he shattered into one thousand pieces.

From high up in the mountains, Yuki Onna watched, eating the old man's liver as his warm blood dribbled down her chin. When she finished, she went deeper into the darkness, in search of an even colder and lonelier village, one that would not tell her secrets.

"Wonderful," I said, crossing my arms. "I hate winter."

Neven had gone quiet and pale beside me. This was too reminiscent of Corliss forcing him to listen to her ghost stories when he was a child. Only this time, we were actually hunting down the ghosts.

"Don't worry, Neven," I said, rolling up the endless length

of scroll. "We'll just put on some mittens and go carve her heart out." I didn't think it would be so simple, but Neven wasn't going to be the one killing Yuki Onna anyway, so it didn't matter if he underestimated her.

"I don't think a simple knife is going to be of much help," Hiro said. He'd tried to argue as much earlier when I'd insisted on finding new knives.

"'Simple' knives are the most useful," I said. "With church grims, for instance. And that Jorogumu we met in Yokohama."

Neven looked away from me at the mention of the Jorogumo, but Hiro only raised an eyebrow.

"A Jorogumo?" Hiro said. "Well, that hardly would have hurt her."

My hands stilled on the scroll.

"What do you mean?" I said.

"Well, most Yokai won't die from stab wounds," Hiro said slowly, as if it should have been obvious. He'd kicked off his slippers and crossed his legs in a half-lotus position, and was rubbing his foot without seeming to notice. "You didn't know that?"

I looked down at the scroll and finished rolling it back up with more force than necessary. Did that mean I hadn't actually killed the Jorogumo? I'd felt so satisfied when I'd slit her throat, but now I felt like a fool.

"I suppose it makes sense that Reapers wouldn't know things like this," Hiro said.

Something in my chest clenched at Hiro referring to me as a Reaper, but I forced the thought aside.

"Most Yokai are not easy to kill," he said. "To destroy

them, you have to destroy whatever gives them their essence. For instance, do you know Kuro Bozu?"

Neven and I shook our heads.

"They're black creatures that feed on the breath of sleeping humans," he said, grimacing. "They suck the breath out of humans' mouths and noses and ears with these long, serpentine tongues. It makes the humans very ill. But I've heard stories of vengeful humans who killed the Kuro Bozu by ripping its tongue out."

Neven shuddered. My own tongue curled up in sympathy.

"Then there's Tenjoname, the gremlin who lives off the filth that he licks from dark homes with tall ceilings," Hiro said. "It is said that the only way to kill him is to get rid of his filth by scrubbing his skin from his bones."

"I don't want to participate in skinning anyone," Neven said, tipping his head back like he was trying valiantly not to vomit.

"Well, Yuki Onna is an ice and snow spirit," Hiro said, "so I imagine her weakness involves heat."

"Then we'll bring enough fire to turn her into Yokai soup," I said.

Hiro nodded. "The village that she's said to haunt has plenty of supplies for making large fires," he said. "They need it to stay warm through the winter. I'm sure they won't mind us liberating some of it from them."

"It doesn't matter if they mind," I said, shaking my clock in front of Hiro to remind him what I could do. "They're not going to stop us. No one will get in my way."

Neven grimaced, but Hiro smiled as if pleased, his dark eyes somehow brighter, as if backlit by a thousand stars.

★ ★ ★

Hiro rowed us back across the river, the city of Yomi disappearing into the perpetual night behind us like a distant candle that had been extinguished. He led us onto the sandy shore and through tall beach grass that prickled at our hands and thighs, shifting restlessly even though there was no discernible wind.

He waved his hand and hundreds of paper lanterns blinked to life, hanging from tiered hooks around an open-air shrine. The lanterns formed a crown of light hovering above the dark and polished wood of the shrine, illuminating the many footprints in the sand.

He picked up a long pole with a hook on the end and used it to hang his lantern among the others.

"Do these belong to the other Shinigami?" I said.

Hiro nodded, setting the rod down in the sand. "Everyone is upstairs working, it seems."

Rather than stepping into the shrine, Hiro walked around the side to a stone tub under a slanted roof. The tub trickled with water from an overhanging system of pipes, and several ladles hung from the rim.

"What are you doing?" I said.

Hiro paused and turned around, raising an eyebrow.

"We have to purify ourselves first?" he said, as if I'd forgotten to brush my teeth or put on shoes. "You can't bring the darkness back to the living."

Neven and I observed Hiro and mimicked as he washed his hands and mouth with one of the ladles. He must have realized that we had no idea what we were doing, but tactfully said nothing. Were we supposed to do this before coming

down to Yomi the first time? I decided out of embarrass-
ment not to ask.

But while Neven washed his hands and only clear water
fell back into the basin, the water from my hands turned a
sour shade of dark green, polluting the rest of the small pool.
Neven jumped back, dropping his ladle as I stood frozen,
hands dripping in water that had turned to sludge.

"It's okay," Hiro said. "Sometimes the darkness clings to
some people more than others. That's what the purification
is for."

I said nothing, watching as the sludge dripped like spoiled
molasses from my hands. Why had the darkness chosen me
and not Neven or Hiro?

Hiro pulled a cloth from his pocket and took my wrist with
a strange gentleness, wiping the darkness from my hands. It
sloughed off easily, like dead skin, but somehow I didn't feel
like I'd been purified.

When we finished, Hiro turned back to the shrine and
slipped out of his shoes, then picked them up and tucked
them under his arm.

"I suggest you carry your shoes, unless you want to arrive
upstairs barefoot," he said.

We copied Hiro and entered the shrine. White candles
lined the perimeter, nothing but night air covering the tiled
floor. Though it had no true walls, the shrine muted the
sounds of wind and shifting grass and running water, as if
we'd traveled somewhere far away. Hiro began to light the
candles with a wave of his hand but hesitated after lighting
only the far wall.

"Actually," he said, "this is your mission, Ren of London. Why don't you do the honors?"

"All right," I said, though I found the idea of carrying three people across worlds much more daunting with Hiro as an audience rather than Neven alone. Not to mention that I wasn't entirely sure how to bring us back to the land of the living.

I turned to the few flickering candles that Hiro had lit. Clearly the answer had something to do with them. We'd descended to Yomi standing in a shrine of total darkness, so maybe the way out was exactly the opposite.

I lit the rest of the candles with a single gesture, casting a golden glow over the stone floor. Then I held out my hands, Neven and Hiro each taking one, the left cold and the right warm.

"Close your eyes," I said.

But I left mine open for a moment longer as the lanterns grew brighter, blending into a star-white cloud of light. The glow of the candles stretched outward, their circles expanding and breathing in all the shadows. For once, light cast the shores of Yomi in broad daylight, the sand white as powdered bones.

All the light began to sting my eyes, so I let them fall closed, let the light in my blood soak up the darkness around me. A warmth spread through the soles of my feet on the stone floor, blooming up my legs and spine and arms, flowing into Neven and Hiro. Then the stone tiles melted under our feet and turned soft and damp. The world smelled of rain and fresh soil and wet grass. The numbness of Yomi disappeared, our new world cool with autumn wind.

I opened my eyes to the gray sky overhead.

CHAPTER 11

From my seat curled up against the window of the train, the seaside village flashed away into sparse cabins over grayed grass, then to winter-dry farmland, then to small inland towns with thatched roofs and snowy mountains on the horizon. Yuki Onna's legend had said that she'd fled to somewhere colder and darker. According to Hiro, that likely meant the village of Shirakawa-go, the snowiest place in Japan that Yuki Onna hadn't already torn through and then abandoned.

Neven and I sat on one padded bench, sharpening my knives on river rocks, while Hiro sat opposite us. A few humans had been milling about the carriage when we'd first boarded, but one by one they'd shuffled into other carriages, probably unsettled by the sound of knives grinding on stones.

A conductor came by as if to scold us, but Hiro shot him a dark look and he immediately turned around.

"You should at least look at your hands when you're using a knife," Hiro said, the angry darkness fading from his eyes as the conductor walked away. I'd begun to understand what Neven meant about Hiro's eyes being darker than black at times. He watched me with unease as I scraped my knife across the rock.

"I know what I'm doing," I said.

Hiro didn't seem inclined to argue with that, turning back to watching the passing scenery. I couldn't help staring at his profile, the slope of his nose and cut of his jawline. Every part of Hiro looked pieced together from shattered glass, deathly sharp and prismatic. It wasn't surprising that his presence unnerved humans, who had likely never encountered someone so exquisitely ominous. I had never seen a Reaper, even a High Reaper, with such an unsettlingly beautiful appearance. Even the Shinigami at the hotel had lacked the same sort of pull. Was there something about Hiro that set him apart from other Shinigami?

I could have continued staring, but Neven's gaze burned on the side of my face, so I turned and looked out the window, as well.

This close to the mountains, it had already started to snow. The landscape around us had turned white and dead, farmers and cattle disappearing in favor of endless spans of snow-white nothing.

"Hiro," I said, still staring out the window into the white hills, afraid my face would betray my thoughts, "what do you know about Yakushima?"

I know who you are, Ren of Yakushima, Izanami had said. That meant I had a home other than London, somewhere my mother had lived, or at least visited. I used to see her as some nameless shadow, but now that I knew where she'd come from, she was alarmingly real. Somewhere in Japan, she could be looking through a foggy window up at the white winter sun, just like me.

"Yakushima?" Hiro said. "It's a tropical island in the south, covered in ancient cedar forests. Sometimes blue fires dance across the sea just beyond the beaches."

I made a mumbled sound of acknowledgment, trying not to betray my fascination. I imagined the snow beyond the window melting away to lush wet forests and burning sun, trees a thousand years tall casting down cool shade. It felt more like a dream than anything that could have been mine. Surely my mother would return to a place as magical as that after being stripped of her title and presumably banished from Yomi.

"Is it close to where we're going?" I said.

But my question must have sounded too urgent, because both Hiro and Neven were staring at me. I turned back to the window so Neven would stop trying to decipher my expression. It felt a bit like betrayal to think of "family" as anything besides Neven, and maybe that was why I didn't want him to know how much I thought about my mother.

"Not particularly," Hiro said. "Why do you ask?"

"I read about it," I said to the window, hoping he wouldn't notice the lie if I wasn't looking at him. It seemed that I would have to wait to find my mother until I'd finished killing the Yokai. In fact, it would be better that way. I would stand before her as a true Shinigami demanding answers, not a lost child begging for her help. She would see all that I'd become without her, and she would have no choice but to respect me.

We got off at the next stop and walked a short distance through the new snow until a valley opened up below us, revealing a small village. Homes shaped like massive triangles carried roofs three times their size, tucked in with a hearty layer of snow. The mountains rose up behind the houses, flanked by an army of snow-dusted evergreen trees. From a distance, the village looked peaceful and perfect, like the Christmas dioramas in toy store displays back in London.

The wind rose in pitch as we descended into the valley, a chorus of dissonant flutes in our ears. The crunch of snow gave way to roads paved in ice and a deeper chill that prickled my eyelashes and stung my lips.

As we drew nearer, I should have been able to hear the soundscape of the village in exquisite detail—small talk in the streets and merchant transactions and the creak of doors opening. Instead, only the keen of wind sweeping through a hollow landscape reached my ears. Lights gleamed through the glass windows but no shadows shifted inside, as if we were in the same eerie quiet of Yokohama in the hour of spirits.

"Something's wrong," I said.

Neven nodded, looking up at the midday sun through the screen of gray clouds. "It's not omagatoki," he said. "Why can't I hear anything?"

I looked to Hiro for answers, but he only frowned.

"Is there anything unusual about this village?" I said. "Do they hibernate for the winter or something?"

Hiro shook his head. "There is nothing strange about Shirakawa-go, other than the heavy snow."

I pulled my coat tighter around myself, the weight of my knives in my sleeves comforting as we descended deeper into the valley.

"Let's go."

We followed the frozen dirt road to the closest homes in the village, buildings half-buried in snow with lamplight burning from the upper windows, great pine trees casting dark, swaying shadows over them.

"Ren," Neven whispered, tugging my sleeve. He pointed to the yard, where a woman in a pale blue coat crouched on all fours, unmoving. I crunched through the snowy yard, waving for Neven to follow me, and knelt a careful distance in front of her.

"Hello?" I said in Japanese.

The woman's eyes were closed, eyelashes twinkling with snow crystals, lips a deathly purple. She remained crouched, fingers sunken like claws into the snow. Her rib cage didn't expand with breaths, nor did any clouds of water vapor come from her nose or mouth. I inched closer, kneeling to examine her face. Her skin glimmered as if coated in a thin layer of glass, leaving her complexion eerily perfect, more like a hand-painted doll than a human. Was this Yuki Onna's doing?

"Can you hear us?" Neven said to her.

But the wind swept his words away and no one answered.

"Ren," Neven said, "is this—"

"Ren? Neven?"

I turned toward the main road, where Hiro's voice called to us.

"I think you should come here," he said.

I took one last glance at the woman, then crossed the yard

and hopped the small fence to walk around the corner to the main road. I took in a sharp breath, pausing a few feet from Hiro.

All the people in the village were frozen.

Villagers paused in the thresholds of their homes, hands on doorknobs. Children laughing as they slid down the ice-slick roads, frozen on their hands and knees. Men frozen midstep on their walk home, eyes cast up at the white sky. We hadn't found Shirakawa-go, but a painting of what it had once been.

Snowflakes tickled my eyelashes and I turned my face to the sky. It couldn't be a time freeze, because the snow was still falling, the towering evergreens still swaying hypnotically in the breeze that shuddered down the mountain pass.

I stepped closer to a young man pulling a sled of wrapped parcels behind him. His skin wore the same clear glaze as the woman in the yard, but unlike her, his open eyes stared straight ahead. His irises were whiter than the winter lake beyond the trees, a thick layer of ice over his pupils. Inside his open mouth, tiny icicles of saliva hung down like an extra layer of jagged teeth.

This was just like the man in Yuki Onna's story. I looked over my shoulder at Hiro, and his face told me he knew it, too.

Neven came up beside me and waved a hand in front of the man's face.

"Hello?" he said. He turned to me. "Do you think they can be unfrozen?"

"I don't know, Neven," I said, even though I was fairly sure the answer was no, especially if Yuki Onna had already eaten their organs. But if Neven wanted to have hope, why take that away?

When the man didn't answer, Neven reached out to set a hand on his shoulder.

"Neven," I said, "don't—"

Neven's hand came to rest on the man's shoulder and gave it a gentle shake.

A loud cracking sound echoed down the silent street, like an ax through a frozen pond. The man's arm snapped off at the shoulder, hit the ground, and shattered into a thousand shards.

Neven screamed and fell back onto the icy ground, scooting away. The sound of his voice echoed forever through the silent mountain pass.

"No, no, no, I didn't, I wasn't—"

Neven kept babbling panicked nonsense, and I wanted to go to him, but I couldn't look away from the one-armed man and the shards of bones and flesh and winter coat spilled across the street, the image so jarring that my brain wouldn't accept it as real. Instead, I could only hyper-focus on the sharpness of each shard, unable to breathe and oddly warm despite the cold.

I knelt down and picked up one of the shards of the man's arm, rolling it between my fingers. The sharp edges pricked my fingers, bitingly cold.

A shadow fell over me. I looked up at Hiro.

"Well, we don't have to worry about whether or not this is the right village," he said, his expression grave.

I nodded, the ice shard slipping from my hands and rolling quietly to the ground. "This must be why Izanami sent us here. She said the Yokai on her list had taken too many souls."

A hollowness opened up inside of me, growing wider as I stared at the shards of flesh and bone. I didn't know if I could ever feel empathy for humans the way Neven did, but I could see the wrongness of ending so many lives at once, of taking so much away from any one village.

Neven let out a sob that bordered on a dry retch. I turned around to find him pressed against a nearby tree, arms folded over himself.

"It's all right," I said, moving the pine branches away so I could kneel in front of him. "He was already dead."

Neven swallowed, his eyes a sickly green. "I… I didn't—"

"You didn't," I said. "Come on." I tugged gently at his sleeve until he got the hint and stood up.

Hiro was gone when I turned around, but I heard movement indoors and followed the sound to a nearby store, where Hiro was busy rummaging through the contents behind the counter. The frozen cashier had dozed off on one arm, oblivious. Neven, following after me in a daze, kept a careful distance from him as we entered.

Hiro popped up from behind the counter and set two gas lanterns on it, then ducked down and retrieved one more, offering it to me with both hands.

"For the lady," he said, leaning across the counter. Up close, his eyes twinkled with Death, magnetic in the way that terrible things often were. The longer I looked at him, the more my pulse raced and my skin flushed. Was this the infatuation that humans wrote about? I'd read Tennyson's love poems with scientific curiosity, unable to grasp the concept and unsure if creatures of Death were even capable of such a thing. Tennyson had written of love and Death as opponents, Death a dark but fleeting shadow and love an eternal light. Surely, creatures made of Death could not love. Even now, was I truly drawn to Hiro, or merely the strong pull of Death inside of him?

I took the lantern and looked away.

"Pillaging already?" I said.

Hiro disappeared behind the counter once more and came back with matchboxes in each hand.

"The humans have no use for these things anymore," he said, smirking.

"You think this is funny?" Neven said. "An entire village is dead."

The smile dropped from Hiro's face. He sighed, dropping a few more matchboxes from his pockets onto the counter.

"I've lived a long time, Neven. I've seen many humans die. Ones that mattered."

"These people don't matter?" Neven said. "How can you—"

"I don't know these people!" Hiro said, slamming his hands on the counter so hard that some of the matchboxes spilled onto the floor.

Neven flinched away, the lights overhead buzzing.

"I told you I was raised by humans. Where do you think they've gone?" Hiro said. His eyes had gone gravely dark, no longer eyes but black portals to Yomi drilled into his skull. How had he gotten so dangerously upset and so suddenly? The lights overhead flashed rapidly from the wrath of Hiro's anger, his shadow growing thicker on the wall behind him, like a black sludge painted across the wallpaper. Was this sudden darkness what Neven saw when he looked at Hiro? Was this why he hadn't trusted him?

Then Hiro closed his eyes and rubbed them with his fist,

letting out a shuddering breath. The lights settled, and when he opened his eyes again, they'd returned to their normal black.

"The heart of a soul collector is too small to hold that many people inside of it," he said, turning to take a few pairs of gloves off the shelf and set them gently on the counter. "It has to be, or we would all end ourselves."

Hiro tossed Neven some of the matchboxes, forcing him to uncross his arms to catch them.

"Yuki Onna has clearly been here," Hiro said. "There's a path up into the mountains that the villagers used to take when they cut down trees. I suggest we go there."

"And what about burning her?" Neven said, his voice much smaller than before. "Should we bring firewood?"

"A lot of wood would be quite hard to carry and slow to ignite," Hiro said.

"Are there any more gas lanterns?" I said. "Could we pour the gas into another container and take it with us?"

"These three lanterns are the only ones left," Hiro said, gesturing to the ones on the counter with a resigned expression on his face. I sighed, glancing around the store for alternatives.

"Because," Hiro went on, depositing a wooden vase on the counter, "I already poured out the gasoline from all the other lanterns into this sake pitcher." He grinned, holding the vessel up as if making a toast. "It appears that you and I think alike, Ren of London," he said, handing me the pitcher with a wink. I didn't know how to interpret such a gesture, but I found myself hiding a small smile as I turned away, holding the pitcher to my chest.

"Only when it comes to plotting a murder," I said.

We each took a lantern and headed back outside, the pitcher of gasoline tucked under my coat, held tight against my chest. With every step we took closer to the mountains, the chilled air grew colder, tiny ice crystals lacerating my face as if warning us away. As the layer of ice on the roads grew thicker and the ground slanted unevenly upward, Hiro snapped a branch off a nearby tree, yanked off some of the smaller sprouting branches, then jammed the jagged end of the large stick into the ground like an ice pick as he walked.

As we journeyed deeper into the mountains, the warm glow of the village faded away and high walls of snow and ice rose up around us, painted gray-blue in the shade. The trees loomed tall and endless in the swirl of white overhead, standing sentinel before a thousand tiny caves and crevices in the mountainside. The snow prickled on the exposed skin of my face like tiny biting teeth. The snowflakes themselves were not helpless ice crystals spinning to the earth but sentient and bitter insects, swarming around our faces, scraping at our eyes and ears.

No human could survive this temperature. Even as a cold-blooded Reaper, I thought the temperature might freeze my blood solid. Floating in the deathly frigid waters of the English Channel had felt comfortable compared to this.

The sound of wind scraping through the mountain pass grew louder in my ears. I couldn't think through the screaming blasts of snow, couldn't remember why I was there, where I was going, except farther and farther into the deadly cold.

A hand closed around my mouth.

CHAPTER 12

A bone-shattering chill stabbed through my lips and teeth. The cold pierced through my gums into my skull and crunched down around my brain, sending burning hot blood out my nose and breaking my vision into flashes of glassy white. Ice shot past my lips and ripped down my throat, into my abdomen, filling my organs with glass shards.

I couldn't move away because my limbs had gone dead with cold. My vision cracked, like I was looking up through the shattered surface of a frozen pond, and through the broken prisms an ethereal woman loomed over me.

She had skin so white that she nearly vanished into the snow, frostbitten blue lips and hair tangled like the blackened and long-dead branches of winter trees. Her face betrayed no emotion, void as the snow-swept landscape. She was going to end my existence, and it meant nothing to her. I had hoped that when I died, it would have been for something that mattered.

"A little foreigner has wandered into my mountains," she whispered. But her words might have been a song of the wind or a dying hallucination. I felt a distant anger at being called a foreigner, but it was hard to truly feel anything other than pain. She had trapped me in her frozen world, nothing but me and Yuki Onna and Death.

With another breath of ice into my lungs, and a sudden brightness that burned across my eyes, I could no longer feel my body at all.

When the brightness cleared, I was standing opposite Yuki Onna on a flat plane of snow, white sky and ice in all directions. I must have been dreaming, or maybe hallucinating as her ice wormed its way into my brain and started cutting wires. This Yuki Onna couldn't be real because, unlike the Yuki Onna who had looked at me with dead eyes as she froze me from the inside out, this one had no face at all, only pale skin as smooth as an egg. The whole landscape blurred at the corners of my vision, like the hazy half reality that I saw in Yomi's darkness. But instead of black, this world was painfully sterile white.

"Where are we?" I said. My voice echoed as if we stood in a great cathedral.

"We're in-between," Yuki Onna said, hundreds of voices speaking in unison. The low voices of men and the light voices of children all tied together into one chorus. Were these the voices of Yuki Onna's victims?

"When my ice touches your mind," she said, "I can see

straight through to all your little secrets. That will help me make my decision."

"What decision?" I said.

"Which part of you I'm going to eat."

She stepped forward and pressed her hand to my throat. I couldn't move at all, like my whole body had turned to marble.

"Shall I take your vocal cords and add your voice to my collection?" she said. Then her hands trailed up to my face, fingers crawling across my lips and forcing my mouth open, tracing up and down my teeth.

"Shall I take your tongue and steal your sharp words?"

With all the energy I could muster, I clamped my jaw shut.

But Yuki Onna seemed to have known what I was doing, for she snatched her fingers out of my mouth just before I could bite them off.

"Were all the villagers in Shirakawa-go not enough for you?" I said.

Yuki Onna said nothing at first. There was no sound at all, despite the shifting winds around us.

"I didn't want to kill them all," she said at last. "I had no choice."

"There is always a choice."

Yuki Onna shook her head slowly. *"I had no choice,"* she said again.

"Why not?" I said, trying with all of my strength to move my arms, even to wiggle my fingers.

"Because of Izanami."

"What?" I said, giving up on trying to move and staring straight at Yuki Onna's blank face.

That didn't make any sense. Izanami had sent me to kill this Yokai because of her crimes against humans and Shinigami. She wouldn't do that if she had caused it in the first place.

"What does she have to do with this?" I said.

Yuki Onna shook her head. "You're not the first that she's sent to kill me, you know," she said. "And you won't be the last."

Then she reached out and pressed a single finger to my chest. It sank through my skin like my sternum was soft butter, until Yuki Onna was wrist-deep in my rib cage. But instead of the chilling pain I'd felt when she'd touched me in the real world, I felt nothing at all.

"I think I will like the taste of your heart most of all," she said. "I don't even need to freeze it first. It's already made of ice."

My breath caught in my throat. Was that some sort of joke? Of course my heart wasn't literally made of ice, and I didn't need moral judgment from a Yokai who had just eaten an entire village.

"I am made from the light that began the universe and the beginnings of time itself," I said, my teeth grinding together. "I am not made of ice."

"It is a blessing," Yuki Onna said, reaching out her other hand to touch my face again. "When your heart is cold, you can have anything you desire. Nothing stands in your way."

"That's not…" I paused. *That's not what I want*, is what I'd meant to say. But the words caught in my throat and wouldn't leave, as if I'd been corked like a bottle of wine.

"I see why she sent you," Yuki Onna said.

"What do you mean?"

Then Yuki Onna looked up, and the black eyes of a Shinigami stared back at me. *Not just any eyes*, I thought as I tried
to back away but my feet wouldn't move an inch, *my eyes*.

I tried to reel away, but whatever mind prison she'd put me
in held me firmly shackled to the snowy ground. She opened
her mouth as if to answer me, and I prayed that whatever
words came out weren't in my own voice, that she hadn't already ripped out my vocal cords and swallowed them into
her endless stomach.

But before she could answer me, she started screaming.

Her hand that touched my face turned to ashes and crumbled away, the pieces pulled up into the spiraling wind like a
swarm of flies in the all-white landscape. She yanked her other
arm out of my chest, but it too had already turned to ashes.

My hands throbbed. I looked down at red veins tearing
through my arms, my skin dissolving until there was only
bones.

"What have you done to me?" Yuki Onna screamed, crumpling onto the ground.

"I… I don't know," I whispered, watching as more and
more of my skin became translucent, the red veins creeping
up my arms, disappearing into my sleeves.

With a feral scream, Yuki Onna ripped herself from my
mind.

I stood back in the freezing mountains of Shirakawa-go,
my lungs full of ice, Yuki Onna's hand over my mouth. Her
eyes met mine, wide and alarmed.

Then the sharp end of Hiro's walking stick pierced the
side of her head.

Her hand withdrew and the ice in my body dissolved instantly, chased out by my body's quick healing abilities and a wave of counter-heat that scorched my throat. I folded forward and the pitcher of gasoline spilled onto the ground, useless. Neven and Hiro pulled me to my feet and dragged my heels through the snow. I coughed out water and scrubbed my eyes, because the whole world still looked cracked and crooked.

Behind us, the Yokai let out a shriek like a mangled bird. Hiro's blow hadn't killed her.

My heels ground to a halt in the snow and I yanked out of Neven's grip despite his protests. I waved toward my abandoned lantern, exploding it into a surge of light and fire that crashed over the Yokai. She screamed again and crumpled onto her hands as the flame sparkled at the ends of her hair, climbing its way up. The smell of fire and rot blew back at us in the wind with a spray of blue embers. For a moment, the flames subdued her. I dared to let out a relieved breath, pulling myself up straighter on Neven's sleeve.

Then a layer of white ice formed across her clothing, as if her kimono had turned into glass. The fire went out, the ice hissing into steam that rose above her in a hazy cloud.

She rolled onto all fours with a thousand tiny cracking noises, maybe from the shattering of her icy skin or the splintering of her bones. I fell into Neven, trying to shudder away from the sound as it scraped the thin tissue of my eardrums. As she rose to her feet, every vertebra of her spine snapped into place one by one until she stood at her full height, looming over us and swaying with the evergreen trees behind her.

She watched us for a moment with the same blank indifference that I'd seen up close. Then she took a step forward, the snow crunching like a thousand glass shards under her bare feet.

Hiro tossed his lantern at her and waved as it arced across the white sky. It burst in a flash of light so bright that a thousand formless shapes danced across my vision before I shielded my eyes. Hiro must have been a more powerful Shinigami than I'd assumed, for his lantern burned sun-bright, far stronger than what I'd used to attack Ivy. The flame singed the Yokai's hair and charred the side of her face as she screamed and collapsed, but once again a swirl of ice wrapped around her, hissing as the flame went out. She barely hesitated this time before standing up.

"Go," I whispered, my voice barely a croak as I tugged at Neven's sleeve. "Go, now!"

I tried to run on the icy ground, but my ankles shook and I clung to Neven's coat just to remain upright. The Yokai lurched closer, one hand outstretched, the temperature plummeting so quickly that every breath hurt, a thousand serrated snowflakes scraping down my throat. I lunged away, the memory of her icy hands lacerating all my organs still fresh in my mind, igniting a panic in my blood.

I stumbled forward, this time dragging Neven down with me when he couldn't catch my weight in time. Hiro appeared next to me and tried to pull me up under my arms, but the Yokai's shadow chilled the snow beneath my palms. There was no time left to run.

I bit my glove off and jammed my hand into my pocket, fingers closing around my clock.

The swarm of snowflakes halted and the blaring howls of wind fell silent. Neven and Hiro stood frozen on either side of me, the only sound my own choked breaths. Yuki Onna leaned over us, frozen in glass, her pale hand reaching out for us, but unable to come closer. My limbs gave out from the sudden drop in adrenaline, nearly throwing me face-first into the snow. Somehow, we had survived. I almost whispered a prayer of thanks to Ankou before I remembered that he wasn't my god anymore.

But the time freeze had not erased the deathly cold, as the frigid silver of the clock in my bare hand reminded me. The metal shot daggers of ice down the tendons of my wrist and threatened to meld itself to my palm.

I yanked off my other glove with my teeth and touched my bare skin to Neven's face. He jolted backward, awakening from the time freeze.

"Ren, are you all right?" he said, grabbing my arm.

But there was no time for that. I stumbled to Hiro and pressed my hand to his cheek. He crashed into me, still trying to run away from a threat that he hadn't realized had frozen.

Neven pulled him off me as Hiro spun around, eyes widening at Yuki Onna's frozen stance, the snowflakes suspended in the air.

"Is this…" He spun around in wonder. "Ren, have you done this? Is this—"

"Not now!" I said, the cold still stabbing through the hand holding my clock. "Over there!" I pointed with my free hand to a cave behind some evergreens a distance away. I'd never managed to cast such a wide circle before, freezing the snowscape and mountains as far as I could see. I might have felt proud of myself, had it not been a desperate accident.

Hiro and Neven tried to help me up, but I couldn't find

enough oxygen to tell them to stop coddling me and run to the cave, dragging me if necessary, before my hand went blue from frostbite.

"Lantern!" I said to Neven, coughing. He released my arm and scrambled to gather our last remaining lantern, sliding to his hands and knees on the ice. I stumbled toward the cave, slowly regaining control of my feet. The hand around my clock felt like it had been stabbed through with kitchen knives, binding the clock to my bones.

Neven caught up to us easily, taking my arm and urging me to walk faster.

I fell to my knees at the mouth of the cave, crawling into the shadows and curling around my frozen hand.

"Hiro, hide us!"

He raised a hand and yanked the darkness over the mouth of the cave. The moment it was safe, I hurled the clock against the wall.

The wind picked up again as my clock hit the stone wall with a hollow clink, spinning around on the icy ground before settling. I collapsed back against the cave wall, trying to rub heat back into my hand. Even in the darkness, I could see that the clock had blackened my palm with frostbite, the circular shape stamped into it.

"Where is she?" I said, eyes closed.

Someone shuffled beside me.

"By the tree line," Neven said. "She's looking for us."

I opened my eyes and looked up at the cave ceiling. Dripping stalactites stared back at me, threatening to gouge my eyes out. Neven took my hand and tried to warm it with his, rubbing the cold away. I could hardly feel his fingers on my skin.

"Are you okay?" Hiro said.

I nodded, cuffing ice crystals from my lips. Ice had scraped my lungs raw, but I would survive.

"So this is what Reapers are capable of."

I opened my eyes to Hiro grinning through blue-tinted lips, even as his whole body shuddered in the cold. "This was well worth the wait," he said. "Finally, Ren of London stops the universe with only a clock."

"Not the universe," I said, my face suddenly warm despite the cold everywhere else. Hiro's contagious smile crept onto my lips, even though I couldn't feel them.

Hiro began to speak, but the wind rose in volume and blasted snow through our curtain of darkness. Neven curled against me, probably more from fear than for warmth, since both our body temperatures had plummeted. He would have been better off cuddling Hiro, but I didn't make the suggestion.

"How are we going to get past her?" Neven said. "We can't stay here forever."

I slid my arm around his shoulders and pulled him closer, even though it made both of us shiver.

"I've lost the gasoline," I said.

"Not all of it," Neven said, nodding toward our one remaining lantern.

"That didn't work the first two times," Hiro said. "As soon as she catches fire, she just ices over it a few seconds later."

"So…" I coughed, still sensing ice crystals scraping up my

throat. "So we need to turn those few seconds into a few minutes."

Neven's eyes went wide as he understood. He reached for his own clock and hissed as his fingers brushed it, jerking his hand away. We couldn't keep our bare skin on our clocks for very long before our hands turned purple from frostbite, so we needed to burn her as fast as possible. I didn't like the odds of trying to explode our only lantern a third time—my control over fire was limited, for I could only wield it as a vehicle of light and not a weapon in and of itself. I could increase the light and heat and pressure in the lantern so much that it burst, but I could hardly control the flames once it did.

But this was what Izanami had asked of me, so I had to find a way. This arctic monster stood between me and being accepted as a Shinigami. I'd traveled across the world to become someone, not to turn into an ice sculpture that decorated a Yokai's backyard.

I closed my fist and looked out the mouth of the cave, where Yuki Onna lurked around the tree line. Her long white kimono dragged behind her, torn from snagging on rocks and ice crystals. How could we smother her with fire so severely that even when the time freeze ended she'd be halfway to a puddle and unable to recover?

I turned away from Neven, coughing out a few more ice crystals. My gaze fell on the wide sleeves of Hiro's coat, dragging in the slush of the cave floor.

I had an idea.

"Give me your coat," I said, sitting up straight.

Hiro looked at me oddly, but slid his coat off.

"I like to think I'm chivalrous, but I believe my core temperature runs higher than yours and I'm less adapted to this climate than you," he said.

"You won't die," I said. "Neven, yours, too."

"What are you planning?" Neven said, taking his coat off anyway.

I ignored him for the moment, putting on both of their coats and kneeling before the remaining lantern. I extinguished it with a wave, then crushed the glass bulb between my hands, shaking the shards out of my palms.

"Ren?" Neven said.

I peered down at the pool of kerosene at the bottom of the first lantern, then tipped it over onto myself, dripping the fuel all along my sleeves and chest.

"Ren," Neven said, "how—"

"We need to burn her quickly," I said. "This way, I can hold her down even after the time freeze ends. I'm strong enough."

"How can you know that?" Neven said, eyes wide.

"I know," I said. I knew it because I wouldn't let her, or anyone, take away my chance of being a Shinigami.

"She'll just extinguish you!" Neven said.

"No," I said. "Didn't you see? She didn't put the lantern out, she put *herself* out."

"That doesn't mean she can't," Hiro said.

I sighed. "Either we try something or we wait for her to come find us. It's not as if we can go back with her lurking out there." I turned to Neven. "How long can you hold your clock before your hand freezes off?"

Neven looked down at the chain hanging from his pocket.

He poked it and hissed at the cold. "I don't know," he said, the words watery.

"Hey," I said, grabbing his jaw and forcing him to look at me. "I need thirty seconds." I probably needed more than that, but I didn't want to scare Neven with an impossible task. "Can you do that for me? Will you help me?"

It was a cheap trick, to always ask for Neven's help when he started to fall apart, but it worked. He straightened up, wiping his nose.

"Okay," he said.

"Hold his hand closed if you have to," I said to Hiro in Japanese. "Until she looks like she won't fight back."

He nodded, his lips pressed tightly together as if he had a great many things to say but knew better than to vocalize them.

I pulled a cord from my wrist and used it to knot my hair back to keep it out of the flames, then carefully pulled my clock's chain with my long sleeve, tucking my clock back in my pocket. "Stop time once my clothes catch fire," I said to Neven. I knew it would calm him down to have a cue, and I didn't exactly trust his timing when he would be peering through the darkness of the cave through glasses that hadn't been cleaned in months. "I need every second of the time freeze you can spare to melt her. But don't wait too long, or she'll shove an icicle down my throat again."

"Ren," Neven said, grabbing my sleeve. His fingers curled tight around the fabric, stiff and trembling from the cold. His lips pulled into an uneasy grimace in the dim light, eyes swirling a murky brew of navy and olive.

Over the near-century that we'd spent together, I'd learned how to hear all of Neven's unsaid words. We never said sentimental things, because that wasn't the way of soul collectors, who were meant to be dispassionate. But we both knew what was real and true, and that some unsaid things could never be captured by words.

I knew, for instance, that I couldn't die trying to destroy Yuki Onna, because I couldn't leave Neven alone in a world he didn't understand with a Shinigami he didn't trust. The resolve spread warmth through my bones and made me stand up straighter.

"I can do this, Neven," I said. "As long as you hold the time freeze, she can't hurt me, okay?"

He swallowed, then closed his eyes and nodded. "I'll hold on. I promise, Ren."

He let go of my sleeve.

I took off my remaining glove and dropped it to the floor of the cave. I didn't know whether the fire or the cold would hurt more, but Neven needed to be able to touch me easily to wake me from his time freeze. I took a step back that felt like a mile, and peered out from the darkness of the cave, where Yuki Onna was looking through another small mountain pass.

I turned back to Neven and Hiro, who stood side by side. Hiro gave me a mock salute and gestured for me to go out. Neven held his clock on top of his long sleeve, eyes fierce and unafraid because he trusted me to come back, even if I didn't quite trust myself. I hoped that, just this once, I could be the person Neven thought I was.

I pulled one of the matchboxes out of my pocket and stepped into the light.

★ ★ ★

Yuki Onna's eyes locked on to me the second I left the cave, a head of black hair on her canvas-white landscape. I stood only a few paces from the cave, close enough that Neven could touch my hand when the time came. The match and matchbox trembled in my hands as she came closer, the scent of gasoline on my clothes burning my eyes.

Fear wanted to wrench open my rib cage like a book, but I held my breath and focused my gaze and shoved it back down. I would do this for Izanami. I would do this for Neven. I would do this because this was what Shinigami did, and I was a Shinigami.

So instead of remembering the sensation of my teeth turning to knives of ice and my organs shattering with cold, I thought about time.

Even without a clock, a Reaper knew how to use time as an instrument and weapon. Reapers had reaction times faster than lightning, and though I'd never excelled in that area, I knew how to time my actions correctly when I focused. I knew that if I struck the match a moment too early, Yuki Onna would run away and I'd have to cross the distance, narrowing the window of time I had to burn her before Neven had to drop his clock. But if I waited a breath too long, she'd fill my lungs up with ice and all of us would die. I visualized the ideal scene in my head as I'd been trained to do, the exact distance between us that would land her right in front of me just as the match ignited.

She crossed the invisible threshold, her frosted white eyes unblinking and blue-tipped fingers stretched toward me. I held my hands steady as I pinched the match between my fingers and poured light energy through my fingertips, igniting it.

The wind tore the match from my hand.

It spun off somewhere into the snow, the flame easily snuffed out in the turbulent winds. The ice beneath my feet felt paper-thin, the world prepared to shatter and swallow me whole.

Now the timing was ruined.

I should have lit the match sooner to account for this possibility, should have told Neven to stop time right before she touched me and not rely on me for a cue. Would he stop it anyway when she got too close, or would he foolishly trust that I was in control? Probably the latter. But by the time she touched me and he realized I was in trouble, it would be too late.

She was already too close. Her white hand reached for my face and my fingers felt too numb and even now I was hesitating, wasting the precious nanoseconds I had left, not fast enough to be a Reaper and not smart enough to be a Shinigami. Was there even time to open the matchbox and light another match? My fingers were shaking so hard I'd probably drop it. I was going to die and it was entirely my fault. I was too slow and stupid and scared to kill a Yokai and I should never have come here.

I held my breath as she came closer and closer. Yuki Onna couldn't stop time, but it felt the same as Ivy with her scissors suspended over my eye for a small eternity, the anticipation of pain and the knowledge that I wasn't enough of anything to stop it and the echo of her words that cut deeper than any of her sawtooth snowflakes ever could: *a little foreigner has wandered into my mountains.*

Foreigner, foreigner, foreigner, ever since I'd come to the place that was supposed to be mine, that was all anyone had called me. Once upon a time, the little foreigner wandered into Yuki Onna's mountains and never made it home, even though there was no home to return to. That was all I would be to her— one sad story out of thousands.

Heat built up in my fingertips despite the cold, but with no light source to flow into, my anger burned into a fever so intense that my whole body felt like glass, a light bulb about to burst. I wouldn't give her my story to add to her collection, because it wasn't over yet.

There was no time to open the box and draw another match, so I crushed the whole matchbox in my left hand. All the anger and light and heat rushed into my fingertips until they burned white-hot, as if I'd closed my first around a shooting star, and all of the matches burst into flames.

My palm began to burn and blister, but I held the flaming ball up to my sleeve, which caught fire instantly. The flames surged around me like a hungry python, winding around my arms and spine to devour the path of kerosene. The heat began to gnaw through the layers of fabric, warming my blood, singeing the exposed skin of my neck and hands.

Yuki Onna saw the fire and stopped in her tracks, but it was too late.

I felt Neven's hand on mine and opened my eyes to snowflakes frozen in place.

I lunged forward, dropping the matchbox, and wrapped my arms around Yuki Onna.

My hands sank into her spine like it was made of cream, great clouds of steam rising off her and swirling us both in their veil. I loosened my grip, careful not to hold her too closely and extinguish myself with the rivulets of water rushing down her body. Already, her white kimono had melted into milk and spilled over my shoes. Her face began to drip, her jaw stretching downward in a silent gaping scream that kept growing wider, the whites of her eyes streaking down her cheeks.

Neven screamed somewhere far behind me, but there was nothing I could do but hold on. Hiro shouted something as well, but I couldn't hear over the rumble of flames searing my ears and the hiss of steam and the endless trickle of water.

Then time came unglued.

Yuki Onna jolted, then let out the loudest, most bloodcurdling sound I'd ever heard.

A thousand stolen voices wailed all at once. All of them cried out in a chorus of agony at the light and heat. I'd heard humans scream and cry at the end of their lives, but nothing resembled the bone-splintering torture of Yuki Onna's voice, the volume blasting my hair back and rattling the flames on my arms.

She tried to push me off, but she had already melted to a cream in my arms and I easily pressed her to the snow. The screams reminded me of humans begging for their lives, and I needed her to be quiet, but she wouldn't stop. Even when I pressed my hand into her mouth and her blue lips bubbled through my fingers, a shapeless sound of pain knifed through the air. I pressed harder and her face splattered into the snow, and finally she was silent. Her soul rose from her melted face in a wisp of white smoke, but it hovered for only a moment before a gust of harsh wind ripped it to pieces.

I sat astride her as the rest of her body melted, unable to breathe through the smell of smoke. Fire still blistered my wrists and neck, but I couldn't bring myself to do anything about it. What did it matter if I was going to heal in a few minutes anyway? Let it burn through my flesh and all my bones until there was nothing left of me.

I kept staring at the swirl of blue and black in the snow where Yuki Onna had been, kept replaying the horrific sight of her face stretching down like pulled taffy. I fell to my forearms, unable to take in any air. My fingers splashed in the puddles of Yuki Onna and the memory of her screams echoed from far away in the mountains.

Someone ripped my coat off from behind and packed snow onto the back of my neck, saying words I couldn't hear over the ringing. Had the explosion of sound ruptured my eardrums?

I lifted one hand as the sticky gray sludge that had once been a powerful Yokai dripped through my fingers onto the snow. The little foreigner had destroyed an ancient monster. The little foreigner was smarter and stronger, had reduced a Shinigami killer into a murky puddle, and it felt *good*.

Your heart is already made of ice, she'd said.

I let out a sharp laugh and realized I could hear my own voice.

"Ren?"

I blinked and turned around. The whispers had stopped crawling through my ears and the air smelled of smoke and flesh. Even though the temperature had risen to survivable level, I shivered so hard that I couldn't see straight. Neven and Hiro stared at me, Neven clutching my singed jacket and Hiro holding handfuls of snow.

"Are you hurt?" Neven said.

I looked down at my hand, suddenly disgusted at the milky

white that coated it. I wiped it on my skirt as Hiro tried to pack more snow onto my neck.

"No," I said, dodging his advances and turning to Neven. "What about you?"

"I'm okay," he said far too quickly. Neven couldn't tell a white lie to save his life.

Before he could protest, I grabbed his wrist and turned his hand over to see the damage.

His hand had turned a rotten color, so shriveled and blistered that a careless touch could have snapped it off like a dead branch. *He did this for me*, I thought, suddenly nauseous.

"It's okay," he said, blackened fingers twitching slightly. His voice sounded pinched, but mostly calm. "It's healing already."

My fingers hovered over his palm, wanting to touch but not wanting to hurt.

"Ren, really," Neven said, pulling his hand back. "It's okay, I promise."

I looked to Hiro, whose own fingertips had slightly grayed. He'd probably had to force Neven's hand closed toward the end. All three of us were damaged, kneeling in a barren village in the soupy remains of a Yokai. It was ridiculous. Something out of my childhood storybooks, but twisted and perverse.

I bit back a laugh that felt like holding down vomit. How could I possibly feel so close to the precipice of unraveling, so powerful yet so untethered? I was a butterfly twisted inside a tornado, the brightest colors between day and night, a little brown bird in the maw of a fox, waiting for the teeth to bite down.

CHAPTER 13

As the night train carried us west, I spread the Book of Hakutaku out before me, unrolling it until I found the story of
Iso Onna. Neven slept beside me, his head on my shoulder,
while Hiro sat across from us, watching the trees flash past.

I ran my fingers across the characters almost punishingly,
as if I could force them to make sense if I glared hard enough.
I read the first sentence three times until I could barely understand what it might have meant.

"Would you like some help?" Hiro said.

I looked up at his reflection, the night passing by us beyond the window of the train.

Hiro must have known. Either from my hesitation or the
look of confusion in my eyes, he knew I was basically illiter-

ate. A Shinigami who couldn't read. Surely Izanami would be pleased.

I shook my head, looking down. "I'm just..." I shook my head again, unable to think of a good excuse. My mind was still spinning with all of Yuki Onna's accusations, my own face staring back at me on the body of a monster, her body that had turned to soup so easily in my hands. *Too* easily.

"This text was recorded thousands of years ago," Hiro said, his voice quiet and warm. "Our language has changed since then. Even for me, this text is not easy to read."

I dared to look up at Hiro's expression. Surprisingly, I saw no judgment or trace of humor in his eyes. He stood up and slid into the seat beside me, barely able to fit with all three of us crammed together. My body still felt thoroughly frozen from our time on the mountain, so Hiro's warm blood burned where his arm pressed against mine.

"You're freezing!" he said.

He laid his hand over mine on the table, scalding hot, but I couldn't bring myself to move away.

"My normal body temperature is quite low," I said. Hiro made a sound of understanding but didn't move his hand. I found myself leaning closer to him, drawn to warmth like an insect to light, even though I'd never found the cold that uncomfortable. With my Reaper's hearing, I could sense the beat of his heart. Reapers had cold bodies and hearts that beat slowly but constantly, and apparently the hearts of Shinigami beat almost twice as fast as mine.

"Read what you can understand," he said, "and I'll fill in the rest." Together, squinting in the pale light of the moon through the train window with Hiro's heartbeat pounding in my ears, we read the legend of Iso Onna.

On the shores of Takaoka lay a beach full of bones.

Sailors passing through the black waters often crashed their ships on the jagged rocks of Takaoka's coast and washed up on the sand, only to die of hunger and thirst when they had no way back home.

One day, a beautiful woman emerged from the sands to greet the seamen who crawled half-drowned onto the shore.

She had hair so long that it dragged behind her on the sand, tangled with starfish and seaweed. When she looked at the men, they fell into a trance, unable to think about anything but her beautiful eyes, as green as sea glass.

When the men came close enough, she opened her mouth and screamed.

The sound shattered every star in the sky and splintered the earth beneath her feet. It was a sound that no human was ever meant to hear, a song that was long forbidden.

Unable to fight against her voice, the men were dragged out to sea by her long hair, like thousands of black arms. She drowned them in the frigid waters and drank their blood, then spit their bones out on the shore.

Iso Onna still ensnares men like a spider. She never has to hunt, because her victims always come to her. And once they reach her shores, they never leave.

I sighed as I read the last word of Iso Onna's tale. Why couldn't Hakutaku have given explicit instructions on how to defeat her?

"What is her essence, then?" I said. "Her hair? Her voice? Maybe her blood?"

"All reasonable guesses," Hiro said. "I'm not sure which one is correct."

I drummed my fingers against the paper.

"We have time to think it over," Hiro said. "By the time we reach Takaoka, it will still be too dark to take a boat. And you're still drenched in melted Yokai."

I grimaced, glancing down at my formerly white kimono, which had turned a sickly shade of gray.

"I don't know that a change of clothing will prepare me to bleed a Yokai like a pig, cut off her hair, and rip out her vocal cords."

Hiro shrugged. "It's your mission to finish as you please," he said, his voice even.

"Nothing about this idea 'pleases' me," I said.

"Doesn't it?"

I frowned and turned to Hiro, his eyes boring into mine with a strange intensity. It was hard to make out his expression in the changing light of the train, but the blackness in his eyes burned more brilliantly than the entire night sky outside the window.

"You don't like it at all?" he said, a chilling edge to his voice.

Do I? I thought about Yuki Onna, and the strange rush that had swept through me when she'd dissolved in my arms, the feeling of destroying someone who deserved it. She had dared to speak cruel words to me, and now she no longer had a mouth to form any words at all. Was it so horrible if that pleased me?

Neven groaned and shifted beside me. I turned away from Hiro, glad for the excuse not to answer. Neven was leaning against the window, so I pulled his glasses off and set them on the table.

Hiro didn't speak for the rest of the train ride, but somehow I felt that he already knew my answer.

The train arrived one hour later at Takaoka.

We stepped out of the station and into the night, the air pinging with the sound of hammers striking metal into shape, sparks and embers flashing up in sudden flurries of light behind the windows of the houses.

Hiro had called this the city of bronze and copper, and now I understood why—it clinked and clanged like one great machine as metalworking continued into the night. Outside, the clear black sky smelled of fire and molten metal. The lanterns of a night market cast circles of light on lattice windows, each one ornamented with metal wares—shiny pots and rice cookers, spoons and chopsticks, tiny Buddhas and flower vases carved with intricate patterns.

Neven still looked half-asleep, stumbling through the crowd, so he and I waited on a short stone wall by the station while Hiro went to find us a place to stay. Behind us, the waters of the East Sea lapped back and forth against the wall, the moon a thin crescent above us and the sky a pale black, the darkness diffused by the lanterns and moonlight. Compared to Yomi, nights aboveground no longer seemed dark. I wondered once more if my mother was looking up at the same moon. I shook the thought away and slid closer to Neven. There would be plenty of time to find my mother once I became a true Shinigami.

The people of Takaoka stared at us as we loitered outside
the station, slowing down and turning around to get a better look. Just how long would it take before Japan became
accustomed to foreigners? To be fair, it hadn't been so many
years since Japan opened to the West, and neither of us wore
jackets in the cool weather, seeing as I'd burnt through all
three of our coats.

Neven's hand hung limp by his side, still a shade of corpse
gray. His other arm wrapped around his legs, pulling them
close to his chest.

"Is it still cold?" I said, gesturing to his hand.

He shook his head, staring with a distant gaze at the crowd
milling around the train station. His silence and the careful
distance between us on the wall told me just how hard he
was trying not to shatter into a thousand pieces. Whenever
he tried to swallow his fear and pretend he was dispassionate,
like Reapers were supposed to be, his eyes grayed and he became nearly catatonic. The Yokai had frightened him more
than I'd realized, and now he was coming undone.

How selfish of me to bring him here, and how cruel of me
to not regret it, even now.

"This city seems to make metal," I said after a moment of
heavy silence. "They might make gears, as well. Maybe you
could find a clockmaker to talk to."

I thought the suggestion might cheer him up, but he only
hugged his knees tighter.

"And how would I talk to them, exactly?" he said, closing his eyes.

I knew how it felt to be weighed down by the world around
you so much that you could barely move your lips to speak,

but I didn't know what Neven wanted me to say, or what might comfort him. I couldn't make Japan speak English for him. I could send him home, but he'd told me over and over that he didn't want to go.

He sighed and let his legs down. "I'm sorry. I just…" He looked down at his grayed hand, curling his fingers. "What if the next one is worse?"

"Then we get rid of them."

He finally looked at me, his face pinched tight with frustration. "You say that as if the last one was easy. As if it wasn't horrible."

"I didn't say either of those things."

But this only upset Neven more. He huffed out a stiff exhale and turned his head up to the sky as if asking God for help.

"What do you want me to say, Neven? That everything will be fine?"

"I'm not asking you to lie to me," Neven said, closing his eyes.

"Then what is it you're asking of me?"

"Empathy?" Neven said, yanking his clock up by the chain and jamming it into his pocket. "Some acknowledgment that none of this is easy for me, perhaps?"

I could only stare, too stunned by Neven's anger to form a reply. I thought he might descend into a rant, but he stared back at me, challenging me to respond.

"I know it's not easy for you," I said slowly. "Is that all you wanted me to say?"

Neven huffed and shook his head. It felt like we were speaking two different languages.

"I don't know anything about these monsters," he said, knuckles white where he gripped the stone wall. "I don't know what they're saying, what anyone's saying except for you, and Hiro when he deigns to speak in English. Everyone is playing by rules I don't understand, and everyone is staring at me. I don't belong here, Ren, I feel so lost and—"

"Stop," I said, holding up a hand as if I could extinguish his words like a lantern. The darkness in my voice halted his words instantly, drawing the attention of a few more passersby. "Are you complaining to me that you feel like an outcast?" I said. "To me, of all people?"

Neven's shoulders drooped, the anger melting out of him. His eyes grayed to a milky blue. "I'm telling you *because* it's you, Ren. I thought you would understand."

"What do you want from me?" I said, rising to my feet. "To congratulate you for living one week the way I've lived for centuries?"

Neven's lips pressed together in a tight line, and for a moment he looked at me like he didn't know me anymore. "You empathize so readily with that Shinigami, but not with me."

My hands clenched into fists, and even hidden beneath my sleeves I could feel them searing with white-hot light. The lights in the train station behind us surged painfully bright for a moment before dimming again.

"'That Shinigami,'" I repeated. "Is that all we are to you?"

"Sorry to interrupt!"

We both turned to Hiro, who jingled a set of keys over his head. "I've found us a nice place. Panoramic views of the coast. No idea how I managed such a feat. Shall we?"

"You go ahead," I said, eyes already scanning the street for possible escape routes. "I'm going for a walk."

"Oh." Hiro blinked and looked to Neven for an explanation.

"Where is it?" Neven said, holding out a stiff hand for a key.

"That red building on the main road, rooms 104 and 5," Hiro said, still looking between me and Neven as if one of us might explode at the wrong word. He handed one key to Neven, who snatched it with grumbled thanks and stormed off.

I turned to walk in the opposite direction, but Hiro grabbed my forearm. I wasn't in the mood to be restrained, but I didn't want to be angry at anyone else tonight, so I let my arm go limp and allowed Hiro to turn me around.

"I'm sorry if I've caused problems," he said, his eyes on the ground. "I couldn't help but hear that last part."

I shook my head. "You're not the problem."

"Somehow I doubt that." A sad smile curled his lips. "But if you're going for a walk anyway, would you like to meet someone?"

He had already linked our arms and started pulling me around a back entrance of the station.

"You have friends here?" I said, nearly tripping in surprise as Hiro held me against his side. I melted against his warmth before I could stop myself. No one but Neven had ever touched me so freely, but for some reason I had no desire to push Hiro away.

"Not a friend, an enemy," he said. "I'm using you as bait."

I rolled my eyes, pinching my lips together as if it could hide the smile on my face.

"You actually have human friends, then?" I said.

"Some special ones, yes," Hiro said, "but this friend is a Yokai."

My heels ground to a stop, forcing Hiro to stop with me.

"Why would you take me to a Yokai?" I said. "Aren't we killing Yokai?"

"Well, yes, but not all of them," Hiro said, raising an eyebrow. "You know that not all Yokai are monsters, right?"

I didn't know that, and it must have shown in my face, because Hiro laughed and adjusted my grip on his arm, somehow pulling me closer.

"That makes this visit even more important, then," he said. "We're starting to build your network. You'll need connections as a working Shinigami."

"Are you going to bribe them with tuna for me?"

Hiro gasped. "I would never!" he said, pulling me across a carriage road and onto the sandy shore. "This one only eats lobster."

We hopped down another stone wall, then kicked off our shoes in the sand and walked down a long strip of rocky beach. By night, the sea was a sheet of black glass broken by the sharp silhouettes of rocks and tiny islands. The glow of faraway lighthouses illuminated the ghostly backdrop of snowy mountains on the horizon.

Hiro sat at the edge of the rock formation, dipping his feet over the ledge into the water and gesturing for me to sit beside him.

I couldn't help glancing down at his foot in the clear water as I sat down cross-legged.

He must have noticed me looking, because he gently kicked

water at me. "It's not polite to stare," he said, though he smiled as if he wasn't actually upset.

"Sorry," I said, tearing my eyes away.

"Don't be," he said. "Actually, it has hypnotic powers, so it's no wonder you can't look away."

"Hypnotic powers," I said, crossing my arms.

Hiro nodded. "Before I was born, my parents prayed that I would have great powers to change the course of the world. The gods granted me the power to hypnotize and seduce any earthly creature I wanted, but at a cost. They broke my foot and vested all of my powers inside of it. Now I have dominion over all beings both on land and at sea."

He lifted his foot, which now had about ten silver fish attached to it, beaming like he expected a compliment.

"I suspect that has more to do with you being a fishing spirit than your magical hypnotic foot," I said.

He sighed and set his foot back in the water, the fish instantly fleeing. "You're ever the skeptic."

"Do you even know the true story of your foot? Or have you forgotten it among your ten thousand lies?"

"I resent that," he said. "I have at least a hundred thousand lies in my arsenal."

A small smile twitched at the corner of my mouth, and this time I couldn't hide it from Hiro.

"Have I done it?" Hiro said. "Have I finally impressed you with my humor?"

I snorted. "Not yet."

He sighed, leaning back on his elbows. "Of course it's hard to impress someone who can stop the whole universe on a whim."

"I told you, I can't stop the universe."

"There's no need to be humble," Hiro said. "You're the first Shinigami who's met Yuki Onna and lived."

"I'm just a time turner," I said, withering under his praise, positive my cheeks had turned a very unsubtle shade of red.

Hiro shook his head. "You were brilliant," he said. "So many Shinigami are soft and dull. They lead the newly dead down to Yomi with their little lanterns and then act like they're the most godly creatures in all the land. But you're worthy of Izanami's favor because you have to earn it. You'll do whatever it takes to become a Shinigami."

"I—"

"Won't you?"

I swallowed, Hiro watching me searchingly as he waited for my answer. Would I really do *anything* to become a Shinigami? Was there any place I wouldn't go, any creature I wouldn't destroy, if it meant I'd have a home here?

"Yes," I whispered. "Anything."

I'd thought that answering his question would lessen the intensity of his gaze, but if anything he only looked deeper, like he was examining all the wheels and pendulums of the clockwork of my mind. A slow smile spread across his lips, his dark eyes still drinking me in as his heartbeat pounded louder and faster in my ears, swallowing up the sound of waves breaking on rocks and trains scraping across tracks in the distance.

"Ren," he said, my name nothing but a warm sigh as it left his lips, so soft that it almost didn't exist, like he hadn't meant to say it out loud.

My face burned with a sudden fever, my heart beating too

fast to be healthy, pushing hot blood to my fingers that felt like white-hot stars in my hands. I was overheating, possibly sweating, even though Reapers weren't supposed to sweat like humans. I had never felt quite so unraveled without any immediate danger, and yet the last thing I wanted was to stand up and leave.

"You're so…" Hiro trailed off, still smiling as he moved closer, like he'd find the right words written on my face.

The thought of what he might say next terrified me. Either he'd say something well-meaning but horrible like *different*, or he'd give me another compliment that made my skin flush with warmth, and I was already about to combust. Having Hiro's undivided attention was intoxicating, but I was sure that my face was an unsightly shade of red and my palms were damp against my skirt, and I didn't want him looking so closely at me when I felt like I was vibrating out of my own skin.

"You wanted me to meet someone?" I said, the words choked and slightly panicked, but at least I'd managed to say *something*.

Hiro blinked, then sat up straight, the empty space between us filling with cool ocean air that washed away the warmth from my face. He looked out across the sea, his lips slightly downturned, as if disappointed. "Ah, right," he said. He cupped his hands around his mouth and called, "Maho!" across the water.

The word echoed back a thousand times, as if the bay was a great plane of marble. The sound crashed into the distant mountains and disappeared, an expectant silence settling over the water.

Then the ocean before our feet began to bubble.

Hiro pulled his feet onto the rocks as a small face with bright green eyes broke the surface of the water, a trail of sea-mangled hair behind her, decorated with kelp. Two sharp white horns on her head curved in toward each other.

"It's been nearly a century since you've visited, you know," she said, bobbing up and down in the waves. Her voice rang like a whisper inside a seashell, echoing dreamily in my ears even after she'd finished speaking.

"You missed me?" Hiro laughed. "Come sit with us. Meet my friend."

A large speckled fin slapped onto the flat rock, followed by another, and then a great sea turtle with the face of a woman climbed onto the rock. Her shell was different shades of brown and black, polished to a diamond shine. Behind her back fins, a broad curtain of green hair trailed into the ocean, like an odd cape or tail.

"This is Maho, the Honengame," Hiro said to me. "This is my friend, Ren of London."

The Honengame inclined her head in a bow, which I copied.

"'Friend,' you say?" she said to Hiro. Then she took a step forward and nudged at his hand with her head. He leaned closer, sliding his hand down her hair to the glossy surface of her shell. He closed his eyes, hardly breathing. Then his face flushed red and he pulled his hand back, hiding a flustered smile behind his hand.

"Maho!" he said, splashing his feet in the water petulantly. "You can't just do that!"

I raised an eyebrow, but Hiro wouldn't look at me, his face still red.

"I can foresee the future," the Honengame said to me. "I can foretell great harvests or warn the people of impending plagues. If you hang my image in your home and pray to it, you'll never get sick."

"Ren is a Shinigami," Hiro said, finally managing to wipe the smile from his face. "She can't get sick. And besides, you know that last part isn't true. You just like the idea of people worshipping you."

The Honengame threw her head back and let out a squeaky laugh, probably the sound a sea turtle would make, if turtles could laugh. "Careful who you anger, fish boy," she said.

Hiro pouted. "Is that what you call your best friend?"

The water beneath Hiro's feet bubbled, and then a lobster flung itself from the water and landed on the rock, twitching. The Honengame wasted no time, opening her jaw wide and taking a great crunching bite out of the lobster's middle.

"Best friend," she repeated, through mouthfuls of lobster shell.

"Would you like one, Ren?" Hiro said.

"I don't think my teeth could handle it," I said over the crunching sounds of the Honengame devouring her lobster.

Unlike the other Yokai, no ambiance of fear and foreboding hovered like a storm cloud over Maho's head. It wasn't surprising that friendly Yokai like Maho had never appeared in my children's anthology. Innocuous Yokai had far less entertainment value than dangerous ones, after all. I eyed the glossy surface of her shell, wondering if it felt as smooth and immaculate as it looked, but I doubted she'd appreciate being petted like a dog.

She finished her food and heaved a satisfied sigh, lying down on the rock and resting her head.

"I've been starving these days," she said.

Hiro frowned. "You have? Why?"

"The humans are overfishing," she said, closing her eyes. "Things have changed since you last visited, Hiro."

"What kind of things?" Hiro said, scooting closer across the rocks.

Maho opened her eyes and frowned into the shifting waters. She turned to me suddenly, far too sharp a movement for a turtle, and looked me up and down.

"You can speak in front of Ren," Hiro said.

The Honengame's nostrils flared, but the tenseness left her face. "No one has died in this town in the last fifty years," she said. "The village is growing too large to sustain itself."

My hands went rigid on the rocks. As a Reaper, the idea of half a century passing without Death was unthinkable. Were a soul collector ever so negligent, the population would balloon.

Hiro's eyes widened. He shook his head, slowly at first, then quickly. "How is that possible?"

"It happens when too many people are dying in other places," Maho said. "Izanami has to keep the death rate steady. If too many die in Tohodu, many more have to stay alive in Takaoka."

"What's happening in Tohodu?" I said.

Maho shook her head. "It's not just Tohodu. It's Shikoku, Hyogo… Wherever there are Yokai with an appetite for humans, too many humans are dying."

Hiro's face turned sickly gray, his eyes glossed over. "Why have the Yokai been overfeeding?" he said.

The Honengame frowned, a deep rumble echoing inside her shell, like an impending thunderstorm. "Go and ask them," she said. "All I know is that my oceans are overfished and my village is overcrowded. Other Yokai are not my concern."

Hiro rubbed his palms across his thighs, pretending to dry them of seawater. "I'll leave some more lobsters outside of your cave before I go," he said, his voice small. "I'm sorry I can't do more."

Maho hummed and nodded. "There's something you should know about your journey," she said, turning to me. "Place your hand on my shell."

"Maho," Hiro said, eyes wide, "I don't know if you should—"

But I had wanted to touch the Honengame since she'd arrived, and I wasn't about to refuse her invitation. Before Hiro had finished talking, I leaned forward and set my hand on the cool surface of her shell.

Blood pours down the stairs of the shrine.

My hand tensed on the Honengame's shell. I tried to pull back, but my hand seemed magnetized, unwilling to release me. When I blinked, images flashed past my eyes—dim stone stairs and syrup-black blood and a white palm turned up to the sky. The Honengame's seashell voice surrounded me, as if I was a grain of sand trapped inside her echoing shell.

Descendent of darkness, this is your fate.

My palm began to burn, and my vision faded until I stood

in the total darkness of Yomi once again, the Honengame's voice raining down on all sides.

That which you seek will never be found. The night will eat your heart and you will wander the darkness for a thousand years.

"What?" I whispered, even though the words wouldn't reach my ears. "What do I seek?"

But there was no answer except for a slight twitching in the fingers of the corpse-white hand. I knelt in scalding hot blood, barely able to catch my breath through the scent of Death. There was so much blood, a river of it spilling through my fingers. Whose blood was it?

Warm fingers closed around my wrist and yanked my hand away.

I blinked, disoriented by the sudden return of light. I caught a glimpse of the Honengame hopping off the rock and splashing into the ocean.

"Ren, what did you see?"

I blinked a few more times and turned to Hiro, who still clutched my wrist, pulling me close to him.

"Blood," I whispered, "and darkness." I wanted to tell him more, but something about the words I'd heard felt too sacred to repeat, and I worried that speaking them out loud would make them true.

"Honengame prophecies don't always come true after they tell people about them," Hiro said. "It gives you the power to change it."

"I don't know what I would change to prevent it," I said.

He sighed and released me. "I didn't expect her to do that. Hearing a Honengame prophecy is a great privilege, one I didn't expect her to extend to a stranger. She must have sensed something good in you."

I stared at the spot where Maho had disappeared into the water. The image of blood and a pale hand and stone steps replayed in my mind. Whose hand had I seen?

"Ren."

Hiro took my cold hand in his own. I couldn't look at him, my vision still flashing with unwanted images.

"Whatever it is, you don't need to be scared," he said, his thumb caressing the back of my hand. "I told you I'd look after you."

I nodded, but my gaze drifted back down to the rocks. Hiro held my hand as we left the shore and headed toward our hotel, but his touch didn't warm me as it normally did. How could it, when my hands and knees still seared from the river of boiling blood? If the Honengame's prediction came true, then someone was going to die in Yomi.

I stared down at Hiro's hand linked in mine for the rest of the walk to the hotel. When I unlocked my room and found Neven asleep, I pulled the sheets back to examine his hands clutching a pillow. But I couldn't remember the hand from my vision clearly enough, so it was useless. I lay awake beside Neven, trying to recall the scene in the changing shadows of the ceiling, hoping that the vision would return in my dreams.

But the night did not betray the secrets of the Honengame, my vision of pale fingers and crimson blood blurring until there was only darkness.

CHAPTER 14

The sea carried us along the coast as if it were one of Hiro's close friends. Hiro sat at the bow of our small wooden canoe, which he'd nervously told us he'd "borrowed" from a local fisherman before dawn. He dipped his oar in the water every now and then, but it accomplished little more than petting the waves the way one might pet a cat. The waters had their own path in mind for us. Far to our left, the shore had turned to jagged brown rocks and hidden caves and cliffside. To our right lay a thousand miles of sea.

Unable to determine whether Iso Onna's hair, voice, or blood was her essence, I'd decided to carve all three of them out of her with my freshly sharpened knives. This time, I'd be able to turn time without worrying about frostbite, so in theory all I had to do was find her, freeze her, and kill her.

It sounded so simple, but the endless stretch of lonely sea and distant shroud of fog around us made me uneasy.

Neven sat behind me, watching the minutes tick by on his clock. He'd said almost nothing to me since he'd woken up, but Hiro seemed all too ready to fill up the silence.

"You're telling me that there are actually fairies in England?"

"It's not as remarkable as you're imagining," I said. "They're more like large, handsome insects that try to con you into making wishes."

"Can you eat them?"

"You *can* eat anything, but that doesn't mean you *should*."

"Then what is their purpose, if not food?"

"To maintain the flora and exasperate Reapers."

Hiro hummed and dipped his oar to the side of the boat, steering us around a rock formation. "I'm not certain I believe that England is a real place," he said. "It sounds more like a storybook. Are you sure it's where you've come from? Or perhaps all of your life was an elaborate dream."

"I've thought the same thing about Japan," I said.

I looked back once more at Neven, who had tucked his clock in his pocket and was staring at the rocky coast. We hadn't had such a serious disagreement since we were children, and I no longer knew how to resolve it. Whenever I looked at him, my fingers twitched with the need to shatter some light bulbs or extinguish a couple stars. I could grudgingly forgive his ignorance for my feelings, since I knew he was busy being terrified by Yuki Onna, but his persistent disdain for Hiro was tiresome. We were one-third finished with my quest thanks to Hiro's help, and he had already saved my life twice. I wasn't sure what else he could possibly do to appease Neven, and I was beginning to suspect that nothing he did would ever be enough.

"The sea won't take us any farther," Hiro said.

Indeed, no matter how much Hiro rowed, the boat couldn't fight the waves pushing us backward. The ocean all around us was jagged with pillars of black rock. To our left, a white fog hovered over a distant shore, taller towers of rock piercing through the haze.

"This seems like a good place for a shipwreck," I said.

"The ocean wouldn't overturn a boat while I'm in it," Hiro said, "but I think you're right." He plunged his oar into the water, changing our course back to shore.

The fog parted to let us through, like a great gate opening its doors. With one final push from the ocean, our boat scraped up onto the shore. In low tide pools around us, garlands of kelp swayed and stuck to the rocks like shiny brown ribbons.

We stepped out onto a jagged puzzle of jutting black stones that wrapped around a rocky cliffside. Rocks the size and shape of eyeballs rolled away as I clambered onto land, the shore cool from the shade of towering boulders leaning precariously against each other. All the rocks had the same ash-black cast, as if the whole landscape had been scorched. Water crashed up against our feet in a white froth, slicking the rocks and soaking our shoes.

"Where are all the bones?" I said, looking to the wet sand. I could smell Death faintly on the island, but this shore had no sign of the skeletons that Hakutaku's book had spoken of.

Neven jolted at the mention of bones, but Hiro only shrugged.

"I don't know," he said, "maybe—"

The edge of his right foot landed on a wet stone and he slipped sideways with a sharp sound of surprise.

I reached for my clock to save him the trouble of hitting his head on a nearby boulder, but the ocean rushed up to catch him in a spray of foam, crashing against his falling momentum and setting him back on his feet, soaked but stable.

"The ocean seems to like you," I said, cuffing salt water from my face where the backsplash had caught me.

Hiro smiled, spitting out a bit of salt water. "I *am* the ocean," he said.

Then another wave came and lapped at my ankles, curling up my calf and tickling the back of my leg.

"Stop that," I said, but there was no anger behind my words and Hiro must have known it, because he kept smiling, even when I splashed water at his face in retaliation. "You could be hanged for that in England." I wasn't sure if that was true, but indecent Reapers had been whipped for less.

"Just that?" Hiro said, grinning. "That's far from the worst thing I've done."

He raised his hands as if to splash me and I took a step back into a tide pool, since my shoes were already soaked.

The water around my feet bubbled like a boiling stew, though the temperature remained cold. The ribbons of kelp tickling my ankles went rigid, as if made of glass, then turned black and crumbled into pieces, turning the tide pool the color of ink.

Hiro grabbed my arms and hauled me back onto the rock.

As I held up the skirts of my kimono to climb up, the veins in my ankles throbbed and flashed a shade of deep red, just like my hands had done before.

"What was that?" Neven said, standing a careful distance away as Hiro knelt and inspected the water. It did not boil at his touch as he scooped up handfuls of murky black sea.

"Did it hurt you?" Hiro said, looking up.

I shook my head. "I don't know why this keeps happening."

"This has happened before?" Neven said, frowning.

I winced, realizing I'd never quite gotten around to telling him.

"A few times," I said, looking away. "Just some plants that withered too quickly." *And Yuki Onna*, I thought, but that would be even harder to explain now, and I knew from the tight set of Neven's jaw that he was already angry.

"You didn't think to mention this earlier?" he said.

"There were more important things happening," I said. "It's not that significant, Neven."

Neven scoffed, and Hiro kept digging around the tide pool.

"This isn't typical of Reapers?" Hiro said.

"No."

Hiro pulled a starfish from the water, its back a bright orange and the tips of its legs a deep violet.

"Would you please?" he said, holding it out to me.

I had an idea what Hiro was thinking and didn't really want to do this in front of Neven, but he would be even angrier if I still tried to hide things from him now.

I reached out and took the starfish. Instantly, all the color vanished from its skin, its arms twitching as it turned bone white and then hung limply over the sides of my hand.

Hiro took the starfish back without comment, his face gray. He kissed it and set it back in the ocean with a quiet apology. "Ren, this may be a problem."

I bit down on the inside of my cheek to stop myself from shouting, *Of course it's a problem!* Didn't I have enough problems already? The Death that spread from my touch must have had something to do with the Reapers crossing out my name in Ankou's book, but I'd prayed that whatever this was, it would fade the farther I got from England. Killing plants and starfish with my touch was the least of my concerns, and easy enough to avoid. But Yuki Onna had started turning to ash just from trying to take my heart and had melted so easily at my touch, so whatever it was, it was starting to affect higher beings as well as lower ones. I didn't like not knowing what would follow, but what choice did I have? I couldn't very well go back to England and ask Cromwell for clarification.

I turned my head at the sound of footsteps on the rocks. Neven was walking in the opposite direction, balancing carefully as he stepped over a small boulder.

"Where are you going?" I said.

"For a walk," he said without turning around.

"Neven, don't be ridiculous. We'll stay together."

He stopped walking, his shoulders stiff. "No."

The word hushed the restless rumble of waves, forcing the waters to recede. This was how Neven spoke as a Reaper, not as my brother.

"I need a moment, Ren," he said. He wouldn't look at me, so I couldn't see the color of his eyes to know if he was sad or angry or scared.

But he didn't wait for my response. He stormed off down the shore, vanishing in the black and unsteady terrain.

I sighed. The waves spilled across the rocks, gently sloshing over my toes. Hiro set a hand on my back but said nothing as we watched Neven go.

"Follow him," I said to Hiro. "Please."

Hiro looked down at me, his fingers tense on my back. "But what about you?"

"I'll be all right," I said, turning to face Hiro and gesturing to the knives in my sleeves, "but Neven's not really a fighter."

Hiro's lips turned down and he pulled me into a gentle hug, my chin resting on his shoulder. I held my breath in surprise, rigid as stone in his grip and praying he couldn't feel how my cold and slow-beating heart had suddenly doubled its pace. Perhaps I was meant to do something with my arms other than let them hang limp, but before I could decide, Hiro pulled away.

"Be careful," he said.

"Neven will hear me if something goes wrong," I said. "Reapers have good hearing."

Hiro squeezed my arm for a moment before his hand fell away.

"Hurry," I said.

He nodded and turned away, following Neven's path across the shore.

I turned in the opposite direction, facing away from the sun, where shadows cast the rocks in an even darker shade of black. I stepped over the jagged cuts of stone and steadied myself as I descended the uneven terrain. The sound of waves grew louder, the air a few degrees cooler, the sharp smell of salt clearing my mind.

I sat down on a smooth rock and looked up at the pale sky. Just for one moment, these few minutes I had by myself, I wanted to be neither a Shinigami nor a Reaper, but just a girl who was very far away from home. I imagined that I was back in London, when autumn made the whole world gold and the nights smelled of charcoal and there was at least one small room where I was safe and my brother loved me. I didn't know what to do to bring Neven back to me, and I especially didn't know what to do about Hiro.

Ever since that strange moment on the shore just before Maho arrived, it was hard to look at Hiro without feeling like my heart was beating too fast. Hiro was supposed to be a tool to get me to the three Yokai. He'd help me, I'd help him impress Izanami, and that was all there was to it. I didn't want to be one of the foolish women in the humans' penny romances. I couldn't afford to be distracted by something as finite and pointless as attraction.

I bit back a frustrated sound, knowing that it might alarm Neven, and got to my feet.

That was when I saw her.

Farther down the shore, a woman sat on the rocks, facing away from me. Her long black hair spilled down her back and into the water like a veil decorated with white starfish, revealing the bare white curves of her waist. The skin around her shoulders pulled tight against her bones, and her whole body blurred around the edges like a dream.

Hair so long that it dragged behind her on the sand, tangled with starfish and seaweed, the legend had said. This had to be Iso Onna.

She sat a bit outside of the range that I could comfortably stop time in, so I held my clock in one hand and began to climb down the rocks, careful to keep my eyes on her. The sounds of the ocean rose up around me, and I wondered if Neven really would hear me if I called for him among the sound of waves shattering on the shore.

A stone rolled away under my foot, sending me sliding down the incline. I dropped my clock to catch myself rather than break my face on the rocks, tumbling until I spilled onto a flat bed of stone. I anticipated the Yokai's teeth in my jugular, or her hair shackling me down, or a horrible screech that would split through my brain like a pickax. But when I rolled onto my knees and crouched in a defensive stance, the Yokai hadn't moved at all.

Her stillness rivaled that of an oil painting, but I couldn't ignore the uneasy shift in the atmosphere that confirmed her realness. I could sense Death nearby, but not in her blood and bones the way Reapers or Shinigami carried it. Instead, Death watched us from across the water, far away and crawling closer.

I pulled on the chain of my clock, but it was caught between two rocks a few feet ahead of me, closer to the Yokai than I would have preferred. I lifted my scraped palm off the rocks and crawled forward.

"Have you come to finish me?" the Yokai said. Her words did not have the magnificent and ethereal ring of Yuki Onna, or the hypnotic echo of the Honengame. Instead, she spoke so quietly that the waves nearly overwhelmed her voice, each word soft and delicate.

"Finish you?" I said.

The Yokai sighed but still didn't turn around.

"I know what you're here for, so why do you hesitate?" she said.

Because my clock is not in my hand, I thought, tugging on the chain to bring it back to me without any sudden movement. Everything about our interaction felt so delicate, and I was sure that any sudden lunges or loud sounds would shatter it.

"I'm here because you've upset the balance," I said, trying to keep my voice even as I crawled closer.

She let out a sharp laugh. I froze, palm outstretched, waiting for her next move. Then she shook her head, hair spilling over her shoulder. "What balance?" she said. "I haven't eaten in half a century."

I frowned, shifting one knee forward. Hadn't the Honengame said the same thing? That would certainly explain why no bones remained on the shore. Surely whatever was left a half century ago had long been pulled out to sea and sunken to the bottom of the ocean.

"None of the humans dare to sail into my waters anymore," she said. "I am bound to these rocks forever, even if it means I starve."

"Am I meant to believe you so easily?" I said, giving my chain another pull with no success. In truth, I did believe her, but I needed her distracted because my clock remained firmly between the rocks.

"What you choose to believe is of no consequence to me," she said. "You can see me here, starving." Indeed, the closer I got, the more I could see of her bones—the sharp edges of her collarbone where it connected to her shoulders, the joints in her elbows. "Your opinion won't change my fate, Shinigami."

Then a cloud of Death numbed my tongue, filling my mouth with bitterness. I realized then why the air around the Yokai felt heavy with an invisible storm, why Death swirled in the sea around us, overhead in the gray cast of the sky and ocean that reeked of shipwrecks and riptides and a thousand things lost.

Iso Onna smelled like someone who was already dying.

"How long will you live if you don't eat?" I said.

The Yokai hung her head low, hair parting slightly to reveal the knobs of her spine.

"I don't know," she whispered. "I don't even know if I'll die at all. Perhaps I'll keep withering like this until the end of time."

"And yet you won't eat me," I said. Surely, if I had smelled like food to a starving Yokai, we wouldn't have been conversing so calmly.

She scoffed and shook her head. "I can't drink Shinigami blood. Believe me, I've tried. You all taste like ash and rot and leave me hungrier than before."

"How did you know I was a Shinigami?"

"I can smell it in your blood," she said. "Along with something else."

"Yes, British Reaper," I said, yanking my clock again. "I'm well aware."

"No."

I paused, letting the chain go slack. "No?"

"I smell a sourness in your blood," she said.

My fist clenched tighter around the chain. "That's because I'm a creature of Death."

"No, it's more than that," she said. "Inside, you are rotting."

I held my breath. What was it that she smelled, exactly? Was it the cloud of Death that seemed to have followed me everywhere since I'd left London, or was it just my soul?

"I can smell your hunger, too," Iso Onna said, tracing a finger across the surface of the water.

"I don't eat."

"Not for food," she said. "You've come here because you think Izanami will feed you. That's why they all come here, and all of them are fools."

"Shut up," I said. "I know you hypnotize people. You're just talking me in circles because you don't want me to kill you."

Iso Onna sighed—a long, sad sound that spoke of the exhaustion of living for thousands of years.

"You would stab a starving creature with her back turned to you?" she said. "How heroic."

"You've murdered thousands of people."

"I was *hungry!*" Iso Onna said, slamming her fists down into the rock and fracturing it into a dozen smaller pieces that somehow still clung together. She panted, as if the outburst had drained all of her energy. "I know what you are," she whispered. "I can smell it on you the way one can smell a rotting corpse in summer heat. You know that you would just as soon drag a man out to sea and drown him if you were hungry enough."

I shook my head, hand rigid on the chain of my clock. I knew that I selfishly endangered my brother and snapped at strangers and was too blunt to humans on their deathbeds, but that was different than being a Yokai, wasn't it? Why did both Yuki Onna and Iso Onna think they could see through me so easily? What right did they have to judge my heart, or my mind, or even my blood?

"Ren!"

I turned around. Neven and Hiro stood at the top of the incline, peering down at us. Neven's jaw dropped and he started scrambling down the rocks.

"Neven, it's under control," I said.

But Iso Onna sat up straight, so sharply that I lurched backward out of instinct, still tethered to my clock's chain. She rose to her feet and slowly turned around.

I didn't know what kind of monster I'd expected, but it wasn't anything like this. Her eyes had the entire ocean inside of them, every shade of blue-green and shimmering fish and bright coral and white sand. The skin under her cheekbones glimmered with hundreds of iridescent scales that resembled fine jewels. Her wet hair hung in ripples around her face, decorated with tiny starfish. She looked more like an enchanting princess of the sea than a bloodthirsty vampire.

She wore no clothing and moved with elegance despite her frailty, every step flowing as if she walked underwater.

Neven and Hiro stood dumbfounded, eyes full of stars and unmoving on the rocks. I wanted to mock them, but even I found it hard to think clearly through the dreamlike ambiance that had settled over the shore. Neven stepped away from Hiro and began to cross the shore, stumbling forward in a magnetized sleepwalk.

"Neven, stay back," I said. But he didn't break from Iso Onna's trance, hurrying closer, eyes only on her.

"What have you done to him?" I said to the Yokai. Under

her trance, I had to fight to form each word, my lips numb and heavy. "You said you wouldn't eat—"

I froze.

She'd said she didn't want my Shinigami blood, but she'd probably never tasted a Reaper before.

"Neven, your clock!" I screamed.

He jumped as if shocked awake, blinking at me in confusion but reaching for his clock instinctively.

Then Iso Onna's jaw came unhinged with a loud crack, and a violent shriek shattered the sky.

Her voice lanced through my ear canal and straight into my brain, scraping down the walls of my skull. Blood spilled hot out of my ears and down my neck. I clamped my hands over my ears, but nothing could stop the sound from knifing straight through my brain, forcing me to my knees. I screamed Neven's name as Iso Onna stepped closer, though I couldn't even hear my own voice.

Neven had fallen to the ground, his hands clapped over his own bleeding ears. Iso Onna's hair began to lengthen, locks of it twisting through the air like swaying cobras. From nearly ten meters away, it wrapped around Neven's wrists, pulling his hands from his ears. He thrashed against her hold, but more locks twisted around his neck, squeezing until his face turned white and his eyes flashed through a panicked kaleidoscope of colors.

I tried to crawl forward, but removing even one hand from my ear multiplied the pain by a thousand, nearly shattering me with its intensity. I could only watch with wet eyes as Iso Onna dragged Neven like a toy across the rocks, and the two of them disappeared into the sea.

I didn't realize I'd still been screaming for Neven until Iso Onna's voice abruptly stopped, my own cries cutting through the ringing in my ears. When I tried to jump to my feet, my chain pulled me back down to the wet rocks. I yanked it with all my strength, but with a horrifying clinking sound, the chain snapped and my clock clattered farther down between the rocks.

"No no no, come back!" I cried, jamming my hand between the rocks and trying to feel for my clock, but my hand was too big and my clock had fallen too far down.

I stared at my trembling hands and dug my teeth into my lip and held back a scream because *I had no idea what to do.* My clock had always bought me the time to think and be rational, but I didn't have any more time when a sea vampire was dragging Neven deeper and deeper underwater. I had to go down after him.

Hiro reached me just as I kicked my shoes off and pulled the knives from my sleeves, tucking them into my waistband.

"I have to get him," I told Hiro, splitting the seams of my kimono as I yanked the top layer off, stumbling toward the shore. "I have to. He's... I don't know how—"

"I'll take you," Hiro said, grabbing my hand.

"Take me?" I said, stumbling after Hiro as he pulled me to the sand. I didn't know if he'd suddenly become searingly hot or if my own temperature had plummeted, but I felt like I'd grabbed onto a shooting star and let it drag me across the sky.

Hiro didn't bother explaining, instead pointing to a giant sea turtle standing at attention on the shore.

"Hold on to me!" he said, lying down on his stomach across the turtle's shell.

I swallowed but stepped forward anyway. There was no time to be embarrassed when Neven could be dying.

I draped myself over Hiro's back and held tight to his shoulders, clinging even tighter when his warmth chased away the shuddering cold in my blood.

"Go!" Hiro said, patting the turtle's head.

The turtle moved excruciatingly slowly across the shore, burdened by our weight. But once we were underwater, it sped through the ocean at a speed I hadn't thought possible of earthly creatures.

The salt water blurred my vision and stung my eyes, but I could make out the silent walls of dark ocean and slowly swaying kelp flying past us. We cut through constellations of tiny silver fish and giant tuna that could easily have swallowed me whole, the smallest of them dying and rising to the surface as they brushed my skin. The sea creatures began to flee as if they sensed something was wrong with me, a mass exodus of squids and jellyfish and stingrays clearing a path for us. There were great tapestries of seaweed below us, flashes of hot and cold water, a slowly intensifying pressure in my skull. And then finally, there was Neven.

He floated limp and white in Iso Onna's horrific shackles. Her teeth had latched on to the side of his neck, her hands in his hair forcing his head back at so sharp an angle that his spine would surely snap, if it hadn't already. His clock floated in the water behind him, glinting silver, still chained to his clothes.

Was he even alive? I'd seen thousands of corpses in my lifetime, and he rivaled all of them in his paleness and stillness. My grip on Hiro's shoulders tightened so hard that I thought I might snap his collarbone, but if I didn't hold on to something, then the dark waters would consume me and drag me down to their lightless end, crushed by the water pressure, brain exploded out of my skull, soupy and formless as Yuki Onna.

The turtle surged closer and Iso Onna looked up, clearly not anticipating any company so deep underwater. As she pulled away from Neven, wisps of blood spun from his neck like billowing red smoke off a burning building. The ocean wiped away the red stain from the Yokai's lips but couldn't clean the rusty tint from the fangs that hung down to her chin. She hadn't neatly tucked her fangs into an artery to drink like western vampires but had gnawed a chunk of flesh out of the side of Neven's neck, severing the artery and tendons.

My brother had trusted me to protect him and now he was bleeding out into the ocean, and for that I hated myself more than I hated the Yokai who'd taken him.

I shoved away from Hiro and kicked through the water, snatching Neven's clock by the chain. Ropes of hair locked around my throat and squeezed, but the pain only lasted a moment before my fingers closed around the clock.

The spinning clouds of blood halted. The serpentine locks of hair stopped tightening around my throat. Neven and Hiro and Iso Onna all turned to statues suspended in the sickly green sea.

I looked at my brother's face, still and corpse-white, and something cold began to swirl in my stomach.

Suddenly, breathless pain shattered through me, like all my organs had been raked open, my abdomen filling up with boiling hot blood, my ribs shattering with the effort of keeping it all contained as the taste of Death crawled up my throat. Whenever I'd felt this kind of rage in the past, my bones had filled up with a violent and irrepressible blaze of light. But this time there was no light at all, only my blood screaming under my skin, a burning pressure fighting to rip open my veins from the inside.

The filtered sunlight at the surface of the water began to dim. Without the warmth of day, the temperature plunged colder, the walls of nauseous green sea turning gray and then black. The sting of Death ravaged my bones and cracked my spine into a rigid straight line, my fingers curling into fists.

I yanked at Neven's clock until the chain tore from his clothes, then clamped the silver between my teeth to hold it still, my mouth filling with brine and blood. I took out my knife and hacked at the hair restraints around my neck, slicing lines across my fingers and throat in my carelessness.

I was not calm and impartial, the way Reapers were supposed to be. I was not skilled and precise, the way Shinigami were supposed to be. I was nothing but Death that bled from every organ and anger so vicious that it could tear the sky to shreds, drain the oceans dry, and crack the universe in two.

As soon as the hair fell away from my neck, I sliced through the locks binding the Yokai to Neven, but so much hair still floated in the water like a thousand greedy fingers. I hated the sight of it, the memory of it stretching longer out of her skull, the metallic texture, so I grabbed fistfuls and cut and cut and cut and cut and wondered distantly if this was how Ivy had felt when she cut my hair. The severed hair floated around us in a tangled cloud of black and the more I sliced, the more my rage expanded inside of me.

Hair, voice, blood. One of those things was Iso Onna's

essence. It didn't matter which, because I was going to take them all.

I wrapped my hands in the long sleeves of my kimono so my skin wouldn't touch the Yokai, then I sliced through the major arteries in her thighs and wrists and neck. She wouldn't bleed until time started again, but I split her skin smooth and easy as butter all the same. Then I pressed my blade to her neck and sawed down and down and the flesh split away, the soft tissues of the trachea yielding to the sharpness of my blade, harder and harder and harder until I was sawing on spine. She would have an awfully hard time screaming with ripped vocal cords gurgling with blood and it had been so easy, why not saw all the way through to the other side? Tear her to pieces, rip her apart, drench the sea with scarlet and make her pay, crack open her rib cage and rip out her soul and slice it to ribbons and feed it to the fish.

That was the price of my brother's blood.

My knife lodged in her spine and wouldn't move, wouldn't come loose, wouldn't release until I kicked her face back and her spine snapped like a piece of kindling. I'd broken her until there was nothing left to shatter and the knife trembled in my hand and my teeth ached from biting down on the silver clock.

And then there was nothing more to do, but the ocean still boiled around me and my whole body convulsed with shivers and only then, when the Yokai was definitely dead and done for, did a warm wave of satisfaction wash over me, a euphoric tingling that fizzled throughout my body because *I had won*.

When I reached out for Neven, my hands were once again nothing but bones and bright red veins. Would I shatter him with my touch, my anger, all the horrible parts of me that had brought him here in the first place?

My throat let out a wretched sound, somewhere between a sob for my brother and a scream at the last remnants of rage that still splintered through my bones. I bit down harder on the clock…and it slipped from between my teeth.

Instantly, the whole world swirled with blood.

I couldn't see outside of the walls of crimson that stung my eyes and filled my mouth, the chunks of black hair, the taste of Death so dizzying that I retched out the water and blood I'd swallowed. Where was Neven? Where was the Yokai? Had I killed her?

Arms wrapped around my waist, and I slashed out with my knife, raking a line across Hiro's shoulder before I realized who he was. Against his stillness, I could feel the uncontrollable shudders still rocking through my body. He pressed something to my hand, and I could tell from the shape that it was Neven's clock, but I couldn't have turned time then even if I'd wanted to.

"Take his arm," Hiro said. Somehow, in the water, I could still hear Hiro's voice as if he'd breathed the words into my ear. A rush of water cleared away some of the blood, and I saw Hiro clutching Neven's arm with the hand that wasn't wrapped around my waist.

I grabbed Neven's other arm and kicked toward the surface, looking down for the Yokai, sure that somehow all of it hadn't been enough to subdue her. But as the blood cleared, I knew we didn't have to worry about her anymore.

Iso Onna lay facedown on the ocean floor, draped among the rocks and algae. Her raggedly shorn hair fluttered around with the changing currents, her whole body wrapped in a haze of hellish red, still swirling from her limbs. The blood that spun toward us tasted of concentrated Death, like cyanide that singed away the skin of my lips.

Hiro kicked harder, clearly still in control of his limbs in a way that I wasn't. We broke the surface, Neven's head hanging limply against his shoulders.

"Take him to land," I said, struggling to keep my own head above water as I dribbled out blood that might have been my brother's or the Yokai's or my own. Hiro held Neven against his side and swam ahead of me to the shore, where he laid Neven down in the sand as I clawed through the violent waves to catch up with them.

Hiro was shaking Neven when I crawled onto the shore next to him, and Neven still hadn't moved. The wound in his neck no longer poured out blood, but the skin still looked raw and mangled. How much blood could a Reaper lose? I didn't know where Iso Onna fell on our power hierarchy, but she'd certainly seemed like someone strong enough to kill a Reaper.

"Neven," I said, my hands on his face. "Neven!"

I lifted one of his eyelids with my thumb, but I couldn't even see the color of his eyes because they'd rolled back in his head. I closed my eyes and let my forehead fall to his chest and imagined another universe in which my brother had asked to escape London with me and I'd said no because I wasn't selfish enough to put him in danger. But that was not the choice I'd made, and that was not a reality I'd ever get to see.

All the darkness had evaporated, and I was hollow. An oyster once the shell had been cracked open and all the flesh had been scraped out with a fork. I closed my fist in Neven's shirt but I couldn't cry, because there was nothing left inside me, so instead the sadness just lodged in my throat and made it impossible to breathe. Hiro's hand fell on my back and traced lightly up and down my spine, but his touch felt far away.

"I'm sorry," I said to Neven's shirt. "Neven, I'm so sorry."

But Neven lay stiff and cold and unmoving. I sat up slowly, my head hanging low and fist still clutching my brother's shirt.

"Ren," Hiro said, his hand on the small of my back. I looked at him, hoping that he had an answer, some secret Japanese potion or benevolent Yokai who could fix my brother. But all he did was pull me into his arms and hold me. My arms hung limp by my sides and my face rested on his shoulder, but none of it was enough, none of it mattered.

Then Neven made a gurgling sound, turning to the side and spitting out foamy brine.

I untangled myself from Hiro, nearly pushing him away as I knelt beside Neven. His head twitched to the side as he drooled out water tinted pink with blood. His eyes flickered open, pale blue.

"Neven!" I said, cupping his face as his eyes tracked the passing clouds and then finally settled on me. He blinked a few times before his eyes started to slide closed again, but I slapped him hard before they could.

"Ow, Ren." One of his hands reached up to touch the wound on his neck. He winced and examined the blood on his fingers, then looked back at me.

I wrapped my arms around him and squeezed so hard that he let out a pained sound, but it didn't matter because he was alive, which meant he would heal.

My breath came back to me all at once, wrenching my

chest open with a ragged gasp of salty air. Every breath came loud and choked, like I was drowning on land. I clutched at Neven, one hand pressed to his spine and the other in his hair, jamming his face into my neck so I could feel his cool breath on my skin. One of his hands drifted up and rested on my back, light as a falling leaf.

I thought of a thousand things I could have said to him, but I could hardly even breathe when every piece of me was about to come unglued, my bones about to collapse into a human puzzle, my organs about to spill onto the rocks.

"It's all right," Neven managed, the words slurred together and whispered into my skin. "Ren, it's all right."

But it wasn't all right, and it wouldn't be all right until my task was finished and I could find a new place for me and Neven to live in Yomi, with lots of lanterns to chase the darkness away.

I thought about Death tearing through my skin and wondered if Neven truly was safe with me. But I allowed myself one moment just to hold him and forget about that, and all the monsters in this new and foreign world, and the blood soaking our clothes, and the darkness slowly but surely bleeding across the sky.

CHAPTER 15

Night fell fast over the shore. The ocean turned dark, as if poisoned by all the blood that had been spilled, and the gray clouds melted together into a stone wall that blocked out the moon and stars.

Neven could barely stand. I helped him stumble to a cave that Hiro had found among the rocks, dragging him most of the way. I'd sent Hiro back into the waters to find Neven's glasses and he'd gone without complaint, his waters bringing them back to the surface in a matter of minutes. Then we'd decided to let Neven rest for a few hours and try to wash the blood out of our clothes so we wouldn't arouse suspicion when we finally headed back to town.

Hiro went to gather firewood while I laid Neven down on the ground of the cave. He curled up on his side in the wet sand, cheek scraping into the ground and glasses knocked halfway off his face.

"How haven't you broken these already?" I said, taking off his glasses and tucking them in his pocket. I tugged at his arm, trying to get him to rest on my leg instead of the ground. "Come on, you'll be eating sand in your sleep. Get up."

"Don't care," Neven said. But he was limp enough that I managed to manhandle him until his head lay in my lap. He mumbled something unintelligible and I ignored it until he spoke again.

"My clock," he said, fingers feeling at the hole in his pocket where I'd ripped the chain away. "Where... Ren?"

"Are you planning on turning time in your dreams?" I said, pulling his clock from my pocket and pressing it to his grasping hands. Teeth marks marred the surface of the silver and I prayed that he didn't ask about them later. For the moment Neven didn't seem to care about the dents, holding the clock to his chest and rolling on his side to curl up around it. I would have to go out looking for my own clock later, but I suspected that I would never see it again. Maybe Neven could make me a new one when he'd recovered, if we found the right materials in Takaoka.

I stroked Neven's hair, despite its disgusting texture from all the salt water and blood. My fingers traced the slowly scarring mark on his neck.

"Stop," he said into my leg, his hand twitching like he wanted to swat me away. "Itches."

I brought my hand back up to his hair and watched him descend into sleep, not wanting to ever let him go again. He'd been my tether to reality in the dreamy haze of Yomi and the

Yokai, but I could no longer trust that he wouldn't evaporate the moment I turned away. I didn't want to sleep, in case I woke to find that Neven's rescue had been a dream, or that he'd never existed at all. Our argument seemed so meaningless compared to the thought of Neven dying. I would have had to carry him all the way back to London so that Ankou could collect his soul. The moment I returned, I would have been shackled and executed. But I still would have done it, rather than leave Neven's soul floating in the ether for eternity.

He shivered in his sleep and curled in on himself, face pressing into my leg.

"He'll recover, won't he?" Hiro said, returning to the cave and arranging a small pile of sticks on the ground.

"I think so."

Hiro pulled a box of matches from his pocket, realized it was sopping wet, then tossed it aside with a scowl. He grabbed one of the flatter pieces of firewood and began the tedious task of starting a friction fire like a human. What a pity that we could use our powers only to ignite sources of light, rather than any flammable material we could find. Sooner than I'd expected, the wood smoked and sparked. Hiro waved his hand over the tiny flame and a fire sprang up, nearly singeing my nose.

"And what about you?" he said, wiping his hands off on his pants.

The fire turned the flat black in Hiro's eyes to warm amber, and suddenly I wanted to tell him everything. *I think Death is eating me from the inside out*, I wanted to say. *I think one day it might break out and obliterate everything.*

"I'm fine," I said, looking down at Neven.

"You're good to him," Hiro said.

I frowned. "If I were good to him, he wouldn't be here." My tone left no room for debate. I didn't want to talk about what Neven deserved. "Didn't you say you had sisters?" Hiro seemed like such a free spirit, I had trouble imagining him linked to anyone the way I was to Neven.

Hiro stared into the fire for a long moment before nodding. "Yes, but they weren't Shinigami. They were the daughters of the human couple that raised me. There was no blood relation, and they're long dead now."

The words grew quieter toward the end of his sentence. He cleared his throat and thrust his hands near the fire.

"Can you not meet them in Yomi?" I said.

Hiro's fingers twitched, a slight grimace curling one side of his mouth. "You have to be rather quick if you hope to find someone in Yomi. It holds all of the dead, expanding infinitely into the darkness. By the time I figured out how to return to Yomi on my own, centuries had passed. I suspect they've moved to the outskirts, since I've never been able to find them in the city."

"Centuries," I repeated. "Just how old are you?"

Hiro smiled and shook his head. "I'm an old man."

"You look my age," I said. "You can't possibly be over three hundred."

"I'm flattered," he said. "I take good care of my skin."

"Six hundred?"

Hiro laughed, clapping a hand over his mouth and glancing at Neven to make sure he was still sleeping. "Let some things go unsaid," he said. "I don't want to scare you off, thinking I'm too old for you." He shot me a leering glance across the fire that I thought might have been a joke, but my face flushed and I looked away all the same.

"How long do Shinigami even live?" I said. "If you're as old as you say, it can't be the same as Reapers."

"Usually quite a long time." Hiro shrugged.

"Do you intend to deflect all my questions?"

He shook his head. "I don't mean to be vague, but I don't know the answer."

"You don't know how long you live?"

Hiro shook his head. "Shinigami live in proportion to the population of Japan. If the population increases, more Shinigami can be born. If it decreases, the weakest of us begin to die off."

"And how can you die?"

Hiro looked at me oddly for a moment, then smiled. "Oh, the tables have turned. *You* want to murder *me* now?"

I rolled my eyes. "I didn't mean you, specifically."

"I'm not sure if I should tell you all my secrets," Hiro said, pretending to lock his lips with a key.

"Will you answer my question or not?"

"As you wish." He leaned back against the wall and crossed his legs. "We can die many ways. A nice sharp twist to my neck would finish the job. As would an arrow to my heart. Or perhaps if you connected a heavy rock with my skull enough times, that would suffice."

I paused, searching his face for signs that he was joking. "But who can kill a Shinigami?" I said.

"Anyone. If you were to plunge one of your knives into my heart right now, I would die." He spread his arms open, exposing his chest. "Now's your chance."

"In England, only superior creatures can kill a Reaper," I said, ignoring his theatrics.

Hiro hummed and nodded, letting his arms fall to his sides. "Then it's essentially the same."

"How is that the same? Anyone can kill you."

Hiro shook his head. "Anyone can *try* to kill me," he said. "Only a superior creature will succeed."

"But..." My head spun. "That means Yokai are more difficult to kill than Shinigami. Aren't we superior creatures?"

Hiro laughed. "Don't tell Maho I said this, but Yokai are base creatures. Strong but not particularly smart. They need to be hard to kill, or humans would wipe them all out. There are thousands of Shinigami, but there is only one Iso Onna. Or, there *was*, until you came along."

Hiro smiled, like me wiping out a rare Yokai was something to be proud of. And maybe it was, but it was hard to feel anything but shame with Neven half-conscious in my lap.

"Your eyes look different," Hiro said, leaning closer and tilting his head to the side.

I looked away, wanting to hug my knees to my chest for warmth but not wanting to look like I was cowering from him.

"Ren," Hiro said, the word so careful and soft that I knew he was broaching something difficult. "When I blinked, back in the sea, the water turned black. Your eyes were black, too, not just the irises, but the whites of your eyes. And your veins..." He took my hand, tracing the faint silhouette of blue lines under my skin. "What's going on?"

I looked away, letting hair fall over my face. Cromwell's

words echoed in my head from my final day in London that felt like a lifetime ago.

Death will find her.

Ever since I'd left, Death had been nipping at my heels, reaching out his crooked fingers to just barely scratch me. I hadn't wanted to think about what it might mean, and it was easy enough to forget about wilted flowers and dead leaves. But whatever the Reapers had cursed me with, it had spread beyond my hands and feet and infected every part of me. Maybe Hiro, who had lived for so much longer and knew so many humans and Yokai, would have an answer.

"I think," I whispered, "I think Death is coming for me."

"Death comes for all of us—"

"Not like that," I said, shaking my head. "Before I left London, the High Reapers did something to me. I don't know exactly what."

I must have sounded delirious, like someone on their deathbed lost to fevered ramblings. Hiro waited for me to continue, his expression blank.

"There's something horrible inside of me," I said, looking down at my trembling hands. My skin remained almost mockingly opaque, my veins a normal blue, as if all of it had been a bad dream. "I think Death is poisoning me from the inside out."

Inside, you are rotting, Iso Onna had said. I had always been blunt and selfish and bitter and now I was decaying, too, a putrid corpse releasing gases that attracted maggots, everything around me rancid and ruined. I felt myself filling up with darkness like a well after weeks of rain, night spilling over the top. But the most terrible part wasn't what the High

Reapers had done to me. It was that somehow, despite everything, I didn't want it to stop.

It had to be a side effect of their curse, or maybe it had latched on to something dark and broken that was already there and grown roots. But how could I not relish the feeling of being able to crush bones like biscuits when all of my life it had been *my* bones breaking? Was it not supposed to feel glorious to finally be stronger than someone, to finally bring someone to their knees and make them feel fear instead of feeling it myself? Did that make me a monster...and did it matter if it did?

"Ren," Hiro said.

I dared to look up, and once again Hiro was staring at me like I was every constellation in a clear sky. What about me could possibly warrant such a look?

"Whatever this is," he said, "is it really such a terrible thing, if it helped you tear Iso Onna to pieces?"

"No," I agreed, far too quickly. I wanted Hiro to be right. I wanted him to give me permission to be this way without apology. "But it's going to kill me eventually. It's going to work its way through my bloodstream and then stop my heart. Why else would the High Reapers do this, if not to kill me?"

Hiro's eyes darkened. "I won't let it," he said.

"How can you stop it?" I said. "The High Reapers—"

"Reapers do not have a monopoly on Death." Hiro's expression turned bitter. "Death is not a dog you can teach to roll over. You can set her loose on others, but she does as she wishes."

"Hiro—"

"I'm not going to let this curse hurt you," Hiro said. "You're too important."

My throat went dry. *Important.* I had never been important to anyone but Neven. Always a scarlet letter to my family and a plaything for my peers. And yet, here was Hiro, whom I'd known for less than a week, and somehow he thought that I mattered. It didn't make any sense.

"Why?" I said. "You saw all that blood in the water. You know what I did."

"I'll admit, this curse and your changing light powers are a dangerous combination," he said, "but they're also powerful."

"And terrible." I looked down at Neven in my lap.

Hiro shook his head. "Everyone has terrible parts inside them, even if they pretend otherwise. You're just honest about it."

"Not Neven," I said. "Not you."

"Is that what you think?" Hiro said, his voice dropping lower. He leaned over the fire, which had smoldered to embers. I couldn't move without waking Neven, so I stayed perfectly still as he drew closer. In the dim cave, the only light was the reflection of the dying fire in his eyes. I didn't dare breathe, afraid that the moment would shatter.

Hiro tucked a strand of wet hair behind my ear. His fingers, hot as embers, grazed my cheek and stayed there, holding me perfectly still while barely touching me at all. My heart beat so fast inside the frozen cage of my body that I thought I might break into a thousand pieces if not for Hiro's touch somehow holding all of me together.

I thought of Tennyson's poems, how love and Death were supposed to be archenemies, light and darkness. But Tennyson had never known Reapers or Shinigami, or the look in Hiro's eyes like he saw the entire universe in me, the darkness in his eyes that somehow looked starving, ready to devour everything, and maybe I wanted to be devoured.

"Ren," Hiro said, the word a reverent whisper as he leaned closer. Not Wren or Ren of London, just the name written on my spine, the one thing that I knew for certain I truly was.

Neven shifted in my lap.

Hiro drew back without a word, so fast that I wondered for a moment if I'd imagined everything, but I could still hear the quick drum of his heartbeat from across the embers.

Neven turned over and lay still again, and Hiro waved a hand to reignite the fire.

He stood up, stretching his arms above his head. "This has been a lovely discussion," he said, avoiding eye contact, "but if we want our clothes to dry by morning, we should wash some of the blood out now."

I looked down at Neven, who still snored against my leg. "I—"

"I'll go first," Hiro said, already walking to the mouth of the cave. "You watch over him. I'll return soon."

Then he strode into the darkness, headed for the sea.

I leaned against the cave wall, dazed by Hiro's quick departure. One of my hands began stroking Neven's matted hair again. More scar tissue had formed in his neck. That was a good sign. I imagined his body regenerating all the lost blood and slowly circulating it through his veins.

I turned my head, and through the opening of the cave, I could see Hiro in the water, partially hidden behind the rocks.

He started undoing the ties of his kimono, and heat rushed

to my face. I should have looked away, but I kept stone-still as Hiro shrugged out of his jacket and cast it to the ground. This was wrong. It was indecent and impolite and I absolutely needed to look away right this instant, but for some reason I didn't move at all, my skin turning feverish as I watched Hiro undress.

The skin of his neck and shoulders glowed even more than what I could normally see around his kimono, highlighting the muscles around his shoulder blades. Like me, he had his name tattooed in kanji across his spine, harsh strokes of black stark against his pale skin. The characters—

—didn't say *Hiro*.

My hand tensed in Neven's hair. I leaned closer, trying my best to get a clear look from around the rocks.

I knew from my studies in London that there were different ways to write *Hiro*, but I'd never seen it written with the characters on Hiro's back. Those characters together were unfamiliar to me. At least, I thought they were. I'd caught only a quick glimpse before he'd moved behind a rock. I wanted to crawl closer to be sure of what I was seeing, but Neven was still sleeping on my leg.

While Reapers had spectacular hearing, we weren't known for having extraordinary vision, if Neven's severe nearsightedness was any indication. Even under the best of circumstances, I wasn't very good at reading Japanese. Hiro was not only distant and poorly lit but constantly moving, preventing me from getting a better look.

I heard a splash as he went into the water and knew my chance had been lost.

I turned my gaze to the ceiling. The more I tried to recall

what I had seen, the less certain I was of the characters. The only thing I couldn't deny was the feeling of shock that had coursed through me when he'd first revealed his tattoo, when whatever I'd seen hadn't been what I'd expected.

It was entirely possible that I'd been mistaken. My Japanese was far from perfect, especially my ability to read kanji. And perhaps Hiro was short for something else. Regardless, there wasn't a way I could ask him about it without revealing that I'd watched him undress. If it turned out that I'd been wrong, or that *Hiro* was simply a nickname, he would never stop teasing me for being a voyeur.

But if I wasn't wrong, that meant that Hiro wasn't really Hiro at all. What could possess him to tell me how to kill him, but not tell me his real name? What kind of power could his name possibly hold?

"What does it mean, Neven?" I whispered.

His only answer was his slow and stable breathing. I closed my eyes to that comforting sound, and the faraway murmurs of cold water crashing against black rocks, and the footsteps of the Shinigami who called himself Hiro crossing the shore, returning.

CHAPTER 16

And last, there was Tamamo No Mae.

Hiro had found us a train to Yahiko, saying his myriad connections had told him Tamamo No Mae was rumored to be there. He'd told me she was a Kitsune—a fox shape-shifter—but every time I asked him to sit down and help me read her story in Hakutaku's book, he changed the subject.

Neven was fast asleep, drooling against the window, while I had unrolled Hakutaku's book and was busy glaring at the characters as if I could translate them through sheer anger.

"You're going to burn a hole in the paper," Hiro said as he watched me reread the same line for the tenth time.

"I don't understand what you're trying to hide from me," I said, my voice colder than I'd meant it to be. But this was about more than Tamamo No Mae. I couldn't help remembering the kanji on his back. It wasn't fair that one warm look from Hiro made me want to unravel, yet he withheld so much from me.

The smile fell off Hiro's face. He stood up and sat next to me once again, smoothing out the paper.

"I'm sorry," he said, his eyes far too wide and far too close to me. "It wasn't my intention to anger you."

I looked away. Hiro's face was too painfully earnest. No one had ever apologized to me before. The only person who cared enough to do so was Neven, and he never did anything wrong.

"Help me read it," I said softly to the paper, rather than acknowledge his apology.

"Of course," Hiro said, nodding quickly. "Anything, Ren."

Then he smoothed out the scroll and told me the story of Tamamo No Mae.

On a cool morning in late autumn, a train arrived in the mountains of Yahiko village.

A man stepped off the train, the shadow behind him twice as long as he was tall, as dark as all of Yomi. He had black eyes like burning coal, and was the most handsome man that anyone in Yahiko, or Japan, had ever seen.

His name was Hiro.

I shot Hiro a flat glare. "That is not what the story says."

"No," he said, grinning, "but it's true, isn't it?"

"You're trying to distract me."

"You don't think it's true? I'm hurt."

"You're being evasive."

"Is it working?"

I sighed, turning back to the paper. "I can read this line," I said. "It says, 'Hiro was beaten to death by his companion for his arrogance and for wasting her time. The end.'"

Hiro nodded in approval. "Yes, he probably deserved that ending."

"If only he hadn't been so impertinent and had simply told her what was happening, maybe he wouldn't have died."

"Perhaps," he said, shrugging, "but we'll never know what might have been."

"Hiro," I said, frowning, "why won't you tell me about Tamamo No Mae? You didn't act this way with the other Yokai."

"Because she's not like them," Hiro said, gaze falling to the story that I couldn't read. "Other Yokai are perpetual, but Tamamo No Mae changes. Hakutaku's book is helpful up to a certain point, but it is very old, and the Tamamo No Mae we will find is very new."

He glanced at me, as if gauging my reaction, then looked back at the table. "There are rumors about what she's like now, but I want to confirm them with the Shinigami in Ya-hiko before I tell you. The things I've heard are...unpleasant."

"I also find it rather unpleasant to walk into the den of a dangerous Yokai unprepared," I said.

Hiro shook his head. "You don't need to storm the village with a knife in each hand. She's not going to hurt us unless we get in her way. There will be time to plan, Ren, I promise."

Something in my expression must have distressed him, be-cause he set his hand on top of mine and leaned across the table.

"I promise," he said. "I told you when we first met in Yomi that I wouldn't lead you astray, and I haven't forgotten that. I won't let anything hurt you."

His eyes had a strangely dark intensity, and there was a bitterness to his words, like the thought of me being hurt actually angered him. His hand squeezed mine hard enough to bruise a human, but for me it only registered as a dull ache.

"Please, trust me," he said.

I swallowed, staring back at maybe-Hiro. He was withholding more information than I was comfortable with, but he had also saved both my life and my brother's, and that warranted a certain degree of trust. Perhaps his real name was inconsequential when it was so easy to see what was in his heart. After all, I too had more than one name.

"Fine," I said. "But you will tell me everything tonight."

Hiro nodded. "I will," he said, leaning back in his seat and crossing his arms. "But soon, you'll wish I hadn't."

Yahiko turned out to be a small village tucked away at the foot of a mountain, sitting low on fertile plains and shielded from the East Sea by smooth green-and-white slopes. We crossed the endless stretch of rice and edamame fields between the train station and village as the sun drew low on the horizon.

As soon as I set foot on the fields, my footsteps scorched the surrounding crops into parched gray. It seemed my shoes were no longer enough of a barrier from the Death that seeped from my skin. Hiro coaxed me into letting him carry me on his back until we cleared the fields, and while I hated feeling so helpless, it was better than destroying a town's harvest and announcing our arrival with a trail of Death behind us. Hiro carried me like I weighed nothing at all, his hands warm and gentle under my knees. I passed the time by counting the beats of his heart against mine. The touch felt bizarrely normal, as if we were humans who held each other because we wanted to and not because we were trying to outrun Death.

Neven could finally walk without my help, though he occasionally lurched as if he was still halfway dreaming. The wound on his neck had scarred to smooth white, blending back into his skin by the hour. I kept a close eye on him, partially in case he fell over, and partially because we now had only one clock between us.

We'd scoured the rocks for my clock by morning, but it had fallen so deeply into a crevice that none of us could see it or move the heavy rocks aside. Judging by the rate my curse was worsening, we didn't have time to forge me a new one. Fine silver and gold were harder to come by in rural Japan than in London. Hunting down the materials and testing their quality would have been a fourth mission in and of itself. It was best to simply share with Neven, since we had only one Yokai left, and forge a new clock after Izanami hopefully resolved whatever was wrong with me.

"This is a sacred place," Hiro said as we drew closer, the ground sloping downward and mountains growing grander as the land peeled back to reveal them. "The great grandson of Amaterasu lived here."

"Amaterasu?" Neven said, stumbling slightly as the ground grew uneven.

"The goddess of the sun and the universe," I said. "One of Izanami's children."

"Izanami can have children?" Neven said.

I waited for Hiro to explain, as he could probably answer Neven's questions better than me, but he was staring at the distant village as if we didn't exist. Whatever horrors Tamamo No Mae had in store for us certainly troubled him.

"Not anymore," I said. "But she had two children without bones after she ruined her marriage ritual, then the next eight formed the islands of Japan. She had a few more that formed minor islands, and the last one killed her in childbirth. When Izanagi went down to Yomi to see her, Amaterasu and the sea and moon gods were born when he washed his face."

Hiro hummed in agreement, gaze still fixed on the village. I wished once more that he would just tell me about Tamamo No Mae rather than let me imagine the worst.

The air grew cooler as we descended into the mountain shade. The village before us felt like a secret, hidden from the sea behind the great wall of Mount Yahiko and all alone among the patchwork fields of rice that stretched to the horizon.

We passed under a great vermillion torii gate and entered the village. Hiro stopped to set me down on the dirt path.

Stepping into Yahiko was like slipping into place in my own story, like I'd been destined my whole life to arrive there at that exact moment. As soon as we passed through the gate, the sky seemed to unfold in endless white, as if some celestial being had peeled open the Earth to look down at us. I didn't believe in any gods that I hadn't seen with my own eyes, yet I couldn't deny that something sacred had passed through this village.

The houses of Yahiko pressed close together, not crammed

and crushed like in Yomi, but huddled like comfortable friends. The trees must have looked lush and green in the spring, but in late autumn only tanned branches and bare trunks remained, the last of the brown leaves crisp under our feet. Death nudged me toward the surrounding forest, so there must have been a graveyard nearby.

"I'm going to look for the Shinigami who presides over this village," Hiro said. "I need to get some information from him."

"All right," I said, starting to wave Neven over from where he'd knelt down to pet a stray cat.

Hiro shook his head, holding up a hand to stop me. "Please understand, the rural Shinigami are more traditional. He may not take kindly to foreigners asking questions."

My face fell into a frown as I realized what Hiro was trying to say. Just how long would the label *foreigner* follow me in the land where I was born? I looked across the street to where Neven knelt, the silver chain of his clock dangling from his pocket like shackles binding him to London. The loss of my own clock no longer stung as much as when the chain had first broken.

Hiro sighed, setting a hand on my arm that felt like lead. "It's not what I believe," he said, "but he won't see you as you are, Ren."

My body stiffened under Hiro's touch. Perhaps sensing my temper, he wisely dropped his hand.

"It's not just you," he said. "He's likely not going to be pleased to see me, either. It's best not to upset him twice."

I thought back to how "kindly" the last Shinigami had

taken to Hiro back at the hotel in Yomi. "You think he'll actually talk to you?"

Hiro shrugged, gaze drifting away. "We're here specifically on the Goddess's business, so he has to listen, at least."

"*I'm* here on her business."

"Ren," Hiro said, "he wouldn't even open his door for you. I'm sorry."

Light surged in my fingertips, but I clenched my fists and held it down. Hiro didn't mean to upset me. He was only speaking the truth. Perhaps when Izanami acknowledged me, the other Shinigami would be forced to follow her will and respect me.

"Come find us when you're finished," I said, my jaw clenched hard enough to shatter my teeth.

Hiro sighed, visibly relieved that I hadn't argued further. "It's not a large village. I'm sure you won't be hard to find."

"Because I look so foreign."

Hiro shook his head. "Because I'm drawn to you," he said, shooting me a wicked smile. I didn't have a chance to feel embarrassed before he turned and hurried off.

"Has he left us?" Neven said, returning to my side.

"For the moment," I said, watching as Hiro disappeared down a side street. "Are you lucid enough to explore?"

"I can do that," Neven said, letting me take his arm and pull him toward a forest path. I didn't like the idea of being boxed into the small village roads, no matter how empty. Besides, Death was pulling me into the woods.

The late autumn light cast the forest in the shade of dried amber, the trees reduced to slender lines drawn from the earth up to the white sky. The crackling of dead leaves beneath our feet resembled the sound of fire as we wove through the trees and found a small trodden path.

We followed the sound of whispers up a grand set of stone stairs that opened to a pebbled courtyard warm with sunlight. A large shrine loomed over the yard, its walls built from scorched black wood and its sloped roof ornamented with gold. An elderly couple meandered around the gravel yard while a family of three took off their shoes and entered the shrine.

"It's beautiful," Neven said, moving closer to the shrine.

Neven's English caused the elderly couple to turn their heads in our direction. For one guilty moment, I wished I were here with Hiro instead, speaking Japanese, doing my best not to draw attention to myself. I let my arm slip from Neven's and drift down to my side. He didn't seem to notice, craning for a better view.

"Let's go this way," I said, wary of the lingering gaze of the couple.

"But I want to see—"

"Later," I said, pulling Neven around the back of the building to the smaller auxiliary shrines. Unlike the majesty of the main shrine, these fell under the silent shade of the forest and what little it retained of its foliage. They formed a ghostly village of tiny houses, all connected by a paved stone path, guarded by stone lions patchy with moss. Maybe it was the lack of humans or the quiet or the sacredness of the whole village, but a sense of calm spread like cool water through my blood.

"It looks a bit like the mausoleums at Highgate," Neven said.

And there, once more, was the constant reminder that I was shackled.

"It's different," I said.

"I don't know," Neven said, strolling down the path, "the arrangement is similar."

His eyes had gone pale purple with wistfulness. He was probably imagining London in autumn and missing it terribly. A good sister would have cared, but instead I felt frustrated that he could see Japan only through the lens of "Not London."

"It's different," I said again. But this time he heard the heaviness in my voice and turned to face me.

"Have I offended you?" he said, a sour look on his lips, just like when he'd snapped at me on the shores of Takaoka. Apparently his near-death experience hadn't lessened his bitterness.

"I don't want to hear about London," I said. "We'll never return, so it's not relevant anymore."

"So we just erase it from our memories?" Neven said, voice rising and eyes darkening.

"You can do whatever you want with your memories, I just don't want to hear about it."

Neven scoffed, kicking some rocks in his path. "Is our heritage so repulsive to you?"

"It's not that simple," I said.

"It never is, with you."

I closed my eyes, consciously swallowing down a sudden surge of darkness crawling up my throat. A village shrine was not the best place to start shouting in English if I hoped to blend in.

"Neven," I said, "I just don't need to be constantly reminded that—"

"That we're Reapers," Neven said, scowling. "Believe me, I've noticed."

I knew he meant it as a fact, but the word *Reaper* had never before stung badly. No one had called me that in London, yet the title had followed me like a curse to Japan, worse than being called a half-breed or a whore. Could he not see that all the blood on my hands was for the sake of becoming a Shinigami? That I would give anything for it? He had done things he hated just to be the perfect Reaper son that Ambrose wanted, so how dare he judge me for trying to become a Shinigami, for wanting to stand before my mother as someone strong and whole?

"Are we?" I said. "Are we really Reapers?"

Neven frowned. "Of course—"

"*You* certainly are. But why am I granted the privilege of that title only now that I'm no longer in London?"

"Ren, don't be ridiculous," Neven said. "Our father is a Reaper."

"I have no father," I said. "You know this."

"Then am I even your brother?" Neven said, throwing his hands up in exasperation. "If you cut all ties to London, then what am I?"

"This isn't about you!" I said. The wind blasted a spray of dying leaves into the air, the sky growing dim. How could Neven, my only companion for over a century, be so incapable of understanding me and so utterly unwilling to try?

The fallen leaves beneath my feet crumbled to black dust, a circle of Death appearing around me. Of course London had followed me to this sacred place. No matter how far I ran, it always found me.

Water splashed somewhere behind me.

Neven and I both turned around as an elderly woman began washing her mouth at the fountain. In all my years collecting souls at the end of lifelines, I'd never seen such an ancient human. Her skin looked like wet crumpled paper, translucent gray and speckled with bruise-purple age spots. Snarled white hair hung down her back, each strand a delicate spider string twisted into a tangled mass. Every gnarled tendon of her neck stuck out through her loose and withered skin. How had she even ascended the steps to the shrine, or approached without Neven or me noticing? It was as if she'd simply materialized at the fountain.

"Come here," she said.

Her voice sounded jagged, sharp as the gravel beneath our feet. I stiffened, looking to Neven, whose eyes had gone wide.

A little girl came around the side of the fountain and took the old woman's hand. I let out a breath. She hadn't been addressing us.

The old woman washed the girl's hands and mouth with splashes of water that soaked the girl's clothes, making her whine and squirm. She grabbed the girl's wrist and turned around, suddenly facing us. Her hazy eyes locked onto mine with startling precision, considering the distance between us.

"And why have they let your kind into this sacred ground?" she said.

I couldn't find the energy to be offended, too transfixed by the odd feeling that had settled over the courtyard. From somewhere far away, Death had begun to pull in all directions, as if tiny hooks had bitten into my skin and lightly tugged, peeling skin from flesh. A faraway static filled my ears, the edges of the world fizzling away. Neven had gone rigid by my side.

"Are you dumb, as well?" the woman said. "Come to these sacred places and you can't even speak our language."

"Grandma," the little girl said, tugging on the old woman's sleeve with impatience. The woman yanked the sleeve away, making the girl stumble and grab her skirt for balance.

"We're just passing through," I said, not able to put much anger behind the words when I was too busy figuring out why the world was crushing down on all sides. The old woman didn't emanate Death like a Reaper or Shinigami, nor did she seem to be dying, despite her age. Instead, Death crawled up from the dirt beneath her feet and pulled color from the sky.

Disregarding the fact that I'd actually spoken in Japanese, the old woman scoffed. "These gods have no interest in people like you. Go trample through a different village."

She took a step forward as if to blaze through us, but Neven moved forward at the same time, standing between me and the woman. He crossed his arms and stood still in her path, his eyes hard purple quartz, his clock gripped tight in his right hand. He couldn't have understood much of the conversation, but he definitely would have noticed the pull of Death around us.

They both froze in an odd standoff—a decrepit old woman and a scrawny nearsighted teenager, glaring like they were about to grab each other's throats. The combined energy of Death began to peel the last clinging leaves from the trees, melting the slender shadows of the barren trunks into solid pools of darkness around our feet. What kind of creature could impact the world so severely?

Hurried footsteps stomped up the stone staircase and all four of us turned. Hiro appeared at the final stair into the courtyard and leaned on a nearby stone lantern for balance. His eyes cast over me and Neven, then slid to the old woman and her granddaughter. Suddenly, his breath caught in his throat and his grip went rigid on the lantern.

"Come here," he said, barely above a whisper. "Now."

I shot one last look at the old woman and slowly edged away. Neven seemed more reluctant to abandon his stance, his limbs uncooperative as I tugged him away, still glaring over his shoulder as if the woman would leap across the courtyard and attack us from behind.

Hiro waited until we'd reached the top of the stairs, then spun around and hurried back down, waving for us to follow.

"I leave you alone for twenty minutes and somehow you find her," he said.

"That was her?" I said, looking back over my shoulder. But the old woman had vanished in the sparse trees. "Why are we letting her get away?"

"She's not 'getting away,'" Hiro said. "She's not running or hiding, and it won't be difficult to find her again in this tiny village. But there's a lot you need to know about her before we go forward. The presiding Shinigami confirmed what I'd suspected."

"Which is?"

"That she's definitely Tamamo No Mae," he said, sounding strangely disappointed.

"That explains why the sky was curdling like milk from all the Death around her," Neven said.

"And why she was so charming," I said, scowling.

Neven checked over his shoulder once more, walking faster. "What was she saying to you?"

"Nothing I haven't heard before. Let's just say I have no qualms about ending her now."

Hiro slowed down, casting me an odd look over his shoulder. "She insulted you?"

"She wouldn't be the first," I said, waving a dismissive hand. "Will you finally tell me how to kill her now?"

Hiro stopped walking, looking between me and Neven like all three of us were speaking a different language.

"You're oddly impassive about this," he said.

"You haven't told us what there is to fear!" I said, throwing my hands up in exasperation. "She looks about thirty years overdue for a soul collection. I'm honestly surprised she didn't turn to dust when the wind changed, so *what*, pray tell, makes her so horrible?"

Hiro's eyes flashed with understanding, then his expression turned sour. "Ren," he said, "Tamamo No Mae is not the old woman. She's the little girl."

CHAPTER 17

The Legend of Tamamo No Mae went something like this:

Long before humans began counting years, a Kitsune was born in a forest in China where tall trees blocked out all the sunlight. She crawled from the darkness of the forest and met the world, and when she saw all of its light and splendor, she knew she had to devour it.

She grew up more beautiful than clear moonlight, able to speak all the languages of the world and recite every book in the royal library. With her beauty and sweet words, she could make men do anything she wanted.

First, she called herself Daji and ensnared King Zhou. She whispered in his ear, and his eyes went dark and hollow like moon craters. He promised her his kingdom and all its subjects to prove his love for her, so she took his hand in marriage and became China's Queen of Darkness.

Her subjects became her toys. She cut the feet off farmers to see why they were so sturdy. She cut out the belly of a pregnant woman to see what an unborn child looked like. When the king's concubine protested, Daji cut her into a thousand pieces and fed her flesh to the peasants. When the people grew to hate her king, and the Shang Dynasty collapsed from her cruelty, she vanished.

Next, she fled to India and called herself Lady Kayo. She whispered in King Kalmashapada's ear, and a feral darkness washed over his eyes, his teeth lengthening like a wolf's. He began inviting children into his palace and locking them in shadowed rooms. Lady Kayo would hold them down while her king ate their flesh with his bare hands and sharp teeth. He swallowed their organs and sucked the meat from their ribs, bit their eyeballs like grapes and drank their burning blood like wine. When all of the children were gone, and her king lay choking on their bones, Lady Kayo grew bored and disappeared once more.

Finally, she came to Japan, this time not as a woman, but as a baby. A human couple raised her as Mikuzume, more beautiful than fields of lavender and wiser than all the court scholars. She recited the poems of oracle shells in Emperor Toba's court in Nasuno, her words so enchanting that he begged her to come closer. She whispered sweet words in the emperor's ear, and a gray fog overcame his bright eyes. He made her his wife and gave her the name Tamamo No Mae: Lady Duckweed, for the dainty leaves that float in lakes.

Then the children of Nasuno began to disappear.

At night, they vanished from their beds, even through locked doors and windows, they slipped away so suddenly and silently that it was like they'd never existed at all.

The emperor grew ill, too weak to speak a single word, his face gray, but his eyes screamed with an urgent message that no one could hear. Every day he grew weaker, and every day the children of Nasuno continued to disappear. The court prepared for the inevitable day when Tamamo No Mae would ascend as queen regent upon her heirless husband's death.

On one foggy night, the palace priest saw Tamamo No Mae leave the grounds, shifting into a nine-tailed fox as she ran into the forest. He prayed to the gods for guidance, and their verdict was unanimous:

Tamamo No Mae must die, or all of Japan will fall.

The imperial army chased after her for months, but she was always too fast, too clever, too strong to be captured.

But after four months and four days, the king's strongest soldiers found the fox asleep in a clearing, lit by pale moonlight. As she slept, one soldier fired arrows through the fox's stomach and neck, while the other severed her head with his blade. The fox did not fight back, bleeding dark blood into the wet soil.

Back in Nasuno, Emperor Toba awoke from his deep sleep. He remembered nothing of Tamamo No Mae, or his strange illness, but the gray fog never left his eyes.

The children of Nasuno were never found, but at night the walls of the castle creaked and groaned as if in agony, and everyone who slept in the palace could hear nothing but the screams of children in their dreams.

No one dared to admit what they all knew: that Tamamo

No Mae had allowed herself to be killed. That she had given up only when her plans had gone awry, and that a creature like Tamamo No Mae would never truly end.

She is not gone. She is waiting.

I put all my concentration into not shattering the porcelain teacup in my hands.

We were sitting on the floor of a small café, a kettle of wheat tea and Hakutaku's book between us on the low table. The other customers watched warily as we spoke in English, but Hiro paid them no mind. I was beginning to understand why Hiro hadn't wanted to mention this in passing.

"You're certain this is the same girl we saw?" I said.

Hiro downed the rest of his teacup like a shot of alcohol, then poured himself another steaming cup. Neven had long since abandoned his cup to stare slack-jawed at Hiro.

"The old woman found her by the side of the road and named her Mikuzume," he said. "It's the same as in her legend."

"You want Ren to kill a child because the old woman picked a strange name?" Neven said.

"The presiding Shinigami here has been watching her since her appearance," Hiro said, turning away from Neven and speaking only to me. "She's already showing signs of unusual intelligence. The humans of the village might be weak and pliant, but I know you can sense Death around her."

I stared at my reflection in my teacup. "If she's already been killed once and come back, then what's the point of killing her again?"

"Time," Hiro said, shrugging. "She's been quiet for seven

hundred years since the last time she was killed. She's a creature of Buddhist origins, so she's always going to be reincarnated, but I imagine that Izanami wants to stop her while she's small and weak."

"You mean 'helpless,'" Neven said, frowning. "Her story might be different this time, since we know who she is. We could keep her far from any royalty. Buddhists don't believe in predeterminism. They think we're in control of our own fates."

I had known as much, but unlike Neven, hadn't wanted to say it out loud.

"Though she may be Buddhist, she's still a Yokai under Izanami's domain," Hiro said, each word chosen carefully, as if to placate Neven. "She must have decided this was too great a risk."

"But..." Neven's fingers twitched like he wanted to grab something. "Does she even remember her past life?"

Hiro's gaze slid to me, grimacing at Neven's line of questioning. "I'm no Buddhist," he said, "but to my understanding, no. One usually cannot access memories of past lives without concerted spiritual effort."

"So she won't even know why she's being killed?" Neven said. I wished he would stop asking questions I didn't want to hear the answers to.

Hiro shook his head, unable to meet Neven's gaze.

"She hasn't even done anything!" Neven said, slamming his fist on the table and rattling the teacups. Everyone in the café turned toward us. I grabbed Neven's arm, my face flushed hot.

"Calm down," I said, my nails biting into his wrist.

He yanked his arm away from me. "You're not considering this, are you?"

I said nothing. It was so easy for Neven to moralize when he wasn't the one who'd suffer the consequences. Of course I didn't want to kill a child. But I also didn't want to live forever in isolation, as neither a Reaper nor a Shinigami. Tamamo No Mae could die quickly and painlessly, and in exchange I would have thousands of years of freedom. And if Hiro was right, I'd be saving a lot of humans, too.

"Neven, just think about this for a moment," I said.

"I have!" Neven said. "That girl hasn't done anything. Tamamo No Mae could just as easily have been reborn in your body."

"Would you stake your compassion on the thousands of lives lost if you're wrong?" Hiro said. But his words sounded empty, and I had a feeling he was trying to redirect Neven's anger toward himself more than actually defend his position.

It didn't work. Neven ignored Hiro, eyes focused solely on my face.

"Ren, is this really what you want?"

I knew in that moment that I was a horrible person, because my heart didn't hesitate to say *yes*. The word thrummed through my bones and blood and every part of me. While I didn't want to hurt the little girl, I didn't want to hurt myself anymore, either. Her life should have mattered more to me. I should have cared more. But I didn't.

"I don't know," I said.

But Neven knew I was lying, and the look of betrayal on his face was ten times worse than the guilt of not caring enough about the little girl.

"Fine," he said, yanking his clock from his pocket and slamming it on the table. "I don't want anything to do with it."

"Neven—"

"Find me when you're finished," he said, standing up and storming out of the café.

I picked up his clock, feeling no joy that he wasn't going to stop me.

"Will you really do it, Ren?" Hiro said.

I looked down at my hands in my lap, turning the clock back and forth between them.

"I've... I've collected children's souls before," I said, trying to convince myself that this was normal.

"That is not the same as killing them," he said. "I'm sure you know that."

"Do you want me to do this or not?" I said, glaring across the table.

He shook his head. "It's not about what I want. Whatever you decide, I will help you."

"What's her essence?" I said. "How do I..." I fumbled for words, imagining myself subduing the little girl the same way I'd killed the other Yokai and growing nauseous at the thought.

"Animal shifters must be hunted and killed like animals, usually with some sort of hunting tools," Hiro said. "Luckily, we have a guide for Tamamo No Mae, since she's been killed before."

"With arrows and a sword?" I said, the clock growing damp in my sweaty palms. "Cutting off her head?"

Hiro grimaced. "This is why I didn't want to tell you," he said.

I took a deep breath. "Well, you shouldn't have worried," I said. "I can do it." My words didn't even sound convincing to my own ears.

Hiro sighed. "I know you *can*, Ren, but—"

"I *will* do it," I said. "I told you before, I'll do anything. If this is what Izanami wants, then I don't have a choice."

Hiro looked at me across the table, his eyes flat. "You do have a choice," he said.

"Then I choose to be a Shinigami," I said, even as my hands shook underneath the table, "no matter the cost."

The new Tamamo No Mae lived in a small hut at the top of a large hill. As Hiro had promised, we had no trouble finding her again, for the scent of Death carried down the hill and dispersed into the streets like some sort of noxious perfume. As we climbed higher, Death's presence crushed down harder and harder, as if we were walking deeper and deeper underwater. Now that I knew how much blood the Yokai had on her hands, the way Death shrouded her made sense—her destiny and Death were forever intertwined.

Hiro had somehow charmed a local ronin samurai out of his katana and bow, or possibly just stolen them. Since I'd never shot an arrow, Hiro kept the bow slung over his shoulder while I wore the katana tucked under my belt. I couldn't fight with it to save my life, but hopefully I would need only a single blow.

We reached the top of the hill, with all of Yahiko spread out below us, the tiny houses lit by moonlight and stars. A short walk away, we found the hut, little more than a dark wooden box with a mossy triangular hat on top. Through the walls, I could make out the muffled sounds of a broom and slow footsteps on weak floorboards. A pale light burned through the windows, shrouded by the spidery branches of a dying maple tree.

Something shifted in the leaves.

We both froze, eyes scanning the dark for the sound's source. While not anywhere near as dark as Yomi, the scarcity of lanterns in the village left the night a swirl of distant gray and formless shapes. The sound had definitely come from the yard, but I couldn't find its source.

Hiro tapped my arm and pointed. I followed his gesture to a pile of leaves on the side of the hut.

A baby fox slept among the crinkled brown and red leaves. She couldn't have been bigger than my forearm, her tiny tail tucked up against her chin, triangular face tilted sideways on a pillow of branches. Another tail swung in her sleep, followed by many more red tails, all waving in a bright fan before settling back to the leaves.

"Mikuzume!" the old woman's coarse voice called from inside.

The fox startled awake, bright blue eyes opening.

Hiro grabbed my arm and pulled me behind a plum tree, drawing the darkness over us. I peered through the veil of night at the baby fox glancing back and forth with star bright eyes, probably wondering where the sound of footsteps had come from. Her large ears swiveled, her tiny jaw opening in a yawn and letting out a catlike squeak. She scooted her front paws forward in the leaves, closing her eyes as she stretched. All of her tails fanned out behind her like a crimson display of peacock feathers. I counted nine of them swinging back and forth.

"Mikuzume!" the old woman called again. "Come to bed!"

This time, the fox hopped to her feet and pranced around the back of the house, out of sight. I heard a door slide open and a little girl's voice calling "Here, Grandma!" before the door slammed shut again.

This was the great monster I was meant to dismember. My stomach felt full of rocks.

Hiro released the darkness around us, stepping back from the tree.

I took Neven's clock in my left hand and the night went still. In the infinite moment before I woke Hiro with my touch, I ran my fingers across the bite marks in Neven's clock and wished he were here. Not to see me become the monster he already thought I was, but to force me to be cold and un-breakable. What a selfish thought, to want my brother to be traumatized just to comfort me while I murdered. I couldn't think about Neven anymore without feeling nauseous shame in my stomach, so I reached out and touched Hiro's hand, breaking him from the time freeze.

He only took a moment to look around at the frozen night before turning back to me. "Whenever you're ready," he said. "I'll wait for you in the backyard." Then he walked around the house and disappeared in the dark.

Standing before the house reminded me too much of my time as a Reaper, when I'd waited in hallways and listened to the humans' mundane conversations and unhurried footsteps, going calmly through their evening routines with no notion that soon I would come in to end them. Their ignorance had always given me a sick sense of power, as if I were Death himself and not merely his puppet. But now that I truly wore the gloves of Death, I felt no self-importance, nothing even close. Instead, nervousness rattled in my stomach in a way I hadn't known since my first collections. I didn't want this power.

I crossed the lawn, my footsteps across the grass the loudest sound in this silent world. The front door was predictably locked, so I walked to the side of the house.

It's just like a collection, I thought as I slid open a paper window and slipped inside. *You've done this thousands of times.*

The hut had only one room, in disarray from the toys and cooking supplies. Tamamo No Mae and her grandmother had gone to bed, lying next to each other on reed mats and blankets. The grandmother lay on her side, stiff and unbreathing from the time freeze, while the girl lay on her back, arms raised up beside her head. I had hoped to find her in her fox form so I could see her as more of an animal, but she lay as a human beside the old woman, dressed in a white nightgown with sleeves that covered her hands and a hem that passed her toes.

I slid my hand behind her head and lifted her up to my shoulder, careful to touch only her clothes and not her skin. Her body was stiff from time freeze, but still warm and soft and smelled of autumn from her nap in the leaves. *I carried Neven like this when he was first born*, I thought, and had to stop walking until I could force the thought down and lock it away. I couldn't think about Neven right now.

I unlatched the door and stepped out into the backyard. Hiro stood waiting with his bow and arrow as I lay her down in the grass a short distance from the house.

"Are you ready, Ren?"

I swallowed, nodding and taking a few steps back. I looked up at the stars as Hiro nocked his first arrow. For a few seconds of tense silence, he took aim. Then the arrow whizzed through the air and cut wetly into a flesh target, my jaw locking as I imagined where it had struck. He didn't hesitate to nock a second arrow, that too sinking into flesh with a wet *thwack*. Was it truly so easy for him, or was he only pretending for my sake?

I heard him set his bow down in the grass, then he approached me and placed a hand on my back. He guided me toward the girl, still peacefully asleep but this time with an arrow stabbed through her heart and the side of her neck. It was easy to pretend they weren't real when the time freeze had congealed her blood and she wasn't awake to feel or show pain. I didn't need to feel sympathy, because I knew this much alone wouldn't be enough to kill her. Nothing truly terrible had befallen her yet.

I pressed Neven's clock to the inside of my wrist and looped the chain around twice, securing it there. Hiro stepped back as I unsheathed the katana and held it in front of me with both hands.

This is easy, I told myself. *It's the easiest mission you've had.*

When I killed her, Izanami would free me from my curse. I could build a safe home in Yomi for myself and my brother. I would wear red robes, and all the creatures in Yomi and Earth would have no choice but to respect me.

It was easy, because she looked like a human and I didn't even like humans that much. It was easy, because I'd time-frozen her and she couldn't attack or run away. It was easy, because all I had to do was bring my arms down.

My arms shook from the weight of the katana.

I am a selfish person, and her life doesn't matter to me, I thought. *Not compared to what my reward will be.*

But if that was true, then why couldn't I move?

I reached for the pull of Death that I'd felt when I'd slain Iso Onna, needing it to wreck and ravage me, awaken an insatiable craving for blood and suffering. I needed to be that person, wild and strong and selfish. But Death stayed tucked away some place deep and small inside me, and instead my heart filled up with nothingness. Why now, of all times, had Death abandoned me?

I closed my eyes and told myself I would count to three and bring my arms down. But I counted to three and then twenty-three and then sixty-three and I still couldn't move, my arms frozen, the blade now shaking violently in my hands.

I made the mistake of looking down at the girl, her eyes closed in tranquil sleep, her cheeks still swollen with baby fat, her bangs cut in an uneven line across her forehead. I thought of Gray Westbrook's face as years of his life were ripped away, and the frozen families in Shirakawa-go shattering to pieces, and the look on Neven's face that said he would never, ever forgive me for this. I tried to see a monster who had ravaged Japan and would do so again, but I could only see a little girl. Just like me, she would suffer not for what she'd done, but for who she was.

I lowered my arms slowly, setting the blade down in the grass as I knelt beside it. Even without its weight, my arms trembled.

"I can't," I whispered.

And with that admission, hot tears burned across my eyes and scorched down my face like acid as I finally realized that I would never be a Shinigami. I'd come all this way, nearly lost my brother, and all of it was for nothing. Without my anger, I was weak and sentimental like a human, and for that I would live and die alone.

Hiro didn't encourage me to do it. He stood beside me while I cried, the sounds loud and ugly in our small sphere of petrified night. After a moment, he picked up the sword.

"I can," he said.

My tears dried up instantly. I choked on a startled breath and shook my head.

"No, no, it has to be me," I said, my hands clenching fistfuls of grass. "Izanami will know, she'll know I didn't—"

"She won't know," Hiro said, his aura oddly dark and stoic, like a shadow that loomed behind you in a dark alley at night. "She'll sense the change in energy when a Yokai's soul leaves Earth, but she won't know how or why."

I shook my head again. "It's my job," I said, wiping my eyes with dirty sleeves. "You've done so much already. If you do this for me, too, then what have I even done to appease Izanami? I haven't earned the right to be a Shinigami. I'm weak."

"Ren," Hiro said, kneeling beside me. He set the katana on his lap and tucked my hair behind my ear. "Do you truly believe that murder is what makes you a Shinigami?"

"If not this, then what?" I said, hiding my face behind trembling hands. "What more could I possibly do?"

"These tests are a formality," Hiro said. "You don't earn

the right to be a Shinigami, Ren. Izanami doesn't have the power to make you what you already are."

But what was I? I had no idea what it meant to be a Shinigami, other than my black hair and eyes and light and everyone in London telling me I was not a Reaper. For all my life, I'd been defined by who I wasn't. What was left underneath when you scraped away all the things I wasn't allowed to be?

"I'll do it for you, if you want me to," Hiro said.

I swallowed, then looked up at him. In the darkness, with the moonlight glaring off the katana in his hand, he looked like some sort of ghostly warrior.

"Why?" I said. "You shouldn't want to do this for me."

"I would do anything for you," he said, as if it were that simple.

"Don't say that," I said, looking away. "You can't just..." I trailed off as Hiro cupped my face, forcing me to look at him.

"Do you think I'm lying?" he said, his breath brushing across my face.

"I don't know," I said. I couldn't think clearly with him so close, his hand so warm on my face.

Hiro pressed his forehead to mine. "I can show you," he whispered, his words warm on my lips. "I'll kill her for you, Ren. I'll kill anyone for you."

I shuddered and tried to look away, but Hiro raised his other hand to my face, holding my jaw still and brushing his thumb across my lower lip. His hands burned with fever, his eyes full of blazing coal. He looked like a nightmare, but I didn't push him away.

"Would you really?" I said. "Anyone?"

"Yes," he said, his fingers pressing harder into the soft skin of my face. "I would drown all the islands of Japan if you asked me to."

"That's horrible," I said, but still I didn't push him away. Was this not how humans showed affection? With grandiose declarations of devotion? I didn't know what it meant to love someone. All I knew was that being around Hiro made me feel dark and infinite, like every star in the universe burned inside the prison of my ribs.

"I am a creature of Death," Hiro said. "Of course I'm horrible. And so are you."

Then he leaned in and devoured me.

One hand locked my jaw in place while the other clutched my throat, my pulse hammering beneath his fingertips. His lips pried mine apart and our teeth clashed together but I wouldn't push him away, not when his hand slid to the back of my head and pressed me closer, inhaling me with his exquisite darkness. Hiro was a molten star in my arms as he pressed me into the dead grass, his bones laid out against mine. He tasted of dark nights alone on a coastal town and half moons and stars too far away to touch. I melted beneath him and he crushed me into the earth, and in that moment, for once in my life, I could not feel the pull of Death in any direction.

I reached out for his hand, my clock pressed between our palms. My other hand cradled the back of his head, but this time my fingers tightened, locking around a fistful of hair and dragging him down to me. I tasted the syrupy darkness of Death, caustic as it seared our tongues. I rolled on top of him and held him hard enough to shatter his bones, locked him in place like I was about to extract his soul, trapped him, a pinned butterfly, *mine*.

The silence of the frozen night amplified the sound of Hiro's heartbeat, his shuddering inhale as I bit and crushed and ruined him the way I ruined every good thing, and he lay there and let me. I leaned down and bit his neck, making him arch his back with a gasp. I thought of Iso Onna and an ocean full of blood.

I didn't realize the clock had slipped from my hand until the girl screamed.

I shot to my feet, heart racing and dizzy eyes casting around the darkness. Tamamo No Mae had sat up in the grass and was yanking out the arrows from her flesh like splinters. They barely had a chance to bleed before the wounds sealed shut, but she wailed all the same, cheeks covered in tears, the sound of her cries shattering the quiet night.

"Grandma!" she cried, tossing the arrows to the side and trying to crawl back to the house, stumbling over her night-gown.

Hiro picked up the katana from the grass without hesitation.

"Stop!" I said, grabbing his arm before he could get any closer to the girl. "Hiro, she's awake! You can't—"

The door to the hut slammed open, the old woman standing in the doorway. The darkness filled in the lines on her skin and sliced her face into sections, making her look like a puzzle barely held together. Since I stood closer to the door than Hiro, her gray eyes locked on to me and narrowed. Even when I'd told thousands of humans that they were going to die, I'd never seen so much rage as I saw in the old woman's eyes. The moonlight glinted on the sharp edge of a kitchen knife clutched in her right hand.

She charged across the yard with a ferocious scream, alarmingly fast for someone with crumbling bones and puckered gray skin. She held the knife above her head, aiming for my face or neck.

My clock still lay on the ground, so I waited for the old woman to come close enough that I could snap her wrist and take her knife.

But the moment never came, because Hiro ran between us and drove the katana through her chest.

The world fell into all its discrete pieces—Tamamo No Mae shrieking louder than Iso Onna, the old woman spilling blood from her lips with a wet retch, and Hiro bracing his left hand against the woman's chest to yank his katana out again. The old woman fell limp on the ground, pouring dark blood into the dirt.

"Why would you do that?" I said, barely feeling the words leave my lips. Tamamo No Mae kept shrieking at an ungodly volume, and I could hardly think above the noise. The old woman convulsed and gagged on her blood as Hiro calmly wiped his blade on the grass.

"She was going to kill you," he said, sheathing the katana.

"Humans can't kill me!" I said. "I've told you that before!"

Hiro said nothing in reply. The old woman twitched and gurgled, her blood running across the ground and soaking the soles of my shoes. I should have cut her throat, or banged her head against a rock, or something to end her feeble death throes. But Tamamo No Mae was still watching and shrieking, and I didn't know if such a display would actually be an act of mercy in her eyes.

"I'm sorry if I've upset you, Ren," Hiro said, his voice oddly measured for someone who had just slain a human in front of their granddaughter. "I just didn't want her to hurt you."

Once again, I didn't know whether to be touched or horrified. My gaze fell on the dark purple teeth marks on Hiro's neck, and my face burned. But it wasn't time to think about that, not when the old woman's corpse lay cooling at my feet, and Tamamo No Mae was...

I turned around, finding the yard empty. My ears rang from the memory of her screams, but she had slipped into the night.

"She's gone," I said, swiping Neven's clock off the ground.

"She can't be," Hiro said, eyes casting around the yard and finally beginning to echo the panic that had hammered through my veins since time had started again. "She was just here! Can't you stop time until we find her?"

"Not for the whole village," I said. "I'm going after her."

Then I took off running down the hill. I knew Hiro couldn't keep up with me and I felt bad for leaving him behind, but I needed to catch the Yokai before we lost her forever. I still felt the distant pull of Death, but if she ran too far from us, I could lose it entirely. She could so easily leave the village and run into the rice fields, dooming us to another century of searching.

As I reached the main road and once again Death began crushing the sky down onto me, I knew there was still time. I ran headfirst into the pull of Death, a headache already growing behind my eyes from the constant changing pressure in the air. But when I finally found the Yokai, the problems before me, once again, increased tenfold.

At the foot of a plum tree, by the light of a dim lantern, Neven sat with a nine-tailed fox curled up in his lap.

CHAPTER 18

"Neven, get away from her," I said, every muscle painfully tense as Neven stroked the fox's fur. Who knew what Tamamo No Mae was capable of when upset? I'd already nearly lost Neven to one Yokai. I wasn't about to watch a magic fox bite into his arteries or scratch his eyes out.

But Neven just raised an eyebrow, looking thoroughly unimpressed with me, and continued to pet the Yokai. She whined at the sound of my voice, burying her nose under the crook of Neven's elbow.

"This is the 'terrible Yokai' you were meant to kill?" he said.

"Put her down," I said. "She's dangerous."

The fox began to glisten, a thousand star flashes bathing her skin, and suddenly a human girl clung to Neven's side, her nightgown speckled with blood and her face wet with tears. She grabbed fistfuls of Neven's shirt and pulled herself up to his level, her mouth near his ear.

She whispered in his ear, and his eyes went dark and hollow like moon craters.

In her legend, this was how Tamamo No Mae unraveled all of the men she wanted to lead astray. But I wouldn't let her take Neven and turn him into one of her monstrous child-eaters.

"Don't listen to her!" I said, rushing forward to tear her from Neven's arms, but he shielded her and turned away with a scowl.

"What did she say?" I said, falling to my knees and grabbing Neven's shirt as he tried to push me away with his free hand. "Neven, *what did she say to you?*"

"I couldn't hear anything over your yelling!" Neven said, managing to shove me away. The Yokai wailed in his arms, far too loudly for such a late hour and such a quiet village, but Neven quickly wrapped his arms around her and petted her hair, eyes softening as he shushed her.

"She's already enchanted you," I said, the words like lead in my mouth as I fell back in the dirt.

Neven rolled his eyes. "She hasn't enchanted me, Ren!" he said. "You knew how I felt about this before I'd even met her!"

"You wouldn't know if she'd enchanted you!" I said. "You heard her story, it's what she does to men!"

He huffed out a breath, shaking his head. "Why is it so hard for you to believe that I'd want to stop an innocent child from being beheaded?" he said. "Not everyone is like you, Ren. I care about people other than myself."

I bit back my next words, too afraid of whatever cruelty would spill from my lips. Of course I'd always known I was selfish, but Neven had never said it out loud before, had never admitted that he saw me the same horrible way that I saw myself. No matter how rotten I'd felt inside, I'd always hoped that I could at least be enough for Neven. How stupid of me to think I could ever even pretend to be someone he deserved.

Maybe Neven was right, and this Yokai was really just a helpless child. She hadn't tried to harm me or Hiro, after all. She'd done nothing but cry like a human, and now that Neven had seen her teary face, he was never going to let her go.

I closed my eyes as the weight of the entire night sky collapsed on top of me—now it was far too late. If I hurt her, or let Hiro hurt her, Neven would hate me forever.

I sat down in the road and stared into the dirt, dazed and exhausted, while Neven rocked the girl back and forth. I didn't even turn around as Hiro approached. I had no idea where to go from here. For the first time in my life, I saw no escape route, no way that I could possibly win.

Hiro came to a stop beside me and surveyed the scene.

"Neven," he said, his voice dark.

"Don't bother," I said to the ground.

Neven stood up, the girl sniffling into his chest. "Where is her grandmother?" he said.

"Dead," I said.

Neven sighed, face twisting like both of us disgusted him. "Then what are we meant to do with her?"

"You know exactly what we're meant to do with her," Hiro said.

Neven hugged the girl even tighter. "Well, you won't!"

"Then your sister will never work as a Shinigami!" Hiro said. "Is that what you want?"

Neven looked at me, his eyes softening with guilt. "Of course not. Ren, I... I don't know how—"

I held up a hand to stop him, shaking my head. There was no point in having this argument. No point to anything at all. I might as well have just fed myself to the nearest Yokai and hoped that my soul ended up somewhere decent.

"Can we trick Izanami?" Neven said, turning back to Hiro. "Make her think that she's dead?"

Hiro scoffed. "You think it's that easy?"

Neven flinched at the anger in Hiro's voice, taking a step back. "I... I don't know, I just—"

"Why do you think she didn't ask Ren to bring back any proof that she'd killed the Yokai?" Hiro said, cutting through Neven's guilty stuttering. "She knows when the souls of her Yokai leave Earth. You can't simply ship her off somewhere else and lie through your teeth to a Death Goddess. She'd rip Ren's soul out on the spot."

"But she's just a child," Neven said, turning to me with wet eyes as if I was the one who needed convincing. "Ren, I'm sorry. I don't know what to do."

I knew he was turning to me for a solution, but I had none to offer him. Hiro went on berating Neven and he started to cry nearly as hard as the Yokai, but I could barely hear their words. I could only stare at the dirt road in the dark night that was nearly morning and accept the fact that all of this had been for nothing.

She knows when the souls of her Yokai leave Earth, Hiro had said. Surely there was no way around such an omniscient power. Unless…

I sat up straight, staring at the Yokai and trying to block out the sounds of Hiro and Neven arguing.

How, exactly, did souls leave Earth? In England, the souls of departed Reapers and other creatures of Death floated up to an unseen void. Japan's monsters probably suffered a similar fate. But that wasn't the only place that souls could go. Every night in London, I'd turned in the souls of departed humans to Collections, where they went through Processing and were tossed into an afterlife that the humans hoped was Heaven. But in Japan, the final resting place of human souls was not nearly as cryptic. In fact, we'd been there before.

"Is Yomi on Earth?" I whispered.

Hiro and Neven fell silent, both staring down at me.

I looked up at Hiro. "Is Yomi on Earth?" I said again, this time more clearly.

Understanding flashed in Hiro's eyes. He closed his mouth.

"It's not," I said, his eyes the only confirmation I needed. "It's on a separate plane, isn't it? So if we bring her there, Izanami will think she's dead."

Hiro grimaced, as if physically pained by my suggestion. "It's not a place for Yokai," he said. "It's bad enough that Datsue-ba is there, and she can't even cross the river. Yokai are not meant to go to Yomi."

"And Reapers aren't meant to kill," Neven said, eyes narrowed at Hiro, "yet here we are." Then he looked down at the girl in his arms. "Mikuzume," he said. She looked up at him, her eyes wide and brown and wet. "Will you come with me on an adventure?" he said in clunky and accented Japanese.

She turned to look at me and Hiro, her expression strangely stoic, as if she was assessing us. As she turned back to Neven, her eyes filled with tears that she smothered in his shirt.

"They won't try to hurt you," Neven said. "I'll protect you."

"He hurt Grandma," she said, sniffling.

"I know," Neven said, shooting Hiro a murderous look, "but he won't hurt you, because I'm here."

The girl didn't respond, lying limp across Neven's shoulder. He knelt to put her down, but she whined and wrapped her arms around his neck.

"She'll come with us," Neven said, as if daring Hiro to challenge him. If the girl had any objections to this, she didn't voice them. Her crying ceased and she fell quiet and limp in Neven's arms.

Hiro sighed and looked to me. "I suppose this will work as well," he said, offering a small smile that looked more like a grimace than he'd probably intended, "but take care that the Goddess never finds out, or she'll tear all of our souls to pieces."

"We can be discreet," Neven said, shifting the girl to his hip as she stuffed her thumb in her mouth. I groaned internally, praying that some of Hiro's "connections" were hoping to adopt a Yokai and could keep a secret. Convincing Neven to hand her off would be a task, but likely an easier one than convincing him to let me kill her.

"We should leave," Hiro said. "It's not prudent to be the

only strangers in a small village when they wake to find an elder murdered in her own backyard."

We headed for the village gates, the Yokai watching me from over Neven's shoulder. Her wide, unblinking eyes cast my own reflection back at me in the weak moonlight, and her gaze did not stray from my face.

We trekked back across the rice fields in the last hours of night.

Even as I clung to Hiro's back, the crops wilted as I passed, leaving scorched streaks of black in our wake, the cicadas falling silent.

"It's not helping," I said, motioning for Hiro to put me down. "It's better just to hurry."

Hiro set me down, and the dirt dried into cracked clay beneath my feet. Neven walked behind us with the Yokai looking over his shoulder.

Now, all that remained for me was to find one of Izanami's shrines and descend back down to Yomi. According to Hiro, there was a shrine a ways north in Niigata, a few hours by train. In less than a day, I would stand before Izanami again. Then I would be free to go to Yakushima and search for my mother in the red robes of a Shinigami.

I didn't feel any relief now that we were heading back to Yomi, too aware of the precariousness of my situation. Any number of things could go wrong now that we'd added another layer of risk with the Yokai.

I glanced at Tamamo No Mae, whose gaze followed me like a magnet no matter where I moved. Something about her dead-eyed stare made my bones itch and my skin prickle. I wished, not for the first time, that Neven wasn't such a good person.

I turned to Hiro instead, but looked away as soon as he met my eyes. I could still feel his hands crushing me into the dirt and my lips tracing his pulse across his throat and a thousand other things I didn't want to think about with my brother walking beside me. Now that we'd crossed an unspoken line, was I meant to hold his hand and insist we never be parted, as the humans wrote in their penny romances? I certainly didn't want that, nor did it seem realistic given our circumstances. But I couldn't deny that I didn't want Hiro to go very far.

Just like the pull of Death—at times a distant longing and at other times a crushing magnetism—I found myself tethered to Hiro. I could no longer pretend otherwise. And while Hiro murdering the girl's grandmother hadn't thrilled me, I would have been a hypocrite to criticize excessive bloodshed. I wanted all the dark and ugly parts of Hiro, even if they terrified me. That way, I knew I could never scare him away.

But I didn't know what to do with my new feelings. Hiro respected the careful distance I kept between us, and the three of us crossed the rice fields in the cool night, the stars beginning to fade overhead.

"When you start work as a Shinigami," Hiro said, "you'll have your own lantern to guide the dead down to Yomi. The Goddess will give you a place to live in a commune of other Shinigami at first. Then she'll assign you to a town, or several towns, depending on where help is needed."

The job of a Shinigami sounded not unlike that of a Reaper. I ached to finally touch souls again, to feel them slide like liquid silver through my hands. I imagined a house of a hundred lanterns for me and Neven, as bright as Yomi was dark. I imagined red robes and dark nights and a place that could maybe one day be a home. Neven would be safe and happy, and I would have Hiro to tell me all of Japan's secrets, to melt away the chill of Death with his voice. In the summer, I could visit my mother in Yakushima and watch the blue fires dance across the ocean. For the first time, I saw a future before me that didn't hurt.

In the village a short distance behind us, a woman's scream echoed across the rice fields. We stilled as more panicked but indecipherable words floated up the hill.

"They found Grandma," the Yokai's small voice said. Was she only guessing, or could she sense the other people in her village?

"You hid the body, didn't you?" Neven said, turning to me.

I looked at Hiro, who shook his head. "We were a bit preoccupied chasing after the Yokai," he said.

Neven sighed, shooting me a bitter look, as if everything was my fault.

The Yokai tugged on Neven's shirt. "Go faster," she said. "They're gonna catch you."

Without hesitating, Neven turned and walked faster into the rice fields. I pulled a sheet of darkness over us, staring at the Yokai with unease. Why was she trying to help us kidnap her?

"You don't want to go back to your village?" I said.

The Yokai shook her head, rubbing her wet nose into Neven's shirt. "They're scared of me," she said. "Without Grandma, they're not nice."

I frowned. "Why not?" After all, Reapers or Shinigami

could sense the pull of Death around her, but humans weren't that sensitive to it. They shouldn't have seen her as anything but a little girl.

"I speak too many languages and have too many tails," she said. "Grandma said people don't have tails, so I should stop having them."

"They've seen you as a fox?" Hiro said, raising an eyebrow. "No wonder they're scared."

"They can't be that scared if they're coming after her," I said, glancing over my shoulder as more and more street lanterns ignited.

"They have to come, since I'm not allowed to leave," the Yokai said, her voice growing quieter as she muffled it against Neven's shoulder. "Grandma said in five years I'll be worth four million yen."

A coldness filled my stomach. I looked to Hiro, whose face had gone gray.

"To who?" I said.

"The yakuza," she said, and stuffed her thumb in her mouth.

Any resentment I'd felt toward Hiro for killing the old woman evaporated. She hadn't been raising an orphan out of kindness, she'd been grooming her to sell off to gangsters. If the other villagers had seen her as a fox and had let her stay, they were probably hoping for a cut of the profits.

"Do you know what the yakuza is?" Hiro said to the Yokai, his expression bleak.

"Kind of," she said. "Grandma said it's a school where I can learn more languages."

Hiro pressed his lips together and said nothing as Neven

hitched the Yokai higher on his shoulder, shooting me a confused look. This was one conversation I didn't particularly
want to translate.

We pressed forward through the fields, this time shrouded
by a translucent sheet of night. More of the villagers began
to wake up, the small village shining brighter in the weak-
ening darkness of early morning. Tamamo No Mae watched
the village grow smaller over Neven's shoulder.

"Bye-bye," she whispered, waving a chubby hand to the
retreating houses. I wondered if Yokai even understood the
concept of "home" the way we did.

Hiro's warm fingers slipped into mine, hidden in our cloud
of darkness, where my brother wouldn't see.

"It's been a privilege to travel with you," he whispered. I
couldn't help but look at him, hoping that the morning shadows hid the heat rising to my face. He smiled, but it didn't
quite reach his eyes.

"You say that as if we won't see you in Yomi," I said, rather
than acknowledge the sentiment.

Hiro laughed, but the brightness quickly faded. He cast
his gaze to the sky. "I can come to Yomi as I wish," he said,
"but once you work for Izanami, you won't see me anymore."

I stopped walking. Neven bumped into me, jostling the
Yokai.

"What do you mean?" I said.

Hiro shrugged. "Izanami doesn't allow other Shinigami to
associate with me," he said.

I thought back to the Shinigami in the hotel hall who had
struck Hiro, and his hesitance to meet the presiding Shinigami of Yahiko.

"Do you really think I would forget you so easily?" I said. Hurt bled into my words, but I couldn't hold it back. Neven looked between the two of us with confusion.

Hiro shook his head. "It's not a matter of what you want, Ren. When you work for Izanami, you follow her orders. You won't have a choice."

Something that might have been tears or darkness or vomit rose in my throat. Just how much would I have to sacrifice to be a Shinigami?

"You didn't think to mention this until now?" I said.

Hiro looked away, over the fields. "Would it have made a difference?"

I bit my lip to hold down whatever wretchedness was trying to claw its way out of me. The happy ending I'd imagined in Yomi would never exist outside of my dreams, now ruined with images of Hiro rowing back across the river alone, humming his sad lullaby. I saw myself as the Shinigami in the hotel, striking Hiro to the ground while he lay there and let me.

"Izanami might change her mind when I tell her how you've helped us," I said.

"It may soften her heart, if she's in the right mood," Hiro said, "but she hasn't made me any promises as she has with you. I'm preparing you for the most likely outcome."

"Isn't that the reason you helped us?" I said. "To persuade her?"

"At first, yes," he said, meeting my eyes. "Then other things became more important."

The heat that I'd tried so hard to suppress rushed to my

cheeks. In the distance, the villagers began to venture into the rice paddies, lanterns and scythes held overhead.

"I trust you'll put in a good word, as you promised me," Hiro said. "I have hope, but I'm an optimist, not a fool." Then he turned back to the horizon. "We should keep walking," he said. "The villagers are coming."

"I'll convince her to take you back," I said.

Hiro glanced over his shoulder, but wouldn't meet my eyes. "You're kind, Ren."

He gestured for us to keep walking, but I stood firmly in the dirt. "You deserve to be a Shinigami."

Hiro sighed and turned around, his face tight with impatience. "Ren," he said, "she thinks I'm incapable. I don't think she's even seen me stand."

"But you can!" I said. "If she knew what you could do with the ocean, or a bow and arrow, she—"

"She'll never know!" Hiro said, hands curling into fists and eyes wet. He spun away from me, looking back up to the sky with a shuddering breath. "None of it matters," he said, "because she'll never know."

Then desperate words bubbled to the surface and spilled out my throat before I could think twice about what I was offering: "So why don't we show her?"

Hiro's shoulders tensed. He turned to face me again, his expression blank.

"Ren?" Neven said warily.

"Come with me to see her," I said, stepping closer to Hiro.

"The guards won't let me in the palace," he said. "You know that."

"We're time turners," I said. "You really think we can't get around that?"

Neven yanked my sleeve. "Ren," he said.

"I couldn't ask that of you," Hiro said, looking down at the soil.

"I want to," I said. "You've done so much for me. Please, let me do this for you."

Hiro looked up, his eyes finally meeting mine. "You would do that for me?"

His words from last night replayed in my mind: *I would do anything for you.* Would I do anything for Hiro? I wasn't sure. But this much, I could do.

"Yes," I said.

Hiro took my hand, and for a moment I thought he might kiss me, even with Neven and the Yokai standing there. But instead he just held my hand tight, his eyes a shade of black more brilliant than the sky of stars above us. No one had ever looked at me with such affection, as if I was something other than a wretched creature of Death.

"Ren!"

Neven's voice made the dead trees quake and crackle, echoing across the fields. His livid eyes spun a thousand colors, his face bright red. The Yokai clung tighter to his shirt while the villagers in the distance looked around in confusion at the disembodied sound.

"I need to talk to you," he said, the words ground out and stiff.

"Neven," Hiro said, "I—"

"I said I need to talk to *Ren*, not you," Neven said. He pointed into the distance. "Walk ahead of us."

"Neven," I said, darkness fizzling in my fingertips. "You can't just—"

"It's all right," Hiro said, holding up a hand. "I'll keep heading north. I'll wait for you by the station."

He gave my hand a gentle squeeze, then turned and walked toward the horizon, pulling his cloud of darkness with him.

Neven stared rigidly at Hiro's retreating form. When he was no larger than a speck of blue on the horizon, he turned to me.

He opened his mouth to speak, but before a single word could come out, the long, curved blade of a scythe hooked around his throat.

"Let go of the girl."

CHAPTER 19

Neven swallowed, the blade around his throat tightening at the motion and scoring a fine line into his skin. Behind him, a middle-aged farmer from the village gripped the long wooden handle of his scythe, his lantern abandoned on the ground a few meters away.

In my distraction, I must have relaxed the sheet of darkness over us enough that lantern light had pierced through it. Now a human was trying to stop us.

I reached for my clock but my fingers brushed over the fabric of my empty pocket. Neven had our only clock, and both of his hands clutched the Yokai.

The situation wasn't dangerous for us, but it was definitely precarious. A lot of noise or light would send the other villagers running toward us, and while we could easily kill them, I had a feeling Neven wouldn't be overjoyed by the bloodshed. But hesitation could mean a scythe through Neven's carotid artery. He would be fine, eventually, but the injury would likely bathe the Yokai in blood, which would probably make her scream, alerting the rest of the villagers and creating another host of problems.

I sighed and withdrew a knife from each sleeve.

"You will kindly set down your scythe, or I will insert one of these into each of your eyes," I said, gesturing with my knives.

"I don't bow down to murderers," the man said, dragging Neven closer and making him wince. Neven still clung stupidly to the Yokai rather than going for his clock, as if someone would rip her away.

My gaze shifted to the Yokai pressed against Neven's shoulder. Perhaps she would give us more leverage.

I moved one of my knives away from the man and pointed it at Tamamo No Mae.

The man scoffed in disgust while Neven shot me a murderous look, as if I would actually kill her in his arms. It took everything I had not to roll my eyes at him.

Tamamo No Mae looked back at me with eyes full of reflected moonlight, her lower lip trembling. Even though she was nothing but an obstacle who might have hypnotized my brother, her show of sadness distracted me when I couldn't afford to be distracted.

"So these are the monsters we've let in from the West," the man said, his blade cutting deeper into Neven's newly healed skin.

"I may be a monster, but I am from Yakushima," I said,

my grip tightening on the knives. Could humans truly see nothing but what I wasn't? They always seemed determined to pin my faults on my lineage, when in truth I was just an innately bad person.

The man threw his head back and laughed, revealing yellowed teeth. "The Japanese don't point their knives at children."

"But apparently they behead teenagers," I said. Neven was almost a century old, but the farmer didn't know that.

Neven had begun to shift the Yokai's weight to one arm, trying to slowly free his left hand. I wanted to scream at him to just drop the girl and grab his clock, but he acted as if she would shatter from a three-foot drop.

The farmer noticed his movement and yanked on his scythe, splitting the skin around Neven's neck and choking him as a surge of blood painted his neck and collar. Neven dropped the Yokai and grabbed at the blade with his bare hands.

I had already let this go on for too long, and now it was getting messy.

In two quick steps, I crossed the distance between me and the farmer and plunged my knife up under his rib cage. Predictably, he released his scythe with a pained cry and Neven fell forward, coughing.

I didn't give the man a chance to scream. I wrapped one hand around his throat and pushed him into the dirt as he thrashed, then held my blade over his left eye.

"I'll have to do them one at a time," I said as his brown eyes blinked rapidly, "but don't worry, I'll keep my promise."

I leaned more weight onto his throat and his eyes opened

wider with panic. His warm blood soaked my skirts where I straddled him, his thrashing growing weaker and eyes beginning to roll back in his head. In his final moments, I would no longer be "the girl from the West" but "the girl who ended his life." All around me, Death swirled in noxious clouds. My skin went translucent and pulled taut against my bones, red veins twisting up my arms like serpents. I pulled my hand back to plunge the knife into his eye and imagined how it would feel, the soft squishing, the vibration of his screams. I would not show mercy again.

A hand closed around my wrist and snapped it backward.

The bone splintered audibly as Neven wrenched me to the ground. I shot to my feet in fury as the bones clicked back into place. One look at the frozen farmer told me that Neven had stopped time.

"Have you lost your mind?" he shouted. If I were a human, his fury might have intimidated me.

"I was helping you, you ungrateful—"

"He was subdued long before you tried to spear his eyes out!" Neven said. "First her grandmother and now some old farmer? Are you just going to murder anyone who looks at you the wrong way?"

"I didn't kill the old woman!" I said.

But this only angered Neven more. "Of course you didn't," he said, "but it's fine, because your beloved Hiro did, and he can do no wrong."

My face burned, darkness pulling at the edge of my vision, threatening to drag me down completely. I had finally found someone who understood me, but Neven only saw a monster.

"Don't pretend to understand us," I said, stepping forward. Neven didn't back away, or even flinch, as I'd expected.

"I know all I need to know," Neven said. "I know that he's somehow convinced you to break Izanami's rules for him, and no one who cares about you would ask you to take such a risk."

"I'm breaking her rules for *you*!" I said, pointing to the frozen Yokai on the ground.

Neven snatched her into his arms and she immediately shuddered into her fox form, climbing onto his shoulder and tucking her face against his neck.

"That's to save an innocent life!" Neven said. "It's not for me, it's because it's right! That Shinigami is using you and you're too infatuated to realize it."

"Stop calling him that like it's an insult!" I said. "That's why you don't like him, isn't it? Because 'his eyes are too black' or some other nonsense."

Neven rolled his eyes, and my fingers twitched with the urge to strangle him. "You know that's not it, Ren."

"And how would I know that?"

"Because you know me!" Neven said, tipping his head back and covering his eyes with a weary hand. "Because *you're* a Shinigami and I've clearly never had a problem with that."

"So now I'm a Shinigami, not a Reaper?" I said. "When it helps your argument?"

"Is that not what you want?" Neven said, his voice echoing across the withered fields. "To pretend you've always been a Shinigami and forget your other half?"

"I don't want to be half of anything!" I said, finally crossing the distance between us and shoving Neven backward. The fox whimpered and hopped down, hiding behind Neven's legs. Hot tears burned my eyes, and I hated him for making me cry. Neven was the one person who was never supposed to hurt me. "I just want to be *something*, not half of something." The words sounded weak and human and everything I didn't want. "Maybe here, they'll treat me like I'm whole."

Neven shook his head slowly, his hands falling to his sides.

"You know that they won't, Ren," he said, his voice gentle even as his words sliced me open. "No one ever will."

My hands clenched into fists. I had never before wanted so badly to punch my brother in the face, feel his bones crack under my hand. He was right, and I would be a fool to hope for anything else. But what else could I do but follow this path?

"There is no other road for me," I said, tears stinging as they tracked down my face and neck. "I can't go back to your world, Neven."

"It was *our* world!" he said, hands tangled in his hair like he wanted to tear it out.

"It chased me out!" I said. "You saw how they treated me there."

"That doesn't mean it never happened!" Neven said. "You're still a Reaper, Ren."

Death surged up all at once, like a wave of violent sickness that tore through my whole body. I tasted it like tar in my mouth, seeping out between my teeth. The sky plunged into stark black, the crops melting away, the stars extinguished. Before I realized what was happening, I'd thrown Neven to the ground and stomped my foot into his chest.

"Don't tell me who I am!" I said, the night spiraling around

us from the language of Death, twisting into a noxious hurricane of black as my foot pressed down harder into Neven's sternum. "That's all that anyone's ever done! I want to decide for myself, for once!"

Neven grabbed my ankle and tried to throw me off, but I leaned more of my weight onto him and he wheezed, eyes furious as they cast around the darkness for escape. The fox whined and nipped at my ankle, but I ignored her.

"You can't just decide where you come from," Neven said through gritted teeth, "or what you are."

"Then who can?" I said, grinding my heel down and forcing a wounded sound out of him.

All my life, everyone had told me exactly who I wasn't allowed to be. Ivy and her friends, the Collections guards, the humans on the ships and in the villages, the dead of Yomi, the Yokai, and now Neven, too.

I leaned all my weight onto my foot, fighting off Neven's grip around my ankle. *"Why am I the only one with no say in who I am?"*

The night sky throbbed in agreement with my rage, and for one moment, I thought I might actually kill my brother. Damn him and his feral pet for ruining the only thing I'd ever wanted. He tossed out moral platitudes like party favors because he had never known suffering, could never understand that light and dark weren't so different when your whole world was cast in shadows, that nothing was easy, that there were no happy endings. If he truly loved me, he would try to understand, he would do anything for me the way Hiro would.

At my words, the anger drained away from Neven's face

and his eyes went wide and complexion stony-white, the same look as when he fled from bloodthirsty Yokai or church grims or nightfall, but this time he was looking at me, the most fearsome monster of all.

As swiftly as it had come, the sting of Death fizzled away, washed out by a soul-deep sorrow. My question would never be answered, no matter where I went or who I hurt. I couldn't punish Neven for a truth he couldn't control.

I stumbled away from him, falling to my hands and knees, bones aching emptily where the darkness had abandoned me. Once again, we stood in a dying rice field under the slowly dissolving stars.

"I'm going to be a Shinigami," I whispered, "and so is Hiro. I won't let you tell me otherwise."

Neven sighed, sitting up and rubbing his sternum. The fox hopped into his lap and started licking his hands. "It doesn't matter to me what you are," Neven whispered. "You will always be Ren."

I shook my head, wishing that I could understand why being just Ren and only Ren was supposed to be enough.

We sat in the soil, six feet apart that felt like a thousand miles.

"I'll do as you wish," Neven said after a moment. "If you think we should take Hiro to Izanami, then we will."

I nodded, but Neven's concession brought me no joy because I knew he still didn't understand.

"You'll take me, too, won't you?" he said, even quieter this time.

I turned around. Neven had curled up around his knees, glasses askew.

"Take you?" I echoed, throat sore and raw, burned from the taste of Death.

"When you go to the palace," he said. "You won't leave me alone outside in the dark?"

I sighed. "Of course," I said, standing up but not offering him a hand.

As we began to cross the shadowed fields in silence, I couldn't shake the feeling that once more, something important had been irrevocably ruined.

CHAPTER 20

The second time we entered Yomi, the sky was even darker than before. This time, the total blackness not only hid us but erased us completely. The night numbed my skin everywhere it touched, as if something unseen was eating it.

Neven's fingers latched on to my arm, and though I didn't want him to touch me, I also didn't want to argue anymore. He didn't release me until I'd lit one of the many lanterns in the shrine at the banks of Yomi's river, though it did little to disperse the heavy darkness. I could hardly see Hiro at the perimeter of our circle of light. The Yokai made no comment on the darkness, holding Neven's left hand and walking beside him.

"What's happened here?" I said, following the sound of Hiro's footsteps onto the sandy shore.

"What do you mean?" Hiro said. He couldn't have been more than a few feet away, but sounded much more distant. Why hadn't he taken a lantern this time?

"The darkness is worse than before," I said. "I can hardly see."

"You'll see better if you extinguish your lantern."

"Hiro."

His feet splashed into water. I followed the sound as Neven stopped to lift the Yokai onto his back.

"The darkness waxes and wanes with the power of the Goddess," Hiro said, slow footsteps dragging through the shallow water. "Now that three powerful Yokai are gone from Earth, the darkness is stronger."

Neven swallowed audibly behind me.

Hiro led us through murky darkness back to the dock and untied a boat to row the four of us back to Yomi. He climbed in first, staring across the black river without expression, then Neven placed the Yokai inside before stepping in himself, sliding over so I could join them.

Hiro pushed off from the dock without comment, his oar pulling slowly through the waters, as if the river had turned to tar. Soon, he began humming the same eerie lullaby that had pulled us across the river on our first journey. The melody tangled with the wind, echoing across the glass surface of water and endless cathedral of the sky.

But this time, after a few notes, the girl began to quietly sing the same melody. It had never occurred to me that the song had words, but the Yokai sang them by heart as Hiro fell silent.

Golden koi swimming in cold waters,
Let the sea carry you far away.
Do not come back home.

Spineless koi climbing the rapids,
Your scales were forged of darkness.
Your gills are filled with ash.

Cursed koi, lonely koi.
May you wash ashore and die.
May the river eat your bones.

When Hiro had hummed the melody, it had felt wistful and lonely. But with the Yokai's voice, the same song sounded more like imminent doom.

I turned to Neven, but he didn't seem to know enough Japanese to understand my unease.

"How do you know that song?" I said to the Yokai. I must have sounded too demanding, because Neven shot me a dark look.

"I don't know, I just know it," she said, shrugging.

I turned to Hiro. "What is that song?"

Hiro didn't speak for a moment, rowing silently through the darkness. "It is a very old lullaby," he said at last, with seemingly great reluctance. "It's no surprise that the Yokai has heard it before. She is not as young as she seems. Memories may be resurfacing."

"But why do you sing it?" I said.

Hiro kept rowing, still facing away from me. "They say that it is Izanami's lullaby," he said. "She sang it to her children, and they sang it to their children, and their children's children. Long ago, Shinigami would sing it on quiet nights when they came to collect from rural villages, and the humans would know to lock their doors. But now it only promises safe passage across the river to Yomi."

Perhaps that explained why the melody sounded so familiar—my mother might have sung it to me when I was a child.

But that wasn't possible. I shook my head to clear the thought, ignoring how Neven raised an eyebrow. It must have been a false memory, for why would my mother have sung to someone she would later give away?

"What does it mean?" I said, staring out across the emptiness.

"You would have to ask Izanami," Hiro said, but his voice sounded too light and far away, and something told me that he knew the answer.

He began humming again. This time, the Yokai stayed silent.

We moved through the town center, the lights slightly dimmer than I remembered. As we left our lanterns at the edge of the darkness and headed once more toward the shrines, Neven latched on to my arm with his right hand and clutched the Yokai with his left. His touch weighed me down like an iron shackle on my sleeve.

Beyond the light of the town, a cool ocean of night swirled around us, every breath filling my lungs with bitterness. The darkness grew heavier as we walked deeper into it, trying to drag us down to the dirt as if warning us not to go any farther.

We'd agreed that I would stop time once the palace guard

opened a portal, in order to let all of us pass through unnoticed. I would have preferred to leave the Yokai outside and as far away from Izanami's knowing gaze as possible, but Neven refused to leave her alone and I'd promised I wouldn't abandon him, which meant all four of us had to go inside. Once again, I was risking everything because of Neven's bleeding heart.

Finally, we stood at the edge of the gardens, where the dirt gave way to the cool tiles of the palace courtyard. I held my breath and waited for the guard to appear, but he didn't come.

"I've come to speak to Izanami," I said into the darkness.

But no one answered. I turned and looked back at the hazy forms of Hiro, Neven, and the Yokai. Neven hugged the girl to his chest and stared uneasily into the darkness, while Hiro met my eyes but offered no suggestions.

I turned and took another step toward the palace.

Something buzzed in my ear. I swatted at it, but the sound only intensified. The darkness swirled into a thousand gnats, swarming around my face, trying to crawl into my ears and mouth.

I spit them out and tried to fan them away, but all at once they fled and converged into the shape of the guard. The vaguely human silhouette loomed over me in a deeper shade of night than the surrounding darkness, pulsing and swirling at the edges.

"I see you've returned," he said.

"I've finished my task," I said, picking at my ears, which still itched with the phantom sensation of bugs. "Take me to Izanami."

I expected him to step back and open a portal in the darkness for me, but he vanished as soon as the words left my mouth.

Then the Yokai shrieked.

I spun around as she slapped at the slithering darkness that pulled her hair, crawled over her arms and wrapped around her torso. Neven held the girl at arm's length, rigid with panic.

"Stop that!" I said, yanking a blanket of deep darkness over the Yokai. The shadow reluctantly withdrew, unable to swim through an even darker black.

"What a lovely child that you've dragged so unkindly into the darkness," the guard said, reforming into a humanlike shape before me.

"I need to see Izanami," I said again, standing between the guard and the Yokai. I forced my voice to sound untroubled, as if her presence was inconsequential. I didn't want him paying attention to her, or worse, asking questions. Already, I was starting to regret bringing her with us. What if the guard told Izanami that we'd brought a child to Yomi? He might be ignorant, but Izanami wouldn't be.

The guard had no face to speak of, so there was no way for me to guess his thoughts. His silhouette ebbed and flowed for a long moment, then he took a step back and tore a hole in the darkness.

"Step inside," he said, pulling back a curtain of night.

Neven stood tense, looking in my general direction and waiting. Hiro gave me a soft smile, which somehow reassured me more than any words could have.

I pulled out Neven's clock and froze the courtyard. Though there was no visible change in the total darkness, I could sense the freeze from the silence, the whole world holding its breath. I touched Hiro and then Neven, whose touch woke the Yokai, and all three of them slipped through the portal. Once they were safely inside, I released my hold on time, cast one last look at the guard, and entered the darkness.

The world flipped and the night pulled at my hair and teeth as if examining me. Its ghostly hands shuddered under my skin and caressed every bone, spreading chills wherever they touched. Finally, the darkness spat me out on the floor of a wooden hallway. I must have been outside Izanami's throne room once more, for the air crushed down with the weight of stone, even stronger than the first time I'd visited.

Hiro, Neven, and the Yokai lay in an undignified pile on the floor, struggling to get up against the crushing pressure of Death. At the whirring sound of the portal beginning to close, I shoved Neven and the Yokai against the wall and stood in front of Hiro, yanking a curtain of dense darkness over the three of them just as the shadow guard stepped through, the portal sealing behind him.

He didn't spare a glance in our direction, just slipped under the cracks in the door to Izanami's throne room like spilled ink.

I let out a tense breath. *We did it.* We'd all made it into the palace, and I was only moments away from standing before Izanami again, from finally getting what I'd wanted my whole life.

But so much could still go wrong. What if Izanami could smell the fear in my blood and knew I was trying to trick her? How much would it hurt to have Death herself tear me open and eat my heart? Too much adrenaline rushed through me and I worried I might vomit all over Izanami's throne room if I didn't take a moment to breathe. I jammed my hand into my pocket and grabbed Neven's clock once more.

The distant sounds of the palace servants halted, the pressure releasing so suddenly that my lungs sucked in a deep and greedy breath, finally unrestrained. I felt around for Hiro and Neven's faces until they woke up, then I knelt down on legs that felt like wet paper as my eyes began to see once more in the total darkness.

Before us were the doors to the throne room, and around us lay a labyrinth of hallways painted with a thousand murals— cherry trees and waterfalls, giant reeds growing between Heaven and Earth, a coral palace and a dragon waiting beneath the ocean. These walls told the story of Japan, but shrouded them in the dark where no one would see.

Hiro stood up and started examining the painting of two gods stirring the sky with a spear and a baby floating out to sea in a reed basket. He ran his hands over the painted walls as if he wanted to dive into the vivid scenes. Neven was clutching Hiro's sleeve, eyes casting around but unseeing, the Yokai on his back.

"So this is what it's like inside," Hiro said, his fingers gentle as they traced the curves of the painted sea.

He turned to the paper doors separating us from Izanami, transfixed at the watercolor images of purple mountains. I followed his gaze, still nauseous at the thought of passing through the threshold. No matter how strong I felt, Izanami would always have more power than me. She could decide she didn't want me anymore, she could deny Hiro, she could find out about Tamamo No Mae and snap my spine the moment I passed through the door.

"Ren," Hiro said, a soft hand on my shoulder, "the hard part is over."

I said nothing, because his words didn't feel true.

"You've done what she asked," he said, his grip tense, almost painful on my shoulder. "Go claim what you deserve."

I swallowed and nodded. After all I'd done for Izanami, I deserved to be a Shinigami, to live in Yomi and find my mother.

"You should hide," I said, nudging Hiro's arm. "Pull down a shadow."

Hiro nodded, drawing back and gesturing for Neven to do the same.

"Don't anger her," Neven said suddenly.

I turned to where he stood by the table, shifting from foot to foot. The Yokai stared at the doors to the throne room as if she could see through them.

"I don't intend to," I said.

Neven sighed, shifting the Yokai on his hip. "Please be careful," he whispered.

I offered him a stiff smile and set a hand on his shoulder, gently guiding him down to the floor beside Hiro.

"Go," Hiro said. The finality of his words felt like shoving me off a cliff into dark waters, nowhere to go but down. He pulled a blanket of deep darkness over the three of them, and I stood alone in the hallway.

I swallowed, turning back to the throne room, and released my hold on time.

The weight of Death forced me to my hands and knees, hard enough to shatter my kneecaps if I were a human. I bit my tongue, tasting blood as my teeth throbbed from the impact.

The shadow guard slid the door open.

"You may enter," he said, moving aside as I painstakingly crawled forward.

I carefully controlled my facial expression when the stench of Death and rot made my throat clench. As I entered the room, the weight of darkness grew heavier on my back, warm and humid as swampland, thick between my fingers and cloying on the roof of my mouth.

As soon as I'd crossed the threshold, the door slammed shut behind me.

"You've returned," said Izanami. Her voice swarmed the darkness from all angles, raining down on top of me and humming through the floor. "I assume that means you've done as I asked," she said. "Otherwise, you wouldn't have dared come back here."

"I have," I said, my voice barely a whisper, words too weak to carry through the thick heat of the air. "The Yokai are dead."

"Yes, that much I know," Izanami said. "You've done well."

Something close to pride swelled in my chest, but it was quickly crushed by what Izanami said next.

"Soon, all of them will be gone."

My throat went dry. I thought of the Honengame, Hiro's friend. Izanami wanted her gone?

"It takes a long time to starve a Yokai," Izanami continued. "I was growing impatient. So thank you, Ren, for helping to move things along."

Thank you, Ren. No one but Neven had ever thanked me before, but somehow her ominous words didn't feel like gratitude. What, exactly, had I helped Izanami do?

"You were starving them?" I said. I thought of Iso Onna's thin frame, her ravenous hunger. That had been Izanami's doing?

"I was taking souls from wherever I please, as is my *right*," Izanami said, her words a low growl that rumbled the floorboards. "If I want to take the souls of all the sailors in Takaoka and leave Iso Onna with nothing, I can. If I want to devour every snowy village in Japan so Yuki Onna has nowhere else to go, I can. Don't you understand, Ren? Death is *mine*."

Her words began to stir the air in the room, like an invisible fire stealing all the oxygen. Sweat beaded on the back of my neck and I started to feel light-headed, like I was falling while kneeling in place.

Wherever there are Yokai with an appetite for humans, too many humans are dying, Maho had said. Hiro had thought that meant the Yokai were overfeeding. But it hadn't been the Yokai at all. It was Izanami cutting off their food supply.

I stared down at the hazy outline of my hands in the darkness and tasted bitterness, my fingers curling into the mats.

Izanami was eradicating the Yokai. And maybe some of them had deserved it, but not all of them, not the ones like Maho. But what mattered to me infinitely more than Yokai politics was that Izanami had used me as a tool and I hadn't asked why. Death was supposed to be sacred, a task we executed to keep the universe in balance, not a tool to feed Izanami's greed.

"You told me there was harmony, even in death," I said. "I thought you had to work together with the Yokai."

"Harmony?" Izanami said, the word hissing across the room with a waft of hot air. "Was there harmony in my husband leaving me to rot down here after I birthed his kingdom of the living? Every day, the population of Japan grows and he becomes more powerful, while I have to share with ghosts and gremlins too stupid to find their own food if it doesn't walk straight into their gaping mouths."

I leaned away, not daring to breathe as the waves of heat and the scent of decay became unbearable.

"I want Izanagi to know that the souls of his precious humans are in my stomach, building my kingdom and deepening Yomi's darkness," Izanami said. "I created Death. I am done sharing it."

The floorboards creaked as if straining against their nails, the wallpaper tearing itself from the walls under the force of Izanami's rage. Had I upset Izanami too much? At any moment, her anger might turn on me, stripping my skin from my flesh and grinding my bones to dust. I didn't dare move, afraid I'd already said too much.

"And you, Ren, are mine, as well," Izanami said. "If you live in Yomi under my care, you will do as I say without question. If I ask you to kill one thousand Yokai with your bare hands, you will."

I bowed down farther to the ground, not out of reverence, but out of despair. I'd never imagined this outcome, but what choice did I have? How could I come this far only to be turned away and homeless in a land of eternal darkness?

"I understand," I said, allowing my muscles to go slack and Death to crush me completely into the mat, my forehead sweaty against the reeds and my legs burning from the warped bow.

The chaos of tearing wallpaper and groaning floorboards settled, an eerie stillness falling over the room.

"I quite enjoy you, Ren of Yakushima," Izanami said at last. "Unlike my Shinigami who were handed their rights at birth without question, you want it so much more… You are far stronger than your mother ever was."

I stopped breathing. All the blood in my body rushed away from my brain and pooled hot in my feet. I played Izanami's words back in my mind, sure that I'd misheard. If my mother was still in Japan, then why had she spoken of her in the past tense?

"Was?" I said.

"As I said before," Izanami said, "she has been punished for her transgressions."

"Punished *how*?" I said, finding the strength to tear myself away from the mat to lean up on my elbows.

"She was sacrificed to the creatures of the deep darkness."

For a moment, the words meant nothing to me. I understood, objectively, that my mother was dead, and yet nothing had changed.

"You killed her?" I said, barely able to feel the words on my lips, not even sure if I'd spoken in English or Japanese.

"Are you so naive as to think she could live after what she'd done?" Izanami said. "She made her decision when she had a child with a Reaper. She knew the consequences and yet she tried to flee."

I said nothing at all, for my mouth had dried up. My hands shook, but they didn't feel like my hands anymore. Nothing about this moment felt like it belonged to me. I'd seen my mother so clearly when I'd pictured the beaches in Yakushima, the blue lights and forests and her house on the shore. How could none of that be real?

"True Shinigami accept their punishments with dignity," Izanami continued, her voice low and bitter. "I could no longer let her live as my child after showing such cowardice."

My nails bit into the reed mats, ripping the fibers loose. All of my life, I had been the girl no one wanted—no one but Neven. And it had hurt but it was *fine*, I was used to it, I knew how to turn that hollowness into a simmering anger that made me fierce and cold, the way Reapers were supposed to be.

But I hadn't really been unwanted.

My mother had tried to run away with me. And Izanami had killed her for it.

All this time, I'd thought I would go to Yakushima and ask my mother why she'd abandoned me. I'd braced myself to hear a thousand reasons why I wasn't good enough, why I'd brought shame to her family, why I shouldn't exist at all, like everyone had told me my whole life.

But she wouldn't have told me any of those things, because she'd never given me away.

Maybe she'd loved me, but now I would never know.

I closed my eyes and imagined a world in which my mother escaped Japan with my father, and a whole different Story of Ren Scarborough began to play through my mind. The Ren in this story never pressed her ear to the wall to eavesdrop on her brother's bedtime stories because her parents read them to her in her own bed and held her until she fell asleep. Her mother taught her to control her Shinigami powers, so she never hurt anyone and never had to flee to Japan to become a murderer. She grew up to be the kind of sister Neven deserved, the kind of daughter Ambrose didn't resent and fought hard to protect. Her classmates didn't always understand her, but her parents hugged her when she cried and her father complained to the High Council when she was bullied, and she never ever doubted that her life mattered.

But that story was not mine, and I would never be anything but this—a walking Death curse with a festering heart—because Izanami had taken all of that away from me.

"So, Ren of Yakushima," Izanami said slowly. "Do you still want to be a Shinigami?"

Tears fell hot onto my hands, splayed against the floor.

No, I didn't. I didn't want to work for someone as terrible as Izanami, the reason that I'd spent the past century and a half as a pariah in London, the one who had killed my mother.

But no one else in the world would take me.

I was no longer allowed to be a Reaper. I could be a Shinigami, or I could be nothing at all. The idea of being nothing and no one was so much scarier than dying.

"Yes," I whispered, holding back a sob as I folded into the floor and my heart screamed *no, no, no!* This was ten times more humiliating than being threatened on a dirty London street with a pair of old scissors. I was a street rat with nowhere left to crawl, and Izanami knew it.

"Excellent," she said. "Now, you may give me your clock."

My tears stopped. I looked up through the heavy darkness, my whole body suddenly numb.

"What?" I whispered, conscious of the weight of silver and gold in my pocket. "How did you know—"

"I know all about the trinkets of Reapers," Izanami said. "I may be old, but I have thousands of eyes and ears that roam the earth. I can say with certainty that my Shinigami have no need for clocks."

I swallowed even though it scratched like glass down my throat, unable to hear anything but the quiet ticking of the clock in my pocket. So this was the true price of becoming a Shinigami.

There was a time when it wouldn't have mattered to me, when I would have sawed off my own hands if Izanami had deemed them the hands of a Reaper, would have done anything to belong in Japan. All I'd known was tiny, broken England and its wicked Reapers with hearts as black as tar. But this land teemed with monsters and was crumbling apart from Izanami's greed. I had traveled all over Japan but could never outrun the darkness of Yomi or the cruelty of humans. Everywhere in the world was its own hell.

"If you choose not to be a Shinigami," Izanami said, "my guards will escort you out of Yomi. You will no longer be welcome in my domain."

I slid my hand into my pocket, fingers running over the nicks and dents in the cool silver of Neven's clock, the bite marks, the links in the chain.

If you cut all ties to London, then what am I? Neven had said. *Am I even your brother?*

I tried to tell myself that handing over Neven's clock was not the same thing as cutting my ties to Neven, but even in my mind that felt like a lie. Without clocks, we weren't Reapers anymore, just humans with unnaturally long lifespans. I thought of my own clock, trapped somewhere beneath the rocks of Takaoka, and shame curdled in my stomach. I'd been so busy hacking Yokai to pieces and swooning at Hiro and giving everything to be a Shinigami that I'd hardly even thought about it. And now I had to give away Neven's clock, too? Perhaps he could figure out how to make a new one, but who knew how long that would take, or if it could ever compare to the clock that Ambrose had given him.

I knew what he'd think of me once he found out—that I'd looked at everything he was and decided it wasn't good enough for me, that I didn't want it anymore. It was impossible to separate being a Reaper from being Neven's sister, because that was what I'd been in the century we'd spent together in London, even if both of us had been outcasts and disappointments, even if I'd tried so hard to erase that time and be reborn as Ren of Yakushima. But if I hadn't once been Ren of London, I wouldn't have had Neven by my side.

How unfair it was that after all I'd given up for Izanami, she wanted more. How dare she ask this of me, when without my Reaper powers, I would have been dead long before I'd even met her. I had defeated Yuki Onna and Iso Onna not because I was an exceptionally strong Shinigami, but because I was also a Reaper.

"My patience is not indefinite, Ren," Izanami said.

I gripped Neven's clock as it ticked even louder in my pocket, like a heartbeat against my palm. This was what I'd asked for, wasn't it? To be something whole, even if that something was vile and dark. I'd wanted so badly to be able to choose for myself what I was, but this wasn't a fair choice.

I slowly unclipped the chain from my clothes.

It doesn't matter, I told myself. *It's fine, you're fine, and it doesn't matter.*

I slid the clock across the mats, and the falling sensation in my stomach as the metal left my hand didn't matter at all.

The metal scraped across the floor as Izanami snatched it, her nails, or perhaps bones, clacking against the silver. I bit down hard to keep from making a sound, my clenched jaw and the skull-crushing force of Death grinding away at my teeth. *This is what you wanted, Ren. Your wish came true.*

"The guards will take you to your new lodging," she said. "You will return here tomorrow to meet an experienced Shinigami who will teach you how we reap. Your brother is free to take any job in Yomi, so long as he doesn't interfere with the work of my Shinigami. Now go."

With Izanami's dismissal, Death began to drag me back toward the door.

"Wait!" I said, clawing at the reed mats. I couldn't lift my arms through the leaden weight of Death to wipe the tears from my eyes, so I tried to swallow the soreness from my throat and ignore the wetness still dripping down my face. I had to hold myself together just a moment longer, because there was one more thing I hadn't done.

"Speak quickly," Izanami said. "I grow tired of this exchange."

"Another Shinigami helped me with my tasks," I said, forcing myself to look up. "I ask that he be rewarded as I have."

For an unbearable stretch of time, Izanami said nothing.

"Who?" she said, the temperature of the room crawling upward.

I swallowed, my throat suddenly scorched. "His name is Hiro."

The temperature of the room skyrocketed, and for a moment I thought I would faint from the rush of heat and smell of rot.

"*Do not waste my time!*" Izanami said, the language of Death splintering the floorboards. "I told you before, I have no Shinigami of that name!"

"How can you deny him, even now?" I said.

"I deny *no one!*" Izanami said. "I have no Shinigami by the name of 'Hiro' and I never have."

The door to the throne room slid open, slamming against its wooden casing. A pale circle of flickering candlelight appeared in the doorway.

"But you have one named Hiruko."

I started to turn toward the sound of Hiro's voice in the doorway, but I froze as his words echoed through the darkness.

"Hiruko?" I whispered.

And then all the pieces began to come together—everything Hiro had ever told me that should have made me suspicious. He was a wounded fishing spirit from a coastal town, older than time itself, called a "leech" by the other Shinigami, wearing a name on his spine that wasn't "Hiro."

Izanami can have children? Neven had said as we entered Yahiko village.

She had two children without bones after she ruined her marriage ritual, I'd said while Hiro had stared at the horizon, reticent from what I'd thought was anxiety about Tamamo No Mae. But his silence had had nothing to do with the Yokai, and everything to do with me nearly uncovering his secret. He'd known perfectly well that the names of Izanami's first two children were Awashima and Hiruko.

According to Shinto legends, before Izanami and Izanagi made Japan, they made a horrible mistake.

They built a pillar of Heaven and a great palace for their marriage, but during the ceremony, Izanami broke tradition by speaking before her husband.

As punishment for her transgressions, her first son was born without bones. They named him Hiruko, leech child, and cast him off to sea in a boat of reeds.

He washed ashore in Ezo, where he was raised by humans and grew most, but not all, of his bones. He became a great god of fishermen who they called Ebisu, and that was where the legend of Hiruko was supposed to end.

But the legends never told the rest of the story—that Izanami's firstborn son had taken a new name and returned to Yomi.

Hiro's footsteps crossed the dark room, and a great surge of sadness caught in my throat. I had trusted him, and he had lied to me. I bit my lip and pressed myself hard into the mat and wished I could melt into the darkness.

"How did you enter my palace?" Izanami said. Heat washed over the room in nauseating waves.

"Is that really the first thing you wish to say to me, after all this time?" Hiro said. "Aren't you so pleased that your first-born has returned?"

"How can you even walk?" Izanami said, her outrage boiling the air. "I thought—"

"I learned to do many things *without you*," Hiro said, scowling and stepping closer, his circle of light drawing nearer and nearer Izanami's hidden form.

"You dare to bring light into my sacred darkness?" Izanami

said, but her confidence wavered, her presence retreating under the threat of light.

"Are you scared of what I'll see when I cast my light on you?"

"Hiro," I whispered. He turned to me, his rage softening when he saw my face in the dim light. "What are you doing?"

"I'm showing my mother what I've become," he said, turning away from me. "Am I worthy of your grace now, *Mother*?" he said. The light flickered dangerously close to Izanami's throne.

"My dearest Hiruko," Izanami whispered. The gentleness of her voice stilled Hiro's rage.

"You were my first and gravest mistake," she said. "I had all the magic of the gods in my hands…the power to create the world…and yet, I couldn't fix you."

"I didn't need to be fixed!" Hiro said. "There was nothing wrong with me! There was everything wrong with *you*! The gods should be ashamed that they gave their powers to anyone so cowardly."

"Hiruko," Izanami whispered. "I'm sorry. I should never have sent you away…"

Then the darkness parted and the light from Hiro's candle inhaled Izanami's true form, half bone and half grayed flesh, thousands of years of slow and tortuous decay. Her empty eyes teemed with maggots and her lips had rotted away to reveal sharp yellowed teeth. She pushed herself up and rose with a shuddering creak, bones clicking and scraping against each other.

"I should have ended you myself."

CHAPTER 21

Death compressed the room, smashing both me and Hiro flat to the floor. Rather than simply immobilizing us, the weight of the universe kept crushing harder and harder on our backs, my joints popping out of their sockets, my bones threatening to splinter. The pressure on my brain sent blood spilling out my nose and ears, forcing my eyes to cross.

Izanami's horrific corpse drew a long katana from a shelf above her throne and lurched toward Hiro, dropping Neven's clock to the floor. The light glinted along the curved blade as if it had been freshly forged in molten white starlight. She dragged it behind her, scraping through the mats and wood as easily as soft fruit.

Hiro's eyes widened when he saw what his mother intended to do, the same wild look of hares caught in traps and humans on their deathbeds when they knew there was no way out, a look I knew so horribly well and had never wanted to see on Hiro's face. My throat dried up and I could no longer draw in breath, but this time I didn't think it was because of Death crushing me to the floor.

"Mother, please!" Hiro said. He was sobbing, his teeth chattering from the high pressure and blood pooling around his face from where he'd bitten his tongue. It was the same as when the Shinigami had kicked him in the hotel, but this was his *mother*. My blood was suddenly burning hot, the curse of Death peeling away the skin at my fingertips as I found myself crawling closer to Hiro, even as the screaming winds tried to drag me away from him.

Izanami staggered closer, the katana carving through the floor behind her.

"You knew to never come back here," she said. "Your brothers are the islands of Japan, the moon and the storms. Your sister is the sun. And what have you become, Hiruko?"

"I—I'm a god of fishermen," Hiro said, blood trickling down from his eyes.

"Fish," Izanami said with disdain. As she limped closer, trails of black rot streaked the floor behind her. "You are proud to be the god of *fish*?"

My fingers scraped at the reed mats, tearing straight through them and sinking into the splintering hardwood beneath. How dare she demean Hiro when he had risked his life just to please her? How dare she speak of pride and prestige after casting away her own child? I thought of Ambrose in his golden chair in the High Council and Izanami hiding away in her opulent palace and my fingers curled with disgust at the gilded cowards we called our parents, splinters stabbing under my fingernails. I dragged myself forward, even as my face scraped along the mats.

"I'm sorry," Hiro cried, the ever-crushing strength of Death pinning his head to the floor and grinding his teeth into the wood. "Mother, I'm sorry. Please—"

"You are a leech," Izanami said. "You dare to bring my greatest shame into my palace? When I pushed you out to sea, I hoped that you drowned."

Her words drained all the warmth from my blood, and they hadn't even been for me. Surely even the sharpest katana in all of Yomi could not cut Hiro as deep. Hiro sobbed into the floor, hugging his legs to his chest and soaking the reed mats with his tears and blood.

My teeth crunched and cracked as I ground them together, Death wrapping around my arms in ribbons and flaying away my skin, and still none of it hurt as much as looking at Hiro come undone. Boiling hot tears, or maybe blood, dripped down my face, and it didn't make sense because I never cried for anyone else, never felt sorrier for anyone than I did for myself, but now I felt like I'd swallowed hot coals and my nose was running onto the mats and if I let go of my bloody grip on the floor I would break into a thousand pieces like the human in Yuki Onna's story.

I clawed my way toward Hiro, even as my eyes kept rolling up to the ceiling, my body threatening to faint under the pressure. With the crushing weight of Death on my back, the few meters between me and Hiro might as well have been halfway across the universe.

The rattling floors shook Neven's clock closer to me, only

a few inches from my hand. I tore my gaze from Hiro and focused on the glimmering silver, even as my vision spun, because *this was how I could save Hiro.* He had lied to me, but I could never let him die.

I stretched out my fingers and the bones instantly snapped under the onslaught of Death, but I gritted my teeth and forced my hand closer.

Izanami finally reached Hiro, kicking him over so he lay on his back. He croaked out an endless stream of apologies, but the gravity of Death tugged at his lips and tongue, the words coming out as sad, distorted sounds. He thrashed against the floor but couldn't escape as Izanami pressed the sharp tip of the blade over his heart.

"Welcome home, Hiruko."

I bit my tongue and wrenched my broken fingers into a closed fist around Neven's clock.

The pressure released. I gasped at the sudden influx of air, the ringing silence of the room. My bones clicked as they re-aligned themselves, the stream of blood from my nose and ears quickly tapering off. Now that the chaos had ended and the space around me was a quiet throne room and not a hungry darkness, I realized Hiro was much farther from me than I'd thought, pinned under Izanami's blade but unharmed.

The whirlwind had torn open the sliding doors to the throne room, revealing Neven's frozen form sprawled on the floor with the fox clinging to the back of his shirt, his feet just beyond my grasp. I crawled the meter between us and grabbed his ankle, yanking him closer to me and startling him awake.

"Ren!" he cried, jolting up and immediately wincing. I heard his teeth clacking back into place and his jaw realigning itself, but otherwise he seemed unharmed. He gasped at Izanami's frozen form and gathered up the Yokai into his arms, then pressed her face into his shirt.

"Are you all right?" he said to me, gaze jumping between me and Izanami's rotten corpse. He swallowed a convulsive gag and pressed his head to my shoulder.

"Yes," I said, my lips numb, my whole body numb as it finished healing.

I turned to Hiro, who still lay on his back, pinned under Izanami's blade. I crawled the distance between us and laid my hand on his cheek, startling him into wakefulness. He gasped in a sudden breath and flinched away from Izanami's blade before he noticed the time freeze. His eyes flickered to me, then back to Izanami, his expression devoid of any discernible emotion. I'd never seen a living creature look so lifeless.

I stood up and unlatched the blade from Izanami's hand, forcing her fingers to release with a series of cracks. I dropped the katana to the ground and knelt beside Hiro, who sat up slowly, staring at the far wall.

The sting of resentment abated when I saw the lost look on his face. There would come a time when I would berate him for lying to me, but how could I keep my anger burning when he looked like such a hollow shell? While I knew how it felt to be an unwanted child, my father had never said anything so cruel to me. Hiro had still wanted Izanami to be proud of him.

"Hiro, I'm so sorry," I said. I wanted to hold his hand the way he'd held mine after the Honengame's horrific vision, but I was too conscious of Neven a few feet away.

Hiro finally looked at me, but his eyes gave away no emotion, as if he knew I was there but didn't quite understand what that meant.

"Don't apologize," he said, and even his voice sounded completely soulless, an anonymous sound vacant of anything that made it *Hiro*. "You saved me."

He got to his knees and pressed a kiss to my forehead, warm and sticky with blood. I tensed, aware of Neven watching behind me, but of course Hiro wasn't exactly in his right mind.

"Thank you, Ren," he whispered into my skin. "Thank you for helping me do this."

"Do what?" I said.

But Hiro didn't answer. Instead, he turned to Izanami, and in one swift movement, grabbed the katana and pierced it through her chest.

I gasped, the clock slipping from my fingers and crashing to the floor.

Death pulled me in all directions at once, yanking my left arm from its socket and smashing my kneecaps into powder and threatening to rip my teeth from my gums, no longer a stable force but a feral energy. Hiro's overturned candle ignited the reed mats, and the darkness peeled away from the walls.

Through the chaos, Izanami's decayed vocal cords let out a harrowing wail, a swarm of flies surging past her torn lips and spiraling into a buzzing tornado.

I clung to the burning mats as the winds and insects whipped my hair around my face and tried to pry me away. Beside me, Neven had caged himself over the Yokai, both of them clinging to the wall even as it grew slippery, the darkness melting into slick liquid.

Hiro stood sturdy as the world broke into pieces around us, the katana still extended from his right arm, his black eyes blazing as Izanami thrashed and screamed.

She lunged toward Hiro, impaling herself further on the katana and scraping her finger bones across his arm, tearing the fabric to shreds and coating his arm in a full sleeve of blood. He twisted the blade a few degrees to the left, and black tar spilled out from Izanami's chest. She tugged at the blade until it began to saw her fingers off and the bony tips fell to the mat.

The winds surged harder, and the mat that I clung to came unglued from the floor, sending me crashing into the wall. I clawed at the wallpaper until my fingers sank into cracks in the wood, splinters piercing under my nails. The Yokai was screaming and Neven was shouting something about his clock, but even if I could have seen it in all the chaos, I wouldn't have been able to reach it.

Hiro yanked the blade out of Izanami's rib cage with a spray of acidic black sludge that singed holes into the reed mats. Izanami collapsed at his feet but still wouldn't give up. She latched on to Hiro's ankles, broken fingers scratching at his feet.

The constant tugging and crushing pressure of Death was like being torn apart by a pack of grims. I could no longer tell if the darkness kept surging over us in waves, or if I was constantly passing out from the raw power of Death. But in the sparse moments of light, I saw Hiro crying as he yanked Izanami up by the hair. He said something to her that I couldn't decipher over the roaring wind and splintering wood, the maelstrom ripping his tears from his cheeks. He pressed his eyes closed, then raised the sword to Izanami's throat and severed her head.

Both her head and body dissolved into a black powder, spilling through Hiro's fingers. The hurricane of darkness and flies and bone fragments inhaled the dust, spinning it around in an ever-tightening orbit above us. The wind grew even stronger, beginning to rip my hair from its roots.

Hiro rose to his feet, unimpeded by the strength of the storm. All at once, the dark hurricane changed direction and spiraled toward him.

But rather than crushing him to the ground, the winds changed direction, and Hiro's body began to inhale the darkness.

His skin absorbed the long tendrils of black that flowed endlessly into his open palms. The flies crawled into his ears and mouth, but he seemed not to notice them, his eyes suddenly so endlessly dark that they seemed not to exist at all, retreating into his skull.

With one final surge of twisted darkness into his chest, the pressure finally relented.

Being released from the torment was like dropping from the sky and landing flat on concrete. I couldn't hold back the small cries of pain as my joints popped back into place and my bones reformed. Neven was groaning and the Yokai was crying, but I didn't have the strength to get up and turn to them. I could only lie on the mat and look at Hiro. His katana clattered to the floor, but he made no move to pick it up, staring at the far wall and panting, face streaked with tears.

The doors opened and servants rushed into the room in a

panic, shadow guards materializing through the walls. They gasped, but no one made a move to subdue Hiro, or any of us.

Instead, they began to bow.

"Your Majesty," they said in haunting unison, foreheads pressed to the mat. They looked only to Hiro, ignoring the rest of us. I gasped, pressing a trembling hand to my mouth as I realized what Hiro had done.

He had succeeded Izanami and become the new God of Death.

I pulled myself to my feet, then crashed down to one side before lurching toward Hiro. He finally turned to me, holding out a hand to help me stand up straight, but I slapped it away.

"Ren," he said, "I—"

"You're a liar!" I said. I tried to shove him to the ground, but the room still spun above me and I could only grab his collar, pulling us both down. The guards loomed closer, but Hiro waved them away.

"This was what you wanted all along, wasn't it?" I gripped the front of his kimono and slammed him back into the floor, my strength rapidly coming back to me. He lay limp underneath me, looking pained, but didn't say a word.

"You didn't even…" I trailed off as tears burned at my eyes. "You didn't even tell me your real name," I said, unable to stop the tears from dropping onto Hiro's face.

"Ren, my real name means 'leech boy,'" he said, his voice barely a whisper, fresh tears welling in his eyes. "That's what she named me when I disappointed her. I showed you everything that I am, Ren, just not everything that I was."

"You used me!" I said, slamming him once more into the ground. He didn't fight me when his head bashed against the hard floor. "You pretended to care about me so I would take you here!"

"I never pretended!" Hiro said, grabbing my wrists and yanking my hands from his collar. I tried to pull my arms away, but he wouldn't release me. "I love you, Ren. That was never a lie."

"Why should I believe anything you say?" I managed to tear one arm free, but he lunged and pinned me to the floor. I didn't know if Hiro had always been so strong, or if he had suddenly become so much stronger with his new status as a Death God, but I felt weaker than a moth under his grasp.

"Because you understand me," Hiro said. When I stopped struggling, he released my arms and cupped my face. "I've wandered this world for longer than Japan has even existed, but I've never met anyone else who understands."

I said nothing as Hiro pressed his forehead to mine. Of course I felt the same, but was that enough to make up for all that he'd done?

"You know how it feels, Ren," he whispered. "When everyone tells you what you're not, even when your heart knows that they're wrong."

My eyes watered, the tense anger melting away from my limbs.

"I just wanted to come home," Hiro said, his tears now dripping onto my face.

I closed my eyes as more tears fell on me like a warm rain. Regardless of Hiro's intentions, killing Izanami wasn't the worst thing he could have done. She'd planned to eradicate all the Yokai, even the good ones, like the Honengame. She'd cast baby Hiro out to sea because he didn't look like the perfect Shinigami she'd wanted. She'd killed my mother and hadn't told me until after I'd murdered for her.

Perhaps Hiro would make a better God of Yomi after all.

"You could have told me," I said, but my words no longer had any anger behind them. "I trusted you."

"I'm sorry," Hiro whispered, kissing my forehead. "I'm so sorry, Ren. I was scared. But there's nothing to be scared of now. We've won."

He sat up, pulling me with him. His eyes sparkled brighter, his grip on my hands tight enough to shatter a human's bones.

"Marry me," he said.

My whole body tensed. I was positive that I'd misheard him. "What?" I whispered.

"We can be the new Izanagi and Izanami," he said, taking my hands and lacing our fingers together. His eyes looked fevered, the temperature of the room simmering with his excitement.

"Hiro," I said, so stunned that I could barely form a coherent thought.

"I'm the new God of Yomi," Hiro said, squeezing my hands, "and I want you to be the Goddess."

Goddess, I thought, the word echoing back a hundred times through the dark cave of my mind.

Once upon a time, I'd lain on the dirty streets of London at the mercy of a pair of scissors, and now I could have a palace made of gold and an army of the dead bowing at my feet. It would no longer matter if I was a Reaper or a Shinigami, because I would be a deity. Those who questioned me would be drowned alive in the tar of deep darkness because Hiro loved me, would do anything for me, would kill anyone for me if I only asked.

Suddenly every part of me burned with black fire. I was all the concentrated light of the sun and the cruelest coldest depths of the ocean. I was every brief flash of life and the frozen infinity of Death, and the whole world belonged to me. Every star of the universe was tied to my fingers by a puppet string.

"Yes," I said. I grabbed Hiro by the collar and pulled him closer. "Yes, I will."

I grabbed his jaw with one hand and leaned in to kiss him, but something yanked me to the floor.

"Are you insane?" Neven said.

My face pulled into a scowl as I rolled to my feet. Of course, I could count on my brother to once again ruin everything.

"I told you from the start that we couldn't trust him!" Neven said, the Yokai clinging to his leg. "Do you honestly believe he had no idea this would happen?"

"You would never understand!" I said, the raw ferocity in my voice startling both Neven and the Yokai into jumping back a few feet.

"Ren, he lied to you so he could kill his mother!" Neven said. "What do I not understand?"

"That she deserved it!" I said. "Or is that too complex for the Patron Saint of Mercy to understand? Did you want to adopt Izanami, as well?"

"Ren, please…" Neven stepped forward to take my hands. I snatched them out of his grasp, and he flinched, the Yokai shrinking into fox form and letting out a high-pitched cry.

All the qualities I'd envied in Neven—kindness, mercy,

humanity—suddenly seemed like such privileged ignorance. Of course it was easy to condemn hurting others when you'd never known the voracious anger that came with being hurt. Neven could so easily stand before us and denounce Hiro for killing Izanami because he wasn't the one who had lost his mother or his home to her. "You don't know what it's like to be unwanted," I said, taking a step back. "That's why you'll never understand."

"Of course I don't!" Neven said, falling to his knees. "But what would you have me do about it, Ren? If I could take your place, I would."

"It's so easy to promise things that will never happen," I said, turning away from my brother and returning to Hiro, who wrapped an arm around my waist.

Neven looked between us, the Yokai circling his ankle. "Ren, don't do this. Please."

"It's not your decision," I said.

"Ren, you can't trust him!" Neven said. "He's not a good person!"

I scoffed, then slid my hand into Hiro's. "Neither am I."

Neven's eyes went wide, his lips trembling. He fell forward onto his hands, head hanging low. I expected him to cry, the way he always did when things went wrong. But his fingers scraped into the floor like claws, and when he looked up again, his eyes seared with blue fire.

He rose to his feet and grabbed the abandoned, bloody katana from the floor.

"Neven," I said. "What do you think you're doing?"

But Neven wasn't looking at me anymore. He looked only at Hiro.

"You won't take her," Neven whispered. "I won't let you."

He'd only taken a single step toward Hiro when a thousand shadows wrapped around his arms and dragged him to the ground. His chin slammed into the floor and blood welled in his mouth, but he still clutched the katana in his right hand and thrashed against the guards. The fox keened and leaped back and forth, trying to gnaw the shadows off him.

Hiro stood motionless a few feet away, arms crossed and expression unreadable.

The shadows swirled over Neven's eyes like a blindfold, but he raked his nails across his face and tore them to pieces.

"Release me!" he yelled in the language of Death, and the shadowy tendrils shivered and loosened their grip just enough for him to slide free.

Neven had never looked so enraged. And for what? To stop me from finally becoming who I was meant to be?

"Stop it!" I shouted in Death, stepping in front of Hiro. "Why do you always ruin everything you don't understand?"

"I would rather ruin everything than watch you turn into a monster," Neven said, stumbling to his feet and slashing the blade at the cloud of hovering shadow guards behind him.

I tried to grab his wrist, but he twisted away from me, accidentally scoring a line across my cheek. The sight of my blood startled him just long enough for me to force the blade from his hand, his fingers snapping in my grip. He hissed and cradled his hand as the katana clattered to the floor, his eyes still a scalding blue that now focused on me instead of Hiro.

"I've followed you across the world," Neven said, chest heaving. "I believed in you. But this time, you're wrong, Ren."

My hands fell away. I closed my eyes and resolved not to cry, even as I realized that I would never have both the life I wanted and a brother who loved me.

I had so desperately wanted Neven to love me as I was, wretched and dark and greedy. But the only person who would ever love me was someone equally as dark.

Hiro's hand fell on my shoulder as he stepped beside me. "Neven—"

"Do whatever you want to me," Neven said, scowling. "Lock me up or flay me or burn my eyes out with your stupid light tricks, but I won't stand by and watch you ruin her."

Hiro's fingers tightened on my shoulder.

"All right," he said slowly. "As you wish, Neven."

The shadow guards materialized once again, encircling Neven's limbs and wrapping tight around his lips to muffle his panicked sounds. The Yokai squealed as the shadows muzzled her, as well.

"Take him away," Hiro said, waving his hand as if to dismiss them.

"Wait!" I said, pushing away from Hiro. My gaze cast back and forth between the shadow choking my brother and the writhing, screaming fox. "Stop it!" I said, but the guards stilled only when Hiro held up a hand.

"Ren," he said, one hand reaching out to caress my cheek, "you don't have to worry about them interfering anymore. As you said, they'll never understand."

I shook my head. No matter how angry I was, I would never want Neven hurt. He let out a plaintive sound before the shadows locked tighter around him, knocking his glasses halfway off his face.

"I don't… I don't want him chained in a cold dungeon somewhere," I said, "or tortured by your shadow guards."

Hiro nodded, tucking my hair behind my ear. "Anything you want, Ren. And the Yokai?"

I frowned down at the feral fox trying to bite into the formless guard. Neven thrashed against the shadows, and I remembered why I'd kept her around in the first place.

"Her, too," I said. "Can you just…keep them at a distance so we can have our wedding in peace?"

Hiro nodded, lifting my hand and pressing a warm kiss to my fingers. "Of course."

"And don't let your guards hurt them," I said.

Hiro squeezed my hand and nodded, turning to the guards. "Do as she says."

Neven wrenched away from the guard's hand. "Ren!" he said, reaching out for me.

But the tearing of the darkness swallowed his cry, and the guards pulled him and the girl onto another plane, leaving only the ruins of the throne room and the echo of his voice where he'd once stood.

Something in my chest stung as Neven vanished, but Hiro erased the thought with his warm lips against mine and his hand on the small of my back, leading me out of the throne room. I wouldn't let Neven hold me back from being who I was meant to be. I would tell Hiro to bring him back in a few days, after we'd both calmed down, and Hiro would do it, because he'd do anything for me.

Hiro led me to a royal chamber, where he tore my clothes off with knives that scored my skin, then bit and scratched at every inch of me. I let him hold me hard enough to leave bruises on my bones, and he let me grip his throat and crush down and down until his eyes rolled back in his head, because this was what it meant to be the most powerful people in all of Japan—to ruin and destroy.

I didn't realize, until much later that night, that I had never gathered Neven's clock from the floor of the throne room.

CHAPTER 22

I woke up to darkness, unable to tell if it was day or night. Hiro was already awake behind me, his arms caged around my ribs, a thin futon beneath us. I couldn't make out shapes in the darkness while half awake, but I remembered Hiro taking my hand and leading me down hallways painted with dragons and spiraling rivers, white lightning and red daybreak over fields of rice. He'd opened a door by the murals of the fire god's birth and sealed us in a windowless bedroom where our shadows cast monstrous shapes on the white paper doors.

Now I felt like I was waking into a strange alternate reality, one where I had never known London and had always woken up with Hiro's warm skin against mine. He pressed a kiss to my neck and pulled me even closer, like he feared I'd run away from him.

"Good morning," he whispered into my skin.

"Is it morning?" I said. "I can hardly tell down here."

"We're gods," Hiro said. "It can be whatever time we want it to be."

Technically, I wasn't a god yet, but I didn't bother correcting him.

"How does it feel?" I said, turning over to face him and combing my fingers through his hair. "Being a god, I mean."

Hiro thought for a moment, tracing shapes into my spine. "Like I'm reading a thousand different books at once, but somehow all of them make sense," he said. "I hear the names of the dead in my sleep, and when I close my eyes, I see their faces. Every time one of them dies, it's like a shot of opium straight into my heart. All of my bones tremble, and my blood rushes ten times faster through my body."

He shuddered against me, as if imagining it. "I can understand why Izanami wanted more," he said.

My hands stilled in his hair. "But you're not going to take more, are you?" I said.

Hiro chuckled, pressing his face into my collarbone. "I'm not going to eradicate the Yokai, if that's what you're asking," he said, mumbling against my skin. "There is only one more thing that I truly desire, and it has nothing to do with the Yokai."

Then he lifted his head and kissed me again. He pulled away just as I began to claw at his shoulder blades.

"Speaking of which," he said, sitting up, "I know you are not Shintoist, but I would like our wedding ceremony to be traditional, if that's all right."

My face warmed at the mention of our wedding, but I nodded. Hiro smiled and kissed my forehead.

"I have a present for you," he said. "Wait here a moment."

He stood up and left the room, the door sliding shut behind him. I wasn't even sure if he'd stopped to put clothes on, but I supposed a god could do whatever he wanted.

Lying in the dark, beneath the elaborately painted ceiling, the depth of the darkness overwhelmed me. For the first time, I was alone in Yomi. Without another soul to ground me, the endless darkness threatened to erase every memory and replace it with nothingness, scrubbing away the features of my face and stripping me of my name, letter by letter. Perhaps Tamamo No Mae had proven useful after all, for at least I didn't have to worry about Neven spiraling into despair from loneliness.

The door slid open and Hiro returned. He pulled me up and placed a piece of cool metal in my hand, a circle of intertwining gold and silver, freezing cold, somehow lighter than air. A ring.

I looked up at Hiro. "Is this—"

"There are no rings in a Shinto wedding ceremony," Hiro said, "but I read of this tradition and I rather liked it."

I closed my fist around the ring. "English traditions are of no importance to me," I said. Was I not Japanese enough for his Shinto ceremony?

Hiro shook his head, sitting on the bed beside me. "It's not only an English tradition," he said. "The ancient Egyptians wore wedding rings. They believed the circle was the symbol of eternity. That's fitting for newlywed gods, isn't it?"

My anger melted away as Hiro gently opened my palm and

picked up the ring, then slid it onto my finger. The gold and silver on the band swirled together in a watercolor design, like two typhoons crashing into each other. It sparkled with diamond flecks, casting light even in the darkness.

"I didn't mean to imply anything," Hiro said. "I only wanted to give you a gift."

I didn't know what to say, so I kissed Hiro's cheek. "Thank you," I said quietly. What an odd feeling to receive a present, much less one so valuable. "Where did you even find this?"

"You would be surprised what kinds of riches are hoarded in Yomi," he said. "To my understanding, offerings from the dead are melted down and forged into new jewelry. I looked through the vault while you were asleep, and this piece reminded me of you."

"Why?" I said, smirking. "Because of the mixed metals?"

He shook his head. "Because it's beautiful."

My face flushed and I turned away as Hiro laughed at me. How could such simple words always disarm me so easily?

"I have to go," he said. "There's a lot to arrange for the ceremony. We'll need to inform the dead of Izanami's passing."

I wanted to cling to him, my only tether to the world above, but I nodded and let him go.

"The next time I see you," he said, squeezing my hand, "you will become my wife."

Servants came in shortly after to run me a bath hot enough to melt bones and scrub my skin raw. All of them called me "Your Majesty" and wouldn't look me in the eye. They looked more like silhouettes than true people, watery abstracts of souls. Was this how all souls decayed in Yomi, or were these servants bound by some contract to the God of Death, my betrothed?

Their stoicism unnerved me. The air of the bathroom filled up with steam that masked their hazy faces and made them look more like ghosts than humans, halfway part of this world and halfway Beyond. It was a strange sensation to be in a bathroom with so many others yet feel so alone.

One of the servants raised a bucket of boiling water to add to the tub, but it slipped from her fingers and poured out too quickly, rocking the still waters with a scalding wave across my face. I frowned and combed wet hair from my eyes as the servant gasped and threw herself to the ground.

"Forgive me, Your Majesty," she said, bowing to the tile floor.

The other servants ignored her, continuing to scrub my legs and feet while the girl lay still as a corpse, waiting for my pardon.

I peered down at her and wondered just how long she would lie waiting for me in foolish obedience. If I told her to wait until the end of time, would she listen? And was it allegiance to Izanami that bound her, or did she truly fear me? I had never had so much sway over anyone, never been anything more important than the soot beneath their boots. I felt like someone had handed me the entire universe in a box with a bow and told me to use it as I pleased.

"Get on the floor," I said.

The servant instantly deepened her bow.

"No," I said, "put your face on the floor."

Without hesitation, she pressed her face to the bathroom tiles, soaked with the scalding water she'd spilled. But there was nothing glorious about her obedience. Instead, a sour feeling sloshed in my stomach and the water around me felt too hot, like it was no longer cleansing me but cooking me alive.

But why? I was supposed to feel smug, or at least feel an ounce of the satisfaction I'd felt when killing the Yokai. Never again would I have to bite my tongue or apologize for wrongs I hadn't done or bow to people who didn't deserve it. Now the world belonged to me, to break and burn as I pleased, and it was supposed to feel better than this. A true goddess wouldn't have thought twice about making her servants look like fools, or the look on her ignorant brother's face when she'd sent him away. So why did my hands shake and my mouth fill with bitterness?

I gripped the edges of the bathtub.

"Get out," I whispered.

The servants exchanged blank looks.

"Your Majesty," one of them said, "we're supposed to help you—"

"*Get out!*" I said, the porcelain rim of the tub cracking under my hands.

The servants scurried out, bowing as they shut the door with a quiet click. The moment they were gone, I hurled a scrubbing brush at the mirror and shattered it, spraying shards across the wet tiles.

I leaned back, placing my shaking hands over my face as the water settled back into stillness.

Even now, Neven was ruining everything. I had everything I'd ever wanted, but because of his childish moralism in the back of my mind, I couldn't enjoy it. Neven was wrong about Hiro and I didn't need to waste my time worrying about him. He would be perfectly fine. That was what Hiro had said, and Hiro wouldn't lie to me. Except that technically, he already had.

I emerged from the water, which had rapidly started to cool, then clambered out of the bathtub and picked up the scrubbing brush from the floor. Shards of broken mirror sliced into my feet, but I didn't even feel them. I stood before what was left of the mirror and scrubbed the rest of my skin until I felt like a serpent ready to molt. I kept scrubbing, even when the brush began to pick up blood. I would heal long before the wedding, so it wouldn't matter if I scrubbed and scrubbed and scrubbed down to the bone.

Neven is wrong, I thought, scrubbing harder. *He's wrong, and I am a Death Goddess, and everything is going to be fine.*

The servants dressed me in my wedding kimono, wrapping me in layers and layers of heavy snow-white fabric.

They pinned my long hair up with clips and combs, then hid their efforts under a great white hat, a semi-circle resembling a moon. I had never worn anything remotely formal in my nearly two centuries of life, and suddenly having my hair tied in elaborate knots and my lips painted with a fine brush felt like a bizarre masquerade. But I let the servants do as they had been instructed, feeling too empty to protest.

The ceremony itself mattered little to me. I'd never dreamed of my wedding day as the humans did—I had never entertained the thought of getting married. But for Hiro, I could play the part of a bride for a few hours, before I finally assumed my role as a goddess.

As the servants rolled white socks onto my feet, I began to

worry about what, exactly, the wedding ceremony would entail. The last thing I wanted was to humiliate myself in front
of a royal court. But Hiro knew I wasn't Shintoist and hadn't
seemed concerned, so it couldn't be anything too onerous.

One servant girl tucked a small purse, a dagger, and a
fan into my belt, then hid them beneath folds of fabric. She
couldn't have been much older than the Yokai.

"What are these for?" I said.

She jumped at the sound of my voice, then straightened
and bowed.

"They're tradition, Your Majesty," the girl said. "The purse
is for beauty, the fan is for happiness, and the knife is to protect your husband."

I doubted Hiro needed protection from anyone, but I nodded and let her finish tying my dress. She led me to the throne
room, where Hiro waited for me on his golden throne.

He stood up and smiled, bright and clear like the first day
I'd met him.

I had never seen Hiro in anything but his blue fishing
clothes. Now, he wore a formal kimono with a shirt and jacket
of clean and unwrinkled black, deep as all of Yomi. From
the waist down, the fabric of his kimono was embroidered
with long gray and silver stripes, elongating his silhouette,
like a birch tree in the dark of winter. How could someone
like this—more breathtaking than all the constellations in a
clear sky—want me? Hiro looked like a true god, someone
carved from the first light of the universe, every part of him
so impossibly beautiful that he didn't seem real. I crossed the
distance between us as if pulled by an invisible string, and
when he took my hand and pressed a scalding kiss to it, I had

to stop myself from melting into his arms to preserve my dignity in front of all the servants, no matter how much I wanted to grab hold of him and never let go.

"You look lovely," he said.

I thought I looked rather like a walking egg, but I kept the comment to myself.

In the short time since last night, the throne room had been repaired, the floorboards once again smooth and wallpaper replaced, every trace of Izanami scrubbed away. Remembering Neven's clock, I turned away from Hiro and looked around the room for any trace of silver or gold, but no metals reflected the dim light.

"Hiro," I said. "Where is—"

His hands cupped my face, turning me toward him. "Later," he said, smiling. Then he took my hand, pulling me to the door. "Come. They're waiting for us."

All the dead of Yomi had come to see the wedding of their new god.

A sea of stoic faces in white kimonos stood in reverent silence across the palace courtyard. The crowds spanned so far back that they disappeared in the fog of darkness, which even a Shinigami's eyes couldn't penetrate.

These will be my subjects, I thought. All of the dead who had ever died and ever would. My knees began to shake under their unrelenting gaze, but before I could fall, Hiro put his hand on the small of my back and ushered me forward. The procession curved around the back of the palace to a shrine dripping with darkness like wet paint, open to the air and exposing us to the endless crowds.

"First, we must be purified," Hiro said.

Nothing on Earth or Yomi could ever make me pure, but I didn't voice the thought. This was important to Hiro, after all.

A man with white robes and a tall black hat, who I assumed to be a priest, bowed as we entered. He lit several ceremonial candles, the sudden light illuminating the round shape of his glasses. I thought of Neven in the shadow guard's hold, glasses askew on his face, and tore my gaze away as the priest began a half-spoken and half-sung incantation.

His words sounded vaguely Japanese, but I understood none of them. I looked to Hiro in confusion, and he took my cold hand and squeezed it.

"The words are ancient," he whispered. "He's asking for the blessing of the gods."

What futility for a human to beseech the gods to bless a different god, I thought.

When the priest finally stopped, a shrine maiden in long red skirts offered him a bough. She looked far too young to be a priestess, her whole form swallowed by the shadows. The priest continued his chant and waved the bough over both Hiro and I, but I kept staring at the young girl. I must have stared far too intently, for she looked up and jolted back at the eye contact, quickly bowing and stepping back into the shadows.

The priest turned to set the bough down, and in the changing light I could see his round glasses, like two bright full moons. I began to feel sick.

The priest poured a clear liquid that smelled like sake into a shallow metal cup and passed it to Hiro, who then passed it to me with both hands.

"You must drink," he said. "It has been blessed."

I stared at my pale reflection in the sake, unable to move my arms, even as all of Yomi watched and waited.

Those who ate or drank the food of Yomi could never return to Earth. Hiro had said as much when I'd first met him, and I'd already read it in the legend of Izanami. It was the reason she hadn't been able to return to Earth with her husband after her death, the reason her rage and sorrow had first brought Death upon the humans.

Once I drank the wine of Yomi, I could never leave Hiro. I would never be able to escape his domain.

"Ren?" Hiro said.

My hands had locked around the cup, unable to move. The priest and shrine maidens watched me in silence.

"I'm sorry," I whispered, "I'm just a bit… I feel—"

"Are you scared?" Hiro said.

I didn't answer, looking across the sea of expectant faces, the eyes of the dead a bright white in the near-darkness.

"Don't worry about them," Hiro said, turning my face back toward him. "It's all right, Ren. I know this all happened rather quickly. I know it's overwhelming."

I glanced at the priest and the small shrine girl behind him, both watching me, eyes white and expectant.

Hiro moved in front of them, blocking them from my view.

"Don't worry about anyone else," he said. "Just look at me. Tell me your fears, and I'll take care of them. I can give you anything in the world."

I shook my head. "I…"

My frigid blood boiled under the weight of my kimono. I could see nothing but the white eyes of the dead, and the soft edges of the priest's glasses lit up by the candlelight, the small girl behind him, and the cup trembling in my hands. I wanted the darkness to open its jaws and devour me.

"Ren, you have to breathe," Hiro said, his hands like burning coal on my face. I was supposed to be corpse-cold, not melting under my clothing. I felt like Yuki Onna as her bones liquefied.

"Ren!" Hiro said, nails biting into my cheeks.

"I want Neven," I said at last. The moment the words left my mouth, the feeling of imminent doom faded away, the night air of Yomi soothing the sweat on my brow.

Hiro's hands fell away from my face.

"I shouldn't have sent him away," I said.

Hiro withdrew, his face shrouded by shadows and indecipherable in the half darkness.

"You mean that you regret agreeing to marry me?" he said, so quiet and fragile.

"No!" I said. I took his hand, but it hung limp in mine. "I want to marry you. But please, let my brother and the Yokai out first. They should be here, too."

Hiro frowned. "Let them out of what, Ren?"

A wave of coldness crashed over me, chasing away the panicked heat under my skin.

"Have you not locked them up somewhere in the palace?" I said.

Hiro shook his head, then took my free hand and gave it a squeeze that was probably meant to reassure me. "As I said, you don't have to worry about them anymore."

"What do you mean?" I said, sliding my hand out of Hiro's. "Where are they?"

Hiro gestured at the night beyond the shrine. "Away," he said. "It doesn't matter anymore."

"Of course it matters!" I said, casting the cup of sake to the ground. The priest and priestess drew back. The dead gasped behind me, but no one dared to interfere. "You told me your guards wouldn't hurt them, so why can't they be here?"

"My guards haven't laid a hand on them, Ren," Hiro said, staring at me with moon-bright and unblinking eyes. "They only took them to the deep darkness."

I had been certain, up until that point, that the defining moment of my life was when I lost control of my light and struck down the High Reapers in the street. That day marked a definitive end to the life I had known, the death of Wren Scarborough and the birth of Ren of Yakushima. After it happened, my home might as well have turned to ruins behind me, because I could never go back and nothing would ever be the same.

But, as all the blood drained from my body and my throat clamped shut, I knew that the true defining moment of my life was when I realized that I had killed my brother.

I couldn't move, my joints locked as if they'd turned to stone, trapping me in a prison of bones while inside I was falling from an infinite height, unable to scream. I sucked in a weak breath and thought back to the one and only thing Neven had ever asked of me.

You won't leave me alone outside in the dark? he'd said. And I'd promised him that I wouldn't.

I imagined Neven stumbling through the darkness, crawling through the slick soil just to keep himself tethered to something real in all the endless night. The Yokai would cling to his back and wet his neck with tears, trusting even when she felt his bones rattling against each other from fear. The monsters would smell their tears and come crawling, shadows licking at their heels with forked tongues. I prayed they'd swallow them whole and crush every bone with a single bite of their gigantic maws, killing them instantly. But Hiro said they loved breaking humans into pieces, so maybe they would suck the flesh off their bones limb by limb, popping out each individual joint to build their nests, fueled by the song of their screams.

My ears burned with the memory of Neven calling for me as the guards dragged him away. He had cried for me...and I had turned away from him.

The lock on my bones unlatched and I collapsed onto my forearms, letting out an inhuman sound of despair. The floorboards quivered at the violent noise, the taste of Death like bile on my tongue.

"Ren," Hiro said, kneeling down before me. "I thought—"

But he never finished his sentence, because I lunged and shoved him into the ceremonial table, the back of his skull hitting the edge with a dull thunk. Flowers and sacred texts spilled across the floor, and the darkness swirled with a sudden swarm of shadow guards.

Hiro held up a hand to stop them.

"Do not interfere," he said. "I'm fine."

His calmness only enraged me more, and I yanked him up by the collar again, then smashed him into the ground. I felt Death surging through my veins, my blood boiling, skin turning translucent.

"He was always going to get in our way, Ren," Hiro said, turning his head as I tried to score my nails through his eyes. "I know that you're upset now, but soon you will see that this was necessary. You will forget him in your eternity as a goddess."

"I could never forget him!" I said, curling my hand into a fist and aiming a punch that would have shattered his cheekbone, but he caught my hand easily.

"You think that I never lost anyone?" he said, his fingers tightening around my wrist. "I had siblings, too, Ren. But centuries mean nothing in the face of eternity. I can't even remember their faces. In our time as gods, this will only be a sentence of your endless story. But our love will be eternal."

My hands shook, horrified by the sincerity in Hiro's voice.

"I don't love you," I said.

"Yes, you do," Hiro said, like it was an absolute truth. I thrashed against his hands and tried to break away because he was right and he knew it. Was this curse really the love that humans spent their whole lives seeking? They could have it. I didn't want it at all.

I lunged for his throat, ready to snap his neck, but he grabbed my hands again before I could.

"That's enough, Ren," he said.

I wrenched my arms away and managed to scratch his face before he grabbed my wrists, this time with more force, snapping them both. I bit down on a sound of pain as the bones healed themselves.

"I said that's enough," he said. "It's time to finish the ceremony."

I spat in his face. "If you marry me, I'll kill you the moment you close your eyes," I said. "Keep me in your bed and you'll never sleep again."

He sighed and pulled me to my feet, wiping his face on his sleeve.

Then his fingers closed around my throat, the darkness plummeting pitch-black all around us, the crowds gone, the shrine evaporated. I felt like my bones turned to dust under the crushing pressure of Death. I hung limp in his grip, suspended by my throat.

"Do you really believe you could kill me, Ren?" Hiro said. "You live because I allow it."

Then the pressure vanished and I collapsed to the floor, wanting to cry for the death of the Hiro that I'd known.

"This has gone on long enough," Hiro said. "Guards, kindly help Ren complete the ceremony."

The shadows wrapped around my arms like sleeves, hauling me to my feet and dragging me forward. Other shadows retrieved the cup I'd cast aside and refilled it with sake. They brought it closer to my face, but I jerked my head away, spilling it down the front of my dress.

My gaze fell on the ceremonial candles flickering on the table. More sake splashed down my neck as the guards tried again, but I stretched a hand out toward the candles and poured all the light inside me into its flame, every bit of warmth and brightness somewhere deep inside the dark cage of my heart.

The light blasted away the darkness, stripping it clean off the floorboards of the shrine. The shadow guards disintegrated under the onslaught of light, releasing my arms.

Hiro stood unmoving by the table, his lips pressed tightly

together. Under the violent brightness of my artificial day-light, he looked paler against his black clothes, almost like the dead that wailed and shielded their eyes from the light.

"What a nice party trick, Ren," Hiro said. "It may work on my guards, but it won't work on me."

I barely dodged his hand as he reached for my throat, his nails scoring lines on my skin. I backed up against the half walls of the shrine, nearly tumbling backward over the edge. Hiro strode closer with the unhurried pace of someone who knew they were going to win.

I reached for my clock, and Hiro didn't try to stop me. But as my fingers touched the fabric where my pocket was supposed to be, I realized why he hadn't interfered.

"Where is Neven's clock?" I said. We'd passed through the throne room where I'd dropped it, but the floor had been swept clean.

"You gave it up, Ren," Hiro said, smirking. "Don't you remember how you wanted to be a Shinigami?"

"Where is it?" I said, bracing myself against the columns as Hiro drew closer.

"You don't need it anymore," he said.

I shook my head. The darkness spun around me, and maybe Hiro was drowning me in the night or maybe I was just faint-ing, but none of it mattered because I had lost. I was going to spend eternity as Hiro's prisoner, all because I'd wanted power. My hands shook, but there was nothing to hold on to. I thought of the dagger in my belt and wondered if Hiro would stop me from plunging it into my own heart. I de-served death even more than he did.

I grabbed my throat, trying desperately to take in air, the

cool metal of my cursed wedding ring stinging my neck. It burned like frostbite against my skin, and I moved to yank it off and hurl it into the darkness.

But my fingers hesitated as they brushed over the sparkling silver and gold. This, I realized, was my solution.

I sucked in a dizzying breath, then tore away a layer of my kimono and pulled the ceremonial dagger from my belt. Hiro watched with impatience as I unsheathed it.

"You think I can't stop you, Ren?" he said. "I am a god."

"And I am a Reaper," I said, stepping closer.

"That means very little without your clock," Hiro said. "Put that toy away, or there will be consequences."

"You don't know anything about Reapers," I said. "If you did, you would know that we don't need clocks to turn time."

Hiro tensed.

"That's a lie," he said, though he no longer sounded certain. "You and Neven always needed your clocks."

I shook my head.

"The clocks are tradition," I said. "They let the timekeepers see our movements so that no one affects the timeline too much. But we don't actually need them."

I pressed the blade to his heart.

"What we need," I said, holding up my left hand, the wedding band sparkling in the darkness, "is pure silver and gold."

Hiro's lips parted in surprise. Death sparkled at the edges of my vision, his power ready to compact me into dust.

But Reapers knew how to use time, and that every second contained a thousand moments.

There was the moment that Hiro understood his mistake, his face washed clean with shock.

Then the moment that he realized he would have to subdue me, and his eyes began to warp with anger.

Next would be the moment that Death crashed over me and snapped apart every vertebrae of my spine.

But that moment would never come.

The instant the world stopped turning, I plunged the blade into Hiro's heart.

Just like before, when I set time turning again, the world fell to pieces.

The dead screamed and ran around the courtyard, the sky filling up with cries of terror and panic. But this time I ignored it, because I could look only at Hiro.

He gripped my sleeves, the only thing holding him upright. But soon his weight was too much for me and we fell to the floor of the temple. He wouldn't look away from me, his black eyes still petrified with shock.

"Ren," he whispered, tears running down the sides of his face as he looked at me and only me, his blood hot beneath my right hand, soaking my white kimono.

"Ren, I love you," he whispered.

Even now, he loved me. I didn't know how he could, how anyone could. But Hiro didn't love me the way Tennyson had written in his poems, a love that was birdsong and golden mornings and endless fields of flowers. Hiro's love was hungry and cold, an empty room that he'd tried to lock me inside of.

I moved to stand up, too shattered by the intensity of his gaze, but he let out a weak cry, his bloody hand grabbing at my sleeve.

"Don't leave me," he said. "Please, Ren, just hold me. I don't want to be alone."

I closed my eyes as tears burned down my cheeks. I wanted to hold him as his soul left for whatever hell awaited creatures like us. But I thought of Neven dying in the darkness, and I couldn't bear to look at him.

I stood up and crossed the shrine, watching the chaos outside as the darkness fractured and tossed the dead back and forth, broke their bones and tore them to pieces in the chaos of a change in power. Behind me, Hiro coughed and cried for me, begged me to come back. But I would not turn around, even as sobs racked my body and I had to hold the wooden banister for support.

When he finally fell silent, the winds picked up, stirring dust into the air. The darkness began to flow into me, the feeling just as euphoric as Hiro had described. For a moment, I saw Yomi in the sunlight, the majesty of all the palace's colors, the trees swaying against a backdrop of blue, the people flushed and alive. But the darkness returned, as it always did, poisoning my blood. I could feel the world above, all the stuttering final breaths and screams of agony and pleas for just a little more time. I could feel the Shinigami, carrying their lanterns throughout the country, facing their eternal servitude. I could feel the Yokai like a distant ache in my bones, shapeless shadows that burned in my blood. The exhilarating rush of power and the compounded sadness of all of Japan's deaths brought me to my knees, heaving a wretched sob into the bloodstained sleeves of my wedding dress.

Death had finally come for me, but not as the Reapers intended.

They had set Death loose on me, but instead of it devouring me, I had swallowed it whole. I'd let it poison every inch of me and done nothing as it decimated everyone that mattered. I no longer had to run from Death, for I had become it.

Yomi had fallen quiet, the dead gathering themselves in the aftermath of the chaotic transfer of power. I cried as they bowed and called me "Your Majesty," a title that I no longer wanted. I looked behind me, where Hiro's body had dissolved to dust. The shrine lay still and empty, the stairs painted with blood, just as the Honengame had predicted.

Then I turned away from the ruins of my wedding ceremony and looked, instead, across the infinite darkness of my kingdom.

CHAPTER 23

"Enter."

The door to the throne room slid open. The shadow guards threw themselves to the floor in deep bows, and that was how I knew it was bad news.

"What have you found?" I said, crossing my arms and leaning against the velvet seat of the throne. "Surely, you've found something, or you wouldn't have bothered returning."

"We're deeply sorry, Your Majesty," the first guard said, his voice trembling. "We searched the depths of the darkness, but there was no sign of them."

I sighed, resting my chin on one hand. "You see, I don't believe that's possible. Do you know why?"

The guards didn't answer, shivering as Death slowly began

to crush down from above, the jagged ceiling sinking lower and lower.

"Do you?" I said.

"No, Your Majesty," the second one said.

"It's not possible," I said slowly, as if speaking to particularly dense children, "because I ordered you to find them, and you must fulfill my orders. Am I wrong?"

"No, Your Majesty," they said in unison.

"Then where is my brother?" I said, the language of Death stripping the paneling from the walls, sending wood planks crashing down on top of the guards. *"You idiotic shadow puppets were the ones that tossed him out there, were you not? How could you possibly forget where you put him?"*

"It wasn't us, Your Majesty," one of the guards said, crying out as a piece of wood fell over his head. "Other guards—"

"You are all the same to me," I said. "Faceless minions. So tell me, why haven't you found him, when I've ordered you to do so?"

"Your Majesty," said the first guard, "if I may, it's possible that…" He trailed off, looking up to me for permission.

"Yes, go on," I said. "What's possible, exactly?"

"It's possible that the creatures of the deep darkness… Perhaps we're too late."

In an instant, I crossed the room and ripped the shadow in half like a sheet of paper. He cried out as I ripped him into infinitely smaller pieces, sprinkling them like confetti over his trembling companion.

"Do you agree?" I said.

"No, Your Majesty!" he said, the edges of his silhouette rippling with fear.

"Then go back out there and find him!"

"Yes, Your Majesty!" The moment he felt my dismissal, he phased through the walls and vanished.

I tossed open the doors to the throne room and stormed down the hallways. The dead servants threw themselves to the ground in bows as I passed, but I ignored them. It had been months since I'd become their goddess, and while they excelled at cowering before me, they had made nonexistent progress fulfilling the only order that I actually cared about.

At first, I'd tried to charge into the deep darkness myself, but could walk only as far as the edges of my courtyard before the darkness turned to lead and crushed me to the tiles. My katana clattered to the ground, suddenly too heavy to lift.

"Your Highness, you cannot go to the deep darkness without a successor," a shadow guard had said. "If you die—"

"I do as I please!" I'd said, raking my fingers through the air behind me. The guard evaporated into the night, but another took his place.

"If you die at the hands of the monsters in the deep darkness," he said, "they will inherit your kingdom."

"They can have it!" I said, trying to charge through the darkness once more, but it formed a solid wall against my hands.

"Your Highness," the guard said, "they would devour all the souls above. Everyone in Japan would die."

I gave up pushing against the unyielding barrier, falling to my knees. How fitting it would be, as my last dying act, to ruin all of Japan, just as I'd already destroyed everything else that mattered. But Neven was worth every soul in Japan and more.

"I have no intention of dying," I said. "Let me through."

"I cannot do that," the guard said.

Darkness boiled in my fingertips. "I said—"

"This is not my rule, Your Highness," the guard said. "It was written by Izanagi when Yomi first came into being."

I slammed my fist into the ground, shattering the black tiles. Of course, Izanami's husband, responsible for the birth of new souls, would protect his kingdom of the living. But ever since Izanami had chased him out of Yomi in a rage of thunder, no one knew where to find him.

The darkness rumbled, raining down in jagged hail around us. Now I was strong enough to smash all the tiles of the courtyard, drain the lake in the garden, turn all the water lilies to ashes and rip every shadow guard to shreds, but none of it would bring Neven back.

I fell onto my hands, hanging my head and letting the darkness inhale my tears.

"Find him," I whispered. "Please."

"Yes, Your Majesty," the guard said instantly. But I didn't want reflexive obedience and empty promises. I wanted Neven.

While I waited for the guards month after month, I had to keep the rest of Japan from falling apart.

In a few hours, I expected some Southern Shinigami to arrive and report on their progress, as they did every few weeks. I could sense the population of Tokyo increasing, so I considered transferring some Shinigami north to compensate. The population of Japan was growing, now that it had opened up to the West, and we had to keep up the pace. More

Shinigami would be born soon, and I would need to oversee their training. I had so many duties that I cared so little for.

As I stormed down the hall, several hundred more deaths absorbed into my bloodstream all at once, spreading a pleasant coolness across my skin. The feeling always calmed me, temporarily sating the mindless hunger for souls that rotted in my stomach. But it never lasted long enough. I could understand, in some terrible way, why Izanami had always wanted more.

At times, I still saw her.

Not in my dreams, or in the hazy half vision of the darkness, but when I sat alone in my room and dared to light a single candle as I brushed my hair by my mirror. While Death no longer ate away the flesh of my hands or feet when I grew angry, she appeared in my reflection, my rotting face of taut gray skin and empty eye sockets. My face still felt smooth beneath my fingertips, so it could have been just a trick of light, but I sensed that it was more than that. It seemed that even in death, gods were never truly gone.

I threw open the doors to the study and locked them behind me. The servants knew better than to bother me in here.

This was the only room facing South, into the deep darkness. I'd had great glass windows built on the far wall, looking out into that impenetrable wall of night. If, one day, someone were to claw their way out of the deep darkness and crawl onto the palace grounds, I would see them.

I sank down against the wall, leaning my head against the glass and spinning my wedding ring around my finger. One day, I would need to take it off. But whenever I went to remove it, I thought about the look on Hiro's face when he'd watched me put it on, all the brightness before everything had been ruined, and I couldn't bear to touch it.

I pressed my hand to the window that looked over the disappointing nothingness, my ring clinking against the glass. Perhaps it was undignified for a goddess to sit on the floor in her expensive robes and cry against a window, but I hardly felt like a goddess. I was more like the creatures of the deep darkness, only with a different sort of hunger.

I wondered if the humans would come to learn about me as they had Izanami, if I would become a part of their religious texts, or if I would forever be Yomi's dark secret. While Izanami's legend had been cruel and bleak, at least she had created Japan, done something of importance before her purpose was served. What story could be told about me, who had so ruined and destroyed everything?

I imagined, that if they were to tell the Legend of Ren, it would go something like this:

Once, there was a bastard daughter made of time and light.

She asked the universe what she was meant to be, but the stars held no answer.

There was only one person who loved her, and she took him across the sea, into the darkness that he feared.

She became a great queen, with a legion of the dead who bowed at her feet and a king who told her she was more beautiful than all the stars.

So she cast the one who had loved her into the darkness, because she didn't need him anymore.

But the king was rotten like her, so she killed him, as well.

And suddenly, in her palace of gold and one thousand servants, she was alone.

She knew then that the fabric of her soul was neither time nor light, but the pattern of stars over a restless sea, and stories whispered in catacombs, and steamship journeys to faraway lands, and her brother's hand in hers. The names that she had fought for meant nothing in the loneliness of eternity.

She combed through the darkness in search of the only person who had loved her without condition, but year after year he was nowhere. She remembered the prophecy of the Hōnengame—*that which you seek will never be found*—and cried for the fate she had written for herself.

But she would not allow her story to end there.

Every day, she ate thousands of souls, and every day she grew stronger. Her servants brought her the creatures of the deep darkness and she tore apart their stomachs with her bare hands, but still she didn't find him.

She knelt in the infinite darkness that was now her kingdom, and swore that someday, somehow, she would bring her brother home.

Until that day, Yomi continued to grow darker, until even the brightest lantern could no longer combat the endlessness of the night.

★ ★ ★ ★ ★

Thank you for reading!
We hope you enjoyed—and survived—your journey
with Ren into the enthralling world of
Reapers and Shinigami.
Don't miss book two in The Keeper of Night duology!

ACKNOWLEDGMENTS

This story would not exist without the love and support of so many people in my life. I once thought that no one would care about a story of an angry biracial girl trying to find out where she belonged, but little by little, the people in my life convinced me that I was wrong. To everyone listed here and so many more, thank you, from the bottom of my heart, for making my greatest dream come true.

Thank you to my parents, who always gave me so many books for Christmas, sent me to writing workshops, always supported my dreams no matter how far from home they took me, and never questioned the practicality of me pursuing a degree in creative writing. Your love is my greatest privilege.

Thank you to Natashya Wilson, not only for being a fantastic editor and making this book ten times better, but also for your incredible kindness and support that encouraged me to come to Inkyard in the first place. Thank you, also, to Rebecca Kuss, Bess Braswell, and Claire Stetzer for supporting both me and Ren with so much kindness and enthusiasm. Thank you to the entire Inkyard team for all the fantastic work that you do!

Thank you to my amazing agent, Mary C. Moore, who helped me tremendously with my outline and early drafts, answered all my nervous silly questions with kindness, and believed in both me and Ren even when I didn't.

Thank you to my wonderful agent-sisters and beta readers Van Hoang, Brandi M. Ziegler, and Yume Kitasei, whose feedback completely transformed this book for the better. Some of the best moments in this book came from your ideas.

Thank you to my teacher, David Samuel Levinson, who gave me the confidence and encouragement to keep going when I first decided to major in creative writing. Thank you also to my professor and advisor Jim Grimsley, who spent countless hours helping me with my first manuscript that eventually got me my agent. Thank you for your patience and kindness.

Thank you to my dear friends who patiently listened to my stories, didn't hold it against me when I canceled plans to stay in and write, celebrated with me, and encouraged me: Ruby, Giang, Jerry, Joan, Kaleigh, Kin, Lina, Nadea, Patty, Sarah, Veronica, Weng-Ching, and Winny. These are the ones who have suffered most from listening to me whine about writing, but certainly not the only ones whose love and support got me this far. To everyone else who supported me through this process, thank you.

And lastly, thank you to my wonderful coworkers in Korea who supported my dreams with so much enthusiasm and took care of me while I was writing this story, living alone in a foreign country: Suhyun, Seung-jin, Jiwon, Mira, Somi, Mina, Jimin, and Jieun. I hope that we'll meet again someday.